# Fire in the Fjord

## M. C. Smith

First published in 2018 by Endeavour Media Ltd.

# Table of Contents

# Note

The Tjierrefjord, with its fishing village of Hemmeligstein and perilous navigational headaches, is a fictional place situated in the more sparsely populated part of Norway somewhere between Namsos and Narvik. The creative intention was to draw elements of the confused campaign of April-June 1940 from both north and south and centre them upon a place where the company of HMS *Burscombe* and others could get to grips with the problems in their own way. The actions which take place out at sea are similarly inspired by true events.

However, more familiar will be the adventure of HMS *Cossack* chasing the *Altmark* into the Jossingfjord, February 1940. For the purposes of advancing the story actual events are more closely observed.

Historians whose work I have read in preparation for writing *Fire in the Fjord* include François Kersaudy, Donald Macintyre, Geirr Haarr and Robert Pearson. I am indebted to naval veterans John Lillywhite, Fred Sutton, Kevin Price and Captain Mike Matthews RN for their helpful comments and suggestions for this novel and the other numerous veterans and colleagues with whom I have spoken concerning procedures, technicalities and general culture within the service. Any remaining irregularities are my fault entirely.

Finally, I must give a special thanks to Stan Kitchener who generously agreed to read through each draft and challenge my writing according to his unique thinking.

# ONE

## Approaching the Leads

*February 1940.*

After what seemed like a lifetime, the Norwegian freighter *D/S Dagrand* was finally about to cross that invisible line of demarcation separating international seas from the safety of home waters. She was a slow steamer, about a week and a half out of New York on her way home to Bergen laden with foodstuffs and her crew had been victim to a palpable tension for the length of the run through the Denmark Strait, north of Iceland. Of course, they would have got home much quicker had they simply traversed the main warzone nearer Scotland but Captain Bakkevig had heard it said that there was less chance of being molested by the belligerents up here. He had no particular wish to run into either the Royal Navy or the Kriegsmarine as there was the distinct possibility of being detained by the one or being sunk out of hand by the other, and he was entirely unimpressed by the desire of both to disrupt neutral trade in their savage contest of the seas.

However, there had been no choice but to try and reach home soon because the *Dagrand* had already been held up in America for far too long with engine trouble and every further delay was costing him and his bosses a lot of money. Now it just remained to cross into the Leads, that long strip of Norwegian coastal water where the presence of foreign warships was forbidden by international law. Once there, he could rest easy.

Bakkevig's temper had been short since approaching Iceland and only he knew the near debilitation that he was suffering from this unwelcome feeling of trepidation. He was not exactly a coward but neither was he heroic. The combined pressures of risks taken in the last war, the stresses of raising a family, the despair of the Great Depression and the torment of once being shipwrecked were all too much for him and he had belatedly come to the conclusion that this life was not for him. Unfortunately for his crew, anxiety had translated itself into temper which had in turn been translated into the tension that now plagued them all.

With sharp orders barked out, he had posted a couple of extra lookouts on the frozen deck above and now stood inside the bridge staring out of the windows at the grey sea shrouded in its dim winter light. The wind was whistling through the small cracks in the wood panelling and the occasional bank of fog drifted weightily about the ship. The sea itself was heaving towards the east making the ship pitch on seven foot waves. Bakkevig knew from long experience that this was fairly calm weather for the time of year.

He was suddenly aware that somebody was trying to catch his attention and, stirred abruptly from his thoughts, he turned and saw young Oskar Fjelstad waiting patiently, meaning to hand him a cup of coffee. Oskar was his latest apprentice and possibly one of the best who had ever worked for him. Not yet old enough to shave, the boy somehow showed wisdom beyond his years. He had a refreshingly willing attitude to learning what this job was all about and was not prone to the absent-minded foolhardiness that seemed to afflict many youngsters these days.

Bakkevig rarely cared for novices and had accepted apprentices on board with reluctance. Even then he only took them when a family member or friend asked if he would offer their son a chance. It was just that this was a hard life and the five boys he had taken on before had turned out to be either disappointing mediocrities or utterly useless. Oskar's skilful defiance of the trend actually made him feel guilty that he had been giving him such a hard time. Oh well, the bullying in itself could only be character-building.

He acknowledged Oskar's gesture and took the coffee. Sipping it carefully and savouring the warmth as it travelled through his body, he continued his personal vigil against the evils that lurked somewhere out there in the gloom. He had kept this poise for a long time and was looking forward to the moment when he could relax. God willing, this would happen before his fatigue got the better of him and gave away the fact that he was as nervous as he was.

That was when he spied a shadow upon the indistinct horizon about a mile off the starboard beam. It was no trick of the light. It was definitely a ship. But what type? He could see a low freeboard with a solid superstructure rising up from the hull. Damn, it was a warship. He could now make out the big guns and high tripod masts. But was it British or

German? It was just then that a message was called down from one of the lookouts up above. The wind-garbled words were relayed by Michaelsen, the rugged first mate who had stepped out on the portside bridge wing. The warship had just been spotted.

'Yes, yes!' snapped Bakkevig. 'Tell that fool up there that I saw it a whole two minutes ago!' My God, but some of these rascals were not worth the money they were being paid.

He took up his binoculars from the shelf next to the telegraph and began studying the approaching vessel. It was definitely heading straight towards them. Fighting to hide his growing panic, he asked, 'Michaelsen, how long until we're in the Leads?'

'We've got less than a mile to go by my reckoning.'

Bakkevig tutted audibly and strained his eyes, trying to figure out what was happening now as the shadow had started growing disproportionately fatter as it approached. Before too long he realised that he was actually seeing two ships, the second emerging from its hiding place behind the first. A few seconds later a message came down from above to that effect. Bakkevig shouted at Michaelsen, 'Tell that bloody idiot to come down now! He's about as useful as a paper lifeboat!'

Concentrating on the dark vessels bearing down upon him, his guts sending unseen shivers of worry down his legs, he observed a morse signal being flashed across from the bridge of the lead ship. "Stop all engines," it read. It was in English. Although his anxiety did not really diminish, he did find time to thank his lucky stars that they were not German. That would buy him time.

'What do you think they'll do?' asked Michaelsen.

Bakkevig was so lost in his own worries that all he could do was cast his old friend a derisive look. What good would it do these people to keep breaking his concentration? Why could they not just let him get on with it?

But it was young Oskar who replied, quite happily, 'They'll likely question us, check our papers if need be, and let us continue on our way. We're not hiding anything.' He had been lapping up naval stories ever since he was little and was clearly excited at the prospect of becoming entangled with the approaching force.

Captain Bakkevig glared at the youngster, holding his naive simplicity in scorn. After all, it was not him who had the responsibility upon his shoulders for the safety of the *Dagrand* and everyone in it.

\*\*\*\*

Within a few seconds of the lookout calling out the bearing of the freighter, Lieutenant-Commander Peterson had evaluated the situation and set the alarms ringing throughout HMS *Burscombe*. The company of this, one of Britain's most powerful light cruisers, came to Action Stations with all the swiftness that their well-practised movements allowed, men expertly clambering past each other in the passageways, sliding down or hauling themselves up ladders and finally slamming shut all the steel hatches behind them. 809 souls, veterans of countless exercises and dawn Action Stations, had made themselves ready without fuss.

The icy wind that had long since been the bane of their lives became more intolerable still when Peterson ordered the sleek, grey ship's speed increased. As she was propelled through the waves by her powerful turbines, he pulled the collar of his duffle coat closer around his neck in a futile gesture.

As Chief Yeoman Ross worked the shutters on the morse lamp, apprising the officers of their trailing sister-ship of what was happening, the captain appeared on the bridge next to Peterson and surveyed the scene with stern, critical eyes.

Until two minutes ago, Captain Charles G. Dollimore had been dozing happily in his cabin just below but had unhesitatingly pulled himself together to full alertness, donned his coat and cap and climbed outside to take up his responsibilities. Indeed, it was for such moments of sudden activity as this that he devoted so much time ashore to sport and his physical well-being. He was about to turn fifty four and neglecting the facts of that age could only be detrimental to the ship. When at sea it was imperative that he did not lag behind the other men, many of who were more than thirty years his junior.

He asked, 'Pilot, you've signalled Captain Craine?'

'Yes, sir,' Peterson replied. He regarded the captain's question as superfluous but knew that he was bound to ask it for he was a very thorough man.

Both glanced over at HMS *Farecombe*, picking up speed off their port quarter at a distance of about two cable lengths. Even though a dusting of snow across her decks and turrets helped to define her outline just that little bit more, her dark silhouette was still something of a smudge against the dismal backdrop.

Just above Dollimore's head, the Director Control Tower, the ship's most vital spotting position for Fire Control, turned towards the freighter with an electrical whirr and, as he spared it a glance, he noticed Rear-Admiral Nicklesworth climbing out onto the bridge behind him.

That grim authoritarian stopped short of the officers doing their jobs and there he stayed so as not to interfere. Casting a look abaft, he was pleased to note that the *Farecombe* was pulling away fast to port in order to approach the target from a slightly different angle according to the pre-arranged plan as laid down by him before leaving Rosyth. This manoeuvre of approaching in divisions was really meant for attacking enemy warships in an effort to divide their fire but it was just as good a precaution against unidentified merchantmen. That freighter over there could turn out to be German, hiding torpedo tubes or guns in false deck housings.

Dollimore took a look through his binoculars and, feeling the tingle of suspicion, asked, 'What do you think, Pilot?'

'Could be, sir,' replied Peterson, raising his eyebrows in hope.

That little exchange made Nicklesworth step forward and take more notice.

Dollimore acknowledged his presence and said, 'Sir, two parts to the superstructure, bridge just forrard of amidships, two masts and one funnel aft ...'

The admiral agreed that this looked promising even though their information on the particular ship that they were looking for was sketchy to say the least.

A couple of months before a squadron of Royal Navy cruisers had chased down the German 'pocket' battleship *Graf Spee* in the South Atlantic and driven her captain to scuttle her. However, her supply ship, *Altmark*, had since disappeared and the First Lord of the Admiralty, Winston Churchill, felt pretty certain about two things. First was that *Altmark* would be trying find a way round the North Sea blockade in an attempt to get home; and second, that she was carrying as many as three hundred British merchant sailors captured from ships sunk. He wanted those sailors back.

But was this the ship in question? The officers of the *Burscombe* only had the blurred photograph from a tattered magazine with which to go by.

Dollimore had the Chief Yeoman flash a signal ordering the mystery ship to stop all engines then waited patiently for them to answer and start losing way. But there was no change to her progress.

With some urgency, Peterson realised what was afoot and said, 'They're trying to make it to neutral waters, sir.'

'Not if I've got any say in the matter,' commented Dollimore with distaste. Cupping his hand over the voicepipe, he ordered, 'Steer one point to starboard and give me maximum revolutions.'

A tinny reply came up from below as he turned to Lt-Cdr Digby, his trusty gunnery officer, who waited nearby for orders. 'Put a shot across her bows,' was Dollimore's expected instruction.

Digby eagerly ordered the observers in the Director Control Tower to fire one round from one of the forward turrets, the only ones which could be truly brought to bear for this particular shot. Down below, in front of the bridge, with spray washing across them thanks to *Burscombe*'s thundering increase in speed, the eight guns of the forward main armament were already prepared. In a few more seconds, the observers had delivered the readings of range, air pressure, wind, temperature, current, courses and speeds amongst other information to the marines of the Transmitting Station deep in the heart of the ship, which held the ship's mechanical Fire Control Table. Once the numbers were entered, the table made its calculation and the resulting training and elevating instructions were fed to the waiting gunners.

With a great boom, the starboard 6-inch gun of A-Turret sent its flame, smoke and shot out across the water. After a short pause, a terrific geyser rose up out of the sea not far from the target's bow and came crashing back down again. The thunder of the explosives detonating in the water rolled back past the *Burscombe* shortly afterwards.

With a practised stance which helped to keep his binoculars trained on the other's bridge, Dollimore read the flashed signal that suddenly started coming over to him but still let the Yeoman standing nearby confirm the words: 'They are the *Dagrand*, sir, en route to Bergen from New York carrying food.'

Dollimore shifted his gaze to the name painted on the bow. He could just about read it and, sure enough, it matched up with what they were saying. There was no sign of any fresh paint which would have been a tell-tale sign of falsification and even some streaks of rust blemished the white lettering. 'Pilot?' he said.

Always knowing what his captain wanted of him, Peterson had already relayed the ship's details to one of his men down below, who was then presently reporting his findings after consulting the *Lloyds Register of Shipping*. Peterson relayed, 'It seems to check out, sir. *D/S Dagrand,* twelve thousand tons, registered as Norwegian. We have no specific intelligence on her.'

But was Dollimore satisfied? He said to the Chief Yeoman, 'Ask him why he's on such a northerly route if he has nothing to hide.'

More than one man standing hereabouts silently wondered, 'Who would want to steam straight through the middle of a warzone when you could skirt happily around the edge?' but nobody ever butted into the captain's business. The bottom line was that his judgment was not just law in this ship, but was fully trusted with a well-earned respect.

As for most neutrals, it had become commonplace to volunteer inspection of papers or even their holds in order to proceed faster and unmolested through the British blockade. It was a point of intense international irritation but the number trying to evade His Majesty's warships was actually dwindling, most skippers resigned to the state of affairs as they were.

As the *Dagrand* finally began to slow, the Norwegian flashed another message.

'He just wants to reach home in one piece, sir,' said the Chief Yeoman with a hint of sympathy creeping into his voice.

'Well,' continued Dollimore, not sharing the sentiment, 'this is precisely where the Germans like to sneak past us. We'll send a boarding party across to get a look at his papers.' He glanced quickly over at the rear-admiral, who immediately nodded his assent without a word said, and gave the orders to manoeuvre the *Burscombe* so that the cutter's crew would be afforded some protection from the wind and waves in the ship's leeside.

Before long, the small grey-daubed boat was being lowered from the davits on the starboard side. For those men down there it must be an unenviable task but they had proved their ability to board ships in rough weather time and time again, always succeeding without any serious mishap.

\*\*\*\*

To Midshipman David Clark it seemed to take forever to cross to the *Dagrand*. Hanging onto the gunwale of the pitching cutter, there was plenty of time to curse this most hideous of winters. Wrapped up in a double layer of heavy clothing, the weathered and tired youngster squinted involuntarily as the spray blew from the tips of the waves into his eyes. Apart from the knowledge that if he fell overboard he was as good as lost, he felt no apprehension about what lay ahead. He was happily in control of his immediate concerns and was thankful for that. This particular serenity did not come naturally to all men when there was the possibility of action.

One could argue that that was just part of being a Clark but that was too simple for him. Belonging to that particular family which boasted over two and a half centuries of great naval heroes, he had decided that there was also plenty to be negative about. His father, the latest to die in glorious battle, had rigidly bred his family for the naval life and that was where David's rebellious side had originated. His reactionary youthful defiance had long since resulted in him being labelled 'difficult' by many of his peers and, having learnt about discipline the hard way, he was now trying to build upon the two positive things that he was sure of. He was brave and the men who went into action with him were confident that he could make sound decisions. He would just have to figure out the rest as he went along.

He looked over at the cutter's commanding officer, his good friend Midshipman Barclay-Thompson – Beatty for short – and wondered how it was he was so less inquisitive about life. The strong, professional way in which Beatty handled the oarsmen was typical of everything in his life. His outlook was as simple as it could get. He was enthusiastic for the navy and all that it entailed, was unquestioning of his station in life and somehow fostered complete confidence from above and below. Sometimes Clark wished that he could be like that.

Anyway, he hoped that they could execute this present job as fast as they could. The spray which had been constantly blowing across them was icing over, making them appear as though they were on an Arctic expedition.

It did not look like there was going to be too much trouble. Once they had decided that this freighter was not the *Altmark*, their excitement had completely subsided. Since the warning shot had been fired, the captain of the *Dagrand* had done everything he had been ordered to and somebody was now calmly lowering a rope ladder down the low side of the pitching ship.

The fenders clumped and scraped against the steel as they came alongside and one of the men grabbed hold of the ladder so that the boarding party's commanding officer could ascend. This was Lieutenant Eddington, a robust young man possessing the full unwavering authority of the navy in his very manner. Clark often looked to his leadership style for ideas but did wish that he would behave a little less like Errol Flynn when dealing with the neutrals.

Eddington was on the ladder as soon as he was able and pulled himself athletically up the side of the ship. Once on the icy deck above he kept his revolver holstered and immediately made for the man who was coming down the stairway from the bridge.

The miserably stressed Norwegian was middle-aged and his dark, tired eyes were almost hidden under the peak of his black cap.

'Sorry for the bother, old man,' said Eddington cheerfully, 'but it really wasn't clever trying to run. Now we'd like to check out a thing or two aboard your ship.'

The captain motioned for him to come up the stairs but Eddington turned back to his men before he followed. The small detachment of marines led by the stocky Sergeant Burroughs had already ascended the ladder and the sailors, tailed by Clark, were on their way up now. He called down, 'I'm going to the bridge! Take yourself down below and have a cursory look around!'

The words had almost been carried away by the wind and Clark, bemoaning the ice on the ladder, only just caught them. 'Very good, sir!' he replied.

He knew exactly what was required of him. He had boarded half a dozen vessels in this manner and mostly they were found to be legitimate and sent on their way. He had once grappled with the Germans, however, and with that experience in mind, it was good to be vigilant.

A close look at the lifeboats and the sparse housings on this blustery deck quickly proved that there were no false fittings, that everything was genuine and not hiding any sinister weapons.

Suddenly a young lad, who could only have just entered his teens, appeared before them. He was clapping his gloved hands together and shivering for the cold but had a big beaming smile on his babyish face. 'Hey, Royal Navy!' he said clumsily in a heavy Norwegian accent, 'Rule Britannia!' There was no hiding the fact that he held the sailors in high regard.

'Well, good day to you, young man,' said Clark with a nod, 'but have a care and stand aside while we search the ship.'

'One day I join the navy as well,' said the boy happily. 'Our navy as good as yours.'

Clark smiled as some of his men chuckled. 'What's your name, lad?'

'Oskar.'

'If all your countrymen believe that then you can make it happen.'

'Not likely,' grumbled one of the men standing nearby.

Clark turned to see who the perpetrator was and gave him a short glare. It was the especially morose Leading Seaman Haggerty, a short, wide-shouldered bulk of a man. The angry face which peered out from the balaclava was bloated and punctuated with a flat nose and unnaturally large slit-mouth. Also, he had no discernable chin and his mates in the *Burscombe* regarded him to be so ugly that they had given him the honorary title of 'The Turtle'. He looked back at Clark with an 'it wasn't me' expression.

But it was time to get on. Clark ordered, 'Martin and Gordy, come with me. Sergeant Burroughs, you take your men aft and see what you can see and Haggerty, you wait here.'

The Turtle watched the men trundle off carefully along the moving deck and had a quick check of the rope which held the cutter to the *Dagrand*'s side rail. He did not envy Midshipman Barclay-Thompson and his oarsmen sitting down there about thirteen feet below, waiting and freezing. He was cold enough himself and this wind was just not letting up. He suddenly figured that, if he just slipped into the gap between these deckhouses, he could get out of the worst of it and still spot anyone coming along.

\*\*\*\*

Clark led the way down the dimly lit corridor within the rolling hull and searched for the ladder which would take them further below. Then came that unbroken voice of Oskar's, 'This way, sirs.'

Detecting nothing untrustworthy about the boy, Clark followed him, saying submissively, 'Much appreciated, young man.'

Able Seaman Pincher Martin commented, 'Reminds me of myself a score o' years back, sir.' A veteran of some seventeen or more years service on the world's oceans in both the Merchant and Royal Navies and an acknowledged character of good conscience, officers and ratings liked to keep him close by. One would have expected him to be a senior rate by now but, for his own peace of mind, he valued the uninhibited company of the seaman's mess more than the responsibility of promotion. 'You still with us, Les? You all right?' he asked of the next man.

It was touch and go whether Les Gordy was ever truly all right. He looked sick and unsure of himself. This young, very white Irish lad always seemed to make headway with his confidence and ability then dropped back into morbid uncertainty once he had burnt himself out. The problem was his meagre intelligence and perception of the world. He just did not get it and he spent his life at a constant disadvantage to the multitude of bullies that prowled the *Burscombe*'s lower decks. Pincher took pity on him and did all he could to convince him that he was a worthy seaman but was beginning to wonder if he was just banging his head against a steel bulkhead. It was perfectly possible that this gentle, lost boy did not belong in the armed forces at all. Unfortunately, in these times of crisis, he was fresh out of choices. They all were.

Soon they were heaving open the creaking hatch which led into the hold. They switched on their torches and shone them inside, illuminating the copious amount of sacks which were stacked all the way to the deckhead. 'You two take a look,' Clark ordered. 'I'll take a look in the next compartment.'

In their respective compartments, they poked and prodded the goods, shifted a sack or two and took a quick look at this and that but they did not give it that much effort. There was nothing untoward here. The Norwegians' only crime had been to attempt to defy Captain Dollimore's order to stop.

\*\*\*\*

Lieutenant Eddington propped himself against the chart table inside the bridge with the ship's manifest and documents laid out before him. Without looking up, he said to the grizzled bridge hand, Michaelsen, as the only man who understood anything approaching English, 'I'm sure you appreciate our concern. Do you know how many merchantmen carrying goods for the Germans sneak round our blockade then go south with impunity in your territorial ... your *neutral* waters? And some of those ships are actually German themselves.'

Michaelsen translated the words for Bakkevig, whose forced reply was, 'We know nothing about German goods. We are simply going home.'

'I believe you,' said Eddington, 'I do, but you would have done better to stop your engines the first time we asked.' Revelling in the discomfort he was causing, he closed the pages of the manifest, pushed it away then turned to Bakkevig with his arms folded. 'With the Germans using the Leads it makes a mockery of our blockade. There's us trying to economically starve the enemy, which can only be a good thing for the world in general, and then your government allows them free passage along your coastline.'

There was no time like the present for a brief evaluation of the captain's politics. Eddington always liked to pick up on the general mood of neutrals when he met them to see if there was anything he could relay to his superiors as intelligence.

Through Michaelsen, Bakkevig said grimly, 'We want nothing to do with your war. Both you and the Germans are putting great pressure on us when all we want is peace. You will bring ruin on all of us. Never in my life have I been shot at just for going about my business.' That was not exactly the truth. The last war should have been coming back to him but the stress of the present was completely overriding the perils of the past.

Having quickly ascertained that he was dealing with a simple sailor of no great intellect, Eddington let his patience end with a dismissive, 'Wanting peace would be an admirable sentiment were it not for the fact that your country is quite happy to make itself wealthy by assisting in transporting millions of tons of iron ore to Jerry.'

'We transport it to you as well!' was Bakkevig's reply.

With a sigh, Eddington said to their translator, 'Please explain to your captain the difference between the good guys and the bad guys.'

Michaelsen required clarification of what he meant before rolling his eyes, wearily telling Bakkevig, 'He's taking the usual line about British virtue and German nastiness. There's no point in pursuing this one. We've heard it all before and he's been watching too many movies.'

Oblivious to the translation, Eddington continued, 'Well, old man, I understand you just want to go home and I won't keep you too much longer, but there is one other thing you could help us with. One of the reasons why we were so interested in you was because of the *Dagrand*'s appearance. She looks very much like a German vessel called *Altmark*. She's a bothersome supply ship for the Kriegsmarine and we mean to find her. Do you know anything you might be able to tell us?'

Michaelsen's face immediately displayed familiarity with the name as he translated Eddington's words for Bakkevig. The two Norwegians spoke together briefly, understanding the British concern about the *Altmark*. They had read the papers in America and remembered her part in the *Graf Spee* affair.

Furthermore, they had seen just such a ship pushing her way through the wintry gloom at a slightly higher rate of knots only yesterday. They had remarked upon her similarities to their own ship but had not thought any more of it. Bakkevig had signalled, enquiring as to her identity as she pulled gradually past them but had received no reply.

'That's the sort of behaviour you should report,' Eddington reprimanded them after listening to their story.

'Well, we didn't,' answered Michaelsen. 'We were just two strangers wary of each other.'

Deciding that they had said too much, Bakkevig was adamant that he wanted nothing more to do with this business and so was becoming more agitated than he had yet been.

Michaelsen, who had sailed with him for years as shipmate and friend, was beginning to recognise the signs of mental strain but was loath to admit that his captain was getting out of his depth. However, as his personal sympathies were actually more for Britain than Germany, he argued that giving up the *Altmark* was the right thing to do.

Seeing that the issue was placing strain on the two old men, Eddington said, 'I do thank you for the intelligence. If it was them then they're well within Norwegian waters by now.' Rubbing his chin in thought and with his eyes alight with the excitement of it all, he continued, 'And breaking international law by transporting prisoners of war through neutral territory.'

Suddenly, the portside door slid open with the sharp crack of wood against wood and a freezing wind swept across them. A panicked man, one of Bakkevig's tired and haggard crew, screamed something in his native tongue, his voice almost breaking into a falsetto. What he said made everybody jolt with surprise, including Eddington. Most of the words may have been a foreign jumble but the word 'torpedo' had been clear.

As his mind deciphered the situation, Eddington began to make his way across to the portside windows to take a look outside while Michaelsen and Bakkevig thought it more prudent to head in the opposite direction, seeking shelter from the impending explosion. Their muscles tensed, their breaths stalled in their throats with hearts fluttering wildly while they waited helplessly for the calamity to ensue.

Eddington looked out, trying to pick out the torpedo track in the uneven sea. He was not sure whether he saw it or not. Was that then a metallic thump against the ship's side, just audible above the angry rush of the weather? The expected moment of impact came and went. Nothing happened.

Sergeant Burroughs appeared beside him having just come up to report on the lack of suspicious cargo. Realising what was happening, he had followed Eddington over to the portside. If the officer was going to face the torpedo then so was he. But he was finally able to declare, 'The bastard didn't go off!'

Stepping outside with the wind threatening to take away his very breath, Eddington scanned the horizon, or what he could see of it with the patchy fog and squalls. He could just see one of the circling cruisers, an ill-defined shadow at a considerable distance but immediately knew her for which ship she was. Without another moment's hesitation, he looked round to find the Yeoman from his boarding party. There he was, standing in the corner of the bridge, white-faced with gawping eyes. 'Get a signal straight off to the *Farecombe* that they have a U-boat somewhere in their vicinity. Then inform the *Burscombe*.'

'Aye aye, sir!' the young signalman snapped back, his training to obey suddenly kicking in, successfully stifling the helplessness that had nearly paralysed him. He joined the lieutenant and started clicking away with the *Dagrand*'s lamp.

Busy with their focus upon what was taking place, they were barely aware that the deck-plates beneath their feet had taken on a new gentle rumble and that the ship was in fact getting under way. Valuable time was lost before Burroughs suddenly twigged, the swish of the bow wave beginning to catch his attention in the swell below them. He turned to Eddington and asked, 'You never gave no engine orders, did you, sir?'

The officer looked down at the water, saw what the sergeant had seen then stalked back into the bridge with fury.

Bakkevig was standing in front of the telegraph, triumphantly seeking to defend the order he had rung down to the engine room. He had decided that he was fed up with this Englishman holding him to ransom in his own bridge and keeping his ship stopped in U-boat-infested waters when he should have been doing something more decisive.

\*\*\*\*

Over on the starboard side, the Turtle remained in his relatively sheltered cubby hole, his arms folded and gloved hands thrust deep into the warmth of his armpits. Every now and then he glanced out to see if anyone was coming and he should have been paying more attention but his mind had wandered. He was miserable. Life could not be much worse and that last hash of a leave he had been on had only exacerbated the difficulties that this bloody war was heaping upon him. Leaves were supposed to offer a respite from the usual stupidity, not make it worse. As his thoughts were about to be overcome with the details once again, he suddenly became aware that someone was shouting nearby. The voice was coming from the cutter.

He rushed out from his place of concealment and skidded across the snowy deck to look over the side of the ship. What the hell? The *Dagrand* was under way and the cutter below was being dragged along by the rope which was still secured to the railing. Now being battered by the bow wave as well as the choppy sea, the men were hanging tight onto the gunwales and thwarts.

All the faces below looked up at him wonderingly. The midshipman, Barclay-Thompson, starting gesticulating with annoyance. 'What the hell's happening up there?' he called in his crisp, well-educated tones.

'Be blowed if I know, sir,' the Turtle answered. 'There's been no word from Mr Eddington.'

'Well, release that line before we're dashed to pieces!'

The Turtle fumbled with the rope, finding himself unable to shift the infernal twisting of whatever knot this was supposed to be. He tore his gloves off and threw them on the deck but he still could not undo it. What did not help was that his fingers were frozen and not responding to instructions from his brain so he reached into his pocket to grab at his knife, belatedly remembering that he no longer had it. It had been lost, sort of.

'Come on there!' shouted the midshipman as the cutter started banging more violently against the ship's side. As the increasing bow wave began crashing a heavy spray over the already wet men, he lost patience and ordered one of his oarsmen, 'Cut it at this end!'

But on the deck above, the Turtle was suddenly shoved away from the railing and a knife being wielded by young hands sliced through the rope in one movement. Staring in surprise, it took the Turtle a good couple of seconds to appreciate that Oskar had come up on deck and, realising the danger, had sprung into action instantly.

Just as it seemed like the men below were to lose control and succumb to the perils of the shifting sea, the rope dropped and the ship made to pull ahead of them. The boat's fenders continued to clatter along the steel side with a series of exaggerated crunches and scrapes which spurred Barclay-Thompson to shout, 'Push her away there!' at his oarsmen.

With all their strength they thrust their oars against the side and somehow managed to put some little distance between them. It was just enough. When the swirling wash created by the propellers went past, the cutter was left bobbing and spinning in their wake, shaken but intact.

The Turtle, who had kept his eyes glued to the plight of the cutter from his vantage point, found he could now breathe a sigh of relief and, as the small boat was gradually left behind, he turned to Oskar.

The boy's face too was a picture of relief.

The Turtle nodded with respect. Oskar might be half his size and not old enough to be considered manly but he had just put this man here to shame. The knowledge that he himself had performed badly made him angry but he should not direct any of it at this boy who obviously had a great future if he lived long enough. What he had done required admiration. 'Well done, lad. Well done.'

The Turtle took his cap from atop his balaclava and removed the tally from its rim, handing it to Oskar. 'You just saved the lives of men from HMS *Burscombe*.'

The boy looked at the gold stitched letters on the ribbon. They simply read, 'HMS'. The ship's name was absent for reasons of security but he would never forget that which he had just been told.

'If all Norwegian sailors have got your guts,' the Turtle continued, 'maybe your navy could be as good as ours.'

Oskar had not understood all the words but he was pretty sure he had the gist. He could not help but smile. This had been the greatest adventure.

****

Without a significant change of expression, Captain Dollimore looked out from the bridge of the *Burscombe*, saying of the hidden U-boat, 'We have ourselves something of a cool customer here.'

Indeed, thought Lt-Cdr Peterson, for it was a tough or a foolish submarine captain who would dare to try and sink a vessel that had two great warships in company. But who knew the full circumstances of the man behind the periscope. Through the squalls and gloom he may have spied the stopped freighter and fired before realising that the warships were there. Unlikelier things had happened at sea.

But as usual Dollimore had already calculated another possible dimension of sobering reality to those around him. 'You can bet your last shilling that he targeted the *Farecombe* too; perhaps even us. We might be needing to thank a shoddy armourer for providing him with dud torpedoes. Anyway, whatever the truth, he's missed out on a fat victory today.'

He had already ordered the *Burscombe*'s speed increased to twenty five knots and steered a course past the stern of the *Dagrand*. Also being careful to pass wide of Barclay-Thompson and his half-drowned men bobbing about in their cutter, this great ship leaned heavily over to port as she sliced through the waves. The crests rhythmically swept across the fo'c'sle giving A-Turret its usual drenching, washing away the fresh soft snow but allowing more ice to form.

Such was the dire visibility of the horizon that they momentarily lost sight of the *Farecombe*. A few seconds ago she had been steaming in a westerly direction about two thousand five hundred yards away, herself having picked up the speed.

Rear-Admiral Nicklesworth, listening to the high hollow ping of the ASDIC repeater against the harsh anger of the sea and wind, knew that his other ship would be going all out to detect that U-boat. Would it not be a stunning end to this difficult day if they could actually sink that wretched thing lurking somewhere beneath them? Jerry sneaked about in such an underhanded way, leaving such misery in their wake that he hated them with a passion.

Unfortunately, the truth of the situation was that they would have to be very lucky to destroy this submarine. *Burscombe* and *Farecombe* were large ships with 6-inch guns, designed for fighting other surface vessels, shore bombardment, scouting and fleet protection. They were not anti-submarine ships. As a result, they only carried six depth charges apiece upon racks which gave the impression of having been affixed to their quarterdecks as an afterthought. So, if they did not bag their prey within two attacks then they would not get him at all.

If ever there was a time that they needed a flotilla of destroyers it was now. This was the situation that the squadrons and flotillas were supposed to be grouped together for and Nicklesworth knew that he was in the presence of a captain who had protested about them being split up. He now felt as though they had been rendered strangely impotent. The odds were stacked in favour of the U-boat getting away.

From the frozen position up in the foremast, there suddenly came a report down the voice-pipe from their eagle-eyed lookout, Able Seaman Smith: '*Farecombe* is coming back into view red zero-one-seven, sir. Range one thousand five hundred yards.'

Dollimore and his fellow officers shifted their gazes a few degrees to port and saw nothing but patchy greys and whites swirling against each other. But they kept looking without any doubts because Smith – or Smudge as he was known below decks – may pretend to be the ship's idiot but he was far from a fool and had consistently proved he had the best eyesight in the squadron.

A few seconds passed and then, of course, there was the shadow of their sister-ship prowling through the waves searching for their hidden enemy. As they watched her, great towers of white water erupted from her churning wake and rose up to the level of her tall masts before they came crashing back down again. The terrific sound of the explosions reached the *Burscombe*'s bridge a couple of seconds later. The ferocity of the pattern of charges going off was evident and must have been hell for the submariners if they were nearby, but it was generally accepted that they deserved everything they got. That was all there was to it.

Dollimore leaned over another voicepipe and ordered, 'Bridge to helm, come one point to port.'

As the tinny acknowledgement came up from below and was whisked away on the wind, Chief Yeoman Ross called from abaft the bridge, 'Sir, signal from *Farecombe*! Target astern moving to port!'

Dollimore gave the distantly flashing lamp a quick glance, reading the signal but glad for the Chief's clarity, and then stared at the murky point where the surface was very slowly settling after the previous explosions. If the U-boat had been properly identified then it should be somewhere between that foamy disturbance and the *Burscombe*.

The ASDIC operators in their compartment in the bottom of the ship, forrard of A-Turret's cordite room, would be getting to grips with this information and hoping to receive an echo which was not the bubbling mass displaced by the last pattern of charges.

Dollimore stared at the waves, wishing he had a superhuman ability to see right through them. His patience was not infinite even if he sometimes liked to give the impression that it was. What should he do? All too quickly, they were steaming over the spot where the U-boat should have been according to Captain Craine's signal in the *Farecombe* and the only sound that was coming from the ASDIC repeater was the steady beat of single pulses being sent into the black depths. There was no hint of an echo and no verbal reports from his experts using the equipment.

Before the war, they had been told: 'The creation of ASDIC has removed the submarine as a viable threat.' Well, I beg to differ, thought Dollimore through the indignation of dealing with yet another serious threat that had been foreseeable.

'Away depth charges!' he ordered, his voice betraying just a small portion of his annoyance.

Down at the *Burscombe*'s uncomfortably exposed stern, two shivering men, already having set the various depths for detonation, released the small gate that would allow their lethal barrels to drop into the sea. For just a second it seemed as though the charges were stuck, retained by the will of the ice that the men had desperately tried to keep clear from the machinery, but then they were splashing happily into the ship's wake.

Not many more seconds later, the surface of the sea trembled and blew skyward once again in multiple detonations, finally to disperse all about the area.

Men at their stations on the outer decks scanned the settling water for signs that anything man-made had broken up beneath the waves – chunks of wreckage or perhaps a slick of oil – but there was nothing save foam, seaweed and a few dead fish.

Dollimore sighed. There was nothing else he could have done. He had dropped his charges upon the hint of what flimsy evidence he had and got a negative result. Though it had been expected it was still disappointing.

Rear-Admiral Nicklesworth immediately took hold of the situation and ordered, 'Captain, order Craine to maintain a search pattern in order to keep the U-boat down while we retrieve our boarding party from the *Dagrand*.'

'Very good, sir,' replied Dollimore, nodding to the Chief Yeoman to get it done. 'Let's hope that the freighter didn't get too far away from us in her panic. If she's taken our men into the Leads we might spark an international incident.'

Nicklesworth looked carefully at the captain, not amused. What exactly did he mean to do?

\*\*\*\*

Bakkevig's brain was locked into survival mode. He was determined that he was going to save his ship from being torpedoed but ultimately he needed to save himself. In the *Dagrand*'s bridge, both the British and Norwegian sailors, most of whom considered themselves old hands at this trade, had rarely witnessed a scene like that which was unfolding in front of them now.

Sergeant Burroughs, who had initially paused because even he was conscious of certain niceties, now grasped Bakkevig's wrists in a lightning movement in order to hoist him away from the telegraph. His vice-like grip squeezed until the captain's whitened hands were forced off the brass casing.

Yelping with pain, Bakkevig swung round in an attempt to hit his assailant in the face, but Burroughs easily blocked the move and brought his fist crashing across the other's left cheek.

The captain almost crumpled under the blow but his racing mind instantly brought him back to his original objective. His order to proceed ahead must not be reversed. Hurt as he was, he was in between Burroughs and the telegraph again before the latter could put his hands on the lever.

Allowing an angry growl to emanate from his throat, the sergeant decided that the telegraph could wait and stepped over to the frightened helmsman at the wheel instead. Grabbing that other hapless man by the shoulder, he shoved him to one side.

Along with the next pained cry there suddenly came a shout of, 'That's enough, sergeant!'

It was Eddington. 'We only need the ship turned around, not this lot beaten half out of their senses!'

'Sorry, sir,' replied Burroughs, catching his breath and expertly hiding the fact that this was the most fun that he had had in a long while. In fact, it was one of the reasons why he liked belonging to a service as tough as the marines. While he was truly patriotic and would do anything for his country and his ship, he also enjoyed heaping misery on those deserving of it.

Disgusted by what he had just seen, Michaelsen raised himself up in something approaching a defiant gesture and said, 'I must think to remind you all of the law, gentlemen. You have no right to assume command of this ship. We are as good as home and you are trespassing, behaving in a threatening manner to us in our own territory. This could get you into a lot of trouble with both our governments, lieutenant.' He pointed to the blurred horizon ahead of them and it took them a few seconds, but they all intermittently saw the rocky shore of Norway through the shifting grey.

Eddington said, 'Well, I'll be damned if I'm getting involved in the legal ramblings of internment just to satisfy you!'

Turning again to the crazed Captain Bakkevig, he continued with, 'Just turn us around and take us back to the *Burscombe* and we can all live happily ever after.'

'Sir?' The voice had come from the open door. It belonged to Clark, who had arrived on the bridge just in time to witness the end of the physical altercation. It had not shocked him; indeed, he looked decidedly calm.

'What is it, damn you?' asked Eddington.

'A suggestion, sir. Just stop engines and wait here.'

If it had been anyone else thinking to be so impertinent he would have been promising the young man a life of living hell but this was David Clark, who had proved in the past that he was equal to any long-standing veteran in capability. He often provided valuable insights and would not have interrupted for anything less than pure common sense.

Clark said, 'You cannot reasonably expect these innocent people to put themselves back into harm's way. To be almost torpedoed once is enough for today, don't you think?'

'Then how do you think we're going to get back to the *Burscombe*?'

'*Burscombe* will come to us,' Clark stated boldly.

'Sure of that, are you?'

'Without a doubt. Captain Dollimore would certainly be tickled at the thought of me being interned but fortunately, I think he would probably want you and the other men back. What's a brief foray into neutral waters when some of his own men are at risk? Especially when there's so little chance of being seen by anyone else? It's exactly what I would do if I were him.'

Eddington shook his head, saying, 'You're very presumptuous, aren't you?' But that was more to get the last word in than to actually berate him.

With the help of Michaelsen, who had at least kept his head, they eventually managed to convince Bakkevig that he was safe and were able to have him order the ship to a full stop.

In a little while the unmistakeable silhouette of the *Burscombe* emerged from the hanging gloom and not before time. The day was drawing to a close and the weak sun in its meagre six hours of revelation was about to set once again. They all knew that any further delay in finding them would have created extra problems.

Everybody's hearts lifted. Clark had been right. Now it would be lovely to see the back of the *Dagrand* and her cowardly captain.

Eddington looked over to the talented midshipman as he prepared to go outside and brave the elements once again. 'You really did know what Dollimore would do.'

With a grin, Clark replied, 'Actually, not for certain.'

# TWO

## Strained Relationships

HMS *Burscombe* thrust her way southwards upon a sea that had fortunately moderated overnight down to State 4. Rear-Admiral Nicklesworth had noted earlier that the captain had been able to order proper ice clearance from the foc's'le as the spray had ceased to be a hindrance to the operation. As it commenced, he had felt no sympathy for the sixty men gathered for the odious job of chipping away the unwanted frozen weight from the deck, fittings and turrets with their shovels and pickaxes.

These men had been luckier than most this winter. The ship had not long emerged from the Rosyth dockyard where hard-pressed engineers, shipwrights, carpenters, welders and others had made good the damage sustained during December's fierce confrontation with the German battlecruiser *Moltke*. This meant that at least they had had the pleasure of spending either Christmas or the New Year with family or friends before heading back out, first for trials, then on the patrol which had led them to the interception of the *Dagrand*. Therefore, as compared to other ships' companies of the Home Fleet who had dealt with persistent cold, fatigue, influenza and bad weather, they were still fairly fresh.

That was why he was unimpressed with their performance. It might have been a different matter if they were dead on their feet and begging for a respite but they were not. They, just like he, had been properly rested and would recently have been made a fuss of by mothers and wives, had a chance to open Christmas presents with their families, eaten a fat roast and cast aside the world's ills for a time. That was what he had done anyway.

This business with the *Dagrand* had come only five days into the patrol and he could see that he was dealing with men who needed to be cajoled back into the swing of things. It certainly looked like it as he made notes for his report. The damning paragraphs told of a fist-fight on the freighter's bridge, a near-fatal incident with the cutter and the breaking of neutrality laws. That last item he had decided to leave out of the main text, thus to be submitted separately and secretly. After all, he personally had ordered the *Burscombe* to follow the *Dagrand* nearer to the coast, albeit at the captain's insistence.

Finally, there was the possible presence of a U-boat which they had not done enough to guard against, though he was having great doubts about the whole sordid episode. Had there been an enemy submarine there at all?

The answer to that did not actually matter. What was bothering him more was the line that he knew Captain Dollimore was going to take about their lack of destroyers. After all, the bothersome man had made his feelings about the breaking up of the squadron known before they had ever left port. He was always commenting on proceedings. Nicklesworth had suspected that working with him was going to be difficult as soon as he decided to raise his flag in this ship, and he had not yet come across any reason to think otherwise. So, then why had he chosen the *Burscombe*?

If anybody had suggested that Charles Dollimore should be his flag-captain three months ago he would have laughed, given a 'harrumph' and maybe even hit back with scorn, but the Commander-in-Chief of the Home Fleet, Admiral Sir Charles Forbes, had tried to force a change in his attitude by recommending this particular appointment, pressing home his point by stating, 'Believe me, you could do a lot worse. You might just find the man more irritating than you can bear but, when push comes to shove, his ability is unquestionable. Listen to what he has to say.'

Well, he was struggling to find the good in the situation. What he had previously known of Dollimore was the story of a high-strung, impatient captain who, seven years before, had driven his ship carelessly to disaster on the River Clyde. HMS *Constant*, a cruiser of no insignificant tonnage, had rammed and sunk a submarine which had resulted in the deaths of three sailors. He had been exonerated by the Board of Enquiry but had been put ashore, out of the way, deemed to be needing a rest.

Nicklesworth had been on the staff of one of the investigating admiral's at the time and had been privy to the details of the case if not active in the judgment. He had been truly aghast at the outcome, believing that an officer of his standing should not have been let off such a lapse of calm professionalism.

Still, Nicklesworth raised his flag in Dollimore's ship. It had either been this one or Captain Craine's *Farecombe*. Craine was a good man with an exemplary record but had not seen the action that Dollimore had. With reservations Nicklesworth had acted upon Forbes' suggestion and was praying that he would not regret it.

This *Dagrand* business was not the best of starts.

****

Dollimore climbed up to the bridge to the acknowledgement of Lt-Cdr Peterson, the Officer-of-the-Watch. Yet more snow had fallen upon the heads and shoulders of the lookouts. Their surroundings were currently a uniform bleak grey as a heavy fog had finally settled but, fog or no fog, they were still watching for specific things such as aircraft, ships and torpedo tracks. The *Burscombe* was not just to be considered the hunter, but the hunted.

Rear-Admiral Nicklesworth had turned them onto this heading of two eight zero degrees based upon the intelligence gleaned from the *Dagrand*'s crew that the German tanker *Altmark* might be nearby. A pointless task it might seem because that ship was undoubtedly in neutral waters but, then again, what if she was not? How frustrating would it be if the damn thing was within hailing distance in this fog right now?

Also somewhere out there was the *Farecombe*. Captain Craine had been given the same mean course and had been steaming a mile or so to the north of them with her engines plugging away at the same revolutions. Even allowing for slight changes in currents and wind, they should not have got too far away.

'Sir', came a voice from behind him.

He turned to see the admiral's youngest steward standing by the hatch. He was lightly dressed, his tunic not very well suited for guarding against the minus temperature that was immediately assaulting his body. Furthermore, his right hand was clenched into a fist, his mouth twisted into a grimace and his eyelids drooped with the effects of a naive worry.

'With the admiral's compliments, could you please see him in his sea cabin, sir?' the lad said. It was more of a statement than a question. The polite delivery was just the navy's traditional way of passing orders between officers.

Without acknowledging the request, Dollimore asked, 'What's the matter with your hand?'

'It's burning, sir,' said the young man, unable to make eye contact. 'It was the ice on the hand-rail.'

'You're lucky your hand didn't stick to it,' Dollimore said sternly. 'Then you would have been in trouble. In future wear your gloves on the outer decks. I can't have men hurting themselves over something that could have been avoided, and your duffle coat wouldn't go amiss when you need to come up here.'

'Yes, sir,' the steward said, an uncontrollable shivering now becoming evident. It only took a few seconds for this wind to penetrate through his thin clothes then through the skin straight to the bone.

Dollimore, purposely detaining him longer than was necessary just to drive the point home, asked, 'Do I have to make a standing order out of something that should, by rights, be common sense?'

'No, sir.' Of course there was nothing else he could say.

After a final pause, Dollimore said, 'Off you go, then.'

The steward then escaped from the bridge as fast as decency would allow.

Dollimore shook his head. He reflected that ten years ago he would have bitten the lad's head off. There had been a period of his life when all these stupid behaviours, coupled with the retrenchment directives of a government determined to lower the standards by which they operated, had truly aggravated him. But he had since necessarily been forced to take a good look at himself, thankful that he was at liberty to do so. From past negative experiences had emerged this calmer Charles Dollimore, forever conscious of keeping things in perspective and preferring the stance of good guidance rather than bullying control.

After taking a last quick look around and satisfying himself that the lookouts and officers were doing everything that was expected of them, he went below.

It was warmer in Nicklesworth's cabin, but not by much. The admiral was sitting at his desk still clad in his heavy woollen jumper with a scarf wrapped tightly around his neck. He looked up when he was aware that Dollimore was by the open door and gave a gesture, saying, 'Please sit yourself down for a moment or two.'

With one hand he shuffled the papers on his desk into some sort of order while with the other, he flipped open a cigarette case and offered the contents towards Dollimore.

The captain took one then lit it with a match struck from the box that he always kept with him. 'Thank you, sir.'

Eventually, Nicklesworth turned in his chair, rested his elbows on the arms and gave him his full attention. 'Charles,' he said, hiding the reservations he had about him, 'I want your honest opinion about what happened with the *Dagrand.*'

'You mean about whether I thought there was a U-boat there at all?'

Nicklesworth displayed a quick flash of triumph, feeling that he was beginning to read the man correctly. 'I knew it would occur to you. However, the evidence doesn't look good. Nobody on the *Farecombe* or the *Burscombe* observed any torpedo tracks and neither were they observed by any of *our* officers on the bridge of the *Dagrand*. Furthermore, when I questioned young Midshipman Clark, who was below decks at the time, he could not swear that there was a thud against the side of the ship. This leaves just one witness to there ever having been a torpedo, and that was one of the Norwegian sailors who, for all intents and purposes, wanted us gone.'

Dollimore just looked at him without saying anything.

'And when we depth-charged the suspected U-boat,' continued Nicklesworth, 'we turned up nothing but a few dead fish. Well?'

'I agree, it doesn't look good, but I believe Clark stated that any one of the sounds that he could hear on account of the ship's motion could have been a thud. My men are not ones for fussing over nothing, sir.'

'There's no suggestion that they are,' said Nickleworth, not so easily hiding the manner which was very much giving the impression of the opposite.

'But something else occurred to me,' said Dollimore, eager to stay one step ahead of this admiral that clearly did not like him. 'A torpedo attack is something very difficult to falsify and Eddington did testify that the man who raised the alarm displayed an unprecedented level of panic as he did so. Furthermore, that particular man had not shown an attitude which could be considered to be anti-British.'

'Yes, but the captain had.'

'The captain was simply a coward.'

'So, what are you saying?'

'Well, sir, just suppose for a minute that what the man said was the truth. I've heard other reports to the effect that the German torpedoes might be failing the further north they go.'

Nicklesworth suddenly put a thoughtful look upon his face, designed to mask the fact that he was actually a little disappointed. 'Rumours.'

'Reports,' Dollimore corrected him, suspecting that the rear-admiral desperately wanted to be right. Or was he just testing him? 'With the effects of the magnetic north getting stronger the closer you get to the Pole, I think it's worth suggesting that the Germans are having trouble with the warheads they're using. We could use this to our advantage.'

'You may be right,' said Nicklesworth, 'but then, if they are having problems, they will simply switch to an alternative type of warhead that will work in these latitudes.'

'Operations of that sort take time ...'

Nicklesworth suddenly screwed up his face in annoyance. 'Are you beginning to delve into matters of strategy, captain?'

Dollimore frowned. 'You asked me my opinion, sir.'

'Yes, on the plausibility of the story brought back by the boarding party,' said Nicklesworth, looking to regain control of the conversation. 'Nothing else.'

Dollimore nodded. 'Of course, sir, you have my apologies.'

He quelled the frustration that coursed through his body. He may have cemented his reputation as a good fighting captain with some admirals but this one here still preferred to remember his doubtful past as opposed to accepting the present. Nicklesworth was not the first admiral to be irritated by his assumptions and comments on the conduct of operations.

Anyway, he had made his point and had already committed his impressions to paper. Nicklesworth still deserved the respect due to his rank so Dollimore inevitably backed down.

But the rear-admiral had not finished. He had control of the conversation so felt free to pursue the subject on his own whim. 'However, as you've brought it up, what sort of advantage are you talking about?'

Momentarily surprised, Dollimore realised that it was going to take most of his wits to deal with this man. He said, 'I should have thought that our First Lord would be keen to land an army in Narvik, up in the north, to secure our source of Scandinavian iron ore.'

Nicklesworth's eyes narrowed. 'What have you heard?'

Of course, thought Dollimore, he's concerned that loose tongues have been wagging, but that's not the way I work. 'I've heard nothing,' he said, 'but a blind man could tell that the focus of this war is shifting onto Norway. Narvik is the key to the iron ore and it stands to reason that either we or the Germans should occupy it thus denying that vital material to the other side. Right now would be a good time to sail a convoy through to do the job while the U-boats are having problems with their torpedoes.'

'It's not clear that they are having problems,' stated Nicklesworth, emphasising the point with the sweep of his hand. 'And anyway, such an act would completely contravene Norway's rights.'

'Well, it would be a rare thing if we had no plan for just such a venture – especially since Churchill must be itching for a fight.' It's in his very nature, he thought. You could read any of his books and pick up on his martial enthusiasm.

Nicklesworth considered his logic. Annoyingly, the captain was quite right about Norway for, unbeknown to him, he had indeed correctly guessed Churchill's intentions. That being said, it was more than Nicklesworth's career was worth to elaborate on the fact; and anyway, the Norwegians themselves were the problem. Churchill could not protect the iron ore without Norwegian consent. The same went for assisting Finland in their new war against Russia. The British could not go forward without the say so of both the Norwegians and the Swedes.

'Whatever the truth is about this alleged torpedo attack on the *Dagrand*,' said Nicklesworth, 'let's hope that the intelligence received about the *Altmark* was more sound.'

Dollimore left the admiral's presence frustrated at the use of the word 'alleged'. Either theory about what happened was as good as the other and he considered it important for both to be put forward with equal weight. But he knew that the main report finding its way back to the Admiralty would clearly express the opinion that the boarding party had been duped by the Norwegian seamen. Dollimore was determined to make sure that the information regarding the torpedoes was attached somewhere.

\*\*\*\*

The sun was finally peaking through the clouds and burning away some of the fog. For the first time in a long while Lieutenant Irwin, the 2nd Officer-of-the-Watch, felt warmer but that was not to say that it could burn away the feeling of helplessness that the war provoked within him. Why was it so wrong to hope for peace? Everyone else in this ship seemed to be yearning for a fight, even the three men he admired most in this world: Dollimore, Peterson and Digby. He had learnt more from those three than everyone else combined but he still could not understand why they thought there was no chance to negotiate with the enemy before things got too out of hand.

Thinking of Lt-Cdr Digby, there he was climbing out of the Director Control Tower, jumping nimbly off the ladder onto the bridge.

Digby noticed that Irwin had just taken over the watch and commented joyfully, 'It's amazing what a little bit of sunlight can do for a man.'

Irwin had to force a smile. Being able to see a few more miles across a calmer sea brought on its own set of problems for a ship at war. He suddenly wished that he was not driven so much by his concern because he knew that his body was expending more energy than he could spare on it. Concern should be translated into extra vigilance but it would be no good if he was to give himself a heart attack in the process. To hide his turmoil, he replied, 'Yes, it's beautiful.'

'Still no sign of the *Altmark*, though,' commented Digby with a clumsy mock dourness. He would not know how to be dour if he studied it for a year.

'I wish we had more to go on,' said Irwin.

'We'll get her.'

Irwin looked at him, struggling with his thoughts. 'Where do you get all this optimism from?'

'From just knowing that we're doing all we can and that everything will turn out right in the end. There's no other truth for me.' Digby, not wanting to alienate his friend, then cautiously asked, 'Is everything all right, old boy?'

'Nothing I can't handle,' replied Irwin with all that fake cheerfulness, but there was much he would tell if only they did not live in a world built on bravado and emotional restraint. No, it was easier to talk about other people instead. 'How are the family?'

Digby laughed at the memory of his leave. 'The children are thriving. They've been mixing with these little terrors evacuated from London. Thick as thieves, they are. In fact, they are thieves. Had to punish them more than once for raiding the larder for extra apples. Can't seem to make them understand that the next harvest is a whole six months away.'

'You make it all sound rather jolly,' said Irwin, showing confusion.

'They're precious little scamps.'

'And your wife is well? Helene, isn't it?'

'Oh, she's well.'

Irwin thought that there must be something truly special about her judging by the look on Digby's face. But whatever the case, he was content just to be happy for his friend's marriage because it was not likely that he would ever be following the same path.

He looked back out at the white-tipped waves and tried to clear his mind but it was difficult. His friend had been right to be suspicious for there was something which presently tormented him. A few months ago, he had initiated the idea of giving a series of lectures on the conduct of the war so that the men of the lower decks could be kept better informed about the progress of events. Every couple of weeks or so, approximately fifty men stuffed themselves into the starboard aircraft hangar in order to hear him speak. It had been a simple affair to start off with but with the rise of more complex issues such as the subjugation of Poland, the German counter-blockade of the British Isles and the Russians invading Finland, Irwin found the lectures more difficult to deliver.

The ship's company wanted to know why they had done absolutely nothing for the Poles; they wanted to know why the navy's sowing of minefields had to be declared to the Germans when the enemy neglected to reciprocate in this international understanding; they wanted to know why Chamberlain had promised to assist the Finns yet no declaration of war against Russia was in sight; and they wanted to know why there was no discernable movement on the part of British troops stationed in Europe.

Irwin's lectures had ceased to be as productive as they had once been and the men were beginning to think that he was just wasting their time; and he knew that his pro-peace stance was one of the root causes of his unpopularity.

An hour ago, Captain Dollimore had dragged him into his cabin to speak to him about his notes concerning the next lecture and, in as friendly a manner as possible, had made observations like, 'Do you not think that our helping the Finns defeat Russia might hasten the defeat of Germany?'

'Well, er ...' was all Irwin could muster.

'In your notes, you've leant heavily towards our fighting Russia ending in total calamity for the West. Do you think the ship's company want British military might to be written off quite so easily?'

'Mm, well ...'

'And you express the hope that our general inaction has bought time for heads on both sides to cool down clearing the way for peace negotiations to take place.'

Irwin was shocked that his thoughts needed explaining and in the face of this grilling his mind had emptied of all the relevant facts that he had studiously filled it with. The captain reminded him so much of the schoolmasters in whose classes his face had never seemed to fit.

Dollimore quickly tired of the man, thinking to advise him to stick to his primary job of navigation, but then decided on a last chance. 'You endeavour to build a strong case for peace, Mr Irwin, but we are playing by the rules of Hitler and Stalin now. They do not possess the same ...*virtues* as Neville Chamberlain and must be planned against accordingly. Your sentiments do you justice but, for the purposes of your lectures, if you cannot create a balanced argument for peace *and* war, then I suggest you stick to the plain facts and nothing more.'

'Yes, sir,' replied Irwin. Having offered nothing in his own defence, there was no other business to hand so he was curtly dismissed.
****
Midshipman Robert 'Beatty' Barclay-Thompson shivered with the cold and kept moving along the port waist. At least the sea was moderating even if the temperature was not. The *Burscombe*'s movements were much less pronounced and he was able to walk without holding onto the railings and lines. His sharp eyes noticing the salty stains, patches of rust and dull brass as he made his way, he knew that the captain would order the seamen to clean the lot as soon as he judged that the weather would not render it worthless.

He quickly nipped into the cross passage abaft the torpedo and divers' workshops and pulled open the hatch which led into the wardroom passage. He stepped inside, closed the door and then slid past the curtain which had been hung to block any light from escaping. Without looking at the stuffy officers who jealously guarded their space against the likes of him, he went through the second door on the portside.

This was the gunroom, the cramped but homely mess for the midshipmen, charmingly lit by the dim lamps. He took his coat off and, after hanging it upon one of the pegs, slumped down into an inviting leather armchair. Only five other lads were here right now. A couple of them were chatting in undertones, another was reading a newspaper and another was fast asleep at the table, his pen still poised over the letter he had been writing where the last unintelligible words had drifted off down the page.

Then there was David Clark, staring into space having given up on his own newspaper. It was he with whom Beatty wanted to share his news. Sometimes he considered their friendship to have an air of 'touch-and-go' about it but, having been cadets together at Dartmouth College, they had known each other since they were thirteen and shared common bonds in wit, entertainment and, to a large degree, temperament. But Clark had come to develop ideas about class issues which were unhelpful to their position and Beatty's attempts to make him see reason forever fell flat.

Today, however, what could go wrong with this news? 'David, I've just been informed that I shall be taking the sub-lieutenant's exam the moment we reach port.'

'Good on you,' Clark reacted wholeheartedly. He happily folded up the broadsheet of the *The Times* and slid it into the paper rack nearby.

'You know that means I'll be leaving the ship if I pass?'

'Well, of course,' replied Clark. Over the course of the last two and a half years or so they had done all their time in training ships, small ships and large ships together. However, they had always known that this sort of promotion came with a complete change of tack, that this was where their individual destinies truly began. That was usual.

'The only thing that bothers me,' said Beatty, 'is that you're older than me and you should really be getting this first.'

'Hogwash,' said Clark. 'Some are more deserving than others. Don't you worry, I shall be a sub soon enough.'

'Yes, but at this rate, not before you're twenty,' Beatty went on, hardly noticing that he was slipping back into the realms of frustration that his friend always seemed to engender within him.

'We can. ...' Clark began but was interrupted by the steward sliding open the door to the pantry, coming out and saying, 'Hot chocolate, sirs?'

'Thanks, Terry,' said Clark.

They paused in their conversation while the steward, bracing his legs against the constant swaying of the deck, placed the cups of steaming liquid down on the table.

It would be nice to get a full cup once in a while, thought David, but in a rolling ship, two-thirds full as a deterrent to any spillage would have to do.

'Wind's abatin', sir,' said the steward as though to comfort them.

'What?' asked Beatty, suddenly realising that the man had addressed him. 'Oh, yes.'

Once the steward had retreated and closed the pantry door behind him, Beatty took out a cigarette and lit it up. Sinking deeper into the dangerously comfortable armchair, he continued, 'You were saying?'

'Just that we can argue the toss about my suitability for promotion until we're blue in the face,' said Clark. 'We both know that I'm a bloody screw-up.'

'And there's only one person who can remedy that situation.'

'Yes, yes, yes. Me.' Clark had heard this many times before and not just from Beatty. But he had made his tone dismissive. He could not see the point in talking about it any further.

Beatty shook his head. 'At times you're impossible, David. You should grow up. The way you approach your duties – some of the time at least – and the feud that you insist on prolonging with your family can only have negative effects. As far as I'm concerned you're wasting your God-given talents.'

'Don't preach to me about my family,' said Clark, taking on that look of indignation that was so familiar to his friend. 'You don't know the half of what they've done to me. So just count yourself lucky that you grew up with a father you respect, someone you idolise, whose lessons were worth absorbing. I didn't have that. Any of it.'

Beatty gave a short, 'Huh!' then said, 'Even if you did I'm sure you'd find a way to ruin it.'

Clark felt his blood boiling over and bit his tongue so that he would not say anything that he would regret. For all Beatty's narrow mind, he still had great regard for him and did not want to ruin what they had. He picked up the hot chocolate and started sipping. That would help calm him.

It was just as well that their exchange ceased when it did because, at that moment, the door opened and Mishipman Farlow stepped inside. This rotund, red-cheeked cockroach had been on all the same ships as Beatty and Clark and had a history with them that stretched all the way back to joining Dartmouth. If there was one person that they wished would go away it was him, but they had resigned themselves to the fact that his constant presence would only ever be addressed by promotion, disease or death.

'Nobby' Clark had become the object of particular dislike to Farlow because of the way in which he talked down their class. They were gentlemen and he did not seem to understand what that meant. There was also an intense jealousy because of the easy way in which Clark rose to heroism.

Farlow was no hero. He often wished that he could be but he was too addicted to self-interest and gossip to recognise when it was that he could be doing the right thing. It was a family trait. He looked at Clark and, in his exaggerated upper class tones, said, 'Oh, you're here. Are you not due on the bridge?'

'I've half an hour yet,' said Clark, 'and what's it got to do with you?'

Farlow huffed a little, narrowed his eyes and flicked his head back but having started on Clark, something one would have thought he had learned not to do, he was now a little put out by his stare. He always stopped short of ruffling Clark's feathers too much because he did not really know how to get the better of him.

He sat down at the table, slapped it with his palm in order to wake up the sleeping junior hunched over his letter, and started stuffing tobacco into his pipe. 'Well, Nobby,' he began afresh, looking back at Clark, 'what was your impression of our Norwegian friends? When are the fools going to wake up and just admit that it would be better if they came into the war on our side? I don't understand this neutral claptrap. Take a side, I always say, take a side.'

Clark shrugged. 'What's the point in even talking to you about it? You're a political nincompoop.'

'Oh, I say!' returned Farlow, offended by the chuckling of the other midshipmen. 'I simply asked you a civil question. I am interested, you know.'

'Really?'

'Yes.'

Clark considered that for a moment and decided to answer with, 'Okay. They're very cautious; possibly even scared and with good reason. They're between a rock and a hard place and it's too easy to suggest that they should simply be better off by joining our side in the war. Even with U-boats sinking their ships without warning they still have to consider the repercussions of going against Hitler.'

'But then they would get the unequivocal support of Great Britain and her empire.'

Frowning, Clark leaned forward and said, 'Poland had our support and we did nothing.'

'Poland's too far away,' Farlow stated in a manner so blasé it was as though he was dismissing the Poles with a sweep of his hand.

'Yes, Poland *is* too far away yet the people of Norway and other neutral countries watched while she was subdued by a lightning German attack against which *we did nothing*.'

'We declared war!'

'How the hell did that help them?'

'I say,' cut in Beatty, aware that the juniors were listening to the conversation with concern, 'there's no reason to get all steamed up about it.'

'Mark my words,' said Clark, 'for right or for wrong, the Norwegians are suspicious of the Germans *and* us; and eventually, they're going to be forced into this war against their will by one side or the other – and they're not going to thank us for it.'

\*\*\*\*

Later that night, after the 'pipe down' had been sounded and the lighting in the officers' cabins flat above the wardroom had been reduced, Clark lay in his hammock unable to sleep. He had finished his stint on the bridge and, regarding the gentler motion of the ship, had actually being faced with the prospect of a night without being swung violently back and forth against a nearby electrical junction box with the smell of raw sewage drifting up out of the nearby heads. He may well have been yearning for the day when he was to graduate to getting his own cabin away from this draughty passage but his conversation with Beatty had set his mind turning again.

It was the matter of his family which perturbed him the most. Mention of them had started him thinking about the contents of the last letter that he had received in Rosyth. Since his attempt to cut off ties with them, his mother had written to him over and over, presumably begging him to contact her, possibly with explanations and excuses for her conduct. He had never read those letters. He had thrown them all away.

This last one was different in that it was from Henry, his eldest brother, who was currently commanding a group of destroyers out in the Mediterranean. Henry was not like all the others. He could safely be considered the only member of the immediate family who had not manipulated him, pressured him into this service, or made decisions that affected his future in what he would consider to be an adverse way. He alone deserved a hearing.

The letter had read:

*Dear David,*

*I can only assume you are well after hearing nothing more of you beyond* The Times *article that appeared at Christmas. Well done – a first taste of action and a news story to boot! I knew that you had a strong dose of the family's heroic streak in you. But I also know that you never did manage to see eye to eye with father before he died and that greatly saddens me.*

*A letter from me is a rarity, I know, so you've probably already guessed I am writing on behalf of mother, who is at her wits end, thinking she has done you a great wrong. You have always been a very passionate person and I fully understand that you are angry, but surely your perception of the situation is exaggerated.*

*Mother needs our support right now. In case you don't know, our sister is presently very low and needs almost constant attention. Patty is pregnant and this delicate time is complicated by the fact that she has lost both her father and her husband. Please spare a thought for her.*

*This family must stand together. We are in crisis and you can only do us all harm by not answering mother's letters, offering your sympathy and support and behaving like a Clark should.*

The letter went on to describe life in the Mediterranean, though being careful not to mention any names of people, places or ships.

Clark's initial reaction upon reading it had been astonishment at his brother's naive tone and righteous pursuit. Henry, for the most part, had escaped the attentions of their father when they were growing up. He was of a more simplistic nature, more accepting and less rebellious, perhaps just more comfortable within himself and it was very probable that he had scant knowledge of the situation which had lately arisen. If he knew more he might be taking a different stance with this attempted reconciliation.

Still, it could not work anyway. Clark had many reasons to resist, not least that he had been forced to join the navy against his will, been singled out as an unwanted nuisance by his father from the moment he had been born and had been thoroughly denied a voice throughout his whole life. Most importantly, however, was the matter which had finally driven him away.

There was a young woman that he had wished to marry, a true sweetheart in his eyes called Maggie, but while he had been away, shackled to this ship, his mother had conspired to remove her from his life. A deal had been struck with Maggie's parents. Money had been spent – a bribe.

But what had been the impediment? Maggie was the daughter of a publican from the village of Welbury, near the Clarks' ancestral home of

North Cedars. Her station was far beneath his and her breeding would never match his.

He considered that idea to be decidedly narrow but he knew he was very much alone in his views; and he knew that it was not just his rebellious nature that insisted he marry such a woman. He liked to think that he met all people on an equal plane, thereafter to make judgments based upon what he found in their characters and conscience. Maggie was as good as, if not better, than women of his own class. Look at how her calm and generous approach to life differed from the demanding and wicked ways of his sister Patricia.

Mother's hope was that, with Maggie gone, he would eventually mature enough to marry a woman of superior breeding. Until she understood what his perception of superior was, he was going to ignore her pleas.

But then, if that was his resolution, why was he lying here awake agonising over the whole affair? If he was to be truly honest with himself, he wanted to be reconciled with his mother. She had been one of the steadfast influences in his tough life until this episode had revealed the dark extent of her prejudices.

No, for the moment brother Henry had sadly wasted his time in making her case.

Clark tried to concentrate on the creaking of the hammock clews as they stretched with the motion of the ship, the whirring of the distant generators or the gentle straining of the steel plates around him. They must bring on sleep.

****

Les was not Gordy's real first name. He was actually an Albert but the young Irishman was often seen with a large, heavy copy of the book *Les Misérables* in his hands. His father had told him it was a classic so he had made it one of his missions in life to read it in order to find out what made it so. He had been going at it for the best part of two years now and was still struggling through the confusing mash of the first few pages. To say that he was stumped was an understatement. He was beginning to think that his father had been lying to him like everyone else seemed to.

His expression of consternation must have been evident as Smudge leaned across the mess table to stare down at him where he lay on the bench, his head propped up on a folded coat.

'What?' asked Les, now even more concerned because he had attracted the attention of the ship's comedian – again. Smudge kept making everybody laugh at him and he had no clue what he had done to deserve it.

'I could ask you the same thing,' answered Smudge, his usual mischievous look not in evidence. In fact, he had adopted a soft but serious expression.

Les noted that his words were not of a ridiculing nature so decided that he might actually be able to help this time round. He cautiously said, 'It's just something I don't understand.'

'Well, there's nothin' unusual there, my son. I've never met anyone with a life as confusin' as yours.'

'No, it's in this book,' said Les. He showed Smudge the spine. 'It's *Les Misérables* ...'

'Get away!'

The boy had clearly forgotten that it was Smudge and Pincher who had bought him this particular book when his last copy had been a casualty in the fight against the *Moltke*.

Les continued, 'It goes on about this fella of the bishopric being a canon. What's that all about?'

From his vantage point at the end of the bench, where he was servicing a small collection of worn lanyards, Pincher already started smiling and shaking his head. It was just that Les always unwittingly provided Smudge with priceless material to get his dirty mind racing. Inevitably, Les's shock was going to be just as funny as the joke.

Smudge did not disappoint. 'You're an Irish Catholic, ain't yer?' Met with nothing but a concerned stare from the lad, he continued with, 'Well, you must know what the bishop's prick looks like.'

Then all Les could do was look from one person to another as a chorus of laughter came from the other nearby messes. Why did they always poke fun at him like this? There were times when he thought that he was one of them and then somebody, usually Smudge, would say something hideously disgusting or complex and he would find himself wondering what he had done to provoke them.

But thankfully Pincher always came forward as the voice of reason, the man who stopped the others becoming too overbearing. He was a decent man, the only one who brought clarity to this crazy, mixed up world. He stopped Smudge before he drove Les back into that hard shell which he had worked so hard to emerge from. 'Come on,' he said, 'Les asked a perfectly valid question and there's no reason to take the mick.'

'Sorry, you're right,' said Smudge. He turned back to Les and sighed, thinking hard to make up for his crudity. 'The canon has obviously been given personification by the bishop – do you understand? – the fella being the embodiment of the work carried out by that canon. It's the same has giving your gun a name. Have you named your gun?'

Les thought about his action station, the battery of 2-pounder pom-poms up on the edge of the flight deck, and wondered why something like that would require a name. 'No,' he replied.

'Well, you should. Mine's called Fred.'

With a suppression of giggles from hereabouts, the other men added, 'Mine's called Johnson,' 'Mine's Barry,' 'I call mine The Beast,' and so on.

'Does that answer your question?' asked Smudge. Regarding Les's blank look, he finally became exasperated and said, 'If ever there was a reason not to let the Irish in the Royal Navy, it's you.'

Suddenly, from the other side of the mess beyond the armoured barbette, there came a threatening voice laced with an unmistakably Irish tone, 'You wanna say that to me?'

Smudge looked over and was a little alarmed to see Paddy Walbrook, the huge leading seaman from Mess 21, stepping through the gaggle of passing blokes to come and square up to him. He had never seen Paddy hit anyone before but he was sure what the effect would be if those fists ever did come into contact with someone's skull. Smudge raised his hands in submission. 'Obviously you excepted, Paddy, old chum. The navy needs men like you.'

'Really?' replied Paddy, unimpressed. 'I only joined your mob 'cause it was the only place I could get a square meal. The only other plus point is listening to idiots like you talk.'

'Ah, so you do find me funny.'

'No, you make me feel feckin' good about myself.'

At that moment Leading Seaman Haggerty, he who was ugly enough to be styled 'The Turtle', clambered in through the aft hatch, walking skilfully against the deck's pitching motion which was always worse up here in the forrard end than elsewhere.

'Turtle!' cried Smudge relieved, for the newcomer was the only man here who could match Paddy's stature. 'Do you mind helping Paddy back over to his own side of the ship?'

'Get stuffed,' mumbled the Turtle.

Paddy took a step closer to Smudge and said, 'You see? 'E don't think you're funny either.' Then, pointing menacingly at Les, he added, 'And you! Stand up for yerself a little more! You're a feckin' disgrace!'

Les, now sitting up, was completely bemused. No matter what trouble there was between others, it always seemed to end up with them abusing him. He watched Paddy disappear back to his own mess, wondering what he had done to antagonise him.

After rummaging briefly in his locker, the Turtle draped a couple of vests and a pair of trousers over his shoulder, threw a lump of misshapen 'pusser's hard' soap into a bucket and turned to leave.

'Turtle,' said Pincher, 'I've finished your lanyard and I'll tell you what; dhobey my white-front and I'll waive the sip of rum what you owe me.'

'Go on, then,' the Turtle replied in his strangely gruff voice which sounded like it came from the back of his neck rather than his larynx.

Les sat up and asked, 'Oh, can you do mine?'

'Get stuffed,' the Turtle said once again. But now Les had attracted his attention. 'How is it you've got time to be lazin' around?'

'I've not been drafted for nothing, killick.'

'Aren't you wanted for deck scrubbin'?'

Les glanced at his watch and said, 'Got another five minutes yet.'

'Your boots are scuffed. Why don't you clean 'em?'

'I ...'

'What I'm saying is,' said the Turtle, rounding on him with gritted teeth, 'is that everybody else around here is doing somethin' useful so get off your bloody backside and do some work or I'll get you some extra time cleanin' the heads or somethin'.' Then he climbed back through the hatch.

Les unhappily sauntered across to his locker, put the book away and found his boot polish just in time to put it back in order to go and report for duty.

Pincher was still thinking about the Turtle. He had found himself considering him a lot recently.

The usually dependable killick had been brooding and angry ever since coming back from leave. One would have thought that he should have been in better spirits having just enjoyed two weeks out, but something had happened to really sour his mood. All the other blokes just accepted the fact that he must have failed to get his end away and then stayed away from him as much as possible. On a ship of this size it was fairly easy to keep a good distance from a man you did not have to work or live with.

For Pincher and a few others, avoiding him was difficult and they certainly wished that they had the happier Turtle they had known before New Year's. What had happened at home?

Pincher had a suspicion which, incidentally, he was keeping to himself because it concerned a couple of gangland murders that had recently been reported in the papers. They had happened in the Turtle's neighbourhood, one of them having occurred at the same time he was there. Pincher had written home, asking his mum to let him know if there was any local buzz on the subject but he had not received a reply yet.

He would not exactly claim to know the Turtle personally but he knew of him since they had been brought up on the same streets, those of Bethnal Green in the East End of London. Pincher was nearly a decade older and had left to join the Merchant Navy when he was fifteen. But even then he had been aware of the ugly young boy who had had to develop a mean streak out of necessity.

He remembered vividly dossing with his friends in the high street during the summer of 1921. One day the six-year-old Harry Haggerty had come walking by. The plump little boy had his shirt hanging out of his shorts, one of his laces trailing from his tatty shoes and a pretty vacant look on his unwashed, chinless face.

One of Pincher's mates, Dan, fancied himself as leader of the pack and, to tell the truth, he was bit of a mean git. Smiling a wicked smile, he casually blocked little Harry's path and announced, 'Have a butcher's at this stumpy little piece of shit.' Then, to the frightened boy, he said, 'I bet your mum and dad 'ate you. Sick dogs usually get put down.' Without any warning, his fist came flying up and contacted sharply with Harry's left ear.

While the lad staggered, the rest of the gang laughed though, Pincher reflected, it was more out of fear of Dan than actual humour.

They had then expected tears and panicked flight but Harry instead closed his eyes, bowed his head and charged at his attacker. In a movement faster than the one that had caught him off-guard he had ploughed his head into Dan's stomach and brought up his fist to crash into his groin.

Of course, Harry then ran away at high speed but had left Dan leaning, ashen-faced, against a shop window, groaning pathetically. The balance of respect had shifted in Harry Haggerty's favour that day and Pincher suspected that he had never looked back.

Sure enough, Haggerty was a leading seaman now and had been holding his own against the world superbly – up until this patrol. Someone who usually handled himself in a respectfully authoritative manner, he was now distant to the point of arrogance. Was it something to do with those murders?

Even if Pincher was totally wrong about that, the Turtle's bad humour was already having other consequences. On the *Dagrand*, he had accused Les of tying that infamous knot to the railing, the one which had nearly done for some of their mates in the cutter. Only a fool would tie a knot like that because of the possibility of the very incident which had occurred; and Les had been easy to blame. After all, he was a borderline fool.

Pincher wished he could be sure about it but he could have sworn that it had been the Turtle who had tied that knot.

# THREE

## The *Altmark* Incident

The small but significant epidemic of influenza that had swept through the Home Fleet was just another insult adding to the men's woes. That was how Lieutenant Philip Dollimore viewed it anyway. They had difficulties enough to surmount in that dreadful weather without God allowing this. It had been one of the worst winters on record, a sick joke on the part of the Almighty. Philip was especially unhappy about it because he had been one of those who had succumbed to the virus.

Just after New Year's it had put him off his feet for the best part of a week and even now his legs still shook when he stood watch on the bridge for too long. The heart of the matter was that the war was not yet half a year old and he could already boast two periods of convalescence in that time. It was not good enough. Though one might ask, what could he have done about either instance?

Was this to be the measure of his luck? He certainly hoped not for he had a score to settle with the Germans and it was of no light nature. Last October his number had almost been up when his ship had been torpedoed and sunk, but the precipitate death of his best friend in the disaster did not sit well with him. It was tough to describe John Bushey as 'killed in action'. He never had a chance to fight. Neither had the other eight hundred plus men who had perished in HMS *Royal Oak*. The Germans had surprised them while they were sleeping, tucked up in what was supposed to be a safe anchorage; and Winston Churchill had had the temerity to stand in the House of Commons and all but applaud their daring. Well, sod that!

So, Philip had been out once with injuries and then again with influenza. Once the surgeon-commander ashore at Invergordon had finally cleared him fit for duty, his superiors had had to have a quick think about where to place him, such was the confusion caused by the epidemic. Some ship's companies had been disbanded in order to plug gaps in others where they were unable to put to sea. But the appointment and drafting processes of the Royal Navy were nothing if not efficient and he was quickly sent to this neat little destroyer, HMS *Cossack*.

This proven workhorse of a ship was undergoing various changes in her complement and Philip had arrived to an atmosphere of healthy enthusiasm even if it was laced with unfamiliarity. As the days progressed, they had gone to sea perfecting their drills on the go, patrolling the unforgiving stretch of sea in the approaches to the German-dominated Baltic.

By now, however, he had hoped to become more comfortable with his brother officers. Somehow it was just not happening. He felt there was something naive about them, that they did not really get what was going on in this war. Over a drink or two in the wardroom, he had tried to explain the cunning that they were up against but the chaps had taken the odd stance of just humouring him and then finding excuses to keep their distance. He knew quite early on that his social experience in the *Cossack* was not going to be the same as that he had enjoyed in the *Royal Oak*.

Certainly what did not help was that the new captain was a difficult man. Upon taking command he was already highly respected as a hard-fighting captain but came to exercise a strictness which arguably did not benefit everyone. If he thought that a man was not doing his utmost in the execution of his duty then his razor-tongued irritation would cut a man right down to size. He was uncompromising, liking or disliking men to the extremes. There was no in-between. He let only a very few subordinates into his inner confidence and, for whatever reason, Philip Dollimore was not one of them.

The only time that Captain Vian had really taken an interest in him was on the day they had started to proceed across the North Sea in heavy weather to their present patrol position. With the spray constantly whipping up over them and the persistent waves intermittently hampering their efforts to keep station with the other ships in company, Vian enquired after his unusual name. He wanted to know what most men wanted to know ever since the *Burscombe* had started making a name for herself. 'Captain Charles Dollimore is your father, isn't he?'

'Yes, sir,' Philip replied.

'If all captains were like him then we'd have no problem defeating the Hun.' This was becoming the generic reaction to the information gleaned.

'I'll not deny I thought him a fool when I met him years ago but I thoroughly underestimated him; and that hardly ever happens.'

Yes, they love my father, Philip thought. He certainly is an act very difficult to follow.

Vian then stated, 'I'm told that you understand Norwegian.'

Averting his face from the freezing water which splashed across him to the *Cossack*'s pitch, Philip stared at him and replied, 'No, sir.'

'So I was lied to, then?'

Philip did not need bad feeling developing over such a minor issue, especially with whoever had given him this knowledge, so he explained, 'I understand a few words, sir, enough to order luncheon and a drink.'

'So, you do speak Norwegian,' said Vian scathingly. 'That's all I needed to know.'

As the captain turned to leave, Philip added, 'Mr Craven, I think, knows more than I.'

'I daresay,' Vian remarked, curling his lips in disgust. He then disappeared down the ladder abaft the bridge.

Philip gave him a glance as he went. He had heard that Vian had all but assumed command of this group of ships in a way that was not entirely ordinary. The buzz was that the *Altmark* was somewhere hereabouts and he wanted to be the one to make the interception. It was a highly unlikely affair in Philip's opinion. If he was the German captain then he would steer well clear of this place.

\*\*\*\*

A couple of hours of tough vigilance passed. There was nothing like hard work to take his mind from the million and one matters that forever weighed down his brain. He looked all around at the brightening horizons as the destroyer's bridge swayed and heaved beneath his feet. Thankfully the spray drenching them had lessened. It had been difficult to shake off the last of that flu while he was constantly soaked to the skin.

The violence of the other ships' rolling was easing as well. Including *Cossack*, there were six of them keeping pace together: five destroyers and the small light cruiser HMS *Arethusa*. It was not a bad little force for hunting the enemy – if the enemy was even there.

Vian's cutting voice came up the voicepipe, 'Dollimore, set us on a course to patrol up the Norwegian coast and signal *Intrepid* and *Ivanhoe* to follow.'

Soon after setting the three destroyers on a mean course of three-four-five degrees with a view to making corrections as they went, Philip was relieved on the bridge and ordered to the captain's day cabin. He entered and found himself standing amongst the other officers gathered. Clutching at the hot chocolate that the steward had just handed him, he knew that he certainly needed to get some warmth through to his bones but considered this to be a far from substantial drink. Not able to join in the enthusiastic speculation on their immediate future, there was the soothing of his indignation to be considered and he wished that he was able to discreetly flip open the top of his hipflask and pour some whisky into the chocolate.

The chatter respectfully died away when Vian entered. Everybody remained standing.

With no further ado, the captain glanced condescendingly across the table at Philip. 'God bless your father. He may have come up trumps again.'

To the lieutenants and subs assembled, he continued in his decisive tones, 'Captain Dollimore in the *Burscombe* has passed on what he believes to be credible intelligence on the whereabouts of the *Altmark*.'

Craven, Turner and McLean shared grins. Their suspicions on what the course alteration meant had been correct.

'It is believed that she has managed to reach Norwegian territorial waters and is using them to get home,' continued Vian in his precise tones. 'As you know, the key to this whole mission are the missing crews taken from our merchant ships. If she is carrying them then she is in contravention of international law. Now, the difficult part of all this is that, if we find her, Churchill has ordered us to edge her out to the open sea, there to board her away from Norwegian interference. That might be easier said than done, quite frankly, and if we can't get her to come away from the shore I don't know at what liberty we shall find ourselves able to act. But, make no mistake, I know what I *want* to do should the situation arise.'

All agreed with him.

Philip pictured the three destroyers steaming right over the line of demarcation and encircling the *Altmark*. His mind's eye showed the deceitful Hun being cut down as they brazenly protested their innocence. What innocence? They were not going to get away with this.

He was not quite sure how long his imagination controlled his body but he was suddenly aware that Vian had been talking and he had not been hearing the words. A sweat had broken out on his brow and his muscles were tense. Damn! He hoped that the end of the briefing had not held anything important.

\*\*\*\*

The day was freezing yet the sea was calm and visibility was clearing up nicely. Philip and his lookouts were relying on their wits for this one because, like everyone else in the fleet, no one was exactly sure what the *Altmark* looked like. He and McLean had looked at a photograph in a tattered copy of the *Illustrated London News* that somebody had dredged up from below, and they had not fully decided whether the vessel in question was the four-masted ship in the foreground or the two-masted smudge behind. They had spied various ships travelling up and down the coast and had eliminated each one as innocent merchantmen.

As he looked along the distant snowy blue-grey rocks of the wild shoreline, periodically raising his binoculars to his eyes, a red-nosed petty officer telegraphist appeared from below and handed over a slip of paper. Philip perused the words and said, 'Thanks.'

With the PO happily returning to his office and protection from the remnants of the wind, Philip alerted Vian through the voicepipe.

Before long, the captain appeared before him and asked, 'So, where is she?' It was characteristically to the point.

Philip made sure he did not mince his words. 'An air patrol has spotted *Altmark* hugging the coast just north of here, sir.'

Vian took the signal paper and read the information.

Philip could almost physically observe the facts being mapped out in the captain's mind – the excitement of the chase and the precision of the interception. The yearning for action was written right across his features. Then, without even looking up, Vian said, 'You don't look well, Mr Dollimore. Perhaps you should go below.'

Alarm bells flashed through Philip's mind. Effectively be relieved at the moment of action? Never. 'I assure you I am perfectly fine, sir,' he protested, though in as understated way as he could.

Vian looked him in the eye. 'As long as you're sure.'

'I am, sir.'

With the slightest of nods, the captain was gone.

The men who knew Vian the best worked to the premise that, as long as they did their jobs as professionally as they could and were not found to be lacking, they would always maintain his confidence. Philip realised that he must demonstrate this also and what better way to do this than distinguish himself in this hunt? But what of his desire for a drink? He wished that he did not have such a terrible thirst. A little alcohol was the only thing which helped him take all this in his stride. He knew it was wrong but there was no helping it.

Vian talked to his officers and a general agreement developed upon where the enemy ship would be sighted.

The three sturdy destroyers cruised on and Philip strained his eyes as hard as the lookouts in the hope of being the first one to see her.

After what seemed like many painful hours, the silhouette of a two-masted merchant ship came over the horizon blending intermittently with the varying contours of the coastline. Philip's breath caught with the excitement and he quickly conferred with the nearest able seaman over the magazine's photograph.

'Aye, sir, that'd be the smudge in the background,' said the stubble-chinned watchdog.

The *Altmark* was moving casually southwards giving the impression of being completely innocent, advancing her everyday business as though on a peacetime cruise. But was the mask of calm and legality hiding three hundred British prisoners? And what of the rumour that she had been fitted out with guns?

Very quickly the *Cossack* and her two sisters were brought to Action Stations and Captain Vian assumed complete control over the proceedings. 'Well done, Dollimore,' he said, before switching his mind to the task in hand.

Philip stood back and felt great relief and bloodlust all at the same moment. This was a moment of reckoning for him. It was the first time that there was the possibility of truly grappling with the enemy. On board the *Oak* there had been no fighting back. He never even saw the enemy, simply fell victim to their shadowy daring, which in due course stripped him of the naive bravado he had shared with his old companions.

He raised his binoculars to his eyes and reported, 'Sir, she's seen us. She's changing course to duck behind those islands.'

'No matter,' replied Vian coldly. 'It won't do her any good. I have just received permission from Churchill to go in and get our people out.'

Philip was impressed. With such decisiveness upon this most difficult of political situations, which was but one of many, how could there be anything other than success?

Then they were doing it. British warships were blatantly hunting their prey in Norwegian waters. Vian took his destroyers around the southern edge of the islands and very soon the rusting tanker, trailing her thin line of diesel exhaust into the light grey sky, reappeared with all the audacity of one who was sure that they were going to get away with it.

'Steer two points to starboard for interception,' Vian commanded.

As the destroyers picked up speed and pushed in closer towards the target, Philip kept his eyes scanning the *Altmark*'s decks for any sign of the guns that she may or may not be carrying. There was nothing apparent though that did not mean that she was not hiding her weapons behind some fake bulkhead somewhere, or stowed inconspicuously behind the lifeboats.

The tanker altered course again. Turning to port, she leaned ever so slightly out of the turn and threw up a little extra froth at the wake as she tried to pick up enough speed to outrun her pursuers. There clearly remained one thing the German captain could do if he did not want to be caught and that was to put in somewhere safe on the Norwegian coast and beg for protection.

Vian ordered a corresponding correction to the *Cossack*'s course while Philip lapped up the thrill of the chase. There was every possibility that they were sparking off a major international incident but they were ploughing onwards regardless. This should make some work for those bloody politicians who trembled at the thought of upsetting Adolf Hitler.

'There, sir,' Philip said, 'she's making a dash for that fjord.'

Vian raised his binoculars to his eyes and briefly scanned the rocky shore whose dark, jagged contours were broken by bright ice and snow. The mouth of the fjord, whose breadth was becoming more apparent the closer they got to it, boasted a flat calm surface and was flanked by high hills. Close into the shore were a few small vessels, fishing boats and what looked like … 'I think I see a couple of Norwegian gunboats. Is it a coincidence that they're here or are they complicit in this affair? Mr McLean, what fjord is this is?'

The other lieutenant glanced across and answered, 'Jossingfjord, sir. As fjords go it's very small.'

This is fantastic, thought Philip. He really, finally believed that Vian meant to follow the *Altmark* right up into the fjord itself. But what about those gunboats? Even with the torpedo tubes that they displayed they were no match for these destroyers, but how far were they willing to push this? Would Vian sanction their destruction?

The crews of the gunboats let the *Altmark* disappear unceremoniously behind the curve of the river bank then began to manoeuvre in such a way as to block the passage of the destroyers. Philip willed Vian to head straight for them and see how fast they got out of the way but was immediately shamed by the captain's actual approach.

He ordered his ships to slow and come up on the Norwegians in a non-threatening manner, saying to those around him, 'Don't worry. The *Altmark*'s not going anywhere. She's trapped in there like her mistress was at Montevideo last December. Right then, let's see what these little men here have got to say for themselves.'

Philip clambered down into the starboard waist and immediately ordered one of the seamen to lower a rope ladder over the side. It was done with unflinching professionalism.

The 'little men' from the nearest gunboat were standing tall, officious and gloating as they manoeuvred their small grey vessel towards the motionless *Cossack*. One man stood at the ready behind the gun on the bow while others waited by their torpedo tubes. The atmosphere became tense, this threat of force almost smothering the strict legal process. The fenders were thrown out and the senior Norwegian officer leapt for the rope ladder as the gunboat bumped softly along the side of the destroyer.

This man was bulky and agile but the white flecks in his hair showed him to be ageing. The way in which he handled himself, his large hands confidently gripping the ropes, proved that he had spent his life at sea. For that alone he should deserve respect except that he curtly refused Philip's offer of help in assisting him over the side rail. If that was the way he wanted to play it, then so be it.

The young seaman who had lowered the ladder then called down to the gunboat's other crew, 'Obstructing justice, mates? You'll be sorry later on, so you will.'

Philip understood the sentiment more than the Norwegians understood the words. Still, that was no excuse. 'Pipe down! That's not for you to decide!' he said.

'Aye aye, sir,' came the dejected reply.

Philip led the foreign captain up the ladders to the bridge. There they found Vian standing very loose and smiling, the perfect image of patient charm.

He dispensed with the pleasantries as quick as was polite then began to insist that the *Cossack* be allowed to proceed. The Norwegian answered at some length in the most haughty manner and young Sub-Lieutenant Craven translated: 'Sir, he says that we've got it all wrong, that the German ship is in these waters legally and we are not.'

'Press the point about the prisoners,' said Vian.

'He already mentioned that, sir, stating that the vessel has been searched by Norwegian authorities and he can confirm that there are no British prisoners onboard.'

Philip was grinning garishly. He knew that some of the others had noticed but he could not help it. It was because they would shortly see Vian's anger erupt, tell this upstart that he was talking hogwash and put him over the side. Then they would proceed into the fjord and force their own resolution to the situation.

But Vian's reaction, when it came, was stunning. 'In that case,' he said, still maintaining his calm, 'there is nothing more for us to do here, gentlemen. Mr Dollimore, if you please, see our friend here to his boat and then take us back out to international waters.'

After Philip, thoroughly deflated, had got rid of the pompously triumphant 'little' man, he returned to the bridge to find all the other officers gone save Sub-Lt Craven. He immediately shrugged his shoulders in a gesture of despair. 'That can't be it. What's the captain thinking?'

The boyish officer before him looked to either side in embarrassment. Conscious of the discretion that should surround the machinations of the officers' minds, he answered in lowered tones, 'If we go in, best case scenario is that we'll cause an international incident; worse case scenario is that we'll make Norway declare war on us.'

'Only if the prisoners are not there,' replied Philip, losing his temper with the sub. 'The captain was all for it fifteen minutes ago.'

'And what if they really aren't there, sir?'

'Of course they're bloody well there!'

Craven looked duly embarrassed at the other's maniacal expression. Why couldn't Lieutenant Dollimore just be quiet and leave it all to Vian?

****

The low-lying sun which had been trying unsuccessfully to throw some warmth on the proceedings finally gave up and sunk below the horizon. The usual deep chill of night descended and cut Philip to the bone. His tortured muscles began shaking again. In a little while, down in the wardroom, he forced some thin strips of warm gravy-covered chicken with potatoes down his throat and supplemented this with a generous shot of whisky. No matter what anyone said about the evils of strong drink, it certainly helped warm the cockles.

Suddenly the shrill sound of the bosun's whistle came through the nearby loudspeaker followed by the voice of one of the chiefs: 'Do you hear there? Officers to the bridge.'

He pushed his plate away and immediately made for the door in company with Lieutenant Turner, who had immediately filed away the work he was doing in order to follow. They quickly took their heavy coats from the hooks by the door and walked swiftly out onto slippery deck, up the ladder and onto the darkened bridge.

Strong moonlight cast eerie shadows over every mysterious corner and Vian's face seemed thinner and paler, his eyes buried deep in the gloom created by the peak of his cap. His expression remained stern, his demeanour powerful. 'Gentlemen,' he said, when everybody was present, 'very shortly we shall be entering the fjord. Our orders are to re-establish contact with our Norwegian friends and offer them assistance in escorting the *Altmark* to Bergen to be searched again. There's to be no doubt as to whether she holds British prisoners or not and she must certainly never be allowed to reach Germany with said prisoners onboard.'

Turner said, 'Judging by the attitude of that chap we spoke to earlier, they're not going to take kindly to that, sir.'

'Frankly, I'm neither here nor there on whether they'll take kindly to it. Make no mistake, what happens here tonight could have severe repercussions, which is why I signalled the Admiralty for further instructions.' He emphasised the point by holding up a small slip of paper that he had been holding in his hand.

'So, what if they don't accept our offer?' asked Philip.

Vian straightened his back and broadened his shoulders, a clear sign that his answer was going to be weighty and definitive. 'Our instructions come from Churchill himself. If we're rebuffed then we shall enter the fjord and board the *Altmark* regardless. If the Norwegians fire upon us we have been given leave to fire back – within reason, of course; more with a view to inform them of their folly than to destroy them. Mr Turner, if this goes the way that I suspect, you will lead the boarding party.'

'Very good, sir,' Turner answered, his glee evident.

'Dollimore and Craven, you will accompany him. It's now or never, gentlemen. By morning the *Altmark* could very possibly have a battlecruiser escort out of Wilhelmshaven and then we'll be stuffed.'

Philip cocked his head to one side. 'But we want a battlecruiser to come out, don't we, sir? That's what all these never-ending patrols have been about.'

'Mr Dollimore,' continued Vian, his voice audibly deepening with distaste, 'this mission is separate to the usual objectives of the Northern Patrol. It's about those prisoners and showing Jerry up for the crook he is, and nothing more. Our fleet might bag itself a battlecruiser but fat lot of good it will do us if the *Altmark* gets away in the confusion, or gets sunk, God forbid. Now, does anybody else have any insightful questions or are you willing to just follow my orders?'

There was silence all round. There was no hint of dissent. Every other man was Vian's to the end. Philip Dollimore was nothing to them.

'Right, let's get on with it then.'

They nodded or voiced their understanding and orders were quickly issued around the ship as to what was expected from every man. The excitement in the air could not be doubted and Philip quickly forgot the tense exchange and found himself buying into it. British forces had to reiterate the point somewhere that they were serious about this war. It might as well be here. He reflected upon the fact that the decision for this action had come straight from Winston Churchill, the only man in the War Cabinet with any gusto. With a little chuckle, he wondered what Prime Minister Neville Chamberlain thought about all this. His strategy so far had been to do everything in his power not to upset Adolf Hitler, so Philip hoped the duff old statesman was squirming in his nice, comfy bed in Downing Street right now.

In his hurting brain, he had conveniently forgotten that he hated Churchill.

After a short time, the grumbling from the *Cossack*'s boilers and engines picked up and her propellers pushed her through the dark grey water towards the coast which was distinctly illuminated by the timely glare of the moon. All seemed perfect. Even the wind and sea were behaving themselves.

The gunboats were still in the entrance way to the fjord and the same squat little vessel with its proud crew made a course to intercept them. Just as before, Vian stopped and allowed the boat to come alongside and the egotistical man who had made such a mark earlier in the day revisited the bridge, confident that he would get rid of the impudent British once again.

From his position on the gun deck forrard of the bridge, Philip heard the tone of the Norwegian's gruff voice become more agitated as the negotiation turned sour. Then Craven translated Vian's final ultimatum of, 'It's really quite simple. If you fire on us, we'll fire on you. My government is quite prepared to take the consequences of any action I take tonight. Now, my good sir, you may retire to your vessel or, if you prefer, you are welcome to stay here and observe – make sure that my actions are proper.' A certain sarcasm lined that last statement.

Caught helplessly between the aggressive agendas of two superior forces, the Norwegian's position was nothing short of symbolic of the plight of his whole unfortunate country. Reluctantly he called down to his men to cast off the gunboat and let the destroyer pass. He himself opted for staying aboard the *Cossack* in the role of miserable observer.

Philip could not find any sympathy for the man's plight.

The ship entered the fjord at a calm pace, the only sounds coming from the machinery and the rush of water being pushed aside at the bows. The officers and men of the boarding party gathered upon the icy fo'c'sle with revolvers, rifles and cutlasses at the ready.

Philip shivered uncontrollably. His muscles were aching and almost taut with the exertion of trying to stay warm. He cursed, fearing that a relapse of the flu was coming on. Not now! Any involuntary spasms could serve to make people think that he was afraid. At least he had managed to sneak another drink down his throat before mingling with the men.

The rocky, snow-encrusted hills would have been considered beautiful under this starlit winter's night had the circumstances been different but, as it was, there was a certain menace in the way the channel got thinner the further they went. There was not going to be much room to manoeuvre.

Finally, there she was.

As the *Cossack* gently rounded the last bend, the *Altmark* was plain for everybody to see. She was lying stopped with exhaust gasses drifting gracefully from her funnel. To lie stopped was her captain's only choice for ahead was not just the distant shore but a large quantity of thick pack-ice making manoeuvrability that much more difficult still. She was completely trapped.

Vian suddenly ordered one of the seamen near him, 'Turn your lamp on her!'

Within a couple of seconds, the signal lamp, which had been held at the ready, was casting its sudden and powerful beam of light over the enemy ship. Everybody momentarily squinted but quickly recovered themselves. What had put them off their stride for no more than a couple of seconds should serve to completely blind the Germans.

A couple of panicked figures were running along the *Altmark*'s deck and distantly, commands were heard to be shouted in the sharp German tongue.

As Vian swiftly guided the *Cossack* into a position whereby the boarding party could do its work, he became uncomfortably aware that the sound of rumbling diesel engines were rising to a crescendo and a heavy froth was building up in the water at the *Altmark*'s stern. He could see in his mind's eye what was going to happen if he did not do something now and, even as the tanker began moving straight towards them, he shouted, 'Hard a starboard! Stop all engines!'

*Cossack*'s speed had been slow enough to prevent utter disaster so in her turn she narrowly missed the *Altmark*'s stern. By a whisker, the German captain's plan of ramming the destroyer's bow had been thwarted. Thus it was only a screeching of steel against steel instead of a hideous crunch which assailed the men's ears as the two ships scraped against each other. However close it had been, there was no time to waste. As soon as this contact was made, Vian shouted, 'Away boarding party!'

The pent-up tension that had welled amongst the men since the moment they had sighted the enemy was released in all its vigour. Lieutenant Turner was the first to leap the gap as the war cries of the rest resounded behind him. Now on the *Altmark*'s deck, he moved forrard with revolver in hand as others threw lines across in an attempt to arrest the contradicting movements of the ships.

The order to attack acted as an immediate tonic for Philip's weary mind and body. All sense of his suffering suddenly vanished in the heat of the moment and he lifted his leg over the side rail, looking about to see that everybody was doing what they were supposed to be doing. He need not have worried on that score. The only words that came to mind on the men's present conduct were 'bloody enthusiastic'.

A little way aft he saw Sub-Lieutenant Craven hanging from the torpedo davit waiting for his moment to leap.

As the ships swung closer together Philip's heart almost strangled itself to a stop. The larger lifeboat davit of the *Altmark* was just feet away from crushing the young man. 'Watch out there!' he yelled.

It was just as well that Craven leapt with promptness because his precarious perch was suddenly crushed and swept away with a twisted screech.

The near tragedy made a fresh anger rise inside Philip. He came here for vengeance, not to lose more comrades, however much they disliked him. He threw himself onto the icy deck of the other ship, maintaining his balance thanks to the practice of many hours standing on the rolling bridge of the *Cossack*.

With an impressive cry of aggression, a petty officer also made to leap the gap but it widened just as he was airborne. His feet fell into nothingness as he reached out. Just managing to grab hold of the *Altmark*'s rail, he lost his cutlass in the black water below.

Watching the other seamen pulling on the mooring lines, Philip realised with alarm that the ships were about to crash back into each other.

'Take my hand!' he shouted at the PO. The urgency in his voice convinced the man instantly that there was not a moment to lose so the two cold hands linked about the other's padded wrists and Philip pulled with all his strength. With split-second timing the PO was sliding along the *Altmark*'s deck on his stomach as the steel bearing the weight of thousands of tonnes scraped and buckled behind him in the very place that he had just been hanging.

'Thanks very much, sir,' gasped the PO with very sincere gratitude, then he was up on his feet and eagerly running to catch up with his mates.

For a moment Philip paused. That last exertion had taken something out of him. He was out of breath and the deck ahead was wavering strangely to starboard. But the fact that the men further along were not falling over told him that this was the illusion of his spinning mind. Then he realised that he was still standing in the glare of the *Cossack*'s spotlight. Everybody from Captain Vian down to the simplest of matelots could see him standing there. With an effort, he drew his revolver from its holster and began running in the same direction as all the others.

That was when a shot rang out. It was from somewhere inside the ship and what started as a single crack soon developed into an answering chorus of small arms being used. Not able to see where the shots were coming from, Philip climbed a set of ladders, wandered into the bridge and happened upon Craven ushering a German officer away from the telegraph at gunpoint.

This adversary had his hands up but still stared at them in furious defiance.

Wide-eyed and grinning, Craven looked over at Philip. 'I've caught myself the captain here, sir!'

The ageing captain looked from one to the other with a ruthless glare. He gave them a condescending smirk and, in halting English, said, 'You think you've won? I have put explosives on board. We're going to blow up.'

Philip saw red. This dirty underhandedness was so typical of what these Jerry bastards were all about. Hiding explosives to kill them all was just like sneaking that U-boat into Scapa and sinking the *Royal Oak*. He shoved the muzzle of his revolver into the man's cheek, pressing it home until the metal hurt the bone. 'You want to mess with me? *You want to mess with me?*'

The captain actually cowered, shocked at the unbridled rage. Probably nobody had ever spoken to him like this in his life. He stammered, 'We... we are civilians! We are not Kriegsmarine!'

'Sir! Sir! Mr Dollimore, sir!' Craven was tugging at his arm, pleading with him to come back to reality. 'This is too much!'

Slowly, Philip's shaking rage began to subside and an embarrassment started creeping in. With gritted teeth, he said, 'You try saying the same thing when they've killed *your* friends.'

He lowered his revolver and stepped away. Suddenly it was as if the German was not there. All he could see was the face of his best friend, now four months in his grave – and the open door from the bridge.

He stepped back outside, his thoughts clearing to bring him back to the word 'explosives'. He grabbed hold of a young man brandishing a cutlass and ordered, 'Go and tell Captain Vian that the Germans say they've rigged the ship to blow up!'

The lad's face showed a quick flash of alarm but sped off to hailing distance forthwith.

Philip's attention was suddenly diverted by the sight of dark-clad figures running along the deck below him. He could see clearly they were not *Cossack* men. When they reached the part up forrard where the bows where hemmed in by the ice-pack, they began hurling themselves over the side-rail, there to escape across the slippery flats. Squinting in the lamplight and feeling as though the air wanted to freeze the water in his eyes, he quickly started on his way down the ladders onto the waist. Just as he reached the bottom a hatch burst open and some men rushed out on deck.

'Where did they go, sir?' asked one of them, the same PO he had earlier saved from being crushed.

'They've gone over the side,' Philip answered, pointing the way.

Within a few seconds there was quite a gathering as ratings of the boarding party watched the desperate Germans half running, half slipping in their escape across the ice by the light of the lamp. Nobody fired. It was not sporting to shoot a man in the back as he was running. The little audience began to laugh at them.

One unfortunate German, slower than the others and clumsier in his movements, suddenly broke through the ice and plunged into the freezing water with a shocked cry. Philip watched the fellow hanging onto the smooth edge of the hole, unable to get any purchase in order to pull himself back up. In the pause that followed, it also became apparent that his friends were not going to return in answer to his cries for help. They continued onwards until they arrived at the point where the shadowy rocks and trees defined the shoreline.

With the action on board having quietened to nothing, all they could hear now was the panic of the man slipping away through the ice. The PO started clambering over the rail. 'We have to help him,' he said.

'Sod him,' Philip said with murderous calm.

The PO stopped long enough to look back with a frown then jumped down onto the ice.

Before he had got very far, there was a sudden flash of light and the familiar sound of rifle fire echoed off the surrounding hills. The whizz of the bullet flying just by their heads was clearly audible in the split second before it struck the steel and ricocheted off with a spark. Then there were more shots.

'Bastards!' somebody shouted as they all ducked. In a moment which lasted no longer than two seconds, the ratings all brought their rifles to bear on the fools who had decided to continue the fight.

The shadowy figures upon the shore had chosen to see what more damage they could inflict before submitting to defeat. Why did they not just carry on running? Pride? Stupidity? They were beaten after all. Philip took careful aim and fired his revolver until the bullet chambers were empty. He took pleasure at the power of the weapon in his hand and was gratified to see at least two of the figures falling in a heap in the snow. Had he hit one of them? He fancied that he had though there were a lot of rifles joining in the fray.

Then there was silence. The Germans decided that they had had enough and disappeared into the camouflage of the tree line.

Partway across the ice, the PO was successfully extracting the remaining enemy from his watery hole in this singular act of goodwill.

Philip then looked aft and took in a remarkable sight. By the light of the powerful lamp, hundreds of men were appearing on the deck of the *Altmark* and were passing quickly and quietly across a couple of hastily rigged gangplanks to the waiting destroyer. These were the British merchant seamen who had been missing since their ships had been sunk by the *Graf Spee* last year. Churchill had been right!

They looked healthy enough for their many weeks of incarceration though their wonder and relief at their sudden freedom was completely apparent.

Philip felt the victory keenly. At last he was doing something to get back at the Germans. What was more, he and his shipmates had played a daring hand and succeeded in a situation that could have gone horribly wrong. That felt good. But now to get away as swiftly as possible. After all, the German captain had stated that he had set the ship to blow up.

The freed prisoners were cramming themselves into every available space inside and outside the *Cossack*, some of them stopping to look back at the hated enemy. The decks had never been so rammed. The little destroyer had been busy enough with her complement of just over two hundred without adding three hundred more.

When the last few men were making their way across, Sub-Lieutenant Craven elatedly appeared in the *Altmark*'s waist pushing the German captain before him at gunpoint.

Vian, watching closely from the bridge of the *Cossack*, called down, 'Who is that you have there, sub?'

'Captain Dau, sir,' the young man answered.

'Let him go. He's made his point and we've made ours. It's not necessary to take prisoners.'

Then to Dau, he said, 'You, sir, can bugger off home and tell Adolf that we're not putting up with any of it. You hear?'

Craven immediately holstered his revolver and stepped away from the dazed German with a respectful bow.

Philip carefully walked across the gangplank, uncomfortably aware that the board beneath his feet was swaying in his vision. But he reached the other side, took a deep breath of freezing air and climbed up to the bridge.

'Well done, Dollimore,' McLean said softly, but it was not lost on them that Vian did not even turn to look at them.

In a very short space of time the gangplanks were pulled in, the lines were cast off and the *Cossack* was being manoeuvred carefully for leaving the fjord. The lamp was switched off and everything went momentarily black as everybody's eyes fought to adjust to the sudden change. Soon the residual glare on Philip's retinas faded allowing the natural moonlight to redefine the contours of the surrounding hills with their snowy outcrops. He looked back at their victim and saw Captain Dau standing alone upon the deck of his ship, forlorn and failed in his duty. He showed no haste to move. So much for the ship being set to explode. Another lie.

Once in the estuary, the choppier waves of the open sea lay spread out before them. The silhouettes of the gunboats and the distant destroyers were clear and they brought a quite forgotten subject back to Vian's mind. With the evident tone of sudden realisation, he said, 'Where's that bloody Norwegian?'

'Here am I,' came a meek voice from the back of the bridge. The official who had been so pompous earlier in the day was completely deflated. He was returned to his boat with the sure knowledge that neutral countries everywhere who thought that they could avoid this gradually widening conflict should beware – these British and Germans were going to do just what they liked in order to achieve their goals. They held the rest of the world in contempt.

\*\*\*\*

HMS *Cossack* steamed jubilantly across the sea to Scotland bearing her precious cargo of 299 freed sailors. The mood, blighted only by the possibility that one of the Far Eastern lascars might have contracted leprosy from somewhere, was triumphant in the extreme.

In the bright light of the following day, other ships of the Home Fleet fell in nearby to assist in escorting her home. Already a great fuss was being made.

As Philip took in the sight, he saw something unexpected and raised his binoculars to his strained eyes. There off the starboard quarter, about two thousand yards distant, was the *Burscombe*. He tutted. The last thing he needed right now was receive a reminder about the existence of his father.

'A great team effort,' came a voice from beside him. It was Vian. 'Your father's signal was the one which set us on our hunt.'

Before Philip could reply in any way, the captain looked around to make sure no one was in earshot then continued, 'Dollimore, you need a rest. You'll be found another appointment as soon as we reach Scotland.'

Philip was appalled. 'With respect, I've had enough rest to last me a lifetime. I'm not ready to be put ashore again. I acquitted myself well last night.'

Vian's face flashed with anger. 'Don't presume to tell me how you acquitted yourself. I know everything about all that you did so I'll be the judge of how you acquitted yourself. In my opinion you're not physically prepared for sustained periods at sea with possible contact with the enemy.'

'You're saying I'm not up to it?'

His voice rising at every syllable, Vian said, 'I'm saying you're bloody lucky that I'm not throwing the book at you. It's because of the *Royal Oak* and my respect for your father that I'm not. My only advice to you, young man, is to have a hard think about what you're going to say and do before you say and do it; and try and shove a little less spirit down your neck. One more thing, I'm your superior officer so you'll address me as 'sir' in future. Understand?'

The captain left the bridge leaving Philip insulted and fuming. But the message had been nothing if not clear. It was beyond 'clean up or face the consequences'; it was 'I want you off my ship'.

****

Already well-known throughout the ship were Lieutenant Turner's words when he had opened the hold of the *Altmark* and the faces of the prisoners revealed in the weak light. 'The navy is here!' he had announced.

'Couldn't have thought of anything better myself,' said Vian, immediately understanding the power of that simple phrase.

Sure enough, they were the words that Churchill and the great propaganda machine back home inevitably latched onto from the outset. They were simple, succinct and provided a stark warning to the Germans.

****

Philip Dollimore gave a couple of brief and uninspiring interviews with Pathé News and the BBC. By the time the story broke on the radio and the newsreels ran before the main features in picture houses around Britain and the Empire, he could not remember what he had said about the *Altmark* incident. The only thing he was sure of was that the images of him were lying on the cutting room floor somewhere – erased as though he never was.

He began to feel more lost than ever. Having left the *Cossack*, he would be at a loose end until new orders arrived. At the same time he would be stuck in the depressing confines of Edinburgh, living in a hotel, his very movements to be dictated by the law of the Admiralty. On a more personal level, he could not even temper this isolation by bringing himself to contact his wife or mother. What could they do to help him now?

But what did he really want? More importantly, what would he be trusted with now that he was on the wrong side of a man like Vian? He would probably be appointed junior officer at some sort of shore establishment somewhere, a supply depot or training ship, working for some rascally old has-been who was worse than everyone else. What a mess.

# FOUR

## A Brief Respite

Clark and Beatty may have quietly partaken in a drink or two last night but they made sure that they were clear-headed and looking sharp this morning. The guest house in which they had situated themselves had other officers in temporary residence and they did not want their trust compromised. The midshipmen may be allowed a little wine in the gunroom aboard ship but here, in 'Civvy Street', they were underage and that was all there was to it.

This Edinburgh guest house had been doing well out of the increased comings and goings of service personnel but was undiscovered enough to prevent it from being unpleasantly overcrowded. That said, it was just close enough to the centre of the city to prevent access to the rail network being a serious undertaking. It was clean and orderly, run by an affable old lady by the name of McDonnall, a widow of a gentle nature and, to many of the young officers, reminiscent of the archetypal mother that should be wished for in any perfect world.

She bade them sit at a table by the window and said, 'Help yourselves to the tea, gentlemen. I just happen to have an extra egg for each of you this morning.'

It would have been nicer still had she managed a table for them next to the fireplace but there was a sour-faced lieutenant-commander already sitting there, smoking a cigarette over his *Daily Mail*. However, they both smiled their heartfelt appreciation for Mrs McDonnall for they knew how difficult it was to come up with extra of anything thanks to the rationing.

After she had gone back off to the kitchen, Beatty gave a short laugh and quietly said, 'I'm glad we don't have occasion to make more of a habit of drinking liquor. My head feels awful.'

'I'm with you on that one,' replied Clark as he poured the tea. 'However, one last night of being silly was called for.'

'Hear hear,' agreed Beatty, taking the cup offered him and sipping gratefully at the inviting beverage.

HMS *Burscombe* had anchored in the Forth at the end of her long patrol two days ago and, after a hundred and one outstanding bits of business had been taken care of, Beatty and a few other boys passed their exams and had now officially left the ship.

After enjoying his last run ashore with his oldest friend, Beatty was to be on the 0933 to London, leaving clad in this borrowed jacket bearing the single gold stripe of sub-lieutenant on the sleeve. While the cut of the jacket looked okay at first sight, it was not particularly comfortable and he could not wait to get a tailor to measure him for his own uniform.

'David,' he continued, 'I just want to apologise for all the times I've misunderstood you.'

'You don't need to.' Smiling, Clark added, 'You've been a narrow-minded fool at times but I forgive you. Besides, they were not misunderstandings. Our views of the world just happen to differ.'

'Narrow-minded?' Beatty said with a frown. 'If that's not the pot calling the kettle black. See here, anyway, I know that I was completely unsupportive when you told me about the girl you wanted to marry – but, for God's sake, why would anyone want to get married at our age at all? There I go off at a tangent again. What I'm saying is that, if you *had* got to marry her – what was her name? Maggie – I would have given you my best wishes in the end. You know that, don't you?'

'It doesn't matter anymore. Mother put a stop to it with some considerable finality. I've no idea where she is and you can bet your life she'll be prevented from coming to find me.'

Beatty put on an expression of sympathy but could not really feel it in his heart. The class difference would have been too much of an impediment to a happy future. One day Clark would know it, he was sure, and then he would be relieved that he had not jumped in too soon.

At that moment, an alluring sight caught their eyes. Both their heads turned along with the heads of the six other officers seated about the room because a stunning young blonde woman had just entered. Her features were of smooth, soft curves with eyes that told of a confident happiness. She had something of a maturity about her that went beyond adolescence yet one could also tell that she was mischievously naive. She wore a pink dress and cardigan of slightly differing shades but then her neck was hidden by a thick red woollen scarf. She was cold and did not give a damn about appearances.

As more than one officer, including Beatty, was clambering to his feet to bid her 'good morning', she suddenly caught sight of Clark.

'Why, David!' she said through her surprise. 'It's good to see a familiar face in this dreary old town.'

She walked over to their table, forcing Clark to rise to his feet as well in order to greet her properly. The other men in the room, all superior officers, showed their chagrin that the lowly midshipman should be the one singled out. The snub towards them would not have happened aboard ship.

Clark gallantly hid his annoyance at this particular intrusion to do the introductions. 'Betty Dollimore, please meet my friend, Robert Barclay-Thompson.'

They gave each other smiling nods, he saying, 'All my friends call me Beatty, so I insist that you do as well.'

Was he blushing?

She then let out a giggle which was for a few seconds inexplicable until she said, 'That would be funny, wouldn't it?'

'What?'

'If we were together we'd be Beatty and Betty.'

But neither man laughed. They were not sure how to take what she considered to be humour. Her tendency to find amusement where there was not any and her self-serving attitude was why Clark was not best pleased about this intrusion. He could not say that he knew her of old but he had met her last year at his sister's wedding and had known straight away that she had been doing everything in her power to latch herself onto him. Unfortunately for her, she was exactly what he was not looking for in a prospective girlfriend or wife. He could not see her keeping up with the conversations and debates that he would want with a partner. Maggie was much more eminently suited to that, working class or not.

After a brief pause to digest her observation, Beatty said, 'Please, you must sit and have breakfast with us.'

Her smile widened as she graciously accepted the offer and sat herself upon the chair which he had pulled out for her.

After acquiring another cup and saucer from Mrs McDonnall and pouring Betty a tea, he asked, 'I gather from your name that you're related to our captain?'

'He's my father,' she said, making a sudden attempt to take on a new sophistication. Having been invited to sit, she had realised that she had just met another gentleman like David Clark. His sort reacted well to a more refined approach.

Beatty looked impressed. 'Well, I must say that I admire him a great deal. He's one of the best captains I've served under. Been with him since commissioning.' Secretly, he would have preferred to be complimenting her but he was afraid of appearing too clumsy or forward.

'I think I was there on commission day,' she said. 'Bit boring, wasn't it?'

'Were you really? I have no, well ... um.' He had no idea how he had not noticed her.

Then she turned to Clark. 'I thought about you after the wedding. We got on rather well and I thought you might write me but you never did.'

He looked at her and saw the mock sadness on her face. She was lowering her eyelids and compressing her brow, very nearly fluttering her eyelashes. It would be a truly inviting look to any other man who was prepared to take the bait but Clark was simply not that man. 'What brings you north?' he asked almost coldly.

Clearing up her expression in an instant, she said, 'My grandmamma's been in hospital in Newcastle and we came to settle her back into her house. It's been boring to say the least but father managed to get a message to us that the *Burscombe* was in for a few days so we decided to come the last few miles to see him. It's my birthday today as well and we should be having dinner on the ship if the war doesn't get in the way.'

'Oh, happy birthday,' smiled Beatty.

But Clark was very serious when he said in undertones, 'Betty, it won't do to talk of our ship so openly. You never know who's listening.'

She looked around the room at the other officers. 'But why would they be interested in your ship?'

'Just don't talk of the ship again.'

Beatty, embarrassed at her confusion and desperately wanting her to feel welcome, said, 'I'm sorry, my dear, he's right; for security reasons. But your birthday! Well, yes ...'

'I'm nineteen!' she exclaimed. 'I can hardly believe it. I feel ancient, though not as ancient as grandmamma. Or father come to think of it.'

Beatty and Clark exchanged a glance. Neither was prepared to offer even the slightest reaction when it came to comments on the captain. It would be more than their lives were worth if he ever came to hear of it.

Suddenly, there came another exclamation from the doorway. 'Betty, you leave those men alone!'

A middle-aged lady was entering the room, her upright stature and sharp eyes a complete contrast to the manipulatively adolescent approach of the young blonde. This lady, possessing a completely different type of charm, which one could tell was made of stern kindness, had an intellectual charisma all of her own; and she obviously felt the need to keep the younger woman in check.

'Mother,' Betty said with a tut. 'This is David Clark. Remember when Phil took me to that wedding last year? Well, he was there.'

Jennifer Dollimore immediately calmed her posture and walked over to the two young officers who had risen to say another 'good morning'.

She knew all about the Clarks even if she had never personally been acquainted with them. Her husband had once or twice offered his own discreet observations, and discreet they would remain for Charles and Jennifer Dollimore talked in complete confidence.

The Clarks were a famous naval family with many credits that they could be proud of. However, behind the scenes, they felt that they had a sense of entitlement that sometimes outstripped their sense of decency. At least that was how this boy's late father had conducted himself. As for David, the jury was still out. He could be more than he was if only he would settle.

Meeting him as though she knew nothing of his character, Jennifer shook Clark's hand and said, 'I am Mrs Charles Dollimore. Please accept my late condolences upon the deaths of your father and brother-in-law.'

'Thank you,' Clark said with full appreciation. He knew immediately that he was dealing with a lady who was a cut above this vacuous blonde sitting here and one who was well worthy of being wife to his captain. For that reason, his temperament changed to very formal. 'I shall be heading over to Rosyth myself in about an hour. I would be honoured to escort you.'

'Your offer is accepted, young man,' replied Jennifer. 'My son, Philip, was supposed to be escorting us but I have no idea where he's gotten himself to.'

Beatty, eager to make this lady's acquaintance, quickly cut in with, 'I heard that he's been in action. I have to say that that was a very fine show.'

'Yes, he was,' smiled Jennifer, though something in her demeanour suggested that she wanted to say no more of the subject. She had known of her son's frailties and doubts for months now and everything was much more complicated than him wanting to be a dashing young officer going into action against the infamous Hun. Recently he had gone silent and that could not be good.

'Er, my name is Barclay-Thompson,' said Beatty, wishing to complete the introductions.

'Oh yes, I've heard of you,' said Jennifer. 'Your friends call you Beatty. A great naval name.'

'You're very well informed, ma'am.'

'I have been a navy wife for nearly thirty years and I'm as inextricably linked to my husband's ships as he is.'

Very soon the four of them were sitting eating breakfast together, savouring the fine fayre provided by Mrs McDonnall and fully appreciative that there were extra eggs to be had. While Clark found great conversation with Jennifer – which doubled as an excellent diversion from the attentions of her daughter – Beatty revelled in the company of this gorgeous young woman that he was sure Fate had brought his way.

\*\*\*\*

With Beatty finally gone off to wherever the Admiralty would dispose of him, Clark led the Dollimores along the grim, icy dockside to where a boat was waiting to take them across to the *Burscombe*. Not far away, hollow-eyed workers toiled ceaselessly with the regeneration of damaged ships. The war was taking its toll.

What was most noticeable to Jennifer was that the *Burscombe* herself was already looking tired. She understood well enough that this vessel had performed far in excess of what she would have done in quieter days. There had been prolonged bursts of speed not required in peacetime, great storms that would otherwise have been avoided and action against a powerful enemy. Her grey structure was greyer for the dismal day and moisture in the air and orange streaks of rust jutted from her seams and rivets, especially around the hawse hole where her cable protruded. The cold men of the side party were presently chipping and painting, chipping and painting. They would do all they could to smarten her up as befitting the state expected of a flagship but it did not look like she could ever seem as young as she had last summer in Portsmouth.

To Betty the ship was as dull as a charmless boffin. She was only interested in the fact that it was full of young men in uniform. True, she had enjoyed Clark's company on the way up here but he seemed singularly unwilling to commit himself to her so she would just have to see what else was on offer. Unfortunately, mother suspected what was going through her mind and was determined to keep her close by.

Jennifer was not fundamentally opposed to her daughter finding a decent young officer but she wanted it all done properly. She wanted the intentions of both parties to be completely correct and – she cursed herself for even thinking it – Betty was just the sort who might go too far too fast and bring the problem of an unwanted pregnancy home.

Captain Charles Dollimore, husband and father, met them on the quarterdeck. Having been notified that Midshipman Clark was escorting them, he was not caught unawares by the irregularity. He did not hate the boy but then he was not enamoured of him either. Here was a lad of the greatest promise who was determined to ruin everything by being over-individualistic amongst his brother officers and having an apparent lack of faith in the navy's hierarchical status quo. Until he knuckled down and learned to embrace the wonderful institution that was the Royal Navy, Dollimore was going to hold him back.

Knowing of the old man's doubtful regard for him, Clark quickly and professionally saluted before making his way to the safety of the gunroom, to the captain's, 'Thank you, Mr Clark.'

Then, in a display of relaxed discipline, Dollimore leaned toward Jennifer and gave her a quick kiss on the cheek. He was wearing the same smile of genuine affection that he wore whenever he saw her after a long absence. He reflected that a few months ago he would never have risked letting any of the men see this personal side of him. Whatever passed between man and wife was meant to be kept private but, since the start of this war, he had opened up more as if to say that there was no time for anything less.

Jennifer was not going to complain about that. It showed that he was still learning and growing even at the age of fifty three.

'No Philip?' asked Dollimore.

'He didn't show,' Betty said before Jennifer could answer.

Dollimore and his wife looked at each other and immediately agreed an unspoken pact that they would not broach the subject again in front of their daughter.

Before too long they were sitting down to lunch in his spacious cabin below. The stewards had been careful to make it as inviting as possible with tablecloth as white as it could be, silver cutlery spotlessly polished, extra lamps brightening up the scrubbed bulkheads and portable heaters raising the temperature to something more manageable. It was not exactly homely but it was relaxing.

The conversation, mainly being held by Dollimore and his wife, covered domestic affairs: how the evacuated children, Jake and Janet, were doing at their house; how her mother was doing; how the war had hardly affected their current home county of Hampshire; had she heard from their other daughter, Victoria, at all? There had been an even longer silence from that one than from Philip.

He told Jennifer as much as he was able to about the Northern Patrol; about the rigours of capturing ships and all the risks that he and his men took in their stride, then finally he turned his attention onto Betty, 'And you, young lady, you had a job.' He could not think of another way of asking about it.

'I couldn't type as fast as they wanted me to,' she said with immediate defensiveness, thinking back to her boss's extreme frustration as he had to let her go. She had tried her charm upon him, a smile and a cheeky fluttering of the eyelashes of the sort that made most men drop their guard, but it had not worked.

'But you know and I know that you *can* type fast,' replied Dollimore, trying not to sound too much like a captain and as much like a father as possible. There was a distinction but he knew he did not always get it right.

'They kept using foreign in their letters,' she complained, 'and if they're lawyers in England then why can't they do law stuff in English?'

Jennifer said, 'Many of our institutions still use Latin. You would have found it very useful to have persevered. Not to speak it, obviously, but to have understood the terminology. After all, Latin was the world's most important language before English.'

'But it's not now,' argued Betty. 'If they want us to be foreign then we should be, otherwise we should be English. And anyway, most of the world speaks English now. I don't remember everybody going on in Italian in Singapore and Hong Kong.'

'Latin,' corrected Jennifer.

'That's what I said.'

Realising that arguing with Betty was steering them fast into a dead end, Dollimore decided to find a more placatory tone. 'Right now I'll settle for just making sure that the next universal language doesn't become German.'

'Agreed,' nodded Jennifer.

'But it doesn't get you off the hook, young lady.'

There was a knock on the door and at Dollimore's instruction to 'enter', a steward appeared. 'Begging your pardon, sir, but your son has just come aboard.'

'Thank you. Please show him straight here.'

A few moments later, Lieutenant Philip Dollimore was standing in the cabin allowing his father to shake his hand. He had decided beforehand that he would rather not but, now he was here, he suddenly felt extremely awkward and embarrassed at having spent so much energy on hating this man who, to all intents and purposes, had not done anything to him.

Captain Dollimore noticed that his son's face was very pasty and that his red eyes were thinned almost to the point that he looked very ill. But, of course, he had not long got over a nasty bout of influenza, as had many others in the fleet. But was that it? He had heard more alarming reports – on good authority too.

After telling him it was good to see him, he then said, 'But what's the meaning of the tardiness? Not only was the meal at 1230 but you told your mother and sister that you would escort them here this morning.'

'And it's my birthday too,' said Betty, stopping short of saying that this had been the worst birthday she had ever had.

A flash of annoyance crossed Philip's face. 'I'm sorry. Sometimes things just get away from me. I was chasing paperwork and completely forgot the time.'

Dollimore immediately knew that for the hogwash it was. Flimsy excuses and no messages being sent was completely against the way he had been brought up.

Philip, thinking that the subject was done and dusted, spied the decanter of port sitting on the cabinet at the aft end of the cabin and absent-mindedly asked, 'Do you mind if I help myself?'

Dollimore caught hold of his arm as he sought to make his way towards the drink. 'I think not.'

Philip stared at him with shocked recrimination. What was this? Being denied one harmless little drink? Was he not a man in his own right?

The disgusted look that Dollimore was getting from his son immediately lent credence to the reports he had had. A conversation was long overdue. How fortuitous that Jennifer just happened to be here as well. She had always been able to get through to him. But what to do with Betty first?

A few moments later, Betty dispensed with, Philip immediately became guarded. It was a sure sign of his insecurity that he leaped straight to, 'Father, whatever this is about, I don't need a lecture.'

'You've changed,' Dollimore stated. By pointing at a framed photograph of Philip, his wife Sarah and baby Charlie that was mounted upon the port bulkhead, he went straight for the jugular. 'Do you remember the night you gave me that picture? That was less than seven months ago. You were happy then, you loved your job, and your family meant everything. The flame in you has gone out.'

'I've had all of this from mother and I'm dealing with it.'

Jennifer quickly said, 'We've not spoken in weeks, Philip, and don't be defensive. We're not taking you to task.'

'Really?' Philip's hands shook as he drew out a cigarette and lit it. He saw his father observing them. 'Don't think this has anything to do with nerves.'

'Talk to me, boy,' said Dollimore. 'Right now, at this particular moment, I am not your superior officer. I'm your father and I am listening to you as such.'

Philip looked at him directly. 'I am angry. I am angry beyond words.'

'Captain Vian?'

Vian was not the full extent of the problem but it provided an excellent starting point. 'I did everything that was expected of me on that operation. I followed every order, was right in the thick of it. I did nothing wrong and it still wasn't good enough.' After a pause, he added, 'Anyway, how do you know about it?'

'Vian and I do happen to know of each other.'

'Of course,' said Philip sarcastically. The world of the navy's commissioned officers was actually quite small when you looked at it. The men's paths crossed here, there and everywhere as the years wore on but that was no excuse for this. 'You've been talking behind my back.'

Dollimore continued, 'It's as well that it was Vian that talked to me than anyone else. At least I have the true facts.'

'Insofar as *he* sees it. He wants to finish my career.'

'You're wrong about that. It's true he's a very hard man and it's difficult to get on his good side. Anybody who can claim to be his friend would have to be very fortunate indeed. But professionalism comes before any personal allowance with him. It always has.'

'It's just as well you're so forgiving. He told me he thought you were a fool when he first met you.'

Dollimore frowned at the pleasure Philip seemed to take in saying that.

'I asked for no favours,' continued Philip. 'I wasn't needing his approval. Maybe just a bit of respect but I certainly didn't get that. My face just didn't fit.'

Dollimore tried to force away the pang of hurt inside that his son should be struggling like this but it kept reminding him of the mental trials that he himself had faced after the last war. He said, 'Listen, Vian told me that he doesn't doubt your devotion. As a seaman, you did nothing wrong, but the shadow of the *Royal Oak* is hanging over you like a cloud and your obvious need for strong drink is making you dangerous.'

Confusion and consternation were evident all over Philip's features. 'All we need to do is defeat the enemy and that's exactly what we did in Norway!'

'But you must replace your anger with calculation otherwise your enemy will eventually get the better of you.'

'But who's the enemy?'

Jennifer said, 'Please, Philip, your father knows exactly what he's talking about.'

Philip shook his head and looked away. He had heard all this before.

Dollimore went on anyway, 'I felt as helpless aboard the *Warspite* at Jutland as you must have felt when the *Royal Oak* was sinking. The big guns were trained upon us and we were mercilessly pounded. I still can't believe the damage, the injuries, the death, the incredible waste. None of it added up in my head and it made me get careless ...'

The accident which destroyed the submarine HMS *Spikefish* ... He could not go there right now.

'Now I focus upon two things in this life which help me to get through it all. First, the family. Without you all I am nothing. Just the other side of the North Sea is a perverse military dictatorship that wants your enslavement and I'm not going to allow that to happen. Second, my skill as a seafarer. I've spent decades working to defend our way of life and this war is going to prove the justification of my efforts.'

Philip tried to battle with all this in his mind. His father made everything sound so simple, like there was no confusion about his aims and he knew exactly what he was doing. Philip wanted to revere him in the way that he had until so recently but he had the distinct feeling that everybody was measuring them up all the time – father against son. Worse still, it seemed to be no contest. Everybody talked of his father with pride, some with wonder, and it was grating on him. Curse it all! How could he tell him that he was in fact jealous of him?

'But there's something else,' said Dollimore, 'if I keep hearing that you're drinking heavily and it's affecting your judgment, then *I'm* going to do everything in my power to see that you remain ashore.'

Philip looked to his mother for help but he knew that she agreed wholeheartedly with that course of action. He looked the Old Man up and down. 'I thought you said you were talking to me as a father, not a captain.'

\*\*\*\*

Betty had been sent on a tour of the ship with Lieutenant Irwin. She considered him to be a handsome man, with dark hair and shadowy eyes that had a gentle blue shine from within. His mouth would have been perfectly formed by her tastes if only he had a propensity to smile. After listening to him talk for a while and observing his features over and over, she decided that he was one of those odd creations that had been given good looks for absolutely no reason whatsoever. In short, he was devoid of charm.

What she could not know was that that was the very reason that her father had assigned him to look after her. There must be no scope for the officer involved to be a target of Betty's romantic desires.

In flat tones born out of fear at her close proximity, Irwin explained what he understood of the workings of the 6-inch guns within B-Turret. The four breeches with their complex mechanisms of brass and steel stood open while overall-clad seamen inspected, greased or polished various pieces. Exhaling clouds of vapour in this awful, freezing box, each man had an imprudent glance at the blonde beauty who had come down to them from heaven but were careful to look away before the Ordnance Artificer in charge and his companion, Warrant Officer Hacklett, noticed that they had been distracted.

'…But that's as far as my knowledge takes me,' Irwin finished. Then acknowledging the presence of the WO and knowing him to be a gunner of many years experience, he asked, 'Mr Hacklett, is there anything more you can add?'

The muscular man, who had just been helping the artificer lift a section of pipe back into position by the right-hand gun, turned and what Betty then saw made her gasp. Hacklett's face was hardly a face at all. Sure, he had a mouth, a nose and a pair of eyes but the skin and the very shape of the features were hideously distorted across several shades of white and pink. It was like he was wearing some sort of mask. The eyes were the only things that seemed to be alive.

'Hello, Miss Dollimore,' he said, in much the same authoritative way as he would have done with the ratings, though he did try to be gentler. This was the captain's daughter and the captain was the only man in the world that he looked up to. 'These guns are good up to twenty five thousand yards,' he said. 'We can obliterate anything within that range except for ships bigger than us ...'

His words meant nothing to her.

'What happened to your face?' she asked, visibly curling her mouth in disgust.

Hacklett was taken aback, immediately reminded of why it was he had stayed in the navy and not ever tried to make any attachments ashore. 'Well ... that's a bit of a long story. There was once a terrible fire on one of the ships I was serving on ...' He looked down. 'Anyway, keep yourself safe and make sure nothing like this ever happens to you. And always listen to your father. Salt of the earth.'

As Irwin apologetically took his charge away, Hacklett turned back to the working men and shouted, 'Ri,'s 'all u'in'a!' He dropped his consonants when he was in a foul or mischievous mood because he enjoyed the way it put the wind up people. When he was a lad he had done it to annoy his superior officers and had since turned it into an art form. 'Is 'o go'a 'e ra'd u' by 'e chay 'asa 'och!'

Irwin decided that it was best if they went to a part of the ship where they could find a normal person of helpful intelligence, hopefully someone she could not upset, so he took her up a number of interminable ladders to the breezy areas that made up the forward superstructure. The draught blowing in from the expanse of the Forth seemed to get stronger and colder as they went so he was happy to step inside the charthouse for a moment.

'Ah, Able Seaman Barrett,' said Irwin upon finding that man there. 'Is Lt-Cdr Peterson about?'

'Gone to the fu ...'eads, sir,' replied Barrett, staring at the unexpected companion that the officer had with him.

Barrett was one of the worst products of the lower decks but was welcome in the charthouse because of his superior understanding of maths and navigation. Well, useful as he may be, if he was rude or crude now he would just have to take the punishment.

'No matter,' replied Irwin, uncomfortable since he fully understood that the young woman hated him. What was worse, he knew that Barrett knew it too. In another life, in another body and with another name, Irwin knew that he would be laughing comfortably with Betty but here, she made him feel as meek as a mouse and he could not conceal his awkwardness. 'Erm, what can I tell you about charts?'

After an embarrassing pause, Barrett said, 'Depths, currents, shorelines, shoals, reefs ...'

'Thank you,' answered Irwin sarcastically.

Betty looked at the tattooed AB who looked back at her. She said, 'You have an odd accent. You're very common, aren't you?'

Irwin sighed and shook his head.

She was completely unimpressed by this tour. She had been bored stiff the whole time and anything resembling a healthy, respectable man inside this steel prison had not dared to look at her twice. She knew that she had to escape from this Irwin person as soon as possible.
****

A little later, Clark asked the permission of his gunroom messmates if Lieutenant Philip Dollimore could sit with them for a short while to partake in a drink. As this room was the only place for these boys to find refuge from the attentions of other ranks, asking permission was the only acceptable thing to do. But of course the answer would be 'yes' because they all knew that the officer in question had been aboard the *Cossack* during that now famous prisoner extraction.

Clark introduced him to the bright new junior midshipmen, Trent and Eccles, and even spared some politeness for his nemesis, Farlow. He then bade Philip sit in one of the leather armchairs.

Drinks were brought in by the steward, one of which Philip was guiltily happy to get his hands on. He sipped at it directly but consciously fought back the desire to finish it in a gulp. He realised that the young men were looking at him admiringly.

Trent, with his thoughtful gaze and straight manner, voiced the collective question, 'So, what was it like, sir, cornering the *Altmark*?'

This actually took Philip off guard. Considering how it had gone in the end, the credit for the operation really belonged to Vian and Turner; perhaps with Craven also. He had just been a spare part, vaguely tolerated on the sidelines. Stumbling over his words, he said, 'Well, er, there's not a lot I can tell you boys. You've all seen action … more than I have, in fact.'

'Not really,' said Trent with a hint of embarrassment. 'The two of us only just arrived yesterday.'

Cutting in pompously, Farlow said, '*I'm* the only one here who was on board when we fought the *Moltke*.'

Then, gesturing sarcastically towards Clark, he continued, 'But apart from that minor article in *The Times* about our hero over here and his late father, *our* story has been swept under the carpet.'

'I wouldn't say that,' reasoned Philip. 'The whole fleet knows about it.'

'Yes, but the country doesn't. Churchill's made a big deal of the *Graf Spee* and the *Altmark* so the fact remains, you've got the best headlines so tell us more.'

'Yes, sir, tell us more,' piped up Trent. To him, being in the headlines was definitely something worth aspiring to. Clark had had his moment and so too had this Lieutenant Dollimore by serving alongside that national hero Captain Vian! He added, 'What was it you said when you got the prisoners out of the ship? "Out you come, boys, the navy's here!"'

Philip shook his head. 'Well, I can quite guarantee you that it wasn't me who said it.'

'Oh, come on, don't be modest,' cajoled Farlow. 'What was it like?'

Philip, now very tense, decided he was not going to give them the satisfaction. 'We searched the ship and got the prisoners out. It all went according to plan and there's nothing more to it.'

Quite suddenly there were disappointed faces all about him but Farlow, as usual, was the one who was outspoken. 'Heard you killed a few Germans though. Least the buggers deserved.'

'There are many deserving of that – not just Germans,' Philip said, casting him the most evil warning glare and taking another sip of the wine.

Clark immediately realised the situation that was brewing. He had only met Philip a couple of times before and the man he remembered – the outgoing, calm professional – was not the taut, stern individual sitting before him now. Clark ran the facts through his mind at lightning speed. When Philip was the best man at his sister's wedding he had been all right but since the sinking of the *Royal Oak*, it was clear he was no longer impressed by glory or heroism. A change of subject was imperative.

He asked, 'I heard that you're at a loose end at present. Have Their Lordships bestowed upon you another appointment yet?'

'They've mulled it over,' replied Philip, 'and decided that I'm to report to some subsidiary office of HMS *President* in a few days' time. I'll be attached to the staff there.'

'London,' said Clark almost jealously. 'Plenty of time to get the wind back into your sails.'

'Listen,' Philip said to him, suddenly becoming a little more animated with purpose, 'once I've gone south, I was thinking of visiting your sister at North Cedars Hall. I sent her a letter of condolence but I think it would help both of us to speak face to face. What do you think?'

Clark's mind drifted back to that last letter he had received from his brother Henry. He was not going to act upon it because he still could not expel the hurt that Mother had caused him. However, he had to admit that, deep down, he was perturbed by Patty's suffering but was sure any word from him would be spurned by her in the most atrocious way. Fortunately, Philip may just have presented him with the next best solution for them all. Here were two people having trouble coming to terms with the same tragic loss, the best friend and the husband. They might be able to help each other.

'Personally, I think that would be a good idea,' he said. 'I don't know if you knew that Patty is going to have a baby.'

'No, I didn't know,' said Philip. The knowledge stirred a feeling that rose almost as a paternal responsibility within him.

'Please help her if you can,' said Clark.

A few minutes later, after the other disappointed midshipmen had split into separate topics of conversation in different corners, there was a knock on the door and Farlow called, 'Come.'

The oak-panelled door slid open to reveal the beautiful, cheeky face of Betty Dollimore peering in. Although she wore that pink cardigan to guard against the cold, the heavy red scarf still caught the eye first. To the young men who did not know her, it was the sign of a woman who knew her own mind and be damned with the conventions of style. It was also as though God had sent an angel into their midst.

She said, 'I thought you'd come in here, Phil.'

'You're not supposed to be wandering around the ship by yourself, you know,' said Philip, obviously impervious to his sister's charm.

She frowned, saying, 'But I just had to get escape from that Irwin man. He kept talking to me like I was a child or something.'

Independently of each other, both Philip and Clark reasoned that that was because she behaved like one.

Farlow, wanting to be nice and win a place for himself in her affections, said, 'Well, do come in and sit down before we all catch our death from that draught.' He was the only one who had no idea that his invitation, well meant, had been delivered in a condescending way which immediately put her off him.

But she entered the room and closed the door, all the men apart from Philip standing up respectfully and ushering her to a choice of seats.

'Would you like a drink?' asked Clark.

But before she could answer, Philip said, 'That's enough of that. She's not old enough. She's not to have any.'

Clark nodded respectfully but noticed Betty's face screw up in annoyance. She exclaimed, 'I'm nineteen and you're a dullard!'

Sighing, Philip stood and gulped down the last of his drink. With evident tension, he said, 'Well, I thank you gentlemen for the invitation. Good luck in your future endeavours and maybe we shall meet in happier times.'

Then he was gone.

'What's his problem?' asked Farlow.

Clark looked at him hard and said, 'Do shut up.'

Betty slid down into the chair just vacated by her brother and leaned towards Clark. 'I'm so glad we met again today. I'll never forget that wedding. It was such great fun. Do you think you might write to me? Wartime is very lonely, you know.'

While the other midshipmen wondered why Clark should be the accessory to stemming this lovely young woman's loneliness, the door slid open once again and, to everybody's surprise, they were faced with the imposing figure of Warrant Officer Hacklett. Now having discarded the overalls he appeared authoritatively in his pristine uniform. Somehow managing to look everyone in the eye at once, he simply said, 'Miss, a message from your family. Would you be so good as to rejoin them? They are about to go ashore.'

She sighed and left. None of the midshipmen said a word to that frightening beast of a man.

However, once he was well out of earshot, Farlow managed a, 'Crikey, things must have come to a pass if they're needing to send *him* to retrieve the fair maiden.'

The juniors were not impressed.

\*\*\*\*

When Irwin realised that Miss Dollimore had disappeared, he immediately suffered an overwhelming anxiety. He had been trying to prove that he could get things right and now he had amply demonstrated that he could not even control a young woman. He should never have stopped to talk to that petty officer by the torpedo tubes.

He had only paused there briefly but, when he turned back to address Betty once more, he found he had to gasp, 'Where has she gone?'

The petty officer had replied, 'She went that way, sir, nearly a minute ago.'

'You should have said something!'

He wandered aft along the waist, into the passageway by X-Turret barbette and the heads, asking men as he went if they had seen her. It was the same everywhere. They pointed and said she had gone that way but every time he asked, he had just missed her. What was worse, his face was now flushed bright red from the embarrassment and he knew that all these men were laughing at him behind his back.

Eventually admitting defeat, he climbed down to the lower deck and walked forlornly to the captain's cabin to come clean.

Oh no! There was the captain, standing there just outside his door and he had Warrant Officer Hacklett with him. This was going to be doubly painful.

Dollimore turned and watched him approach. 'Mr Irwin, something the matter? You look ill.'

'Sir, I ... I ... your daughter, sir. She got away from me.'

'It was a simple job I gave you. Simple, you understand?'

'Yes, sir.'

'I don't want to hear of anything like this ever again.' All present understood that it was not just this incident which was enshrouded in this warning. It also encompassed his performance as an officer full stop in this ship at war.

'No, sir. But I can't find her.'

'Luckily for you, Mr Hacklett happened upon the fact that she was in the gunroom, so I now have her safely back here with me.'

Irwin looked at Hacklett. The scarred man did not gloat, just stared at him murderously through that dead mask of a face.

\*\*\*\*

Sub-Lieutenant Grierson-Day had only just been appointed to the *Burscombe*. He had immediately been given the unenviable task of taking charge of the midshipmen and, having been one himself not that long ago and knowing what they could be like, had decided to show that he was a disciplinarian from the off. He had spoken to them about respect, trust and orderliness and considered that he had got his point across rather well.

Now, on the very following day, he had to deliver another message. He stepped into the gunroom and looked about at the sixteen boys that had somehow crammed themselves into the small space. How disappointing that he had to take this tone on such a wonderful ship. He said, 'This comes direct from the captain. Under no circumstances is there to be a repeat of this afternoon's indiscretion.'

'What indiscretion was that?' asked Farlow, aghast.

Grierson-Day barked, 'What indiscretion was that, *sir*!'

Clark frowned. 'You're talking about us entertaining the captain's daughter in here without permission, sir.'

'Yes, I am. It's a serious matter, you know,' said the angry sub. 'An unchaperoned girl with you lot? It's just not the done thing.'

'She was hardly unchaperoned, sir,' said Farlow. 'Her brother was in here as well.'

'Yes, yes, I know,' Grierson-Day conceded though he did not want to, 'and that's the only reason why the captain isn't going to take any further action. Now, take heed. I don't want to see any more women in here because this is not where they belong. They belong elsewhere, where they can't cause trouble. Believe me, no good ever came from having one in the gunroom. So behave yourselves. Just remember, I have the authority to cane you and I will if I have to.'

With that he left, knowing that the midshipmen would only dare to snigger and laugh once he was well out of the way. Well, that could have gone better but really the captain should have thought about the consequences of allowing his daughter to escape in a ship full of healthy young men.

# FIVE

## Affairs of One Sort or Another

When Philip Dollimore was standing before his wife once again, he immediately felt guilty. What with everything that had been troubling him he had completely neglected the fact that she existed at all. It was entirely his fault. There was nothing she had done wrong just as there was nothing wrong with her but, while he had been fighting to survive the rigours of a service that no longer agreed with him, he had not been able to imagine what she could possibly have done to help him.

While he had been away, the idea of her had not even been real. While travelling from Scotland, he knew that this terrace in Fulham was where he was aiming for but he could not quite convince himself that he would find anything here he recognised. It was only when he was finally standing here, looking at her that he realised she was an actual person who had his best interests at heart and, just as important, a person who needed his attention as well. 'I'm sorry,' he said.

Sarah's eyes were sad as she regarded him – something which troubled him further because he could not believe that he had done this to her – but she decided that she did not want to make things more difficult for him. She knew well enough that he had seen and done things that she would never understand so was conscious that she did not want to do anything to drive him away. Their distance from each other needed to be addressed and she needed to get him onside in exactly the same way her mother-in-law Jennifer had done with her own husband years ago.

'It's good to see you,' she said, 'no matter what you might be thinking.'

'You should be angry. Why are you not angry?' he asked forcefully.

She knew that it was going to take a while to judge his moods. She had not initially been able to when he came home last time and only his mother had breached his defences, which thankfully paved the way for an understanding between them. But more had happened since then and all

89

that they had achieved now seemed wasted. A phone call from Jennifer had warned her of what she might face this time round – confusion, self pity, perhaps even drink-fuelled animosity.

Sarah said, 'What good would anger do? We need an understanding. We managed it before, we can manage it again.'

'But I never wrote to you once,' he said, his self-disgust evident. He would never be able to tell her that he had sat a considerable number of times with pen and paper in front of him trying to find the words to communicate but instead had allowed a few swift drinks to blot out the attempt. That was before he had come down with influenza. Since then he had hardly known much more than what was going on immediately around him, so picking up a pen at all had been far too much to even contemplate.

She leaned forward to kiss him, to reassure him. He accepted the kiss but it was a distant, almost unreal affection.

With an awkward grin, he said, 'Well, listen, I'm going to be in London for a while. They put me ashore ...'

'That's a good thing,' said Sarah.

'Is it?'

'Yes,' she said strongly. 'You've done more than most in this war and it's not going to end anytime soon. You'll get back into it when you can. Whatever they've got you doing here, it's just as important. Remember that.'

'But I'm no pen-pusher or filer.'

'You're going to have to be.'

Philip accepted her tone in lieu of the anger that he should have expected. Her definitive stance actually calmed him for the first time in a long while. This was strange. He thought he had reached his threshold with anybody telling him what to do. He reflected that he had married this woman for what he used to know of as love. That must have counted for more than he had recently been giving credit.

He noticed that the sadness was disappearing from her eyes. She could have been much harder on him and had a perfect right to be, but she had kept complete control of the situation.

This reunion had been much easier than they had both anticipated. They could be a good team but they would have to learn that all over again.

She then said, 'Sometime in the next half an hour, little Charlie will wake from his nap and start crying for his food. Babies have a routine, you know; and he has a lot of his teeth now. He eats solids.'

90

Philip tried hard to hide his momentary confusion. So focused had he been on trying to wake up from the nightmare of his service that he had almost completely forgotten about Charlie. 'Oh, good. Er, is he walking yet?'

'No, he can pull himself up on his feet but not for too long. He gets overly cautious and sits back down again.'

'Ah.' So even the baby was having doubts too.

\*\*\*\*

The plush Victorian terrace in Fulham was Sarah's family home. Philip had moved her and Charlie to their smaller place near Heathrow Hall at the beginning of the war but they had come back here after the expected bombing had not happened. Now, with the peaceful streets a continuing fact of life, they hardly thought anything of the threat from the Germans.

He travelled through London to take up his new appointment at Deptford. It had been many years since he had been this close to the city so he took some extra time to view his surroundings, all the while fighting the urge to swig from the hip flask he was carrying. He had a terrible thirst raging but somehow he understood enough to know that word of his drinking may well have preceded him to his new commanding officer and he wanted to disappoint him by turning up entirely sober.

There were uniforms of every service all over the place – in the streets and stations, in the cafés and pubs, in the museums and libraries. Piled against the most important buildings were heaps of sandbags, ready to soak up the bomb blasts. Above those the windows were crossed with white sticky tape to limit the prospect of flying glass and, standing sentinel over the lot, were the occasional great silvery barrage balloons.

It was a shame that this great city should have started to resemble an armed camp but nobody looked particularly worried. This was the world of the 'phoney war'. Well, let them enjoy it, thought Philip. Great centres of population were not sacrosanct where the Nazis were concerned. The stories that had seeped out about the destruction of Warsaw had been horrific in the extreme. But you never know, he thought, maybe we'll never experience what happened in Poland.

Before catching his final train at London Bridge, he worked his way down to the river front until he was amongst the bustling, smelly heart of the Pool of London docks. Cranes were working in their never-ending rounds of loading and unloading merchant ships. The vital food and material stores that Britain survived on were waiting upon the quaysides before their respective warehouses, ready to be moved to where they would be bought, consumed or utilised. Standing amidst all this sweating labour as a clear message that London's diversity was firmly entrenched either by accident or design, was Tower Bridge and the medieval bastion and prison of the Tower itself.

Philip's imagination took hold as he pondered the scene. The architecture of warehouse and towers could not be more different and yet they signified Britain's combination of the old and the new, the functional and the decorative, the wealthy and the poor. Their interdependency was of paramount importance if they were to put a stop to Adolf Hitler's little games.

He was pleased for this sudden understanding and was coming to notice that his craving for a drink was subsiding. So far as it would seem, both Clark and Sarah had been right: London was a chance to get the wind back into his sails and whatever it was that they could find for him to do must surely be as important as holding a gun up to a German's face. He was almost glad that he had not pulled the trigger.

'Here we count things,' said his new boss, Commander Derek Crawshaw, as they wound their way through the near ancient corridors of the *President*'s offices at Deptford.

The ageing but suave commander delivered his speech in an unapologetically tired way. 'We collate the information from the various commands – the Nore, Rosyth, Gibraltar, Port Said and much further afield – and we check over budgets and supply. Is there enough food, fuel, ammunition? Are the accounts settled? Does everybody have all the paperwork they need to generate more paperwork? Does everybody have enough toilet roll to wipe their bums on? There's only two types of people working here: those that were born to count and those that have annoyed someone; and since I know a little bit about you, I gather that you're not of the former. Don't be offended by any of my deductions, but who did you upset?'

'I'd rather not say, sir.'

'Really? Well, I'll tell you who I upset. I upset your father but I suppose you know all about that.'

Philip shook his head. 'No, sir.'

Crawshaw chuckled in genuine surprise. 'He always was a tight-lipped bugger, that one. I was his executive officer before this appointment.'

'Yes, sir, I remember you. We met in Northern Ireland just before the war.' In a whole other lifetime.

For a moment, Crawshaw stopped and let his gaze wander across the ceiling. His look was still blank when he said, 'Sorry, young man, I don't recall that. Anyway, I've no qualms about the fact that your father thinks me untrustworthy but if you think that it's going to affect the way you work for me, you'd better tell me now and we can sort it out.'

'No, sir,' replied Philip with confidence, 'I don't stand here in his name. I stand here in my own.'

'Good,' said Crawshaw, staring at this young Dollimore who looked so much like the other. He gauged that relations between father and son might just be cool enough for him to be able to get inside this one's head. 'Now, who did you upset?'

A little more at ease, Philip replied, 'Captain Vian, HMS *Cossack*.'

Then Crawshaw let out a hearty laugh. 'Did you, by God? Well, anyone who raises *his* blood pressure is all right by me. The man's an insufferable fruitcake.'

Before the day was out, Philip felt that his rapport with Commander Crawshaw was already such that he could broach the subject he had originally intended to put off for a week or two until he firmly had his feet under the table. 'Sir,' he said, 'I was wondering if I might talk to you about a spot of leave. Just a couple of days.'

'Already?' asked Crawshaw, scrubbing out a calculation that he had messed up on the open ledger in front of him. He was initially surprised at the front of the lad but then remembered that he could be a useful ally. He softened his look and asked in a more placatory tone, 'Why do you need leave so soon, Mr Dollimore?'

'I need a couple of days to visit the Clarks of North Cedars Hall. Beyond that, sir, the matter is a tad personal.'

'You mean the widow of Rear-Admiral Harper Clark and her daughter Patricia?'

Impressed at the commander's knowledge, Philip replied, 'Yes, sir.'

'I can help you with that straight away.'

'You can?'

'Yes, they're not at North Cedars at present. They're here in London, living at a house in Belgravia. I know them well.'

Philip thought that over for a couple of seconds. He knew that the late admiral had been Crawshaw's squadron commander but he had thought the familiarity stopped there. Though, come to think of it, he recalled David Clark once complaining about some sort of bad blood between them all. Whatever that was about, it must have all been sorted out. Furthermore, this man here was not half as arrogant as David had suggested. He must have got this fellow all wrong.

'Right, well that would solve an awful lot of problems, sir,' said Philip.

Crawshaw was about to ask what his interest was then remembered that he had described the matter as 'a tad personal'. It was best not to push too hard at this stage. Anything he did not know at the moment he would find out anyway after some digging about. Still, not for the first time he cursed himself for failing to take a closer interest in things that did not immediately concern him but had to concede that his brain had always worked that way. He tried to think of what the common link was between Philip and the Clarks. Philip had once served on the *Royal Oak* as had Patricia's late husband. That was as much as he could fathom. Damn it! Why did he not pay more attention to gossip?

Philip walked past the approaches to Tower Bridge that evening noticing for the first time that the breeze was beginning to warm up. Spring was not all that far away. What a boon it was to be something other than cold, confused and lost. Even more important was the fact that he had finally met somebody who simply took him for who and what he was, and who was not expecting him to measure up to the legend that was his father.
****

The noise of the traffic gradually died away the further he walked down the avenue. By the time Philip reached the great Belgravia house set back from the road behind these tall iron railings, he was almost entirely engulfed by the peace. He quickly thought about those people who had donated their gates and railings to the war effort and decided that Dorothy Clark would not do so until she was good and ready, if at all.

He remembered her to be a very forceful, headstrong lady, intelligent and charismatic. Some said that she had often got the better of her late husband as their relationship had become strained towards the end and everybody knew that he had been no pushover. But Philip did not know the truth of it and did not want to judge. He really knew as little about the one as the other.

What he did know was that their daughter, Patricia, had been married just three weeks to his best friend when he had been drowned in the *Royal Oak* and, by all accounts, the blow had been more severe for her than it had been for him.

The maid told him that he was expected and showed him into the lounge to wait.

'Would you like a drink, sir?' she asked.

Good question. He was not at ease and was feeling his thirst coming on. What would be the harm in letting a small whisky or something take the edge off the situation? By the time the maid was delivering the drink to the coffee table he had managed to convince himself that he would not need to sip it just yet. It should be fine to have it sitting there ready in case he needed it.

He was still staring at the glass of amber liquid when the lady of the house, Dorothy Clark, entered. She must have noticed his vacant stare but he pulled himself together as quickly as he could.

'Mr Dollimore, how nice it is to see you again.' She stood tall and commanding, her clothes and hair well ordered and neat. She would allow nothing of her look or mannerisms to suggest that the loss of husband or son-in-law was affecting her in any way, especially in front of a man she did not really know, no matter how well meaning his intentions.

Philip took a step forward and said, 'Thank you for allowing me to visit, ma'am. It was through my concern for Patricia that I felt I must come.'

'And for yourself,' she stated, her eyebrows raised. When he did not answer, she said gently, 'I haven't been checking up on you or anything like that, Mr Dollimore. As soon as I came in the room I noticed that you had the same look of confusion that Patricia wears. Furthermore, I remember a much more outgoing character fulfilling the task of best man last year. You have evidently been suffering as she does.'

He nodded, fighting back the urge to thank her profusely for her instantaneous understanding. 'You're right,' he said. 'You're right. I can still hardly believe what's happened. It had crossed my mind many a time that I should like to talk to Patricia about John and, when David informed me of her agony, that very much settled the matter for me.'

For the first time she almost dropped her guard. 'You've seen David?'

'Yes, ma'am. About three weeks ago I was aboard the *Burscombe*. I saw him there.' After a pause, he said cautiously, 'I gather that there's some sort of bad feeling between you all, of what cause I can't imagine, but it's troubling to me that a decent family such as yours should be torn like this.'

She realised that he obviously knew nothing of the Clarks. 'Yes, we have problems, Mr Dollimore, which I do not consider to be insurmountable. Therefore, my main concern is that David does not have the good manners to answer my correspondence, but I'll not bore you with the details.'

Philip's face then lit up. 'Perhaps a letter from me as intermediary would help to bring him to his senses.'

That was a possibility but she decided it was too much too soon. 'Thank you, but no. He is as stubborn as the day is long and I fear too much intervention will drive him further away.'

She should not really blame David for his stubbornness. She possessed it in abundance as had his father. But, although she was stubborn, dismissive and selfish about many things in this life, when it came to her children, she had the heart to give them almost anything they wanted – within reason. After all, it was her who had chased away the silly little girl that David had wanted to marry and she fully acknowledged that that was what this feud was all about. Unfortunately, as much as she wanted her son back, she felt entirely justified in her actions.

There was presently nothing more that could be said on that subject. 'I'll just see if Patricia is ready to meet you,' she said. 'Before she does, though, you have to understand why it is we're in London. We are here to see a doctor. A particular type of doctor and with that knowledge I must ask you to be discreet.'

'Of course, ma'am,'

'It wasn't just John, you see. She was very close to her father as well and when he died, it was just too much for her to bear.'

'I see.'

Patricia had always given the impression of being a very independent woman. She was opinionated in many subjects and had been forthright in advancing those opinions even if she was never overly concerned about the flaws in her logic. She had ploughed straight ahead regardless of the challenges and taken what she needed wherever she found it. She had been strong, people had thought.

But in truth her world was a tough place and, though she would never have admitted it, she had spent her life living in the shadow of, and at the mercy of, her men. Her father had been a rascally type as was her brother Thomas. It was they from whom she had adopted her outward persona, thinking to get further in life with razor-witted brashness. Her oldest brother Henry was a decent and solid man and any attempts of hers to dampen his resolve had not worked. If there was any man who made her ashamed of her ways it was him. It was just as well that he spent most of his time away with the navy. Her youngest brother, David, was completely different, just a flea to be crushed between the thumbnails.

She had truly loved her husband, Lieutenant John Bushey. While she had seen him as a passport to further independence and future position in society, she had respected his ways and was prepared to let him into her heart. It was no wonder that she was having such trouble coming to terms with his death. The façade that portrayed her as in control of her own destiny had been definitively breached.

She came into the lounge and the three of them sat and took tea.

Philip still did not touch the whisky which sat next to the gleaming tea service. The Patricia that was before him was pale, hollow-eyed, nervous and shaky. More of a contrast between this apparition and the strong woman of last September it would be difficult to find. Just like what had happened to him, except that she was a lot worse.

'Think about the future,' he told her. 'I know that John would want you to concentrate on the baby. When is it due? June?'

'Yes,' she replied weakly, hardly gathering her thoughts on the subject.

Dorothy immediately noticed that his words were having an effect that had been different from those spoken by her and the doctor. Although Patricia was still pretty vacant, she was not tempted towards violent irritation at the advice given about the baby. It did not take much to figure out why. Philip Dollimore was the first man she had spoken to who was a true link to her loss, somebody who had known John as well as she did. This made his words more valid and soothing.

Philip spent the next couple of hours in their company, sometimes talking, sometimes listening and sometimes sitting in gloomy silence. He called to her mind memories of John as he was, the confident leader of men who had taken the bit by the teeth and heroically gone forth to face the enemy in defence of his country. This appealed to her fractured imagination, filling her with a positive feeling before he moved onto to the subject of his death.

'You know,' he said, 'when they found him he was clutching a photograph of you. He was completely aware of what was important to him right up to the end; and he'll be looking down now, willing you to gather your strength for the baby.'

Patricia looked at him sorrowfully then purposefully. 'And what of you? Will you kill the people that did this?'

Dorothy wanted to interject but thought better of it. The direction of the conversation may not be entirely appropriate but she could not doubt the progress Philip had made. Better communication was more important than worrying about the content of her thoughts for the moment. Today had been the first time that Patricia had not demonstrated utter helplessness and irritable despair.

Philip answered, 'Yes. Mark my words. The Germans will pay.' He had no desire to go into any detail about how he had grappled with the enemy so far. That was his problem.

Patricia had been wishing for many weeks that her father could have been here to play his role but she was more than happy that this relative stranger had appeared and was as understanding as he was. Here was a man who was able to guide her through her grief in a way that, she suspected, no one else would be able to; and secretly she was always at the mercy of her men. She put her hand upon his. 'Philip, God has sent you here. Please call on me some more.'

Philip looked at Dorothy. She nodded even though she looked a little uncomfortable with it.

'It just so happens,' he said, 'that I am working in London for a while, so I will endeavour to visit. I'm glad if I've done anything at all to set your mind at ease today.'

Then she actually smiled.

When he was leaving, Patricia had already retired. She had finally been exhausted by her efforts. Dorothy stood with him by the lounge door beyond which the maid waited to show him out.

He asked, 'Should I tell Commander Crawshaw that I found you well?'

Momentarily, Dorothy looked a little surprised. 'What do you know of Commander Crawshaw?'

'He's my new CO, ma'am. It was he who informed me of how I might contact you.'

She suddenly realised how this man here really might truly be a Godsend, somebody who could be well placed to further her plans, but he required a little nurturing first. 'Thank you, but no, Mr Dollimore. I shall see him myself presently.'

Once Philip was walking back down the avenue, the sound of the traffic ahead growing in his ears again, he felt markedly clearer in his mind. He had achieved something today which was civilised and constructive, something which he decided was difficult to do on the Northern Patrol – and he had not touched that drink after all.

\*\*\*\*

Many years ago, Dorothy and her husband had been good friends to Derek Crawshaw's elder brother, Paul, until heavy drinking and fevered imaginations had paved the way for a major falling out. The biggest culprit in the drama, as ever, had been Harper Clark. Through violent actions the fool had created an enmity between the two families which had lasted for the next twenty years.

Both Harper and Paul were deceased now and, with Patricia the way she was, Dorothy had not spared a single thought for all that irrelevant past. That was until Derek Crawshaw had seen her across the dining room at the Savoy last month and had made his move on her.

With a great deal of grace and charm he had offered peace now that the main protagonists of their troubled history had passed away. But from the smooth way in which his talk developed it was clear that he had more on his mind. He must have thought he could have any woman he wanted. Even this woman.

Knowing something of his character, she had recognised immediately that he was attempting to manipulate her just as he had manipulated many others in the past. Also, given her eminent position, she would be a fantastic trophy in his hall of achievements. Finally, she had reason to be suspicious of how far peace would go since David reportedly had had significant trouble with this self-same officer in the *Burscombe* just a few weeks before. That alone demonstrated Crawshaw's real lack of sympathy to the Clarks.

With all that in mind, she had been about to warn him off there and then except that she suddenly saw a way in which his presence could be useful to her. She hid her distaste and said, 'Yes, please sit. Let's talk.'

The smile of the unsuspecting man stretched almost from ear to ear.

\*\*\*\*

Hundreds of miles away, in the Firth of Forth, the men of HMS *Burscombe* were almost ready to go out to on patrol once again. The ship's stores, ammunition, water and various fuels were all topped up and now they were just working their way through the commander's list of exercises as steam was being kept up in one boiler on four hours notice for sea. Conditions were cold and damp but manageable, a good sign that winter was beginning to draw to a close – here in Scotland at least. Things would be worse the further north they went.

From the quarterdeck, Captain Dollimore, standing solitary and casually smoking his pipe, observed some of the boat drill, witnessed a smooth landing of the Walrus reconnaissance aircraft upon the flat water, stood by while ropes and wires were run out across the deck for Tow Aft Drill and noticed the new midshipmen diligently learning their semaphore up on X Gun Deck. All was careful bustle with the odd scream from an angry chief occasionally thrown in. Very satisfying.

Then from the starboard side amidships, he saw a cutter pulling away, heading out towards the distant quayside. He narrowed his eyes in an effort to see who the occupants were. His sight was still very good for his age but faces were a bit fuzzy over three hundred feet away. He grabbed at the telescope which he had held clamped in his armpit and extended the brass tube while tobacco smoke drifted lazily about.

Yes, just as he expected, the cutter contained Midshipman Clark and Leading Seaman Haggerty, heading off to conduct the doubtful business which had been sprung upon them just a short while ago. He retracted the telescope and dug his teeth gently into the wood of his pipe. There were a thousand other issues to take care of and this was an unwelcome distraction.

About five hours ago he had summoned Commander Locklin, the executive officer, to his cabin to inform him of a dispatch he had received. Not able to hide the fact that he was unimpressed, he had said, 'The police have asked permission to question one of our company. Leading Seaman Haggerty.'

Locklin was surprised. 'Indeed, sir?'

'Yes. It would appear they think he might know something about a crime that was committed in London a few weeks ago.'

'Do they say whether he's under any suspicion or not?'

Dollimore replied, 'The message is a bit vague, but they're not coming to arrest him at any rate. It's just that he happened to be on leave at the time it occurred. This Haggerty – he was one of the men on the *Dagrand* boarding party – do you know what he's like?'

'A little, sir,' said Locklin, picturing that unfortunate man's naturally ugly face in his mind. 'He's being urged to put in for petty officer; a proficient seaman, though I've heard complaints that he came back from leave less enthusiastic than when he went. That could be suggestive.'

'Has he been pulled up for anything else?'

'No, sir, clean as a whistle.'

'Have you picked up on any buzz circulating of any connection he may have to the crime?'

'Again, no, sir.'

'We don't need this, EXO. Inform him and his divisional officer quietly that they're going ashore. I'll arrange for the questioning to be done there. I don't want the police anywhere near the ship and I don't think the Regulating Branch need get heavy-handed either. I don't want the ship's company concerning themselves with this.'

'I understand, sir. Absolute discretion.'

'Hopefully he's innocent of any wrongdoing,' said Dollimore. With nothing more to go on he refused to believe the worst about Leading Seaman Haggerty and he did not want the men making a story up and spreading it through the ship like a virus through the ventilation system. He needed them to apply their efforts to fighting the war.

Soon after, upon Locklin discovering that Haggerty's DO, Lieutenant McPhee, was already ashore engaged on some other business and was not expected back until just before they were sailing, Dollimore asked, 'Then who should sit in on the interview?'

He had ruled it imperative that somebody should be with Haggerty for the simple reason that the police should not be tempted to make more of it than it was. Whether they liked it or not, he was a *Burscombe* man, therefore it was *Burscombe* business.

'I asked him if he'd prefer the bosun or Number One,' said Locklin, 'but he requested Midshipman Clark instead.'

'Really?' asked Dollimore, surprised.

'Seems to think that he's the fairest of the lot of us, sir.'

'Does he?'

Dollimore considered Clark's conduct aboard of late. The boy's previous reports from college and training ships had been awful and his service in the *Burscombe* had been unpredictable in as many bad ways as good. But it had to be acknowledged that he had quietened of late, had been able to strike a balance between popularity and discipline – since his father had died in fact. His father, the old admiral, had not been the most forgiving of men and had been hard on his family. There must have been something significant in that after all.

\*\*\*\*

Clark, once he had got over his surprise at being requested to sit in on the police interview, pondered the sparse facts. There had been some sort of crime in Haggerty's hometown of Bethnal Green while he had been on leave, but the man was claiming he had absolutely no idea what they were talking about. Yet something was niggling at the back of Clark's mind so he came down from the bridge to find young Midshipman Trent. 'Do you still have those papers I gave you?'

'Some of them,' Trent replied. He had an addiction to crosswords, something he considered essential to the constant testing of his mind, and Clark had happily given him his read copies of *The Times* before he discarded them. Generally, Trent had taken the pages he wanted and thrown the rest away but some of the papers were still intact in his sea chest. 'Looking for something specific?'

'Yes. Not sure what date, though I'll know it when I see it.'

He quickly thumbed through the half dozen papers from January as Trent gave an embarrassed, 'I really should clean my things out a bit.'

Clark, spying what it was he was looking for, gave him a friendly pat on the shoulder. 'You're an unforgiveable hoarder but thank God that you are. I do believe this might give me the heads up.'

'On what?'

'Sorry, mum's the word.'

Near the bottom of page two of the paper in question, almost submerged in the sea of printed words was an article entitled: *London Gangs Go To War?*

*While the rest of the population prepares for the approaching confrontation with Adolf Hitler, Bethnal Green has been rocked by no less than two murders, the latest of which was perpetrated just two nights ago. Cliff 'The Fox' Parker, a man alleged to be complicit in six counts of burglary since last September and suspected dealer in black market goods, was found dead in the back room of Garry Wilson's Butchers in Green Street. Police stated that the cause of death was due to a single stab wound to the abdomen and an investigation is under way to find the murderer, based upon links made to the death of rival gang member Peter Averell last week. Without a doubt, it is in the nature of such men of no conscience that their personal impulses come before the needs of the communities in which they live.*

Good. This was more information than the Admiralty or the police had sent to the *Burscombe* on the affair.

****

So it was that, a little while later, Clark and Haggerty went ashore by cutter to meet with a representative of the police in a damp, musty old office at the naval base.

Clark sat off to one the side of the desk which was dominated by the paperwork of a middle-aged, moustachioed, red-headed man who looked tired and bored. His crumpled brown coat and scuffed shoes seemed to bolster the idea that he was well beyond his best years. Perhaps he was just going through the motions. Is this what policing had come to in wartime Britain?

Harry 'The Turtle' Haggerty was under no such illusions about the man's run-down state. While his personal experience of the police were the sometimes not-so-tolerant beat bobbies who were quite prepared to do whatever it took to keep the streets quiet with fist or truncheon, he knew that they were backed up by doggedly determined inspectors. He was not fooled by this man's indifferent appearance. He prepared himself for the worst.

After silently and slowly writing headings for his notes, the man looked crookedly at him, screwing up his right eye as though the light was too powerful. 'Mr Haggerty, thank you for taking the time to speak to me,' he said. 'My name's Detective Sergeant Crosbie. Crosbie, like that awful yankee crooner but without the 'y'. I probably sing better than him as well.'

Clark frowned. The man's face was deadly serious. Why would he waste time on a joke?

Crosbie continued, 'Just to make sure I have the right man, you are Harold Haggerty of Pott Street, Bethnal Green, London?'

'I was christened Harry, not Harold,' Haggerty stated with outward disgust.

'Of course,' conceded Crosbie with a shrug. He noted that upon his paper then looked back again. 'Now, I've been charged with asking you a couple of questions.'

Haggerty shook his head. 'And is a sergeant the best that they could come up with?'

'*Detective* sergeant,' Crosbie corrected him with a sigh.

Clark's initial instinct was to tell Haggerty to clean up his attitude and be more respectful to authority but realised all too quickly that he was seeing a completely new dynamic that his own life experience had denied him. This detective's authority might be bona fide in the eyes of the law of the land but it had not yet been accepted by the man opposite, whose civilian manner had temporarily ousted navy discipline. It was wonderfully refreshing to see.

'I don't know if you're aware,' said Crosbie, 'but there were two murders committed in your home town at the beginning of the year.'

'It'd be hard not to know.'

'And how did you find out about them?'

'I was on leave, wasn't I, and I know you know 'cause you've got that in your notes.' Haggerty leaned forward and tapped the papers impatiently with his fingers. 'A fella gets murdered a couple of roads away from where I live. I think I might pick up on that somehow.'

'The first was a Mr Peter Averell, murdered on the second day of January,' continued Crosbie, glancing at his notes unperturbed, 'and the second a Mr Clifford Parker, murdered on the tenth. A couple of regular hoodlums you'd be hard pressed to find elsewhere but that's beside the point. Now, I wish to ask you how you were associated with them.'

'I wasn't,' Haggerty said definitively.

'Oh, come off it. You were arrested in connection with a robbery which had been carried out by Parker's crew.' When Crosbie noticed Clark's expression change to one of concern, he quickly added, 'In November 1934.'

Haggerty gritted his teeth and stared hard at the detective. 'So, you should know then that I was released without a conviction, because I didn't do nothin' and I didn't wanna spend my life being accused of stuff I wasn't involved in. That's why I joined the navy.' He turned to Clark and reiterated strongly, 'That's why I joined the navy, sir, so I wouldn't have to put up with this anymore.'

Crosbie asked, 'Do you deny a connection with the Parker gang?'

'Yes! Well, no. I thought about getting into all that back then. We were always poor, me and my mum. Dad's always in the boozer. It seemed like I might make some easy money but I knew mum would kill me if I did anything like that. I drank with some of Cliff Parker's boys a couple of times then scarpered for the navy.'

'After you were arrested.'

Haggerty nodded his reluctant agreement of the statement.

'And that ends the connection?' asked Crosbie. Frowning at Haggerty's nod, he continued, 'Then how do you account for the night of the tenth? The night Parker was murdered?'

Haggerty's expression visibly became sterner. 'What about it?'

'Well, for starters, one of our beat constables, new to the area, filed a report that he came across a sailor with blood on the side of his face walking along Birkbeck Street in the blackout – and before you start objecting, both you and I know there was enough moonlight to see by. The constable didn't know you but when he described you at the station, there were five others who could testify that he'd just met Harry Haggerty.'

It's true, thought Clark, he does have a very distinctive face.

'That was at 11.15pm,' said Crosbie, running his finger along the many notes before him. 'Now, we just happen to know that you were involved in fisticuffs with some of Parker's gang inside The Camel public house just after ten. What were you doing in the intervening hour?'

'Well, I was walkin', wasn't I. I was proper hacked off and needed a breather.'

'So, what was it all about?'

'Usual gash. They were laughin' at my face.' He was not going to give this copper the satisfaction of knowing that they had been trying to coerce him into doing a job for them and that his persistent refusal had been the reason for them attacking him. They had complained that he thought he was better than them. Well, he was, and he had handled himself well too. Then, his mind moving on, he suddenly looked alarmed. 'You ain't getting round to sayin' that I'm a suspect for murderin' Parker?'

Crosbie sighed. 'Luckily for you, we've got the exact time of the murder on record. As Parker fell, fatally wounded, his watch cracked against the side of the chopping table in the butcher shop where it happened and it stopped at 9.58. You were drinking in The Camel at that time.'

'So, if I'm not in the frame for it, why are we doing this?'

'Just to establish your links with the gang, if any – and to ask to see your knife.'

'My knife?' asked Haggerty, his palms upraised in a wondering fashion. 'I thought you just said I didn't do it.'

'Your knife, please,' said Crosbie.

Haggerty drew his folded jack-knife out of his pocket and threw it impertinently onto the table with a clump.

Crosbie extracted the blade. 'Yes, this is exactly the type of knife that the post-mortem examination showed would have caused the wound. You see, Parker had a bloody knife in his hand, supposedly having withdrawn it from his own guts before dying, except that the knife he held was too large. He had a nasty hole just down here on the right side' – he held his hands to the same point on his own abdomen – 'but it didn't match up with the knife he was holding.'

Clark interjected with, 'Perhaps you should be looking for whoever *was* hurt with Parker's knife, then. Haggerty clearly wasn't.'

Crosbie turned and looked him up and down condescendingly. 'How old are you, son? All the blood in the place was from Parker. There was no evidence that anyone else had actually been hurt, no blood going out the door, none on the ice outside. So, just keep out of it.'

Clark, irritated but deciding silence was perhaps better, noticed that a sweat was forming on Haggerty's brow. It was very slight and his expression was otherwise calm, but did he know more about all this?

'So,' continued Crosbie, 'that hour ...'

'I said I was walkin',' Haggerty asserted, clenching his fists.

'All right, son,' said Crosbie, folding the blade away and handing it back. 'That's all for the moment.'

Clark nodded when Haggerty looked at him, 'Wait outside, killick.'

'Thank you, sir,' said Haggerty respectfully, and retreated from the office as quick as he could.

Clark stood and folded his arms. 'Well, you obviously have nothing on him. I can vouch for the fact that he's a first class seaman and valued member of this ship's company. He's been fighting the Germans right from the beginning of the war.'

Gathering up the loose papers clumsily into the file, Crosbie said, '*Fighting?* One could hardly call this a real war. Nothing's happened yet. It's a phoney war.'

'For you, maybe,' returned Clark, biting his tongue to prevent himself from going further. This whole 'phoney war' business was a matter of serious contention in the navy.

Crosbie continued, 'Know something about life, do you, son? I've been dealing with scum in East London my whole life. The only reason I haven't nicked Lizard Face – and that's what they call him in Bethnal Green – is because he has an alibi at 9.58. Otherwise, I'd bet a month's wages he knows more about this than he's letting on. When I find out how he done it, I'll have him.'

'Well, you'd better have something more than circumstantial evidence.'

'Don't you worry about that,' said Crosbie, positively happy at the prospect of making the arrest.

Then Clark adopted a condescending look to ask, 'If you're so serious about it, why has it taken you so long to come looking for him? The murder was two whole months ago.'

Crosbie frowned. 'Do us all a favour and don't get above your station, boy.'

'You have no idea what happened that night and you can't get any information about the real perpetrator, so you've come looking for the next best thing, a victim of circumstance.'

'Good day to you, sir,' said Crosbie with disgust. 'You pootle off and fight Jerry. *I'll* handle the police work.'

\*\*\*\*

Returning to the ship, Clark attempted to speak to Haggerty about his history but received a curt, 'Sir, I know you're well meaning an' all but I really haven't got any more to say. I hate where I come from but I can't very well turn my back on it. My mum still lives there.'

Clark nodded and said, 'I appreciate that,' and did not push him any further.

However, there was a curious streak inside the mind of the midshipman which was fuelled by the fact that Haggerty had been miserable ever since that infernal leave; and surely somebody like Crosbie could not have spent all those years in his profession just to conduct his business with baseless suspicions. Then again, he had called the criminals 'scum' and had been far from polite in the interview. Maybe he saw all the people of East London in that light. Had the detective succumbed to the worst prejudices against his own class? That would be truly disappointing because Clark had always considered the honest bobby a man to be venerated.

\*\*\*\*

Later, after counting rum barrels down into the stores, a task which had etched the brass-bound words 'The King God Bless Him' unwelcomingly onto his conscience, he decided to see if he could learn more from Pincher Martin. He knew it was the wrong thing to do but then he had a feeling that the problem with Haggerty was just not going to go away that easily. If there was anything he could do to understand more and make things better, then surely he should try it. There would be hell to pay if the captain found out what he was up to, though.

'Martin, you once said that you came from Bethnal Green.'

Pincher immediately looked troubled. He had earlier seen Clark and the Turtle go ashore suddenly and inexplicably and had suspected the reason. 'Yes, sir.'

'And Leading Seaman Haggerty does too …'

'Can I be frank, sir?' asked Pincher, desperate to be away and up the ladder to whatever task was coming next. He had spent well over a decade in this navy keeping his nose clean and he did not want to get embroiled in anything now – especially not this.

'Absolutely.'

'The lads trust you, sir. Leave it at that.'

'You don't even know what I'm going to say.'

'I can't talk about my messmates, sir.'

Clark fully understood what Pincher was saying and knew he was right according to convention yet cursed the fact that there have to be such a gulf between them. They may as well be foreigners to each other. Why could nobody else see that, but for their different pecuniary circumstances, they were all the same damned creature.

Looking at the disappointment on Clark's face, Pincher reiterated, 'Seriously, sir, leave it at that. By the time you reach my age you'll see the world differently, might even be able to change things a little, you know, but right now? Let's just fight the war and hope that Hitler don't win, 'cause then we really will have problems.'

Clark smiled. 'A good philosophy. Your clarity truly strikes me at times, able seaman.'

'Brains do work on the lower decks, sir,' returned Pincher before heading off to do further work.

\*\*\*\*

Of course, working ships with hundreds of men going to and fro were not very private places. There was always somebody just up a ladder or just the other side of a hatch with ears wide open and brain closed shut.

So when the Turtle caught up with Pincher later on, he confronted him and said, 'What was you saying to 'im about me?'

'Back off, Turtle,' Pincher replied, 'I never said nothing. In fact, what do I know? Nothing. I never talk to no officers about my mates, but I'll tell you what: if you want me to think that there's nothing going on then you ain't going the right way about it.'

'I'm watchin' you,' warned the Turtle and stalked away.

# SIX

## Suspicious Activity

April 1940.

The remainder of the month of March had passed with the *Burscombe* engaged on yet another routine patrol. After the usual boarding of neutral merchant ships in varying weathers, the checking of papers and cargoes under the constant threat of superior enemy action followed by many more questions on the effects the blockade was having, Captain Dollimore was suddenly very pleased by a significant change in their situation.

It was upon an issue for which he had been fighting for months and concerned the composition of the 25th Cruiser Squadron. There were now no less than a satisfying six ships designated to work closely together under Rear-Admiral Nicklesworth. At last, it seemed that the Admiralty's intention was not to allow them to be scattered across the sea on distant tasks.

Better late than never, thought Dollimore. This eventuality was the only thing that made sense. Ships operating singly or in pairs had been at a constant disadvantage considering one of their objectives was to guard against the German use of battlecruisers. But now there were enough British Armed Merchant Cruisers – passenger liners and the like with big guns hastily fitted and manned almost exclusively by sailors of the reserve – to take care of the suspect merchant fleets while the proper warships could regroup and get back to guarding against their greater adversaries.

Spread out in a line to starboard of the *Burscombe*, their bows pitching and throwing out foamy spray every which way, were her sister ship *Farecombe*, the smaller eight-gun light cruiser HMS *Marsfield* and the three battered ships of Commander Fulton-Stavely's faithful destroyer group: *Crayhorn*, *Catterley* and *Castledown*.

On *Burscombe*'s bridge, Lt-Cdr Digby turned his camera upon the pleasing sight and captured the image for the sake of his great personal sense of historical undertaking and posterity. 'God help the Jerry that comes across this little lot,' he grinned, his voice raised above the crashing of the waves.

Irwin, sneezing out the salty contents of his frozen nose, shook his head and wished that some of his comrade's optimism would work its way into him. He could not help but feel that they were engaged upon a thankless task to no good end. He would have liked the governments of Britain and Germany to forge some sort of deal for peace right now while they still had a chance. Neville Chamberlain could only become a national hero if he managed to do this but he seemed to have his hands tied behind his back.

'Chin up, old boy,' said Digby.

'I'm doing my best, I truly am,' replied Irwin with the most false smile imaginable.

The captain suddenly appeared and said, 'We keep veering two degrees off course.'

'Yes, sir,' said Irwin, stiffening somewhat and looking at the compass. 'I've already informed the helm and he's making his corrections. There we go, he's back on course again, sir.'

'Very good, Mr Irwin.'

Aware of the very different attitudes that his officers possessed, Dollimore still felt the need to keep a closer eye on this lieutenant. Notwithstanding his pacific leanings and his faltering style with both men and women, the man's performance as a navigator and watch officer had been otherwise fair. There was still promise if only they could arrest his growing lack of foresight and push him to operate more independently. Unfortunately, this war had not taken kindly to him just as he had not taken kindly to the war.

The admiral's steward then climbed out on the bridge, moving stiffly in multiple layers of padded clothing. 'Sir, with the admiral's compliments, could you meet with him in his cabin?'

Dollimore let his head hang to one side as he looked at the comical figure. 'Don't you think you've overdone it a bit?'

'Sorry, sir?'

'The uniform, man, the uniform. Perhaps double balaclavas and jumpers may have been useful when we were in the Arctic Circle in winter but off Scotland in spring? This might be seen as a little excessive.'

'Aye aye, sir.'

Dollimore tutted and shook his head. He made his way past the steward and disappeared into the hatch.

'Doesn't feel like spring,' muttered Irwin to Digby.

'Of course it does,' replied the gunnery officer. 'This is the first patrol since December that I've not had to stuff newspaper into my boots for extra warmth. Anyway, hopefully Jerry will come out and we'll have ourselves a decent scrap. That should warm us up a bit.'

Irwin's face fell. 'I think you shouldn't be so hasty on that front. I mean, you shouldn't hope for these men to lose their lives.'

A couple of lookouts glanced at each other and shook their heads.

Digby looked a little nonplussed. 'Why would I hope for that?'

'At least the Finns and the Russians have had the sense to call it a day,' Irwin finished.

Very bloody fighting had been going on between Finland and Russia during these awful winter months but they had just agreed upon a ceasefire, a move which made a relieved sense to the peaceable likes of Irwin. It was nothing less than the scaling back of a major problem in a world on the brink of Armageddon.

But Digby had his own view on the subject, one which he was confident was the more popular. As patiently as he could, he said, 'Russia only called for a truce because the Finns turned out to be stronger than expected. The bastards are just trying to save face.'

He had been in favour of British forces landing in Norway on the pretext of helping the Finns but it had come to nothing because of the Chamberlain Government's continued policy of waiting to see what would happen. That and not having an appetite to fight the Russians as well as the Germans. Well, he thought, the one are just as crooked as the other. The Russkies stole half of Poland for themselves. Why haven't we declared war on them?

The policy, or lack of, had set men like Irwin and Digby at opposite poles.

\*\*\*\*

Two decks below, Dollimore stepped into the cabin where Nicklesworth was sitting in his customary position, studying the many bits of paperwork that continually came his way.

Immediately acknowledging the other man's presence, Nicklesworth leaned back and handed Dollimore a slip of paper. 'Charles, please have the squadron deploy according to this order.'

'Very good, sir,' Dollimore replied. He read:

*To Rear-Admiral Commanding 25th Cruiser Squadron,*
*RAF Bomber Command reports heavy concentration of shipping in*
*Baltic ports and Heligoland Bight. Patrol south of BERGEN no further*
*than 4° East.*

Dollimore's mind began turning. This would put them many miles to the south west of the southern tip of Norway, definitely not close enough to interfere with that shipping if it decided to head up neutral waters. 'A German invasion fleet ready to hit Norway?' he suggested just as fast as he had given it consideration.

Nicklesworth immediately tightened his mouth. He had had a gut feeling that this captain would be drawn into assumptions. Testily, he said, 'There's absolutely no way you can say that for certain. Whatever they are – and there's no evidence to suggest that they are an invasion force – our first priority is to stop the enemy surface fleet from breaking out into the Atlantic. That's been our objective all along and there's no reason to change it.'

'Of course, sir,' replied Dollimore, his concern heightening over this rigid attention to such a narrow course of action. He believed that they had already lost the initiative by not following up on the *Altmark* affair and striking for Narvik before the Germans could be ready; and while they were having difficulties with their torpedoes. Did it not stand to reason that Captain Vian's action in February might have turned Hitler's mind onto Narvik too?

Whatever the reality of the situation, the Home Fleet had done little more than indulge in seven extra weeks of cautious patrols.

'Until somebody comes up with something solid,' continued Nicklesworth, 'we continue as we are, and that's direct from Admiral Forbes and concurred by the Admiralty.'

Dollimore looked at his superior and asked, 'But what do *you* think, sir?' already suspecting what the uninspiring answer would be.

'The same, captain.' Nicklesworth stared hard at him. 'I will not move forward on conjecture. We are here to follow orders.' He found that he had to remind himself daily of Forbes' reasons as to why Dollimore should be his flag captain. So far they had not achieved anything significant together so the basis of their relationship was beginning to wear a little thin.

Dollimore pushed no further and went back to the bridge, there to issue the orders that would put the six ships in their new position closer to the Baltic. He then looked out over the grey sea and hit his fist upon the bridge casing.

He did understand Forbes' motives. If they moved in to intercept what could have been an invasion force but it turned out to be a false lead, they could leave the way open for enemy warships to break out to the Atlantic. But on the other hand, if there was an invasion fleet out there then they could give it a seriously bloody nose in the opening stages of the battle.

Dollimore knew Forbes to be an intelligent man. He was at sea somewhere further north in HMS *Rodney*, thinking of how best to disperse his forces. He could not be in two places at once and he had long since learned that he was going to get no more ships than he already had. Dollimore just had to have faith that he would be making his decisions based on better intelligence than a mere captain could get his hands on but, even still, he could not shake off his doubts. He decided that there had to be a way he could help force the situation.

Digby and Irwin said nothing as they observed their captain muttering to himself on the windswept bridge. They knew that when he looked like this, there was bound to be some trouble on the horizon.

Then, when a new message was delivered to Dollimore, it very suddenly came time for thoughts to be turned into action. He ordered, 'Mr Irwin, pipe for Lieutenant Hanwell to report to my sea cabin,' then quickly left the bridge in order to go and tell Nicklesworth what his intentions were.

'Very good, sir,' Irwin replied, immediately thinking that any attempt by their air officer, Hanwell, to launch his Walrus aircraft in this weather was extremely foolhardy.

\*\*\*\*

Smudge flapped his arms about his midriff in an effort to get warm. Four hours on the bridge staring at the grey was still a daunting experience even if the mean temperature was improving. The incessant wind created most of his problems, exacerbated by the occasional rain which forever permeated his waterproof coat. He climbed stiffly down a series of ladders. His mess was five decks below and, crammed as it was with sweaty, seasick men, he found it warmly inviting in a relative sense.

'Up Spirits' had been just a few minutes ago and his tot of rum was waiting for him with the Turtle standing guard over it. After gulping it down, relishing the way the taste and consistency stimulated his body, he sighed and said, 'My oh my, I always said the navy was good for something.' Then he began taking off his coat. 'Well, lads, I reckon we'll be fighting Jerry shortly,' he announced as he opened his locker.

A few of the men looked up from their various corners. For a few seconds they ceased their food preparation, sewing or polishing and wondered what more he knew. They had all heard the earlier pipe put out by the captain explaining that they were heading closer to the Baltic because the enemy was on the move, but there had been no particular urgency.

For Smudge, just having people listening to him was the most important factor. Exchanging his wet clothes for dry, he said, 'Yeah, what the captain neglected to mention was that there was an invasion force setting out for Norway.'

'You seem to know a lot about it,' said Paddy Walbrook, casting him a warning look.

'Me an' the captain's like that,' replied Smudge, crossing his fingers to demonstrate their alleged closeness.

At that moment, about half of his audience returned to what they had previously been doing. Smudge did have the reputation of being the only man in the whole of the ship's company to have ever made Captain Dollimore smile at a joke but his other boasts were just hogwash. Some of the more gullible or bored seamen still wanted to know more, however.

Smudge, having seen the captain return from the admiral's cabin more annoyed than when he went, had simply put two and two together and quite shrewdly had come up with, 'The captain wants us to steam right in and knock the bastards brown bread so's we can sail home and get medals and all the girls we want, but the admiral's called for a bit of decorum and what not. "Your men might be heroes but they'd be useless to me with the clap." That was the admiral's exact words. Standing next to him when he said it, I was.'

Les, highly upset these days at Smudge's entire approach to life, said, 'I don't believe you. That's just filth.'

'Says the master of filth! Have you told the boys what that 'artissifer' said to you in the gland compartment? "Do it, Les, do it! Remember the old adage, "One up the bum, no harm done!"'

Then the Turtle was on his feet. 'That's enough!'

'All right, all right,' said Smudge, raising his hands in a gesture of submission. He may have been smart with the words but he was not handy enough with his fists to go up against the Turtle. The ugly old killick was so miserable these days. He had lost all of his sense of humour.

They sat, a little calmer. Pincher asked, 'Here, Turtle, when are you doing the Fleet Board?'

'Dunno,' the Turtle replied defensively. He was still not feeling particularly sociable at the moment and hoped his tone would inform them that he did not want to be drawn out on the subject of being examined for promotion. He had already had a couple of POs and chiefs on his back saying that he had better buck his ideas up otherwise he would find it hard to fit into any petty officers' mess. But, you know what? Sod the lot of them.

Peace amongst the lads was beckoning but, unfortunately, the rum was still fresh on Smudge's lips and his mouth was ready to go into overtime. 'The Turtle as a senior rate? Not until the police have finished with him. Found a corpse up the frog and toad they did ...'

He stopped mid-sentence because the Turtle was now staring into his eyes. 'I don't actually give a stuff whether I make PO or not, so takin' a chunk outta your face wouldn't matter much. Catch my drift?'

Smudge stayed silent. What else was he to do?

But the buzz had already gone round the lower decks that the Turtle was a murderer, a relapsed East End hoodlum. He had gone home on leave and settled an old score; that was what they were saying. It was certainly more interesting than the idea that he had simply failed to dip his wick on leave.

No one was quite sure where the information had come from but the Turtle guessed that Pincher might have something to do with it. He was the only one on board who knew anything about his neighbourhood and background. Don't worry. He would get what was coming to him.

So would that midshipman too. The Turtle had requested Mr Clark's presence for that interview because, knowing him to be more liberal-minded and conscientious, he thought he would be more discreet than to go bleating straight to Pincher. You can't trust anybody in this life.

At that moment CPO Doyle entered through the hatch at the aft end of the mess. He had his cap off so nobody moved to stand. He looked around as though disgusted at the sight of this sorry-looking lot and announced, 'I'm looking for a volunteer for something special.'

Around the compartment leading seamen, able seamen and ordinary seamen all, looked down. Why could the chief not just say what and who he wanted? In a couple of seconds he would pick somebody anyway and then the chosen man would find himself having drawn the short straw for some horrible job.

Smudge, also having looked away, noticed that Les was messing with something under the bench. Oh, he was tickling Felix, the ship's fluffy black and white cat, and had not even noticed the chief come in. Suppressing a laugh, Smudge whispered, 'Here, Les, chiefy wants you.'

Les's face immediately went whiter than it already was as he turned and saw CPO Doyle standing there waiting. He jumped up quickly and smartly and said, 'Yes, Chief?'

'Yes, you'll do,' said Doyle shaking his head. 'Follow me.'
****

Les was taken up to one of the workshops immediately abaft the forward funnel, observing as he went a miserable gathering of stokers and mechanics persevering against the wind and rain all about the Walrus. That should have been clue as to what they were expecting of him but unfortunately his wits did not take him that far. It was only when he was standing in the workshop itself and was face to face with Lieutenant Hanwell, the ship's air officer, that the penny began to drop.

'Oh, good stuff,' said Hanwell enthusiastically, though otherwise he looked dreadfully unwell. Although he had served at sea with the Fleet Air Arm for close on two years now, he had never got over his tendency to suffer from seasickness even in calm weather. This having been noticed by all who came into contact with him, he had started to become known as 'Boris' behind his back for he often resembled one of those horrific creations of Boris Karloff's horror films. 'And what's your name?' he asked.

'Ordinary Seaman Gordy, sir.'

'Right-o. Chief, have you briefed him?'

'Not as yet, sir,' replied Doyle.

'Very well.' Then, to Les again, Hanwell said, 'There's a coat, boots, goggles, all the usual paraphernalia. Get suited up. My man's somehow got himself on the sick list.'

'Am I going up in the plane?' asked Les, a smile appearing on his face.

'Well, it's not for fancy dress, lad,' said Doyle impatiently.

As Les began to prepare, the hatch opened and a wet gust of wind followed Commander Locklin inside. Everybody quickly turned to acknowledge him.

Looking from one man to another in his customary calm manner, Locklin skilfully gauged the characters before him. He understood a lot about body language and decided he was satisfied that he had a good crew in front of him. Even that strange lad he had observed on one or two occasions who perhaps would have been better off in some other service looked confident and happy. 'A short while ago our fellows in the wireless office intercepted some garbled messages about a confused action north of here and, to cut a long story short, the *Hipper* may very well be at sea.'

Even Les knew what that meant. The *Hipper* was one of the German heavy cruisers that everybody had been so desperate to find and destroy these past few months. That had been one of the priorities of these long patrols. But come to think of it, though it was a great adventure, he was not particularly sure he wanted to get involved in actually finding the enemy. He had not been on board when *Burscombe* had engaged the *Moltke* and, from the descriptions of the battle given by his messmates, he was pretty glad about it.

Locklin continued, 'So, just get yourselves up there, fly northwards – you won't be alone; the *Farecombe* is flying off another Walrus on a more easterly course – and report back on anything you find. The captain also wants you to keep in mind that earlier signal we received about the build-up of enemy shipping. He and the admiral are not happy about it. Any questions?'

Fighting back an urge to vomit right now, Hanwell said, 'Yes, sir, the weather. Launching and flying is going to be difficult enough as it is. Don't get me wrong, it's not impossible but you retrieving us is. I can't land on this sea and you'd never be able to lift us back inboard anyway. If we expend all our fuel on this search, what are we to do?'

Locklin's face took on a very serious expression. 'Land in one of the Norwegian fjords.'

'But we'll be interned.'

'Make no mistakes about this. The captain ...' Locklin stopped himself to make a correction. It was just that he knew that all this thinking had come from Dollimore, not Nicklesworth, though the latter had reluctantly endorsed it. '... the *admiral* is taking a calculated risk that you'll only be interned for a couple of days. He believes that a German invasion is underway and that Norway will shortly be on our side in the war.'

His correction had not fooled these men but that worked for the good. Just the very idea that Captain Dollimore was taking the calculated risk was enough for them to go forth without any qualms. He had always had a way of coming through all right in the past and they trusted him completely.

About two hours later, Hanwell was pushing on the Walrus's throttle to pick up the windspeed on the propeller. He, Les and the co-pilot were eager to be off because they had been sitting in the cold machine completely inactive for most of that time simply waiting. They had not bothered trying to find out why. Every now and then the navy threw inexplicable hours of waiting at the men for unknown reasons.

The small explosive charge set into the catapult trolley underneath the plane went off and the crew were jolted breathlessly back into their seats. In a lightning manoeuvre, the Walrus was thrust out from the starboard side of the ship and Hanwell was immediately fighting against the weather for control.

Les felt the pull of gravity and then a sudden weightlessness as it seemed as they were going to crash and then another drag on his body as the plane eventually climbed away from rolling sea. His legs were tense with nervousness for a few moments but beyond that he was too excited about the chance for going up in a plane to be overly concerned. The other blokes did not know what they had missed out on.

He looked down and saw the other five ships keeping pace with the *Burscombe* in the gloom and reflected upon how they looked like little toys from up here. No wonder it was so difficult for the Germans to hit them when they dropped their bombs. He waved out the window and wondered if anyone saw him, then they were on their way northwards, the windscreen wipers doing what they could to keep the intermittent rain from their vision.

'Keep a sharp eye out!' came Hanwell's voice through his headphones.

His shivering forgotten, Les put his thumbs up to Hanwell and noticed that the pilot already looked in better health now than the whole time he had been on that shifting deck.

\*\*\*\*

Rather pleased that he was back at sea again and following the path to the future that he dreamed of, Oskar Fjelstad slavishly inhaled and exhaled the smoke from the very fine cigar that the captain had given him for his birthday. It travelled through his mouth, nose, throat and lungs with nothing short of a smooth sensation, much better than the cheap cigarettes that he normally had his hands on. This was just one of the many types of cigar that the captain often picked up on his visits to New York and was the closest thing the Old Man had to a pastime.

Bakkevig himself had told Oskar to light up right here, right now in the *Dagrand*'s bridge and had lit one for himself at the same time. 'With these you cannot go wrong,' he said as though that was all the explanation required.

At fifteen, Oskar saw himself as much of a man as Bakkevig. He had been working on the *Dagrand* for nine months now and was becoming as proficient a seaman as any of the old sweats. He was certainly more eager than a lot of them. The only thing that still gave away his age, apart from his boyish looks, was the fact that he was not yet ready to move on to drinking spirits. In that he was cautious. Blowing out blue smoke, he said to Bakkevig, 'I really appreciate this, sir.'

'I told your father I would look after you and, as much as anything else, see this as a reward for your hard work.' Bakkevig gave a quick frown, saying, 'Believe me, I've had some hopeless idiots on this ship but you seem to have a brain on you.' He motioned to the cigar. 'This is me telling you that you have a bright future.'

'Thank you, sir,' replied Oskar, trying to sweep away his guilty thoughts about the captain being out of his depth when it came to war matters.

'Let's hope that this stupid conflict between Britain and Germany peters out before we get caught up in it,' continued Bakkevig as if to prove Oskar's doubts. 'If anything's going to affect your chances it will be those two dragging us into their affairs.'

Oskar gave him a thoughtful look and hesitatingly said, 'Sir ... I think we should expect trouble ... and I also think we should firmly side with the British. They're the only ones that will treat us fairly if there's to be a new order.'

Bakkevig's calm exterior crumbled and the indignantly worried man appeared from inside. 'When you've lived a few more years I might possibly listen to your words of wisdom but until then, shut up. You've much to learn about the world of men.'

I certainly don't want to grow up to be like you, thought Oskar, though duly silenced.

The *D/S Dagrand* was just a few hours out of Oslo to carry a new cargo back across the Atlantic. They were crawling along at a speed of less than ten knots in order to conserve the coal that his stokers were busy shovelling into the furnaces down below, and would soon be turning north.

Bakkevig was going to take the ship up the Norwegian coast until he was as far as possible from the British warships and the German submarines. Even with what happened last time it was still considered safest.

Oskar retreated from the bridge and out into the blustery cold. There were many things that he did not admire about Bakkevig and his excessive caution and inability to understand the war were just two of them. However, Oskar was not the type of loudmouth lad who entered into a work situation thinking that he knew more than the bosses. For better or for worse he recognised Bakkevig's strengths as well as his weaknesses and fully appreciated that he had given him a job when plenty of others would not have.

He climbed down the ladder and began working his way along the waist towards the cabins that he was expected to be cleaning and cast a look out at the sea. The grey waves were rolling with some little violence making the *Dagrand* sway back and forth but he was used to all that now. Only the biggest storms made him sick and then half of his sickness had been worry about the old tub's stability. He better understood now just what this ship was capable of. After all, both he and she were still safe and well.

Suddenly he saw something bobbing about on the waves at some distance. A quick bout of concern surged through his body for the very first thing that came to mind was that he might be looking at the periscope of a U-boat. But he was soon able to discount that. What kept on appearing and disappearing between the wave crests was the wrong shape and behaved too differently to be a periscope. Did he see an arm wave at him? What was it?

He ran back up to the bridge where Bakkevig and a couple of the other men shot him annoyed looks for he had already been dismissed. But before any of them could say anything, he shouted, 'There's something floating out there to port!' Then he grabbed a pair of binoculars from the rack just above the chart table.

He and Bakkevig moved out onto the bridge wing after first trying to look through the window and deciding that there were too many droplets of water upon the glass. A quick scan of the sea revealed what it was he had seen and the truth of it made them relax. It was just a lifeboat. Because of the dimness of the light it was not possible to see exactly who was in it, whether they were the castaway passengers of some liner or just the crew of a doomed merchant ship, but they waved enthusiastically nonetheless.

Bakkevig called back inside, 'Bring us to port forty degrees! Head towards that boat!'

'Aye!' answered the apprehensive helmsman who, by straining his old eyes against the gloom, picked out the bobbing target.

Fifteen minutes later, Oskar and Michaelsen threw the rope ladder over the side, the one they always had ready to hand now for situations such as this. As the men below steadied the ladder to their boat as much as possible against the heaving sea, Bakkevig's men confirmed what they had been suspecting as they had got closer and closer to them. 'They're German!' Michaelsen called up to the captain on the bridge wing.

What could this mean?

The wet, shivering men climbing up over the side rail were large, tough specimens and their field grey coats, webbing and weapons confirmed that they were soldiers. Although perfectly calm, they were extremely pleased to have been picked up and more than one offered their thanks respectfully to their saviours. In fact their freshly shaved faces displayed good humour in an almost innocent way.

Bakkevig did not like it one little bit. His stomach began churning as his imagination turned over pessimistic scenarios. Yes, he was afraid for his ship but more than that, he was afraid for himself. He cursed his quivering legs and climbed down the ladder onto the waist. He could see just over twenty men standing hereabouts and no matter how polite they were, they made him much more uneasy than those Englishmen that had stood here a couple of months ago. He considered that it was best to placate them at the very start. He said, 'Oskar, take them into the mess and prepare coffee.'

One of the soldiers stepped forward, taking off his grey life-jacket and handing it to one of the others. From the way they deferred to him, he was clearly in charge. He came to attention in front of Bakkevig, clicked his heels and smiled, 'Leutnant Meissner at your service. On behalf of myself and my men, I thank you for picking us up.'

Bakkevig's grasp of German was very good, having served the Baltic trade routes to a much greater extent than the Atlantic in the last twenty years. 'You're welcome. I am Captain Bakkevig, but ... well, how do you come to be ...?' Failing to produce the words from his dry throat, he had to make do with the quizzical gesture of his hand and confused expression.

'We're part of the 7th Division heading north to protect Bergen,' said Meissner matter-of-factly. It was brazen and he seemed not to understand the import of what he had just said.

Out the corner of his eye Bakkevig noticed Oskar's face take on a concerned expression. He knew the boy's mind and became afraid at what his beliefs might lead him to. He quickly put his hand on the leutnant's shoulder and guided him away. 'Please come to the bridge.'

The two of them climbed the ladder and, once in the shelter of the bridge with the door shut, Meissner, a very young officer himself, suddenly betrayed a true relief. 'Ah,' he sighed, rubbing his eyes. 'How good it is to be out of that wind, out of that boat.

'Now,' he continued, hardly taking a breather, 'it is imperative you take us back into the shipping lanes to the east so that we may catch up with the rest of our division. Time is of the essence if we are to bring Bergen under our protection before the English get there.' It was not exactly the ruthless German that one might have expected but he certainly meant business.

Choosing not to take any accusatory stance with the German, Bakkevig said feebly, 'The English are invading Norway?'

'Any day now. We must get there before them. It is bad luck that our transport was sunk by an enemy submarine, but you have helped redress the balance by your timely arrival. Now, turn the ship around and head to the east so that we can join another transport.'

He then gave Bakkevig a strange look. It was pleasant enough but, at the same time, it seemed to be saying that he had been delayed for far too long 'and if you prevaricate further, then I shall kill you and I know exactly how I'm going to do it'.

Bakkevig agreed to his demand straight away.

****

Oskar just managed to squeeze the soldiers into the mess where they happily laid down their life-jackets and equipment and sat down to laugh about their good fortune. He retreated to the small adjoining galley and set about boiling the water for the preparation of an urn of coffee. He listened to their chattering as he worked, understanding about half of the words being uttered and being sure to keep a dopey look of naive indifference upon his face.

Once he had served the drinks he waited for a moment or two while he was sure that the soldiers were disregarding his presence then left the cabin. He made his way along the passage to the radio booth behind the bridge and peered cautiously around the edge of the door that was swinging in an unsightly fashion on its bent rollers. The captain had promised to get that fixed before the last trip but either had too many other things on his mind or did not care.

For the moment it was fortunate that it was neglected because he could see if anybody was inside without having to knock and alert anyone but the operator to his purpose. The slovenly radio man, Bernie, was sitting, leaning back in his chair with the heels of his worn shoes up on the desk. A long cigarette protruded from his heavy greying beard. He appeared not to be paying any attention to the mixed signals of voices and morse code coming through the small array of systems in front of him, but Oskar knew that he was actually digesting every word.

With a quick glance along the passage, and aware of the proximity of Bakkevig with the German officer next door, he quietly entered the booth.

'Hey, Bernie,' he whispered.

Bernie turned his head lazily and gave the boy a dirty look of impatience. 'You know you're not allowed in here, son.'

Motioning with his hand for Bernie to keep his voice down, Oskar said, 'Bernie, seriously, what do you think of what's happening?'

'Can't say as I give a shit,' the old man mumbled.

'Yes you do,' returned Oskar vehemently. 'You're no idiot. The Nazis are making a play for our country and these people seem to think we've got no choice in the matter. Well, we have.'

'Boy,' said Bernie, looking into his eyes with the most earnest expression he had used in some years, 'take my advice. Shut up and go away.'

'But you've got to warn the British!' he hissed. 'I'd do it myself if I knew how to work this equipment!'

'Oskar. Go ... away!'

'For God's sake, you fat old dinosaur ...'

Bernie grabbed Oskar's collar and pulled him close, saying with smelly breath, 'I've already sent a signal to London, you little bastard. Bakkevig knows nothing about it so don't go blabbing. Now, get lost and act natural – anything else is more than your life is worth. Got it?'

Oskar nodded. 'Thanks.' No clearer message was required and he left the booth happy in his mind that his sentiments were in tune with Bernie's: these Nazis were going to get what was coming to them.

\*\*\*\*

Rear-Admiral Nicklesworth stood in his swaying bridge on board the *Burscombe*, staring out at the mysterious and unforgiving sea. He was suspicious of the horizon because he had heard nothing from the Walrus or anybody else about the *Hipper*'s whereabouts. The original signal which had made Dollimore insist on aerial reconnaissance had suggested that HMS *Glowworm* was in contact with the German cruiser. The *Glowworm* was a destroyer, markedly smaller and inferior to the other ship, completely outmatched in every way. Nobody had heard from her for hours now and that was not a good sign.

He walked over to the voicepipe and called, 'Captain's bridge, admiral's bridge.'

'Captain's bridge here, sir,' came the reply from above.

'Is Mr Dollimore up there?'

'Yes, sir.'

With no more further ado, Nicklesworth passed the plot and chart house and climbed up to the open bridge above. He came to stand next to Dollimore. 'What are you thinking, Charles?'

Dollimore had come to know that the admiral only called him Charles when he needed his help to clear matters up in his mind. 'Just waiting like everybody else, sir.'

'But the *Hipper*'s definitely out there.'

'Without a doubt, but I am also giving equal consideration to those ships sighted in the Baltic and Heligoland, sir.'

Nicklesworth glanced away then gave Dollimore a hard stare. 'At this moment in time, based on what we know, the *Hipper* is more important than Norway. You understand?'

'Of course, sir. I just have one question, though. Assuming that the Germans are well aware that we have various powerful squadrons *and* a battlefleet patrolling these waters, don't you think it's completely ludicrous that they would send out the *Hipper* alone to what would be her sure destruction?'

\*\*\*\*

Visibility from above was not good. Everything was a swirling grey mess and Lt Hanwell had had to bring the plane down quite low if they were to spot anything at all. Aside from that he was in his element. He had spent far too many weeks in the *Burscombe* feeling inadequate because he was so rarely given the chance to perform his primary task. In that the weather had been the biggest obstacle to air operations.

Just behind him, diligently looking out the window, was Les Gordy. He was cold again. These days there were some times when he was less cold but he realised that he had forgotten what it was like to be truly warm. Still, would he have passed up on the chance to fly in this billowy plane just because he might have got a bit cold? Not likely.

But the constant sweep of grey was beginning to annoy his eyes. For a stretch of water that everybody wanted to control so much, it was remarkably empty. Except for that ship down there…

Because his mind had wandered, he had almost not noticed the solid black silhouette down there on the left, but he swiftly came back to reality and tapped Hanwell on the shoulder.

Hanwell looked about and then followed the direction in which Les's finger was pointing. He nodded and immediately turned the steering column and dropped the flaps. Circling down but being sure to keep a safe distance from their target, the ride got a little bumpy as droplets of water sprayed across the glass.

Tutting and straining his eyes, Les stared hard at the ship. It was definitely a warship, with a high fighting top, single large funnel set a little way back behind the forward superstucture and two large triple turrets, one each facing fore and aft. 'A *Deutschland* Class Battlecruiser!' Les cried excitedly into his mask.

Hanwell picked up in his earphones the accented words from the Irish lad, and asked, 'Are you sure it's not the *Hipper*?'

'Certain, sir. I seen it on a postcard.'

'No mistake?'

'No, sir.'

Hanwell put his thumb up in acceptance of Les's assessment and told the co-pilot to send the signal.

Suddenly white tracer bullets began winding their way up into the sky in their direction and the muzzle flashes from the ship's secondary armament were followed by some jolting explosions near the Walrus.

'Oops,' said Hanwell, almost impossibly calm. 'Time to skedaddle.'

Les nearly lost control of his bladder and hung on to the seat as Hanwell began to manoeuvre the plane. He had not signed on for this! But then, of course, he had in a weird way, so he only had himself to blame. He closed his eyes and hoped this pilot was as confident as he thought he was.

\*\*\*\*

Their weak signal was picked up by the ships of Nicklesworth's squadron and quickly deciphered for the officers' consumption. The admiral, having already ordered his ships to turn north, asked Dollimore and Lt-Cdr Peterson to join him in the charthouse where he put the slip of paper containing the information down on the table.

Peterson conferred in undertones with AB Barrett, the problem-solver from below decks, until Nicklesworth finally said, 'Well, spit it out, man.'

The navigating officer stood and marked an X on the chart with his pencil. 'If this is correct then our battlecruiser is approximately a hundred and ten miles north, heading away from us at a slow speed. With the speed we're making in this weather, we might make contact in five hours.'

'A night action,' commented Dollimore, adding, 'if present courses and speeds are maintained by us *and* the enemy.'

'We can't do better, I'm afraid,' continued Peterson. 'This wind battering us on the port bow is detrimental to the tune of about four knots and too much way on in this sea could be dangerous for Fulton-Stavely's destroyers.'

Nicklesworth nodded his head and said of their target, 'I wonder if this is the ship that the *Glowworm* encountered.'

'I would be inclined to operate on the assumption that the enemy has two heavy units at sea,' said Dollimore, 'and very probably more.'

'Norway again? Drop it, captain. There's still not enough evidence for that.'

Peterson shared a little glance with Barrett. These two very different men had judged the respective abilities of their superiors long ago and knew which one of them they trusted in.

\*\*\*\*

The 25th Cruiser Squadron spent the night pushing its way to the north between eighty and a hundred miles away from the coast. All of Dollimore's best intuition pointed to this being a mistake but it was the distance that Admiral Forbes had dictated to them based upon the idea of intercepting a German battlecruiser trying to break out to the Atlantic.

Nicklesworth had no desire to contradict the Commander-in-Chief.

Dollimore could not help but feel that not far off to the east ships containing soldiers of the Third Reich were making their way towards targets in Norway but believed that he had said all he could upon the subject. There was nothing more to do except resign himself to the fact that each passing hour meant a much greater effort to retrieve the situation later on.

These cautious decisions were at least consistent with the way the Chamberlain Government had pursued the war thus far. He would have to content himself with the understanding that in war, although the British always got the upper hand in the end, it would have to cost the lives of many servicemen in blunders first. This was the price of a democracy's peacetime approach to defence.

\*\*\*\*

When Nicklesworth received a signal from the Admiralty in the early hours of the morning that German soldiers had been picked up from a sunken transport who claimed that they were on their way to Bergen, he bit his lip and thought hard about whether to pass this on to his opinionated captain. It seemed to back up everything the infernal man had been saying and, to make matters worse, the origin of the information appeared to be well over twelve hours old. He supposed that it must have taken that long to get confirmation of the reports that it was a Polish submarine that had sunk the transport. Had it been one of His Majesty's subs then they would have known sooner.

But was an invasion of Norway really in the offing? The only complaints he had been aware of coming out of Oslo were of British ships sowing mines in the Leads up north.

It was all very confusing but would any of it change his objective? Thankfully, a timely signal arrived from Forbes which solved the dilemma for him. Intercepting the battlecruiser was the priority. Therefore they would continue on as they had been.

Good. Dollimore need not know anything about the soldiers, the Polish submarine or the mines. He may well be a talented officer with worthy insights to offer but he was not in charge of this show – and one must not forget his past record.

# SEVEN

## Confused Encounters

The expectations of the ship's company were waning by the time the sun began to rise again. There had been no night encounter and it was reasonable to assume that whatever ship had been sighted was long gone by now. Still, everybody was ordered to their Action Stations. Dawn was historically one of the most dangerous times for any ship at war so they wanted to be ready.

The gunners made their way uncomplaining to the cold turrets fore and aft and the blustery open gun mountings above the waists, the torpedo men manned the tubes amidships, the stokers and artificers took up their stations on the various pieces of machinery throughout the ship and the damage-control parties closed up in their strategic positions, ready to counter the unwanted effects of any fight.

Dollimore was standing on the snow-swept bridge, shivering under the bite of the growing storm. It made a complete mockery of the many layers of clothing that he was wearing and he wished that he still had youth on his side to help combat it. Thinking on it, one or two of these younger chaps would do well to take his hints about doing more to keep fit.

The emerging horizon ahead was just a sad continuation of the smudged grey of yesterday augmented by these intermittent gusts of snow. He was practically praying for the enemy to show himself now to take his mind off it but the distraction, when it did come, was in the form of an order from the admiral's bridge.

Nicklesworth called up the voicepipe, 'Bring the squadron onto a bearing of zero-nine-zero.'

'Very good, sir,' replied Dollimore and immediately set the orders in motion, wondering what intelligence the admiral had come by. Beyond that, his patience with this patrol was almost exhausted.

The Chief Yeoman of the Signals hoisted his flags for the benefit of the other ships as the *Burscombe* heeled over for her starboard turn and, as they were completing the manoeuvre, Nicklesworth climbed out onto the bridge to crunch his way through the thin layer of snow underfoot.

'Signal from Forbes,' he said in a monotone. 'We're closing towards the Norwegian coast approximately fifty miles before patrolling back towards the south. He wants us back in our old position, watching for German troop transports as we go. Norway may be under attack.'

Dollimore did not even grace him with a look.

Lt-Cdr Peterson peered out from the hood of his duffle coat. Disliking the tension, he was pleased to have another matter to raise. 'The sea is worsening, sir.'

'Thank you, Pilot, I can see that,' replied Dollimore. 'Reduce speed accordingly.'

He was as frustrated as he could ever hope to feel, his anger growing as though spreading through his arteries on his very blood. He consciously fought for its subsidence, knowing from long experience that his anger led him to do rash things. He had come too far to allow it to get the better of him.

Then, about an hour later, came an order that threatened to tip the balance.

They had been closing the coast with half the company stood down for normal watch-keeping routine when Nicklesworth, who had long since returned to his own bridge, called up that the squadron was to turn one-three-five to starboard.

Set the squadron upon what was in effect the opposite course? Dollimore began to see red. He hissed the order down to the helmsman and took a deep breath. As calmly as he was able, he said, 'Pilot, you have the bridge.'

Peterson and Digby watched him go as the *Burscombe* leaned out of another sharp turn, waves running up along her port waist. Digby had served under him once before, in the destroyer HMS *Stoat* eleven years ago, and was recognising the signs of the troubled man that Dollimore had once been, the old irritable being that he had taken such pains to banish. Digby sorely hoped that he remained in control for Dollimore was the captain that they needed and wanted.

'Come in,' said Nicklesworth above the whistling of the wind when he became aware that the captain was waiting. He had known he would come down here so kept his face stern so that the man would understand off the bat that he was subject to the admiral's wishes and not the other way round.

Ignoring the three staff officers that were present, Dollimore enquired as politely as he could, 'Are we no longer looking for enemy transports, sir?'

'No, we are not.'

Dollimore felt a tightness about his chest, so angry was he. 'Forgive me for my inquisitiveness, sir, but if this new course was a reaction to the sighting of an enemy, you would have already said so. So what are we doing?'

Nicklesworth curled his lip in disgust. So here was the Dollimore that Forbes had taken such pains to promote when he had been deciding which ship to raise his flag in. Well, the Commander-in-Chief might see his bluntness as acceptable but he did not. 'Modify your tone, captain, or this will not go well for you.'

'I must beg for my pardon, sir, but what we're doing does not go well for Norway. Here we are steaming back and forth as casually as revellers on a pub crawl and in the meantime the enemy will be executing his will elsewhere.'

'That's enough,' interrupted Nicklesworth, his voice full of menace. He had come across one or two commanding officers like this before and they had inevitably come to a bad end. In fact, Dollimore was beginning to demonstrate that he might not be fit for this command after all, something which Nicklesworth had suspected all along. 'Captain, you will take yourself away from this bridge and see to nothing more than the fighting efficiency of the *Burscombe*. Matters of strategy and policy you will leave to those who have the necessary qualifications.'

Dollimore took a breath and stepped back. The catching of that breath contained every ounce of willpower he could muster to stay calm. He reminded himself that rank was as important as skill – or at least it should be.

He may not have rated this admiral as professionally high but Dollimore's devotion to the service dictated all respect to a superior. It was as much as he required from his own men. 'I'm sorry, sir, it should not be for me to question Forbes' strategy.'

Dollimore turned to go back to his own responsibilities, his suppressed anger dragging at him like lead weights.

Nicklesworth found the climb-down almost disappointing. Those six years ashore really had taught Dollimore some humility. Therefore, he deigned to add, 'Captain, for your information, the order to turn about didn't come from Forbes. It came from the Admiralty. It seems that, in London, they are more worried about the German battlecruiser fleet than they are about Norway. There it is, plain and simple. All we need do is obey.'

Dollimore nodded. He was determined not to continue the confrontation for he knew that pursuing the matter would get him absolutely nowhere. Whatever his achievements had been since he had taken command of this ship, he should never forget that he still had as many enemies amongst Their Lordships as he had friends, and Nicklesworth himself was clearly far from a friend.

He stepped back out into the relatively welcome lashing of snow and wind and presented himself as a model of calm for the rest of the men on the bridge while, inwardly, he wondered how it could be that the Admiralty was superseding the orders of Forbes who must have had a greater understanding at what was really going on out here. He resolved that no matter what happened, the navy would not find the *Burscombe* wanting when push came to shove. That much he could control.

\*\*\*\*

Even though Smudge's ego was well oiled by the knowledge that the captain regarded him to be the best lookout, he had decided that constantly living in this shivering hell was getting ridiculous. How much longer could he stand here on this bridge? Why had he spent months with icicles hanging from his uniform when other men got decent postings in the Mediterranean or the Far East? They said spring had come and now it had started snowing again. Bloody liars!

He glanced at the other ships conforming to yet another manoeuvre in this long morning of turning every which way and, raising his binoculars back to his eyes, began to think of how a mild, undetectable poison could get him out of work for a while. Maybe the Turtle had an idea or two about how to put him in hospital without too much pain. Ah, but it was all the work of pipe dream stuff. He would never voluntarily put himself out of action. He had too much pride and was simply trying to justify the meaning of his suffering.

Tel, the lookout standing a couple of feet to his right, leaned in close and discreetly asked, 'What do you think about all this to-ing and fro-ing?'

'Same as a flippin' yo-yo.'

'I reckon Nicklesworth's lost, mate. Nebulous Nick, that's what he is.'

'Nebula what?'

'Nebulous Nick. Confused.'

Smudge stared at Tel in wondrous condescension. 'Don't ever, ever use big words in front of me again.'

'Pipe down!' shouted Lt Irwin from behind them. 'Stop talking and keep a look out!'

Immediately looking back out at the grey, Smudge decided he had heard a hint of stress in Irwin's voice. That useless man's days were numbered. That was surer than all the rest of this malarkey.

No sooner had he regained his concentration than he was certain he had spied that which he was here for. 'Ship bearing red zero-one-eight!'

Immediately Irwin turned toward the port bow and stared hard through his binoculars, straining his eyes to see what AB Smith had seen. For a few seconds there was nothing but grey matted across everything, broken only by the intervention of white-tipped waves or snow and he was beginning to wonder if Smith had finally been the victim of a trick of the light. Then he too saw a shadow.

It was definitely a large ship crashing through the waves on an eastward heading, steaming about two thousand yards away. He pressed the alarm button, reflecting that he should have done so the very second Smith had called his sighting. Then he ordered the nearby Yeoman to flash a signal to the rest of the squadron. Managed to remember that, he thought. He looked out at what he could see of their friends. The *Farecombe* was clear off the starboard quarter and he could just see the *Marsfield* beyond that but there was no sign of the destroyers in the gloom. No matter, the signal would be passed from ship to ship until everybody was apprised of the situation.

The Fire Control team just above him trained their Director Control Tower and started observing the target. This was why half the ship's company were kept at Defence Stations, fatiguing as it was, so that their guns could be ready to fire at a moment's notice. The information from the DCT had already started to filter through to the Transmitting Station thus allowing the guns to be trained to the bearing in question.

Captain Dollimore emerged from the hatch still pulling on his coat and immediately looked in the direction indicated by Irwin's outstretched arm.

As soon as the target's forward superstructure and gun arrangements became apparent, they were in no doubt.

'Chief,' said Dollimore to his Chief Yeoman of the Signals, 'have the battle ensigns hoisted.'

'Aye aye, sir,' replied CY Ross, happy with the way things were turning out. Within a few seconds he was hoisting one of the great White Ensigns on the foremast showing off England's red cross and union flag, using all of his strength to prevent the halyard being dragged from his grasp by the wind.

The next order came from Nicklesworth in the hastily organised admiral's plot down below. He had immediately appreciated that the guns of his other five ships could not be brought to bear because the *Burscombe* was in the way, so he ordered, 'Squadron line ahead bearing zero-nine-zero and engage'.

The manoeuvre was going to take a few minutes. Dollimore ordered the wheel put hard over to port and speed increased to twenty five knots so that he could clear *Farecombe* and *Marsfield*'s range quicker. The sooner they had forty 6-inch guns ready to train rather than sixteen the better. For the moment, the *Burscombe* would have to provide the opening shots. 'Guns, fire when ready.'

'Very good, sir.'

As Digby's men made their final calculations, Dollimore turned to Peterson and asked, 'Pilot, what do you make of her?'

Having been studying the shadow carefully as it became clearer and clearer, Peterson experienced a feeling of déjà vu. The two triple 11-inch turrets trained fore and aft definitely gave her away as a *Deutschland* Class ship, exactly that which had been seen from their Walrus yesterday, but there was more to it. 'Do you think it's the *Moltke*, sir?'

'She's had time to make good her damage,' replied Dollimore. It had been the best part of four months since they had left her running with a smashed aft turret and holed superstructures. He kept raising and lowering his binoculars, now and then wiping the irritating snowflakes off the lenses.

Suddenly Lt-Cdr Digby called over to the captain, 'Sir, the officer of the DCT says he thinks we're looking at the *Moltke*.'

'Well, are we or aren't we?' asked Dollimore testily.

A few seconds passed. 'We are, sir.'

If anybody was going to come up with the correct answer it was the man in the Director Control Tower who was in possession of the most powerful optical sights in the ship.

Dollimore, forcing away his frustrations of the last couple of days, focused on his unfinished business of last year. Running the way she had, *Moltke* had thwarted his chance to declare a victory comparable to the destruction of the *Graf Spee*.

Digby said, 'Range two thousand three hundred yards, course zero-eight-zero, speed eighteen knots and increasing.'

Down in the turrets, the guns were ready to fire. There were about thirty men squashed into each of the armoured working spaces as they crowded around the gleaming breeches. Shivering a little from the freezing temperature that was pervading the steel boxes, these men suddenly knew the excitement of the chase as they felt the hydraulic motors of the turret turning them towards the target. Meanwhile, the gun-layers eagerly elevated the barrels to their required angles in the shortest amount of time possible.

A few seconds later, they informed Fire Control that the guns were ready to fire then stood back waiting for the inevitable eruption and the cue to begin the process of loading all over again.

The tension of the morning's indecision and foul weather was shattered by the sound of eight 6-inch guns flashing up and spitting their fire and shells out across the heaving sea. Even the most ready person jumped as the explosives sped on their way towards the enemy.

In the ensuing pause, the sea sent rippling shudders right through the ship. The bows rhythmically crashed through the peak of every wave encountered. The violent water ran across the fo'c'sle and thundered up over the breakwater and guns of A-Turret. The very structure of the ship seemed to be distorted as she proceeded.

Dollimore turned and saw some of the Carley Floats torn from their mountings on the starboard side and knew that it would not take much more for some of the steel fittings to go the same way.

Looking back at the *Moltke*, he observed the sea explode in eight thunderous fountains, ascending from her bow to her port beam. A good opening shot but, when the sea came back down to a relatively calm white froth, she was still steaming ahead unscathed. This was not a problem. A direct hit on the first salvo would have been extremely lucky.

'She's running, sir,' came Peterson's understated voice of surprise.

Dollimore was in turn stunned to see the great German ship leaning over sharply as she continued to increase speed, unapologetically showing them her stern and throwing out a magnificent wake. She was fleeing without firing a shot!

'Helmsman, steer starboard zero-seven-zero degrees! Maximum revolutions!' shouted Dollimore.

The helmsman repeated the order from below and the *Burscombe* rolled violently back the other way. To the astonishment and fury of all the men on the bridge, the shadowy *Moltke* was already being swallowed up by the lingering blanket of grey white.

'Give her another salvo!' shouted Dollimore, hardly believing how it was turning out. This was no battle, nor even a skirmish.

The guns flashed out again, this time not just from *Burscombe*'s forward turrets but those of the *Farecombe* as well. At the last moment she had been in a position to fire. Their shells plummeted through the surface of the sea and blew it skyward but once again there were no hits on the *Moltke*.

Then she was gone. Just as in their previous encounter, she had made the most of her speed to escape.

'Bloody cowards!' cursed Digby.

'Cowards be damned!' said Dollimore, giving his gunnery officer a crooked and terrible stare. 'They have somewhere else they need to be!'

Digby stayed silent trying to think beyond his remit to understand what he meant. Although his instincts were good, he knew his captain's to be better.

Dollimore kept his gaze directly on what he could see of the horizon, willing with all his mental power that the *Moltke* would reappear, but logic told him that she would not. If she was prepared to run without engaging them then she clearly had some other priority which was more important than attempting to destroy this squadron. His earlier thoughts about the plausibility of a lone ship such as this putting herself at the mercy of the British battlefleet came back to him. No, he just did not buy it. She had no intention of breaking out to the Atlantic; she was heading in the wrong direction. Everything in Dollimore's mind still pointed to Norway as the objective.

Nicklesworth flew up onto the bridge in a whirlwind of rage and disappointment. 'What the bloody hell are they up to?'

'Sir, I insist that we get in near the coast as quick as possible,' said Dollimore, his teeth gritted and cursing every wasted moment. 'I'll eat my hat if we don't find transports taking troops to Norway.'

Nicklesworth paused long enough to reflect upon the message that he had read during the night stating that German soldiers destined for Bergen had been plucked from the sea. If the information was correct, they had been picked up the best part of twenty hours ago now. But still he said, 'Admiral Forbes has not given us leave to do so.'

Dollimore turned his back on Nicklesworth and ordered, 'Keep up the chase until I order otherwise. I want to find that ship.'

There was no interjection from Nicklesworth. Despite the other differences of opinion, an effort to regain contact with the *Moltke* was fully justified. So he retreated back to the plot thinking through the reprimand that he was going to give the captain and the report that he was going to write thereafter. Dollimore's words had been very close to insubordination.

A short while later, he was handed a signal which prompted him to alert the captain through the voicepipe. 'If there is still no sign of the *Moltke* in the next thirty minutes, you will turn the squadron due north. Forbes is concentrating the fleet.'

At the end of the allotted time the 25th Cruiser Squadron turned and slowed its speed so as to prevent further sea damage and headed away from what Dollimore considered to be certain action as his superiors attempted to make head or tail of the new strategic situation which was building up along the coast of a slowly waking Norway.

\*\*\*\*

It had been a long while since the ships at either end of the line had seen each other. The *Burscombe* always took the lead and the ship that was always tail-end charlie, unseen but not forgotten, was the destroyer HMS *Castledown*. Lieutenant-Commander Small was her captain and he stood upon his open bridge with heavy spray from the fo'c'sle making conditions uncomfortable. This bridge was much lower than those of the great cruisers up ahead, serving to make him feel like they were underwater. Of course, this challenging sea was always more menacing to the smaller ships.

The icy deck rolled and pitched but that was no matter because the ironically large, swarthy captain reasoned that his discomfort was outweighed by his love of the service and patriotic duty.

'What's the fuel situation after all that ridiculousness this morning, Number One?'

Turning away from the compass where he had been making a note of their bearing, Lieutenant Ursham ducked to avoid a heavy smattering of spray. 'We have approximately twenty hours if we maintain this present speed before we have to think about heading back, sir. Sullom Voe would be our best bet for oiling.'

Small nodded his acknowledgement.

'Sir,' continued Ursham with an inquisitive tone. He and Small were at ease enough in each other's company to brook a certain familiarity. 'What do you think about Norway?'

'I'm trying not to think about it, Number One,' replied Small, taking on a grim expression. 'We'll just have to trust in the admiral.'

Ursham smiled, thinking of the funny pencilled line that weaved its way across their chart. It had seemed like the epitome of British policy, all that coming and going to very little effect. As he thought on it, he looked astern and felt a little better. He pointed and said, 'At last, we might be in for a spot of good weather.'

Although the wind did not abate and there was still a tendency for the ships ahead to be swallowed up by snow squalls, the sky to the south was clearing, letting the pale sunlight shine through. The heaving sea started taking on a better definition in the improving light.

Suddenly, that sunlit hole was filled with a large number of aircraft flying up fast from the south east. As the dark clouds kept moving further apart to help display them, Small and Ursham were shocked out of their complacency in the same heartbeat.

'Shit!' gasped Small. 'Sound the alarm!'

The rattlers and bells sounded throughout the ship and the company abandoned their daily chores below decks and sped to their Action Stations.

'Aircraft astern! Aircraft astern!' Ursham announced through the loudspeaker system. Most of their anti-aircraft gunners had been retained at their stations throughout the morning anyway so there should be no reason for them not to be ready – not that there were many of them. Apart from the main armaments of 4.7-inch guns, *Castledown* and her sisters were equipped with a couple of batteries of 2-pounder pom-poms each along with a few Oerlikons and some 0.5-inch machine guns. They now seemed woefully inadequate when Small evaluated what they were up against.

'Thirty plus at least,' he said. He had already discounted the idea that they could be RAF bombers. The way that they were turning in towards their prey said it all. Besides that, he had long ago given up on support from Bomber Command. They always seemed to have other priorities which did not include watching over the navy.

'High-level bombers,' said Small. Spreading the wisdom of his experience further, he added, 'Very inaccurate. Open fire!'

Very soon the bombers were flying above them.

The weapons of the *Castledown* sent their small shells and bullets up into the sky in a deathly cacophony but it was immediately apparent through observing the white tracers that their accuracy was way off the mark. Not all the guns had the required elevation in their mountings to be considered decent anti-aircraft guns at all and worse, the ship's movement was so detrimental that every attempt at aiming was ruined the moment they thought they had a solution.

Bombs came down from the lead formation of aircraft. As last in the line and the most vulnerable, *Castledown* was the bastards' entire focus.

Small gritted his teeth and watched the small black bombs heading straight for him. He managed a token, 'Hard a port!' before the bombs struck the water all around them. The waves heaved themselves skyward, propelled by the reddened detonations just under the surface and the great geysers of water also unleashed burning fragments of steel which clattered over the ship's side and superstructure.

One of the lookouts, Murphy, standing nearby cried out and fell to the deck. The flattened snow beneath their feet now had a spread of bright red blemishing its sheen. Small stooped down and lifted him to his feet. He was conscious and clutching the right side of his face. A hideous flap of bloody skin was hanging through his shaking fingers. Small noticed a burned scratch mark across Murphy's tin hat as well. Thank God he had been wearing it.

'Let me have a look!' ordered Small.

Murphy groaned as he lowered his hand and revealed the pulped cheek.

'It's not as bad as it looks,' said the captain. 'Go below and get a dressing on it straight away.'

'Aye aye, sir.'

With the eruptions now dispersed and swallowed by the sea, man's destructive efforts no match for nature, Ursham was able to report, 'No direct hits, sir. We've splinter damage only.'

But the guns were still firing their highly inaccurate bombardment into the sky.

'Sir,' said Ursham, 'the ship's too unstable for this sort of firing. We must slow down so that they can aim better.'

'Of course,' Small agreed. He called down the voicepipe, 'Helmsman, bring us back to a heading of three-five-zero and reduce speed to five knots!'

\*\*\*\*

Alarm bells suddenly rang throughout the straining hulk of the *Burscombe*.

Dollimore had only just sat down in his cabin with a cup of tea, the first hot beverage he had managed to get his hands on since yesterday, but immediately forgot about it when he heard the alarm. Too much had happened already and he had far too many things on his mind to allow need of a relieving tea to take his mind off the game. He jumped up out of his seat, grabbed his waterproof coat and raced for the ladder.

Appearing on the bridge with the other men who belonged here, he said, 'Mr Irwin, report.'

'A signal has just been flashed from *Crayhorn*, sir. Enemy planes are approaching from astern.'

Dollimore spun round and raised his binoculars to his eyes. There was the *Farecombe* just over two cable lengths off the starboard quarter, a morse lamp flashing from her bridge – probably repeating the message that the eagle-eyed Chief Yeoman had already read from the little destroyer nearly a mile back on the other side of *Marsfield*.

HMS *Crayhorn* was Commander Fulton-Stavely's ship and leader of the small flotilla vessels. He would be able to see much better what was happening to his stern. Certainly Dollimore could see no aircraft from here.

Suddenly, the sound of muffled explosions and heavy machine gun fire came to him on the blustery wind and he fancied he could see a couple of flashes of light on the snowy horizon. He tried to tune his ears out of the sound of the wind and sea so that he could concentrate on the fighting. At one point he thought he could hear the drone of airborne engines but he was not sure until Irwin said, 'Sir, a formation of aircraft bearing green one-one-zero heading east!'

'Dropped their bombs and running for Norway,' said Dollimore. He shook his head. 'I don't know how much more proof we need.'

'What do you mean, captain?' came a voice from behind him. He had not observed Nicklesworth just climbing out the hatch.

Barely hiding his exasperation, Dollimore replied, 'We have proof, I rather think, that the Germans are already operating out of Norway, sir. Those planes do not have the range to be operating from Germany and we know that their navy does not have aircraft carriers; therefore the only possible deduction is that they are in Norway already. *In Norway, I say!'*

Nicklesworth desperately wanted to hit back with some fantastic evidence that the captain's theories were just hysterical fantasies, but he could think of nothing. This contemptible man before him was correct. Always correct. It was just his tone which was wrong.

Chief Yeoman Ross, not interested in officers' woes, interjected with, 'Another signal's being flashed from *Crayhorn*, sir. "*Castledown* is dropping out of line."'

'Is she damaged?' asked Nicklesworth, working hard to try and be a step ahead of the captain.

The chief stood up to the lamp mounted at the aft end of the bridge casing and began flicking the shutters. The answer that came back was, "Not damaged."

'Then what's Small playing at?'

\*\*\*\*

The *Castledown* was practically beleaguered. Small's evasive action had effectively cut her off from a common defence with the other ships in line and she was now steaming at such a slow rate of knots that she was almost hove to. With everything else about this situation dangerous, only her pitching and rolling had improved thereby making her more of a stable gun platform. She might now have a chance of hitting or deterring their attackers.

The next wave of bombers was coming in and *Castledown*'s guns were throwing their 2-pound shells in amongst the planes but still nothing was hit. The aircraft kept coming on without loss, happily singling out this ship.

Small, now understanding his folly, watched with dismay as the bombs fell towards him and ordered, 'Hard a starboard!' He just had to hope that this evasive action would see them all right until the Germans had expended their payloads.

The bombs whistled down and the ensuing destruction was as sudden as it was horrific. The men were still sitting or standing helpless at their stations when an explosion blew fire from the boilers' air intakes and shook the funnels until they too spewed flame and black smoke. At almost the same moment a white-hot maelstrom of fire and steel swept away the forward gun mounting along with its crew, leaving a hole which in turn poured its own conflagration.

All the men on the bridge were blown off their feet, half concussed. One or two of them disappeared over the side, there to sink under the waves, never to be recovered.

Small shakily grabbed hold of the brass binnacle and endeavoured to pull himself to his feet. The flames burned hot and bright all around him and he saw some of his men lying unconscious or dead. He knew all of their faces. They had been the best company a man could have had these last few months; and the now the Germans wanted to do away with them? Like hell!

He shook one of the lookout's shoulders. It was AB Barts. No response. What about PO Victor?

'Is that you, sir?' asked Victor weakly. 'I can't see anything.'

Heavy black smoke now poured across the bridge from the burning funnels as Small looked around. 'Ursham? Has anyone seen Number One?'

A short man appeared on the bridge, moving amongst the dishevelled men and instruments with the utmost of calm. 'You all right, sir?'

'Bosun!' Recognising Chief Petty Officer Cale, he answered, 'Yes, I'm all right. Have you seen Number One?'

'That's a negative on that one but don't you worry, sir, I've got some of the lads running out fresh hoses. Some of the others were slashed but we'll soon be sorted out. The fire mains are okay. Pressure's up thanks to the generator. Boilers have had it, though. They're gone so we've lost way completely, sir.'

Standing on wobbly legs, Small asked, 'What are the Germans doing?'

'Well, they seem to have gone for the moment, but we're keeping an eye out.'

Small coughed and braved the heat of the fire forrard of the bridge by looking out and trying to assess the damage. 'That doesn't look good, bosun. Is the magazine okay?'

'Got someone looking now, sir.'

'Good. Report to me the minute you know.'

Cale climbed down the ladder and disappeared into the wall of smoke.

Small looked around at the horizon. With the cloud cover having come back in force, cutting off the sunlight, it was difficult for him to get his bearings. He needed to know if Fulton-Stavely knew what had happened or whether they were on their own. Straining his eyes because of the smoke, he was suddenly heartened to see help coming and it was not just *Castledown*'s faithful sisters that he could see but the cruisers as well. God bless Rear-Admiral Nicklesworth.

\*\*\*\*

The admiral was making sure to dominate this part of the operation. Whenever he was this frustrated, he found that he could focus his mind easier. It was a strange state of affairs but perfectly true so there was no need to defer anymore to Captain Dollimore.

With the *Burscombe* circling the burning wreck at a safe distance – having been informed that the status of *Castledown*'s magazine was unconfirmed – Nicklesworth made his dispositions. 'Chief Yeoman, signal Fulton-Stavely that he is to take off the wounded and then, when we know about the magazine, take the *Castledown* in tow.'

It seemed like a lot of work for the *Crayhorn* but the destroyers were almost at the end of their endurance and would shortly need to depart to find oil anyway. The cruisers still had many more days' worth of fuel and probably had greater tasks ahead of them by far.

'*Catterley* is to circle with the cruisers at a thousand yards until we're finished here,' continued Nicklesworth. 'And I want ASDIC sweeps by everyone. I don't want to be targeted by submarines as well.'

'Aye aye, sir,' said Chief Yeoman Ross and began to click away with the shutters on the lamp.

\*\*\*\*

Lt-Cdr Small looked down from the scarred bridge of the *Castledown* and watched the wounded being lowered into the grey-painted boats which clattered against her side. It was a tricky task they had down there as the groaning men, most of them burnt and in pain, really would have preferred not to been moved at all. They did, however, have the incentives of morphine and spreading fire to push them along.

Then CPO Cale climbed up to report to him. Still the model of calm, he said, 'We're in some deep shtook – pardon my expression, sir.'

'Go on, bosun.'

'We just lost the generator, sir, so that's our electrics done for. The fire's creeping toward the magazine and we've lost water pressure, two watertight bulkheads beneath us have been holed and hatches are distorted on three others. I've taken the liberty of having the Oerlikon ammunition from the ready use lockers moved further aft so that it won't explode all over us while we're doing the necessaries. But with the main magazine, sir, we're pretty much standing on a volcano.'

Small nodded through his conflicted thinking. 'Can we not flood it?'

'Fire's preventing us from getting anywhere near the sea cocks, sir.'

'What's your recommendation?'

Cale's eyebrows went up in surprise. His very gaze had 'What sort of stupid question is that?' written all over it.

'Of course,' said Small. 'Once the wounded are away, we'll abandon ship.'

'Aye aye, sir,' said Cale, taking himself back off to the heavy work being done below.

Small picked up the hand-held morse lamp and signalled his intentions to Fulton-Stavely in the *Crayhorn*. An acknowledgement was flashed back along with a wave of good luck from the shadowy Commander standing atop his bridge.

\*\*\*\*

Fulton-Stavely wasted no time in requesting more boats from the *Burscombe*. Captain Dollimore had seen fit to think through the possibilities of this situation some while ago and the cutters were already swung out on their davits, ready to be lowered into the water.

Midshipmen were quickly assigned and Clark climbed stealthily into one of them. The oarsmen and coxswain were waiting for him there and he signalled to the men in charge of the davits that he was ready. 'Hang on,' he said, for the *Burscombe* barely had time to slow or turn so that they might be sheltered from the wind. It was going to be a bumpy ride.

The electric motors whirred, letting the ropes slip through the blocks and then, at the last second, the lines were detached, allowing the cutter to fall onto the crest of the next wave. Spray saturated them immediately but Clark wasted no time in motivating the oarsmen so that they could close on the *Castledown* directly. He was the only man who spoke, as was custom in this situation.

Looking off to starboard, he noticed Farlow in the next cutter. His large frame larger for all the clothes that he wore, he was almost on his feet urging his men to pull with all their might. It was almost as if he was trying to race Clark to the scene of action. Very well, if it was his intention that the men be too exhausted to do anything else when they got there then so be it. Clark would not rise to the bait; and anyway, that idiot regularly complained that other boys always got the lion's share of the excitement so it was just as well that he was making the most of this opportunity.

Clark soon became aware that the fires in the fore and mid-sections of the *Castledown* were spreading and that the hoses were lying on the decks completely impotent. That was the moment he realised just how dangerous this rescue was going to be.

Heavy black smoke was pushed down and across them by the wind and he choked on the fumes as he prepared to throw a line to the chief standing at the ship's railing. That chief was blackened all over but his eyes were clear and calm as he caught the line, pulled it taut and watched the boat clatter against the steel, made safe by the buffer of the fenders.

Another man appeared through the haze on the destroyer's deck, a tall man stepping through the throng of waiting sailors. 'Any more wounded?' he asked.

'No, sir,' said the chief. '*Crayhorn*'s got them all.'

'Right,' said the officer, whom Clark rightly assumed to be Lt-Cdr Small. 'Abandon ship! Everybody abandon ship!'

Farlow, in the next boat along, looked up and down and registered that the destroyer's hull was completely intact. She was showing no signs of sinking so he called up to the chief, 'Is it really that bad?'

The chief gave another of his frowns. 'In a word, sir, yes.'

As though to emphasise his point, there was a massive explosion over on *Castledown*'s other side. Whatever it was, it was not the magazine. Not yet.

'My God!' Farlow exclaimed. He began shouting at the survivors to climb down quicker. What was all the dithering about? Did they not understand the precariousness of their situation? He was clearly unimpressed with the explosion *and* the chief.

'Oh, shut up,' grumbled a tired petty officer, too exhausted to care what retribution this stupid 'snotty' could bring down upon him.

Clark and his oarsmen helped a couple dozen or more men down into the pitching cutter, trying desperately to keep their feet against the excesses of the sea. They clambered past him in the most orderly fashion, some of them sparing a moment to thank him. The lack of panic always impressed him. Soon, the boat was full and Clark ordered the line thrown back to him.

The chief obliged him and in the boat there was a brief chorus of, 'Mind out of the way, mate', 'Budge up a bit,' or, 'Push us off there,' as the oarsmen settled amongst their charges and tried to find the room to pull effectively.

'All right, pipe down!' called Clark as he sought to regain proper command of the boat. The men fell into silence as he established the oarsmen's stroke. Each rhythmic lurch and each wave crest passed was a lessening of the tension that had been with them from the moment they had observed the state of the ship up close, and well might they be thankful that they had started on their way back because the world suddenly erupted all about them.

The wind turned into a veritable furnace as a visible shockwave tried to flatten the sea. It thrust Clark forward onto the men sitting in front of him. The coxswain went with him and they suddenly found themselves in a crazy mix of flailing limbs. Their ears nearly burst with the cacophonous roar that accompanied the force and flames then a startled gaggle of choice phraseology came from mouths all around him. He probably screamed a profanity or two himself.

Fire seemed to pass right over their heads and Clark felt no particular urge to look up. With the heat powerful upon his back, he eventually mustered the courage to turn and find out what he was not sure he wanted to know.

It was incredible. The hull of the *Castledown* had split wide open just under the fore part of the shredded superstructure and a mighty column of fire was reaching skyward. The sound of steel screeching violently against steel emanated from the wreck between the mass of secondary explosions. The foremast shed its radio aerials and then collapsed into the sea whilst, further aft, the blackened funnels sat imperiously on their bed of flames. The ship was settling fast. Her keel must have been blown out as well.

Clark, his heart racing with the utter shock of what had happened, gathered his thoughts and looked out for the other cutters and whalers that were nearby. Amongst other pieces of debris and bodies were cracked strips of planking. They told him part of the story. Then, when some of the swirling smoke had drifted on, he noticed the bottom of a capsized boat nearby. There were shouting men scrabbling about it, trying to cling on.

'Cox'n!' Clark said, thinking that raising his voice was necessary to counter the ringing in his own ears, 'Steer us back over that way!' Then he cajoled the oarsmen to take their eyes away from the dying ship and concentrate on their jobs.

As they edged their way back toward the upturned boat and inevitably closer to the maelstrom, the coxswain asked, 'What if the depth charges go up, sir?'

'Try not to think about it,' was all Clark could answer. The thought of surviving that last explosion just to be killed by the next was a harrowing thought but he decided it was insignificant next to the duty he owed the men in the water. 'It's going to get a little crowded here.'

'What, it ain't already?' muttered the coxswain.

They got in close to the survivors and all the men started to help pull their mates from the oily water. Clark leaned out and grabbed hold of the lifejacket of a man lying motionless, his arms outstretched, his head lolling from one side to the other as the waves buffeted him. The man was hardly recognisable at first because of the cut that had spread its blood from the hairline but it did not take Clark too long to figure out who he was. 'Farlow! Farlow!'

Clark slapped him about the face, hoping for some sort of response. His gunroom nemesis might be a tediously pompous and obstinate little bastard but he did not deserve this. 'Farlow! Wake up!'

After a couple more slaps, Farlow's eyes opened. It was a slow and painful movement and he did not immediately show signs of understanding his whereabouts. But he then stated drunkenly, 'Nobby Clark. You... completely detrimental... to harmonious... running of the ship.'

'And you're the most undoubted buffoon a man could ever meet!' laughed Clark.

Once they had lifted inboard all the men they could – clinging hard onto the men for whom there was no room – Clark had the oarsmen take them away as fast as possible. It was a very real threat that they could be susceptible to further explosions from the stricken destroyer.

As the sea rushed into the ship, the bow broke away along the seam of the earlier damage and floated away leaving her hissing, gurgling stern to rise up into the air. Smoke swirled and clung to the dripping propellers and rudder as the compromised compartments up forrard filled with water and dragged the *Castledown* to her grave. Depth charges clattered out of their racks on the stern and splashed into the sea and before too long, the ship was gone. All that remained was a hideous, bubbling froth which sucked in wreckage and bodies and spewed out filthy oil fuel.

'Don't stop pulling!' shouted Clark at his oarsmen.

After a few seconds, the barely settled sea shuddered again and great columns of water blew towards the sky to crash down again, drenching further all those in the saturated boat.

In the ensuing silence, Clark became aware for the first time that the clouds were darkening. The day was coming to an end already. He saw another cutter nearby and was pleased to recognise Midshipman Trent standing in it, staring at him with a look of abject horror on his naive young face. Apart from his oarsmen and coxswain, his boat was empty.

'Trent!' called Clark. 'Get yourself over here!'

As the boats neared each other, Trent felt bound to explain in scared tones the meaning of his lack of survivors. 'We were not quick enough! The ship exploded before we got anywhere near!'

'It doesn't matter,' answered Clark. 'Just take some of my lot and be mindful that we haven't got long before they're going to start to freeze to death.'

\*\*\*\*

Captain Dollimore manoeuvred the *Burscombe* in amongst the wreckage as soon as he was able and ordered the engines stopped. As the boats were attached to the lines and the davits initiated to hoist them in, he reflected that it was lucky they were still being watched over by the other circling ships. To be torpedoed now would just be the crowning insult in this debacle.

When Rear-Admiral Nicklesworth climbed down to the port waist to where the wretched survivors were being gathered and given blankets and cigarettes, a young man of no discernable rate looked at him, half-dead from fatigue, and said, 'What a shit day.'

'Truly it is hell,' replied the admiral, 'but do get a grip of yourself.'

\*\*\*\*

The squadron then steamed on through the night, their numbers now depleted further for having released the destroyers in their objective to find fuel and deliver the *Castledown*'s wounded to safety.

The next day saw them joining the flagship of the Home Fleet, HMS *Rodney*, and all her attendant battlecruisers, cruisers and destroyers. An impressive force. What would Admiral Forbes do with it all? Dollimore was none too impressed so far and as a result had gone into a bit of a funk.

His officers left him alone. They knew from experience that when he was like this, no immediate good was going to come of it.

\*\*\*\*

Standing with the pom-pom gunners at their Defence Stations near the portside crane, Clark was also too despondent to be inspired by the strength of the battle fleet. Too much had happened with too little positive effect. His mood must have been evident as Pincher piped up with, 'Just be glad it weren't us yesterday, sir. Could easily 'ave been.'

Clark looked over at the able seaman standing ready by the elevated gun barrels. Life always seemed so simple to him. Not so simple, perhaps, for Haggerty who was standing next to him.

'We're gonna get the bastards what sunk her, sir,' Pincher continued.

Yes, we're getting off to a flying start, thought Clark.

But Paddy nodded. 'Too right. Jerry's an 'orrible, sneaky git and if there's one thing I can't stand, it's sneaking about. And I'll tell yer something else. Get me in a room with Hitler and I'll crush him, and if he ever leaves that room, he'll know he's been crushed.'

Trying to soak up the enthusiasm in Walbrook's tone, Clark wished it really could be that simple. 'Something tells me, if we're going to have a chance to crush him, we're going to need to do something about our air cover.'

'You what, sir?' asked Pincher.

'The Luftwaffe just bombed the *Castledown* with impunity, Martin. Don't you think it might be wise for us to have air cover?'

Paddy laughed sarcastically. 'We're better than any of them clowns. It's us they call the senior service. We can take care of ourselves.'

At that moment, Commander Locklin walked by clad in a duffle coat. 'Keep your men quiet there, midshipman.'

'Sorry, sir,' replied Clark, giving the gunners a warning look. But Paddy's last few words left him reflecting on their tragic over-simplification. Getting back at the enemy required nothing more than ships and personal vengeance?

It was not too far removed from the way the Admiralty looked at it. The ship was still supreme. For submarines there were ASDIC and depth charges; for mines there were paravanes and degaussing; for battlecruisers there were big guns and torpedoes; and for aircraft there were anti-aircraft guns. They really thought they had it all figured out.

# EIGHT

## Tests of Character

The Germans were in Norway, attacking multiple targets along the coast, landing troops and capturing their objectives. That British and French forces were being committed to get them out was as much as Jennifer Dollimore understood of the situation from the news broadcasts on the wireless. She knew that the public could never be told the whole story but the government sounded quite positive about the eventual outcome so she did not concern herself too much with it. The Germans needed to be taught a lesson. It might as well be there.

She knew in her heart that her husband was involved somewhere in the fray. Was she apprehensive about his safety? Yes she was, but knew him to be one of the most resourceful men she had ever met. His determination and skill would see him through everything save the attentions of a direct hit by bullet or shell, of that she was certain.

She looked around the dim church hall at the dozens of young, smartly uniformed men dancing, chatting and joking. They paid compliments to their pretty young ladies, most of whom they had only just met for the first time tonight, and wondered where this war would take them. She tried not to think about which of these fine lads might die before too long but she had been a young wife during the last war and understood the chances. She personally knew nine women whose fathers, husbands or brothers did not come home last time around. The current escalation of hostilities was looking set to make that happen again.

On this pleasant evening, the lighting, soft music and attention paid to the decorations served to put everybody at their ease. The organisers – Jennifer being one – had put up a simple affair of paper streamers, coloured lamps and flowers. They were an effective combination. This event for Portsmouth's junior officers had been planned for two weeks but was now considered to be all the more poignant for considerations of morale because of Norway. These officers knew that there could be appointments of great importance coming up soon. One or two also thought about death but they did not dwell upon it – being killed was something that always happened to the other chap.

Jennifer had offered to help set up this event after hearing about it from their old family friend and landlord, Commander Stanley. He appreciated her efforts, not just because she understood the navy's ways so well, but that she volunteered after his original enquiry to her was that a certain number of fashionable young ladies were required to meet their eligible young men; was Betty interested?

Jennifer had answered in the affirmative in her daughter's name but decided that she would also get involved in order to keep an eye on her. So now she and Stanley kept low profiles on the peripheries of the dance so that they could keep a discreet distance from the youngsters whilst observing their conduct. This was not a wardroom so there was to be no tomfoolery.

Thinking she had ditched her mother – completely unsuspecting that it was by her wily elder's design that she had – Betty wandered through the dance hall exhilarated by the sound of the band playing a mid-tempo piece showing off strings, brass and saxophone. The tone was such that a girl might get close to an officer without actually being too familiar.

She stood for a few moments taking in the sight of the wonderful men laughing and joking with their choices of partner. There was one man brazen enough to kiss a girl on the cheek and she to answer by fluttering her eyelashes at him with no hint of shame! Woe betide them if they got caught.

Though, to be honest, she was secretly hoping that somebody would kiss her. She had no idea what a kiss was like but other girls seemed to enjoy it.

As she was about to venture further into the happy room, she was startled by a voice behind her saying, 'Well, it's Miss Dollimore, isn't it?'

She turned her head to address the man who had such pleasing male resonance and immediately recognised the young officer who had sat to breakfast with David Clark in that guest house a few weeks ago. 'Oh, I remember you,' she said.

He paused while she looked like she was going to say his name but then butted in when he realised that it was not going to happen. 'Sub-Lieutenant Robert Barclay-Thompson – you remember, Beatty – at your service; and these are my friends Marriner and Cantell.'

She giggled nervously, looking the other two men up and down. She had not expected to be so flustered when approached. 'Marriner? That's a good name for a sailor, don't you think?'

'It's been noted,' answered Marriner, an amused smile threatening to break out on the tall man's lips. Sipping at his drink, he looked her up and down in return and made his judgment instantly. A stunning beauty but thick as two short planks.

'How is David?' she asked of Beatty.

'Your guess is as good as mine. The last time I saw him was when you saw him too. I must assume that he's all right. I've not heard anything to the contrary.'

'I often thought he might have the decency to write me, but he doesn't.'

'Yes, you said that once before,' replied Beatty with waning pleasure, 'but he doesn't really write to anybody.' Not wanting to lose out on his chance with this girl because of idle chatter about somebody who was not even here, he quickly started to say, 'Would you like to da– ?'

But she had inadvertently jumped to, 'What's that funny stripe about?' before he could finish. She was pointing at the gold stripes which travelled round Marriner's cuff in a sort of chain-link pattern; not like Beatty's – or her father's, come to think of it.

Finally stretching his thin lips into a patronising grin, Marriner explained, 'This stripe is of the Royal Navy Reserve, my dear. I grew up around merchant ships. Of course, my father and his father were often ribbed for their apt name too. Anyway, now I serve the Royal Navy for the duration.'

Betty looked confused. She screwed up her face and then asked, 'The duration of what?'

His smile complete, Marriner answered, 'I couldn't possibly say.'

Beatty looked a little uncomfortable. 'Don't listen to him, Miss Dollimore. You know what they say about the Reserve officers? Sailors trying to be gentlemen and doing it very badly.'

'Where does that leave me?' piped up Cantell, the shorter, less obtrusive man who had, until now, been standing half concealed behind the other two. He showed off his cuffs which sported a single wavy gold stripe each. 'The Royal Navy *Volunteer* Reserve. But I truly am a gentleman.' His exquisitely polished words seemed to confirm it.

Marriner goaded him with, 'A gentleman, yes, trying to be a sailor and doing it very badly; and poor old Beatty here? Trying to be a sailor *and* a gentleman and doing both very badly.'

Beatty's two friends laughed their fill while he stood there unimpressed. He felt strange. This was the first time in the few weeks he had known Marriner that he had not been amused by his sharp wit. He was hardly ever at a disadvantage in social situations but suddenly here tonight, with this girl, he could not think straight. He quickly asked himself what it was he was attempting to do here and managed to reach the conclusion that, at the very least, he wanted to dance with her and to hell with the chaps. 'I insist we dance,' he said more forcefully than he would have liked.

She immediately warmed to the idea and put her hand in his. Taking her into the crowd already swaying gracefully to the mellow tunes, Beatty put one hand on her shoulder, the other on her waist and felt the warmth travel through his hands into the rest of his body.

She likewise put her hands upon him and tried to settle her thoughts upon what she liked about him. He was tall, dark and handsome. Apparently, they were great virtues so she had heard. Her own fancies seemed to bear out the theory but there was more. She was intrigued by his command of the situation. He was staring happily at her and his hands were gentle but firm in their grip. As a result, she felt her rebellious nature being smoothed over towards a willingness to submit. The only other man who had ever come close to making her feel that way had been David Clark.

'It's a lovely tune,' she eventually said of the ensuing romantic music which had been given just the hint of a swing feel for the occasion.

'It's called *Somewhere Over the Rainbow*,' said Beatty. 'It's about a place where all your dreams can come true.'

'So, it's not about Portsmouth then,' she said.

He moved his head back a little and studied her eyes. She was infuriatingly pretty and stupid – no, he would not say stupid – pretty and daft all at the same time. He explained, 'It's from a film about a magical land called Oz. I'm sure one of the picture houses around here must be showing it. Would you like to go with me someday?'

Her heart leapt. Was this handsome officer actually asking her to be with him? She suddenly saw Beatty as a man who would care for her, protect her, give her money, confidence and respectability. She thought he was wonderful. 'Yes, I'd like to go. I've heard all about them.'

'What? Picture houses? You've never been?'

'No.'

Beatty held her closer and they danced with their bodies almost touching. Betty began to enjoy the proximity but both understood to get no closer. At this moment in time it would be more than etiquette would stand for.

An hour passed during which Beatty started to get comments from other officers about the fact that he was hogging the girl for himself. He fended them off for a while until he finally said, 'Betty, do you think you might dance with one of the other chaps for a few moments? It would appease them greatly.'

'And watch you go off with another girl?' she asked with a frown.

He realised at that moment that she was happy to be his girlfriend and smiled his reassurance. 'I'm going to be just over there having a smoke.' Then he handed her over to a circling lieutenant.

He was standing by the door, puffing on his cigarette and sipping at a lemon squash when he heard the words, 'Mr Barclay-Thompson?' being spoken at his side. It surely could not be another girl who recognised him. Portsmouth, or 'Pompey' as the men called it, was still relatively new to him and he certainly had not been doing the rounds.

He looked round and was more than a little surprised to see Mrs Dollimore standing there next to him. Although her gaze could not be said to be reproving, neither could it be said to be accepting. But he covered his surprise well, something of the fighting man that was not rattled by the sight of a German battlecruiser appearing on the horizon.

'Good evening, ma'am,' he said quite smoothly. 'It's nice to see you again. Nice to see Betty too.'

'As I can gather,' Jennifer replied, staring at him intensely with a glint of intelligence that would be worthy of old Captain Dollimore himself. No wonder they were such a good couple. 'You seem to like the company of my daughter.'

This is getting strange, thought Beatty. Surely this was a matter between boy and girl. But then, he reasoned, if I had a beautiful daughter, I might be a little protective myself.

It looked like it was possible that, to get to Betty, he would have to fight his way through her mother first. He said, 'Well, I would just like to say that I've had occasion to admire your daughter and would consider it an honour if I could strike up a correspondence and see her once in a while.'

Jennifer tilted her head to one side and asked, 'Are you satisfied with all that you've admired, sub-lieutenant?'

'I'm not sure I understand, ma'am.'

Jennifer looked out onto the dance floor where another young man now was whispering something into Betty's ear and making her laugh. 'She's a highly impressionable young girl with rather more of an adolescent streak than one would like to admit. To cut a long story short, she's not the type who could be left alone to make the right decisions for herself. If she was in fact left to her own devices, everything would end in tears.'

Beatty allowed his utter confusion to show. 'Mrs Dollimore, I could understand it if you were warning *me* off as an undesirable wretch but let me get this straight. Are you telling me that *she* is not good enough for *me*? I beg to point out that I think you do her a disservice.'

Jennifer softened her expression a little. This young man had passed her first test. His confusion and persistence over this initial step had told her that he was not the type of person who was looking to take advantage of the girl for one night and then cast her aside. 'Mr Barclay-Thompson, some might think me a little over-protective of Betty but as you get to know her, you will understand why. She needs a guiding hand to keep her grounded. Do you follow me?'

He leapt straight on the words 'as you get to know her'. 'Are you saying it would be okay for me to see her?'

'I assume she's already answered that question?'

'She said 'yes', ma'am.'

'Then I concur.' Jennifer smiled, put her hand upon his arm and gave him an almost apologetic look. Her words said the rest. 'Good luck, Mr Barclay-Thompson.'

Betty had not noticed that her mother had walked along the edge of the hall, spoken to her new man and slipped away again. She had danced with a couple more fun-loving officers, felt flattered for the attention but found that her mind kept coming back to Beatty. He had promised to take her to see a film.

There he was by the door, leaning over a table, putting his cigarette out in an ash-tray. He looked up and she caught his eye. He smiled and headed back towards her. Upon taking her hand once again, he asked, 'Another dance?'

'Well, I should hope so!' she exclaimed.

They started swaying back and forth, he running her mother's warning through his mind while reasoning that Betty seemed to know what she wanted all right.

'Is everything okay?' she asked.

'Just fine,' he said with a smile. 'Who ever said that war had to be miserable?'

Eventually, she asked quietly and perhaps a little breathlessly, 'A kiss?'

'Steady on,' he said, looking about. What if Mrs Dollimore was watching?

She stepped back. Why should he be embarrassed? In stories, young men and women were so independent that they always ended up kissing each other without too much effort. The feeling was always mutual when romance filled the air; and romance was filling the air, wasn't it?

****

Later, in what would have been the dead still of the blackout if it was not for the occasional distant sounds of urgent dockyard work echoing out, Beatty walked with his two friends back to their rooms on the base.

Marriner was thinking on Beatty's thoughtful silence and so decided to voice what he and Cantell were thinking. 'You're not serious about her, are you?'

'And why shouldn't I be?' countered Beatty a little too defensively.

'I just think you could do better, old boy. Sorry, just saying.'

'Yes, well you don't need to.'

Did that mean he was or wasn't interested?

The damp April air was crisp and biting after the closeness of the church hall and Beatty walked along the street completely confused as to whether he had just begun to woo a prospective wife or just plucked a chick from its nest far too early. After running this through his mind for a while he settled upon the point of view that he had nothing else to lose. He would continue on this course and take her out, then if it did not work out, so be it. After all, he was not yet even twenty years old. God knows there were enough senior officers who had been advising the young men not to get embroiled in serious relationships too early in their lives. Maybe they were right, maybe they were wrong.

He would have to balance the arguments carefully, he decided, for he did know that he wanted to be a serious Royal Navy officer, but look at how she had distracted him already.

Then there was the disapproval of his friends, a disapproval that had not existed before tonight. He greatly disliked their stance.

However, he was uncomfortably aware that he himself had been just as ungracious when David Clark he had been serious about a girl. Clark had lost her in the end, which was admittedly the best result for all since she was working class and uneducated to boot, but Beatty knew that the loss had killed something inside him. Was it not better to live and let live after all?

\*\*\*\*

The five ships under the command of Rear-Admiral Nicklesworth finally came into Scapa Flow through the Hoxa Sound. Dollimore stood grimly on the *Burscombe*'s bridge watching the sentry tugs pulling the anti-submarine boom open and could not help but think upon the disaster that had occurred here last October, the sinking of the battleship HMS *Royal Oak*. It had been a difficult time for him because that was where all his son's problems had started.

Afterwards, the fleet had necessarily been dispersed into other bays and estuaries around Scotland and Northern England but now, the deficiencies in the Flow's defences having been properly addressed, they were back. Around them, between the scattering of islands, were more blockships, booms, anti-aircraft guns and patrols than ever with procedures tightened up on the lot. The anchorage was finally what it was intended to be – a safe haven.

Once *Burscombe*'s anchor was dropped in the clear water, Nicklesworth made ready to head across to the Commander-in-Chief's mammoth flagship, HMS *Rodney*, which sat imperiously amongst her smaller companions.

Dollimore watched him go, wondering what the tone of their conversation would be like when they spoke of relations in the command structure of the 25th Cruiser Squadron.

When they had joined up with the fleet they had spent a whole week off Norway reacting as and when they could to a growing series of encounters. They had skirmished with the enemy and given them something to think about in the north but essentially the Germans had landed troops everywhere unopposed. Slow Swordfish biplanes from the aircraft carrier HMS *Furious* had flown and fought valiantly but they had been too little too late. A bigger effort had been needed and Dollimore now understood that, in the last few days, British troops had finally been landing in Norway.

He climbed down the ladders and walked out across the fo'c'sle. It was a nice to see this part of the ship above the waves for a change and it was a good spot to stand for all that it had picked up a great deal of rust. The side party were going to be chipping and painting this afternoon to make her appear spritely again but first they had to deal with the tons of anti-aircraft ammunition that had just come alongside on a lighter. Mr Selkirk, the first lieutenant, had cleared the lower decks to get the replenishment done. Dollimore reflected that, during *Burscombe*'s first engagement with the Luftwaffe, a whole forty per cent of the ammunition had been fired for the shooting down of only one aircraft. It was almost too staggering to comprehend.

As he stood there pondering it, Warrant Officer Hacklett, that terribly scarred veteran of the last war and associate of his distant past, appeared before A-Turret ostensibly checking the hydraulic dampers – those which prevented the guns depressing below horizontal while facing forrard and so stopping one from blowing one's own bow off.

Checking that no one else was in earshot, Hacklett took a few steps towards Dollimore and spoke in the very fashion which justified why it was that he had never become a real officer. 'I beg pardon for stepping out of line, sir, but all the blokes on the ship know who it is that's got us this far, and it ain't the admiral.' Then he stopped himself.

'That's enough, Mr Hacklett,' said Dollimore. The navy was strange at times and often presented the men with stranger leaders but its organisation was supreme and not to be messed with. 'While I appreciate your confidence, I do not like your words. They're out of place.'

Hacklett replied, 'Very good, sir,' and went aft to terrorise the lads hauling the ammunition to the hoists.

Dollimore would have been harder on anyone else who had dared to speak so but Hacklett was different from all the others. The WO's personal loyalty to him knew no bounds and he would have gone away taking the warning most seriously. It was a dogged trust which had grown out of a past experience. When Hacklett's body had been ravaged by fire in the *Warspite* at Jutland back in 1916, it had been Dollimore who had saved him for the future he was living now. It was a good life even after all the pain, anger and perseverance that had prevented him from having ties with the shore. His entire focus was upon the well-being of the *Burscombe* and because of that, Dollimore knew he could give him a little leeway.

However, once Nicklesworth's complaints were aired over there on the *Rodney*, Dollimore could not be certain that Admiral Forbes' sentiments were going to match WO Hacklett's.

\*\*\*\*

Much later, Nicklesworth returned, climbing the steps back up to the quarterdeck of the *Burscombe*. He was clearly in a huff. Clutching his document case and ignoring the sound of the bosun's whistle, he quickly marched past the Quartermaster and the two men hosing down the deck to disappear into the hatch that led down to his quarters. The skylight had been opened as part of the spring airing and the strong smells that the ship had been accumulating during the last patrol were thankfully dispersing.

Throwing his case down on the large table, he all but shouted at one of his flag-lieutenants, 'Get the captain in here now.'

'Very good, sir,' was the reply, though the message that would actually be delivered was, 'The admiral kindly requests your presence,' etcetera.

A few minutes later, Captain Dollimore was seating himself at the table while Nicklesworth stared hard at him from the other side. Not having been invited to smoke, he left his pipe in his pocket.

'I'll make no bones about it,' said the admiral, forcing himself to look distastefully into the other's eye, 'I've noted in your record that your manner has begun to appear unstable. However, that's as far as we need go with this for the present.'

'I can only apologise if that's how I appear, sir,' said Dollimore, more relieved than anything else. 'I know I have stressed my indignation at the way this campaign has developed but it is never my intention to demean the efforts that *are* being made.'

Curling his lip in disgust, Nicklesworth said, 'The development and the efforts are the domain of men senior to you and I'm sure I don't need to reiterate the chain of command to someone of your rank and experience. Luckily for you, Admiral Forbes likes you. He recommended – and I say *recommended* – that you and I work out our differences for the good of the squadron.'

While he was saying this, he thought of how much further Forbes had actually gone. He had actually hinted vaguely at Dollimore's superior intelligence, speaking of him as possible material for flag rank! That had seriously ruffled Nicklesworth's feathers, especially since no particular praise for anything had come his way. I might have been a little less decisive than I would have liked, he thought, but I haven't really put a foot wrong. Even the loss of the *Castledown* and thirty two brave men cannot be laid at my door.

He now decided that attack was the best form of defence. 'Many years ago, captain, you were put ashore because it was felt that you needed a rest. Your mental state was unsound and, quite frankly, I think we have witnessed the beginnings of that again.'

Dollimore felt the surge of anger that was living in his heart every day; that which Nicklesworth was talking about. He thought of the crushed *Spikefish*. He had paid for that accident and had spent all these intervening years mastering his moods in order to build himself back up again. Now this inadequate man here sought to undo it all.

He took a discreet breath. What Nicklesworth was really doing was bullying him to cover for his own ineptitude. He had seen it many times before and would undoubtedly see it many times again. He absolutely abhorred it. Surely a man as wise as Admiral Sir Charles Forbes could see all this. Ah, but then Nicklesworth was not just a favourite at the Admiralty. He also had friends at the palace and those sorts of credentials still held sway for all of society's drift towards that funny thing one might call 'equality'.

He calmed himself and said, 'I can assure you, sir, that my mental state need not be questioned.'

'I should hope not,' said Nicklesworth, satisfied that he had at least brought it up. He knew it would give him something to think about. 'Now, here is the reason that you must remember your obeisance. First thing in the morning we are heading for Rosyth. Once there I will give you the details of our forthcoming mission; and it's an important one.'

'Carrying more troops to Norway?' asked Dollimore.

'Where do you get your information from?' Nicklesworth shouted, almost reaching the end of his tether.

Dollimore frowned and said calmly, 'It's the only logical thing to do if we're going to do anything at all, sir.'

The admiral stared hard at him. If only he could see half of the things that Dollimore did then perhaps he would be the one lauded by Forbes. He sighed and drew a sheet of paper from his case. 'Here are the written orders for Rosyth,' he said. 'I'll elaborate further once we have left there.'

'Understood, sir,' Dollimore replied, glancing over the words.

Nicklesworth very much wanted this interview to be finished, so he said finally, 'Just one last thing. Forbes asked after Midshipman David Clark. He wants to know why he hasn't been examined for promotion yet.'

Dollimore should not have been surprised that Forbes might ask. This would not be the first time that the admiral had enquired after a society favourite. 'Don't get me wrong, sir,' he said, 'Clark is one of the most promising seafarers that ever went through any of my ships but there is a level of boyish insolence that he's had difficulty in shaking off. That said, he is in the next batch of boys set to take the exam. It just needs a time and a place.'

Nicklesworth understood the problem of establishing any sort of timetable in war, especially at this moment of crisis. But his mind went straight to something else. 'This Clark sounds very much like you.'

Dollimore was aware of the similarities but felt the differences to be more telling. However, he was pleased to be finally dismissed. There were many matters to attend to if they were to weigh and proceed at first light, not least hound Commander Locklin to hound the rest of the ship's company to work harder.

Nicklesworth watched him go and muttered, 'Damn.'

Great things were afoot and he desperately wanted to succeed. Deep down he knew that he was going to have to stay one step ahead of this infuriating captain if he was going to make his mark. If Dollimore was going to eclipse him then he only had himself to blame.

Suddenly, a jet of gushing water crashed through the skylight and drenched him where he sat. Stunned, frozen and gasping, he jumped up thinking that the most horrific storm must have just erupted out of nowhere. Then he remembered the two fools hosing down the quarterdeck above him.

In a fit of anger he stalked out of the cabin, past the open-mouthed lieutenant and maintenance men and clattered heavy-footed up the ladder.

The two young men with the hose, ordinary seamen both, had already partially realised what they had done and now looked fit to die as they saw the state of the admiral. They felt like dropping the hose and running but they were rooted to the spot in abject terror.

Nicklesworth walked towards them with clenched fists and screamed, 'Give me the hose!'

He snatched it from their inanimate, leaden hands and instantly turned it upon them. Drenched, coughing and spluttering, they fell against the railing and very nearly went over the side. Then Nicklesworth threw the hose down to let it spray its water wherever it chose, screaming at the perpetrators, 'How do you bloody well like it?'

At the other end of the deck, the Regulating Petty Officer and the Quartermaster looked at each other and completely failed to suppress their laughter.

\*\*\*\*

The admiral's quarters still had a faint dampness about them when Nicklesworth hosted a dinner for all of his captains that evening. But it all went well despite that and the fact that his nose had earlier been out of joint. He had buried the issues that were giving him such a problematic time and, as a result, had been gracious company.

That set alarm bells ringing in Dollimore's head for he could not quite put his finger on the nature of his good humour. To the best of his knowledge, no good news had arrived to lift his spirits.

But the admiral's good cheer meant that the only sombre moment of the evening had been the occasion of the toasts drunk to the memories of Lieutenant-Commander Small and the other gallant men who had lost their lives in the worthy little destroyer, HMS *Castledown*. Furthermore, they knew that across the flotillas, a total of six destroyers had now been lost in this campaign and they had all gone down fighting hard, the enemy well aware of their fury.

Commander Fulton-Stavely, one of the finest specimens of a destroyer captain, drunk his port and lit a cigar as the formalities gave way to general chatter. He was in his mid-thirties and set for great things in this service if everything worked out well for him. His round face had a peculiar whiteness about it but a life all of its own in intelligent eyes. He was a jovial chap, very comfortable in this present company and very fit, even though that might not have been immediately apparent. Observers had noted that he had a slight podginess but it was clearly kept in check by the rigours of the service.

He and Dollimore had an affinity which was born out of shared experiences. Their paths had crossed a couple of times before and in circumstances which had not always been of the best kind. But neither held grudges and their mutual appreciation had been cemented during last year's encounter with the *Moltke*. That day they had both proved that they were clinical and persistent fighting captains.

He leaned closer to Dollimore. 'Sir, I've heard that your son is without a ship at the moment and doing menial work in the capital. How would it be if I requested for him to be sent to the *Crayhorn*?'

Remembering the difficult confrontation with Philip over his drinking amongst other problems and also knowing that Fulton-Stavely must have heard the rumours, Dollimore replied, 'I appreciate that. In fact, I recently received a letter telling me how he was doing very well in London.' He did not divulge the fact that the letter had come from Philip's wife, Sarah, not he himself. 'I should judge that he is ready to face seagoing duties again. An appointment in your ship would be welcome if you could swing it. Perhaps I could back your request with Admiral Forbes.'

'I'm sure it can be managed without. It's just that one of my lieutenants is on the sick list and another is being held back from a staff course until I can get replacements. If I could push it through quick enough, I'd be happy to have your son with me.'

'And you're not worried about Vian's evaluation of him?'

'I heard that he didn't fare so well there but, you know, we're not all like Vian. I have my own ways and means, and doing a favour for your son is the same as doing a favour for you; and nobody can truly doubt, he was right in the middle of that *Altmark* affair and he did do everything that was asked of him. To me that says a lot. Even better if his spell ashore has agreed with him.'

'Vian had good reasons for saying what he said about Philip,' said Dollimore carefully.

'But he didn't shy away from the task in hand,' Fulton-Stavely reiterated.

'No, he didn't.'

'So he should be back out there where he belongs and not in some counting house. Vian is indisputably a great man and makes choices based upon his temperament, but I am not Vian. I think this can work.'

Dollimore smiled one of his rare smiles and said, 'Thank you again.'

Fulton-Stavely nodded but still felt a little guilty at a minor deception he was hiding. His father, retired because of ill-health a couple of years ago with the honorary pensionable rank of rear-admiral, had actually written to him urging him to put up this suggestion in the first place and now he was bound to secrecy over the matter. He could not be certain of the reasons but apparently the Dollimores were establishing strong and benevolent allies in Admiralty circles. Fulton-Stavely was quite happy to play his part. 'Well, I'm going to need good men out there. I've a gut feeling that Norway is going to be nastier than anything we've yet seen.'

So, you've guessed what we're doing next as well, thought Dollimore.
\*\*\*\*

A few days later, having got some well-earned hours of respite from his gunnery course, Beatty immediately phoned the Dollimores' cottage and asked Betty if she would like to go into town to see the film he had told her about. Her enthusiastic 'yes' happily set his mind at ease from the earlier worry that she might have forgotten all about him and had found some other interest. It seemed like forever since they had danced. Guns, gun drill and the science of gunnery could be a terrible chore when one had a girl on his mind.

Her jolly nature was one of the things that he liked about her. She had a light coming from within that so many other girls did not seem to possess. Maybe she epitomised the fun-loving youth which he had entirely missed out on in his pursuit of duty. Whatever it was, it was attractive.

He borrowed a motor car from one of his friends at Whale Island and picked Betty up at the cottage during the afternoon. This was the best way to get about and, of course, it would impress her. How many men of his age had access to a car?

He drove her down to Pompey and parked it round the corner from the picture house that he had identified as the one still showing *The Wizard of Oz*. As they watched spellbound at the land of Oz suddenly appearing in grand colour on the screen, the magic was heightened by his taking her hand and holding it throughout.

Afterwards, they walked through the darkening streets to find somewhere to eat. There were many other couples about, each comprising mostly a sailor with a girl in tow. The war could not put anybody off from having a good time. It probably assisted one or two of them in having a better time.

Beatty was saying, 'The colour in that film was incredible. I swear only the Americans could afford to do anything like that. It must have cost a fortune to make.'

With a beaming smile, she said, 'Is that the sort of thing you normally watch?'

He grinned, 'No, you'd usually find me catching the latest Errol Flynn. Basil Rathbone is one of my favourites as well.'

Betty's expression faltered as she tried to understand what he was talking about.

He asked, 'Do you mean to tell me you don't know who Errol Flynn or Basil Rathbone are? What sort of a world are you from?' Then he noticed that her look had started to change dramatically. The happiness that had cloaked her until now was transforming into something else, something unsure. He said, 'I forgot, you told me before that you'd never been to a picture house.'

She then let the smile come back, trying to make a conscious effort not to make a fool of herself but the damage had been done. He had seen her uncertainty and her smile was failing. She mumbled, 'There just hasn't been occasion to.'

'Not even with your friends?'

She looked down and said, 'I've not really lived in a place long enough to make proper friends and, when I do find somebody I like, they get annoyed with me and then find that they have better things to do than be my friend.'

'I'm sorry,' he said, feeling awkward, 'I never realised.'

After a pause, he put his hand under her chin and gently raised it so that she came to look at him properly. He said, 'I'll tell you what, one of my instructors is this ancient chief who keeps telling us, "There's no such thing as a stupid question." How about we eat dinner, you can ask me anything you like and I promise I won't make fun of you in any way.'

'It's not that I don't want to understand things,' she protested, 'but everything is so confusing when all I want is a normal life.'

'You know something?' he said. 'A normal life sounds just fine to me too.'

She smiled and immediately put her arm in his. He having quelled his brief moment of pomposity, she thought that he could be the one to make her happy and, if he could calm her nerves that easily, there should be no reason why they should not enjoy each other's company a great deal. He seemed to be willing to meet her on a level that she could understand.

\*\*\*\*

At almost ten o'clock on the dot – the time that he had promised Mrs Dollimore he would have her daughter back home – they arrived at the cottage. It was just as well they had left themselves a little extra time for the return journey because he had had the devil of a time driving and navigating the pitch black lanes with minimal headlights. Plus, of course, Betty did not have a clue where she was so could not help. It was not her fault. She evidently led a life wrapped up in cotton wool to the point where she could not be self-sufficient. He decided that when they were married she would have her chance to shine and show the world what she was really capable of.

When the car came to a stop she hardly wanted to get out. Beatty had been so kind and so thoughtful to her this evening, more so than anybody had ever been before, that she had this sudden idea that she need not go back to her mother. They could run away together. In books the lovers always developed their bond without anybody else's input – unless the girl had an evil step-mother but that was not the case here.

Then she brought her head out of the clouds and resolved to start behaving like an adult. Her mother often spoken to her about needing to be realistic, and being realistic meant that Beatty could not take her back to the base. He did not have a place of his own that he could whisk her away to, at least no place nearby. His family home was in Berkshire, wherever that was. No, unfortunately this was the end of the evening.

'Thank you for taking me out,' she said. 'I had a wonderful time.'

He smiled and said, 'It was good for me as well. You must allow me to see you again soon.'

'Well, of course,' she said, the shock of any other eventuality clear in her voice.

'I'll call again when I have more leave.' Then, hesitantly, he added, 'And perhaps we might talk about what happens next.'

Her heart filled with joy. 'The answer would be 'yes' of course.'

He furrowed his brow and raised a hand to silence her, 'Hold your horses, Betty.' Suddenly thinking that his wording had not been the best, he was thankful that her mind had leapt to the idea of marriage. What might her reaction be if she thought he was talking about sex? Now he was thinking about sex. His only experience of that had been when he and a maid had somehow seduced each other at home three years ago. It had all been so clumsy that he had never really decided which of them had done the most seducing.

Betty was the first girl who had aroused such feelings in him in all this time since. She must be special.

He said, 'Let's not rush into any ideas of getting married now. We can talk about it some other time.'

'Beatty,' she said almost sullenly, 'what if you get killed in the war?'

He quickly replied, 'I don't plan on being killed. Don't you worry, we have our whole lives ahead of us and Hitler's not going to get in the way of that.'

'Hitler?' she asked, suddenly concerned. 'Who's that?'

He took hold of her hand. 'Oh Betty, I find that I could talk to you forever. There's so much you need to be told. But don't you worry about Hitler. If he comes around, we'll send him packing, you understand?'

She would just have to trust in that. 'Okay,' she said. 'I suppose I must go in or mother will come out here to fetch me, then she'll write a letter to father complaining about me and he'll be all horrid and disapproving.'

'Your father's a great man. He, and your mother while we're about it, only want the best for you,' he said, but immediately realised that speaking too highly of her parents might not be such an attractive thing to her. To redeem himself, he said, 'Anyway, put them aside as well. With your permission, I'd like to kiss you.'

'You don't need to ask,' she said, all of a sudden feeling breathless. An excitement was coursing through her body which was making parts of her tingle that she did not understand. The only truth was that it felt right.

They leaned into each other and the kiss, when it happened, was the most natural and satisfying thing that had happened all evening.

Beatty felt himself being driven to distraction. His mind was being overtaken by an animalistic urge to get even closer to her but he knew this to be completely wrong so allowed the gentleman of reason to regain control of the situation. Drawing away from her, he smiled as though nothing had been getting out of hand and said, 'I'll walk you to the door.'

Getting out of the car and walking around it in this brisk night air to open her side was fortunately just enough to dampen the tension, good though it had been.

He saw her to the porch and she went inside. Then he took himself away, amazed at how the damp, blustery night could not diminish the warmth that he felt within.

\*\*\*\*

Betty wandered into the living room and found her mother sitting reading a book by lamplight. The soft glow behind the seated figure was almost enough to put her face in shadow whereby Betty might have missed the warm smile she gave.

Always to the point, Jennifer said, 'He's different, isn't he?'

Yes, he is different, Betty thought, and something is different about you too.

'I can see it in your face,' said Jennifer softly. 'He respects you, doesn't he?'

Betty sat down in the armchair opposite and leaned back. 'He's been such a perfect gentleman, I can hardly describe it.'

'You'll be seeing each other again?'

'Most definitely.'

'Good,' said Jennifer. 'Well, it's time for me to get to bed. Please make sure you turn off the lamp before you retire.' With no more further ado, she was gone.

Betty stayed sitting for a while before realising that she too was tiring and could do with some sleep. It was just that she had spent so much of this evening in a dreamlike state that she had not recognised her tiredness until now. As she moved to turn off the lamp, her mother's demeanour suddenly struck her. She had been odd. She had enquired in a compassionate way about her evening. There had been no stern judgment and she had taken her word for what it was without needing to rectify anything. What was going on?

Confused, she turned out the lamp and moved carefully through the darkness towards her room. By the time she had reached it she had forgotten her mother and was thinking again about that kiss.

****

The Turtle hardly wanted to know what was in the letter that he had just received. He had picked up the envelope from *Burscombe*'s mail room earlier in the day and had instantly recognised his cousin's handwriting. If she was writing to him it could not be good news.

He had not had enough time to read it straight away as he had much work to do greasing, oiling and maintaining those well used anti-aircraft guns. When he had finished that task he had been set to work painting over the rust on the flight deck – not the most ideal way to treat corrosion. In a couple of weeks the steel would look terrible again.

Now he was back in the mess, hygiene chores dispensed with and hungrily wolfing down his scran before the Last Dog Watch was due to claim him once again. As he chewed on the vegetables, he eventually brought himself to tear open the envelope and steadied his nerves for whatever words the paper held. She had written:

*Dear Harry,*

*I said I would let you know if anything happened at home. The police have questioned me about C.P. They don't know much but somebody's grassed about something. You must believe me when I say I'm truly sorry for all of it,*

*Love Mary*

He screwed up the page and shoved it into his pocket. Damn it all! Yes, she did say that she would write but did she have to be so bloody obvious? What if someone else read the letter? He sighed, thinking that he did not have a lot of choices left.

At that moment, Smudge walked through the mess, saying in all innocence, 'Evenin', Turtle, I was just thinkin' about catchin' up with an old bird on the dog an' bone ...'

'Get stuffed!'

'Oh, well that's charmin', that is.'

# NINE

# Going North

The sight of Tower Bridge opening, its road being lifted to let the merchant ships slip in and out of the upper reaches of the Pool of London, was now so commonplace to Philip Dollimore that he hardly noticed it. He no longer thought of that bridge as the beautiful marvel of architectural and technical wonder that it was and his deepening ignorance of the finery was an indication of just how his mind had drifted away from the things that he thought he had loved. The complacency that now ruled him here was exactly the same as that which ruled at home. Going home to Sarah and the baby each day had lost its appeal. They appeared colourless and dull and he could not put much effort into his relationship with them.

It was as though his heart was going blank – all except for where Patricia Bushey was concerned.

He knew it was wrong and not fair on his wife but his visits to see Patty – to *help* her – were the only moments that were giving his life purpose.

He had found a way into her soul that the other men of her life had not been able to and he had seen her old strength returning, that which had been temporarily crushed. He believed that all she needed to pull herself back together was to be offered tangible security from one who understood her particular pain.

He admonished himself even as he thought about it and walked on along the winding streets, oblivious of his surroundings until he had finally reached his office and was sitting at his desk, seeking to deal with the stack of reports that had found their way to his attention. Even then he was finding it difficult to concentrate.

He desperately did not want to do anything to hurt his wife but, for all her care and patience, he could understand nothing of her world. The shine had definitely gone from that part of his life. All he knew was struggle and pain. This might be reason enough to start drinking again except that he did not want to present that slovenly persona to Patricia. She would see through it straight away and know him for the weak fool that he actually was. Her mother, a shrewder judge of character by far, already knew it but she tolerated him because of the positive effect he had had on her suffering daughter.

A shadow crossed the open doorway and Commander Crawshaw came into the office to sit down opposite him. Philip looked at him, confused. 'Good morning, sir.'

Crawshaw knew that coming in here in this way was an unconventional thing to do considering he was bearing a message of great importance. The usual thing would have been to summon Philip to his office and deal with it there but then he prided himself on the fact that he was anything but conventional. The navy had not dealt fairly with him so he was not going to deal fairly with it, though only so far as to not bring any further disgrace down upon his own head.

'Good morning, Dollimore,' he said. 'I'm almost sad for the fact that our acquaintance has been so short-lived.'

'I beg your pardon, sir?'

Crawshaw handed over the slip of paper that had been lodged amongst his items for attention that day and said, 'You have new orders.'

'So soon?' Philip asked, astonished. This appointment had not lasted much longer than his time in the *Cossack* and as far as he could tell, he had not upset anyone in the same way he had upset Captain Vian. He certainly had not upset Crawshaw here, who seemed to like him a great deal. He quickly read the words and looked up again. 'I'm to go back to Scotland and join HMS *Crayhorn*!'

'Yes, I read it. Commander Fulton-Stavely is quite able, so I've heard. If I remember rightly, he turned up with his group of destroyers at the end of our little fight with the *Moltke* last year and was of some assistance.' Crawshaw did not elaborate to include the fact that the *Burscombe* had been in trouble at that point and Fulton-Stavely's timely appearance, to engage and sink an enemy destroyer, had tipped the balance back in their favour.

'Of course, it would be an honour to serve in the *Crayhorn*, sir,' Philip said, his face betraying mixed feelings, 'but this has got to be my father's doing.'

'What do you mean?'

'I shouldn't really be going into it except, well, you seem to understand, sir.' Philip thought for a moment then continued, 'I need to be able to serve free of my father's influence. Do you see? While I was in the *Cossack*, all I kept hearing was how wonderful he was and now *he* has secured this appointment for me. The *Crayhorn* regularly supports the 25th Cruiser Squadron, so he's going to be breathing down my neck the whole time.'

Crawshaw nodded. 'And you want to be an officer of your own style, in your own right.'

'Yes, and not living in his shadow.'

'And not being judged according to *his* abilities.'

Philip was suddenly embarrassed. He stood up and said, 'Forgive me, sir. It's not my place to complain. The war is hotting up now and I'm to do what I must and go where I'm bidden.'

'Absolutely,' agreed Crawshaw. 'Let there be no suggestion of anything less. But remember something else, young man. I suspect that Norway's where you're bound and it's an ugly business which is going to take a monumental effort to sort out. But you were there before any of the others, including your father.'

The determination that Crawshaw was right appeared on Philip's face and the commander took pleasure in that. After all, if it would cause further aggravation between father and son then he would have achieved a victory of his own. Thinking on it, there was something else that he could do to stir the pot of hypocrites that had relegated him to this backwater. 'Philip, when you get there, no doubt you'll be seeing young David Clark at some point. Could you convey to him a message from me?'

'Certainly, sir.'

'Tell him that his mother desperately wants him to answer her letters. This feud has gone on for far too long and it's about time he grew up. She's willing to come to terms with him about his grievances.'

Upon this matter Philip immediately agreed. He already revered Dorothy Clark as a woman of exceptional character – perhaps even greater than her daughter – and he would be pleased to be able to help bring mother and son back together again. He then added, 'And should I mention your diligence in looking out for the ladies while they've been in town?'

Crawshaw smiled what appeared to be utter pleasantness with no hint of the malice that actually lurked below. 'I would be greatly disheartened if you didn't.'

\*\*\*\*

Patricia had been looking forward to her next meeting with Philip. Now heavily pregnant, the earlier morning sickness that had struck in a thankfully mild manner had disappeared and, with the calming of her mind, the world was looking to be a much rosier place. That was why she felt so betrayed when he informed her that he was going back to the Home Fleet.

Seated as usual in the living room in the family's Belgravia residence with her mother in attendance, a very cross look spread across Patricia's face. She said to him, 'What do you mean by telling me that you're going? It's been but a few weeks since you told me you were going to stay.'

Her accusatory tone immediately served to make him feel guilty. While he stumbled over his words, it was Dorothy who spoke up. 'Patricia, my dear, you are not at liberty to admonish the lieutenant for his necessity to follow duty. You know better than most the constraints that he is under. Our men have always gone where they have been told to go. That is the nature of the service.'

Philip was pleased that this lady was here to be able to explain everything in the only reasonable light. She was able to put words to the things that his conscience was making him falter over and while he could not help feeling that he was letting Patricia down, Dorothy was expertly getting him off the hook.

It was a shame that there was so much unfinished business here for it was not that long ago that Patricia had been a mental wreck. It had been a very unhealthy situation that she had found herself in and he knew that he had helped her to begin to rejoin society again. What would happen when he left? Would she be able to take care of herself and continue what they had started or would she relapse? He was perfectly earnest when he asked, 'Patricia, are you going to be all right?'

'I'm going to have to be, aren't I?' she snarled, her old defence mechanism of anger covering the sense of dread that had come over her. This man had come into her life, a man who had known her late husband well and who was able to empathise on a level nobody else was capable of. He was abandoning her, leaving to go back to the war where he might die too. Her men had all been exposed to the most intolerable risks and she had already lost two of them. She could lose no more.

Unfortunately, she had no way of channelling any of that into a measured response.

Dorothy did not fully understand this but, being one of the most hard-headed and logical of ladies that a person could ever be out to meet, she did not put up with it for a second. 'That's enough, Patricia. Mr Dollimore will agree to write to you, I'm sure. He has helped you immeasurably these last couple of months and you must allow him to leave thinking only of your good progress.'

Philip waved his hand in a conciliatory gesture. 'That's okay, Mrs Clark. I've simply not been able to live up to the guarantee I made. But as you say, I have to go where my orders state. Patricia, I will write and I shall look forward to seeing the baby when it's born. I regard the child as though it were one of my own family.'

Straight away his guilt hit him. His own words made him think of the family he was already neglecting – of his son, Little Charlie, just beginning to coast along the edge of the settees upon his own two legs and of Sarah; poor uncomplaining Sarah. God, how she should complain. He had been next to useless to her.

Tears were appearing in Patricia's eyes. All she could sense was that she was going to be mourning another loss so before her emotions burst forth she stood and ran from the room as fast as the weight of her unborn child would allow.

Philip and Dorothy stood and, once they had both accepted that Patricia was not going to come back, they looked at each other.

He decided that he was not going to embark upon any ridiculous small talk with Dorothy. She was far too intelligent to have time for it. He simply got down to his last point of business, saying, 'Ma'am, as long as you are agreeable, I shall speak to David when I see him and impress upon him the need to talk to you. Commander Crawshaw said that I should do it but I thought to have your opinion before I committed myself to what might be construed as meddling.'

'I thank you, Mr Dollimore. You must only do what your conscience dictates – and I know it to be good – but do remember that there is strong reason behind his anger with me.'

'I still think his treatment of you is quite disgraceful,' he stated. Then, with a fond farewell, he was away.

Dorothy stood in the hallway for an extra minute or two, silently contemplating Philip's slavish devotion to her and Crawshaw's blindness brought on by his incredible egotism, not to mention the unquestioning loyalty that other hapless men in the service were disposed to show her.

She had manoeuvred them expertly; they were all so easy to manipulate. But that was where her triumph paused because David was not half as stupid as the rest of them.

\*\*\*\*

Hundreds of miles away, hasty preparations for the very late attempt to try and influence the outcome of the Norwegian situation were being thrown together. HMS *Burscombe* had been moored at Rosyth's quayside and hundreds of nondescript soldiers in khaki bearing heavy packs and weapons were slowly filing their way across the narrow gangway onto the port waist just abaft the torpedo tubes, there to be dispersed fore and aft. For the next couple of days there was nothing for them but the prospect of a cramped, uncomfortable and cold trip up the North and Norwegian Seas but, finally getting the chance to fight, they mostly seemed to be accepting their lot.

Smudge, who was on the deck above helping operate the derrick by which they were busily hoisting ammunition crates aboard, called down to a cocky-looking lad on the gangway and asked, 'What regiment, my son?'

Between puffs of his cigarette, the man called up, 'KOYLIs.'

'I had a girlfriend once called Koyli. Perhaps you knew her.'

It was as though Smudge must have sniffed out a kindred spirit because the soldier was equally not at a loss for words as he remarked, 'And there's me thinking that the navy was nothing but a bunch of fairies.' Looking off to Smudge's left, he noticed a man standing there with one hand on his hip and so pointed at him, 'See? That's a Doris if ever I saw one.'

Smudge looked over to see who he was pointing at and his grin was immediately wiped from his face. It was only Warrant Officer Hacklett!

Hacklett looked down at the soldier with his frightening face and said, 'It's up to you if you want this to be difficult voyage, lad, but I promise you, if you call me Doris again, I'll shag you. You'll get the full six inches right up your arse.'

Stunned by the man whose hard stare emanated from a face that was nothing more than a mash of twisted, discoloured flesh, the soldier chose to shut his mouth and walk on but not without a nudge in the back from his sergeant, who said, 'Come on, you, stop upsetting the locals.'

Hacklett called after him, 'Na, 'o a' uh orf!' Men were often rattled when they could not understand what he had said. That was why he did it.

These men of the King's Own Yorkshire Light Infantry were being crammed in all the way along the 2 and 3 Deck passageways and messes. It was a shame that they could not make better use of the upper decks but they knew that the weather was going to be awful. The *Burscombe* already had a problem in that, when she had been designed, she had only been furnished with enough space to accommodate a complement of 772. That had already swelled to 819 because of changing operational requirements and now they were taking on a further 343 soldiers – three under-strength companies.

Most took the conditions in their stride but one of the immediate problems was one of hygiene. The soldiers had been on the go since being recalled from France and were not as clean as one might have wanted them to be. There was some complaining and some selling of pusser's hard and coal tar soap but, inevitably, the smell that pervaded everything was just a cross that they all had to bear.

There was also a queue for the heads. There was never a queue for the heads and one or two of the seamen were not impressed with how the place had got messed up so quickly, commenting on the army's poor dietary condition. Their dismay, however, turned to satisfaction when it came time for 'Up Spirits'. It always got the army going when the navy was issued rum in front of them knowing that they were not eligible for a single drop.

Both soldiers and sailors mutually agreed that it was fortunate this was only going to be a short voyage.

\*\*\*\*

It had been hoped that the squadron would be steaming out of the Forth by sundown but such was the hasty organisation of the coming expedition that it took longer than expected to get all the extra equipment stowed away. Even further behind was the loading of the freighter *Corona Lawrence*, which was sailing under the protection of the 25th and bound for the Norwegian port of Namsos. She was to carry large amounts of heavy equipment for the troops already on the ground, including caterpillar-tracked bren gun carriers, heavy machine guns, heavy mortars and a few Bedford trucks. The loading thus went on after dark and a strained moonlight tried to illuminate the last of the proceedings.

Partway into the First Watch, Pincher and Leading Seaman Paddy Walbrook finally closed the loading hatch on the flight deck and fastened the screw clips into place. They looked about themselves, acknowledging with exhaustion that the ship was much quieter now and relieved that the first great effort was over.

Paddy glanced every which way again and asked, 'Did yer see where the Turtle went?'

'No,' answered Pincher, 'I thought he was ordered away. Wasn't he?'

'He's a shifty so and so that one. The idea of him becoming a PO's a feckin' joke.'

Pincher did not want to comment though he did agree with the statement. Some of the men had become quite horrified at the thought of the Turtle being promoted.

A few weeks ago Pincher himself had asked his mum to feed him titbits of Bethnal Green gossip so that he could try to work out the Turtle's involvement in that blasted murder case and she had written him something very interesting:

*The police have been questioning Mary Sewell about the murder. You remember her, a lovely girl before she got mixed up with that lot...*

Surely this was proof that the Turtle knew more than he was letting on concerning the murder of Cliff Parker. Mary Sewell, a pretty but headstrong young woman who had somehow been attracted to the dubious courage of the gangster fraternity in East London, just happened to be Harry Haggerty's cousin.

This having given Pincher plenty to think about, he was still far from decided what he was going to do about it. But, whatever it was, it had to be for the good of the *Burscombe* before everything else.

He was suddenly jolted out of his thoughts by CPO Doyle's sharp command of, 'As soon as you've finished there, Martin, get yourself down to the main gate and pick up a delivery that's just arrived for the KOYLI's commanding officer.'

'Me, chief?'

'Your fault for being the first person I come across.'

Pincher tutted and asked, 'What is it, chief?'

'How the hell should I know?' Really, thought Doyle, these men ask for a lot sometimes. Even if he did know what the delivery was, it had nothing to do with him. The only important thing was that it should meet up with its recipient.

Pincher, more than familiar with unhelpful answers from senior rates, decided not to dwell on it but, instead, remembered something else he wanted to know. 'Chief, has there been any word about Les? I mean Gordy?'

Paddy stopped and looked expectantly to the chief as well. Not that he had any liking for Les Gordy, but the Irish really did need to stick together in this Godless place.

'Not yet,' replied Doyle, suddenly appearing more human. 'As soon as I hear anything I'll let you know.' Privately, it was a matter of concern to him that the Walrus had had to touch down somewhere in Norway, possibly in a place since captured by the Germans. What bothered him most was that he might have been partly responsible for getting that stupid lad incarcerated in some prison camp somewhere or possibly even killed. Incompetent as he was, he did not deserve that.

'Thanks, chief,' said Pincher.

He wandered along the deck and then off down the gangway, quickly explaining to the Regulating Petty Officer what he was about and then made his way forlornly along the quayside to the gatehouse in the black-out. In a way he should have been pleased for the few moments of freedom that this stroll was offering him but he found that he would have much preferred to have been sitting back in the mess scoffing down his supper. He was not as young as he once was.

After the lieutenant at the other end had given him the small crate that he had come to collect, he started to amble back, looking carefully at the ground so that he did not trip on anything unexpected.

Suddenly, out the corner of his eye, he thought he saw a shadow within a shadow creeping alongside a nearby building. An unwanted chill made his spine tingle. What if the Germans had somehow got into the base? It was not likely but then it was not impossible either. He called out, 'Hello?' and looked back to see if there were any sentries about. He was alone and still two hundred yards from the ship.

The moon was briefly laid bare by the drifting clouds and Pincher definitely saw the outline of a man and what was more, he thought he recognised the shape and movement. 'Turtle! What the hell are you doin' here?'

'Pipe down there!' hissed the Turtle as he stalked menacingly out of the deepest shadows and advanced on him. 'You'll cause trouble.'

'Oh yeah? I could cause some trouble anyway. Why ain't you on the ship?'

'I'm doin' a job.'

'What job? Stop giving me all the chestnuts, Turtle. I know what you're about and there's no way you're runnin'. Not now. Not right when we're goin' into action. Even if you got out of the base, they'll catch yer and then you'll 'ang from the yardarm. Unless, of course, they're gonna do it anyway. Have they got reason to do it?'

'Get out of it. You don't know nothin',' said the Turtle.

'Oh, don't I? You forget that I come from Bethnal Green an' all. You've been a miserable bastard since those murders so there's no way you're telling me you've got nothing to do it. Not anymore.'

Quite suddenly, the Turtle launched himself forward.

For all his wariness, Pincher was not expecting to be slammed in the chest the way he was. He fell backwards sharply, the wind thrust out of his lungs, his crate falling first on him then on the ground with the sound of breaking glass coming from within. As he lay there groaning at the pain in his chest and ribs, liquid began seeping from the crate onto the ground and the smell of strong wine filled the air.

The Turtle, incensed and hardly knowing what he was doing, stepped forward and prepared to put his boot heftily into the side of Pincher's head. That was just the way he would have dealt with the situation if he was on the streets of London. It was the way he had had to handle himself for as long as he could remember.

He was suddenly stopped by the sound of a man shouting, 'What's going on there?' followed by the heavy clicking of more than one pair of boots upon the concrete as they came towards them. Before he could say anything, three men of a shore patrol were standing alongside him looking down at the shadowy form of Pincher lying on the ground.

'Is he all right?' asked their senior rate, a Scotsman.

'He fell in the dark,' said the Turtle. 'Proper dangerous, this blackout.'

Pincher rolled over and began to haul himself to his feet. The Scotsman gave him a hand and sniffed the air heavily. 'You been drinkin', fella?'

'No,' said Pincher, holding his ribs. 'The smell's the wine what's in that crate, PO.'

'Where are you takin' it?'

'HMS *Burscombe*. The major's gonna go nuts.'

'Mm. Good luck with that. Well, clear up the gash then go on and get yourselves back to your ship.'

'Yes, PO,' said the Turtle.

A few minutes later, walking back along the dockside with the dripping crate, Pincher said to the Turtle, 'Listen, running ain't the best thing, mate. Talk to Midshipman Clark.'

'What, like you talked to him?'

'I never talked to him about you; and I know you only asked for him for your interview because you think he's a pushover. But he ain't. He can find you a solution. You can trust him.'

'I don't know what bloody world you're livin' in, Pincher. Stay outta this, I'm warning you.'

'I coulda turned you into that patrol back there. In fact, I still might, except you didn't do the murder, did you? You're coverin' for the person what did.'

The Turtle stopped and squared his shoulders. 'Leave it, Pinch, you're gettin' into stuff you don't understand.'

'So make me understand, then.'

But the Turtle fell silent.

They eventually walked up the gangway onto the ship but before they reached the domain of the Regulating Petty Officer, Pincher said, 'By the way, you'll not be catchin' me off my guard again. You try anything else like that and I'll knock your bloody 'ead in.'

'Yeah, right,' scoffed the Turtle disrespectfully.

****

'We're all ready for sea and everything done with only the one casualty, sir,' Commander Locklin reported to Dollimore.

'Very good, EXO,' the captain replied, then adding that the admiral had set their time to cast off as 0001.

The casualty had been a man who had fallen off a ladder and broken his leg. It was said that he had been distracted by the sight of a Wren who had been walking along the quayside. Dollimore had had to berate Lt-Cdr Digby for his light-hearted quip, 'That's what happens when you let women near ships. That man could have gone on to win a Victoria Cross or something.' The many cuts and bruises picked up by other members of the ship's company, like those sported painfully by Able Seaman Pincher Martin's ribs, had hardly been worthy of note.

With all the Special Sea Duty Men at their stations for leaving harbour, the ships of the 25th, their accompanying destroyers and the *Corona Lawrence* carefully edged out into the blackness of mid-river and began to work up power and speed for departure from the Forth. Horns sounded out intermittently from all directions as they manoeuvred without navigation lights. They were not worried about waking anybody up in the nearby town. Secrecy had been difficult anyway and dockyard workers and other servicemen had been saying 'good luck' to them all day. Norway was a fact and that was all there was to it.

A cold wind blew down the estuary making the men draw their collars and scarves tighter around their necks. The men took it all as they could, demonstrating bravado in the sober mood of the small convoy, fully aware that they were stepping into the unknown. Dollimore's private appreciation of the situation was centred around wasted time and the enormity of the extra effort now required to redress the balance.

This was not to say that the Germans had had everything their own way, as Nicklesworth explained once he had gathered all the relevant officers in his quarters down in *Burscombe*'s shaky stern. He had waited until they were many miles out past the old Victorian railway bridge and turning north with the Scottish shore somewhere on the port beam, before summoning them.

He explained what he knew of the developing situation, that the highly organised attack perpetrated by the enemy had seen much of the southern part of Norway swiftly falling into their hands. The mid-section was now in hot dispute with the British Army already on the ground ready to move on the port town of Trondheim in a pincer movement. The north of the country was still relatively untouched except for the town of Narvik, the gateway to the Swedish stocks of iron ore. A significant number of German destroyers had initially captured the fjord leading to that town but the Royal Navy had charged in and expelled or destroyed them. There were still German soldiers holding out there but they were cut off and sure to be destroyed soon.

'We have everything to play for,' he said enthusiastically, looking at the navy, army and marine officers standing about the great dining table. They were all serious. Two or three of them had seasickness thrown in on top of everything else though that was not surprising. This part of the ship, chosen because it was one of the few cabins large enough to accommodate the sixteen asked for, was not far away from where the propellers were powerfully pushing the *Burscombe* on her way through the rough sea. So, not only was the deck swaying but the reverberations were making everything that much more uncomfortable.

He said, 'Gentlemen, the time has come for me to reveal our intentions. For those of you who have not met him, this is Major Binkley-Walling.'

The pristine, smooth-skinned army officer standing next to him with his finely pressed uniform and extremely tidy moustache nodded his acknowledgement of the present company, expertly hiding the fact that he too was struggling with the ridiculous motion of the cabin.

Some of the older naval officers reflected privately that he seemed a bit young for the responsibility he had been given. He would not have agreed. He was twenty nine after all.

Nicklesworth continued, 'He has been tasked with taking his companies ashore in order to take control of a valley to the north of Namsos, the town which is where preparations are being made to move on Trondheim. Originally, we were told we were going to Namsos itself but the valley I have mentioned has now come under scrutiny as a possible landing site for German parachute troops, nasty little buggers that they are. If they get there before us then they might be able to hit our forces in the flank and rear and they would also control the land route – difficult as it is – to the north.'

A few eyebrows around the cabin had been raised at the mention of parachute troops and this was not lost on the admiral. 'Yes,' he said, 'they've trained hundreds of soldiers to jump out of aircraft, who then float down and attack from all quarters – quite brilliant, really. But back to our contribution to prevent that from happening. Lieutenant-Commander, the chart, if you please.'

This was aimed at Peterson, needed here in the capacity of navigating officer. He stepped up to the table and unrolled the large chart depicting a confused plan of islands and fjords, made more daunting by the frequent numbers and lines which defined contours, tides or depths. To those with untrained eyes, it seemed hopeless to begin to understand it.

'As you can see,' said Peterson in his usual patient manner, 'this is a chart of the waters in and around the Tjierrefjord. This is where we have our revised orders to land. It's all very simple really. Its width fluctuates between two and five hundred yards along its length and is flanked by mountains or hills all the way, thinning the most at these series of bends halfway up. Our landing point is the village of Hemmeligstein at the far end of this lake at the top of the fjord, just over twenty two nautical miles from the sea.'

Binkley-Walling then took advantage of the natural pause to ask, 'That damn place looks like a veritable bottleneck. Is it big enough?'

'The lake is two and half miles wide, sir,' replied Peterson, 'a natural bowl scooped out of the earth by falling glaciers thousands of years ago. I am confident that we can manoeuvre our ships in there. It has to be said, though, that our information on the exact depths beyond the estuary is hazy but this chart does indicate that we have at least six fathoms even at low tide. We'll be taking soundings as we go.'

'Thank you,' said Nicklesworth. 'Now, our valley is on the other side of the hills due east of Hemmeligstein and,' – he looked at Binkley-Walling – 'you will have to cover approximately two miles overland to get there.'

'Child's play,' commented the major.

'Good. Now, the *Corona Lawrence* will continue to Namsos as originally planned, escorted by *Crayhorn* and *Catterley*. That's the nearest place with the facilities to unload her heavy equipment and vehicles; and the three cruisers will head straight for the Tjierrefjord; *Burscombe* and *Marsfield* will go in to make the landing, *Farecombe* patrolling and securing the estuary.' He turned to Dollimore. 'Captain, your dispositions please.'

'Very good, sir. Mr Eddington, you will be in charge of our boats at Hemmeligstein; every whaler and cutter will be employed so that we can effect a swift landing; six from us and four from *Marsfield*. Captain Avery, you and your detachment of marines are going in with the army and will be under the major's orders.'

'Very good, sir,' replied the stern officer, his head crooked slightly forward and his uncompromisingly angry expression ready to turn to disgust at a second's notice. He and his men knew that they had an uphill struggle in making the army respect them. Even a couple of centuries on from their inception, the marines were still looked down upon and that was why he held himself in as superior a pose as possible in front of the collected army officers. He made sure to ask Binkley-Walling, 'Sir, what is your standing on assaults from the sea?'

'Can't say we've had much occasion to consider it, captain,' replied the major, sensing the hostility and standing firm. 'Been busy digging trenches the last few months.'

And eating in fancy restaurants, no doubt, thought Avery. He nodded, satisfied that he had the upper hand in a fundamental aspect of this operation. His seventy two marines would be there to show the army the way.

Dollimore observed the dynamics between the two men but was not particularly concerned. Avery might have a bit of an ego but he was a hundred per cent for doing what was needed to be done to succeed. There would be no catastrophic clash. He continued, 'As soon as the major and his men are ashore, both ships will withdraw from the fjord. As you know, sea room for manoeuvring is *our* best defence. Eddington, you will stay at Hemmeligstein, in command of the beach and the signallers. Mr Peterson, what is your calculation for how long all of this will take?'

'Well, to be sure we get the best out of the depths and tides known, we'll enter the fjord at dusk tomorrow and steam up twelve knots on the flood. Light winds should be coming in from the northwest and we should expect the air temperature to be around 37° Fahrenheit. There will also be three inches or more of snow on the ground. As long as we start getting the troops over the side as soon as we're anchored in the lake and get out as soon as we're done; with the number of men and volume of stores to move in the conditions forecast, I calculate a minimum of six hours in the fjord providing everything proceeds with no hitches.'

'And how many hours of darkness will we have?'

'At that latitude the night, such as it is, is presently only three and a half hours long, sir.'

'So the operation will continue into full daylight,' Dollimore finally stated, looking around the cabin to see if the realisation of what that meant was sinking in. The thoughtful expressions told him that it had made an impact. Knowing that he was entering onto a point of contention between the forces, he turned to Nicklesworth and asked, 'Is there any information on air cover, sir?'

The admiral was pleased to be able to say, 'I have been told that, yes, we are getting air cover. HMS *Furious* is still lurking about nearby with her bombers and I understand that they're also busy establishing an airfield ashore – with Hurricanes, I think.'

The cabin suddenly lurched to starboard with the sound of a wave breaking heavily against the steel hull. It made the less experienced of the officers clutch at the table to prevent themselves from falling over and one or two were evidently fighting back the urge to vomit.

Unmoved, Dollimore continued, 'How many?'

'I don't know.'

'Better than nothing,' said Binkley-Walling, then running his mind over another point that was integral to his success. 'Are we certain that there are no Germans in that valley yet?'

'The latest intelligence I've had is that they have not been observed in our area of operations so a slick landing is required so that we can dominate it before they get there.'

'Right, and I'd like my company commanders to have the opportunity to study this chart before we go in. I know that it doesn't tell us much about what we'll find inland but it's all we have. The War Office has not had time to dig up any maps of this Hemmeligstein place.'

There were a few frowns from the assembled company but Binkley-Walling himself seemed completely unsurprised. Perhaps the deprivation and disorganisation he had lived with in the army was worse than the navy's.

Dollimore, knowing that it would ruffle feathers even more, felt bound to ask Nicklesworth, 'Far be it from me to comment on matters beyond my remit, sir, but is our effort large enough and co-ordinated enough to expel the enemy from Norway?'

The admiral, uncomfortably aware of some of the arguments that had flared up in London on this very subject of commitment but more irritated by his captain's never-ending opinions, was able to answer definitively, 'It has been decided that the battalions available are enough to do the job. We've scoured Britain for men and withdrawn as many as we dare from France so there's nobody else to call upon and that's that.'

There was silence for a couple of seconds while Peterson, Avery, Irwin, Eddington and some of the others shifted their gazes back and forth. They did not want the briefing to end on a bum note and were finding the ensuing silence disconcerting. With their respect for Nicklesworth a little touchy, they cautiously looked to Dollimore for inspiration. He was the one who instinctively knew how to balance reality, fantasy, truth and lies and lead the way with the advantage of a superior imagination. It was from him that they wanted the last word.

He did not disappoint. 'Major Binkley-Walling, we will be holding the fjord open for all eventualities and will remain in contact via short-wave radio. I will also place a string of semaphore signallers along the length of the fjord as a contingency. Let it not be said that we didn't offer you all the support that we might.'

'Thank you, old man,' the young major replied, visibly heartened.

'Finally, please take with you the words of our motto: *Forward without fear or regret.*'

'I am touched,' said Binkley-Walling, nodding to one of his company commanders, Captain Tomlinson, who suddenly proceeded to pull the cork out of a bottle of wine that had been placed alongside a tray full of glasses on the side cabinet. As he poured a mouthful into each and prepared to serve them out, the major continued, 'I took the liberty of procuring an 1805 Madeira, just to wet the lips and toast our upcoming success; and, on a personal level, to mark my first taste of action. There were two bottles but it seems as though one of your *able* seamen couldn't negotiate the black-out.

'Anyway, that aside, I thought the 1805 to be poignant as we Yorkshires could not succeed without the help of our brothers-in-arms, the Royal Navy, heirs of the great Admiral Lord Nelson of Trafalgar. Captain Dollimore, you have shared with us your motto. Now let me share with you ours: *Yield to none.*' He and they then drank the wine.

After the meeting had broken up and the officers dispersed throughout the ship, Dollimore stayed behind at Nicklesworth's request.

The admiral closed the door and stared hard at him. 'I appreciated your words there, captain, but do remember your place. I should be the one to brief on the squadron's purpose.'

'You're right. Sorry, sir,' said Dollimore, fighting to hide his agitation.

After a couple of seconds of studying the other's face, Nicklesworth bared his teeth and growled, 'Just say it, man! We're on the same side!'

Dollimore frowned, pleased that there was no audience to this embarrassing confrontation. 'It's all been thrown together too hastily, sir. We didn't plan ahead, then unforgivably squandered more than a week while the Germans played a stunning hand against us. We've behaved like novices and if there's any deficiency in that air cover you spoke about then many men are going to die out there.'

Nicklesworth's mouthed curled into something approaching an evil grin. 'That's very, very pessimistic of you, captain, to predict failure even before we've had a go. Would you prefer to run? Turn tail? Give up?'

'Quite the contrary,' said Dollimore, his disgust showing clearly, 'I'm going to do what I always do, use every asset I have to let Jerry know that he's not going to get away with it scot-free. It's no less than I would expect from every man in this ship.'

'Very well then, but remember I've warned you before about dabbling in affairs of policy and strategy. There are only a certain number of times that I'll warn you off. Dismissed, captain.'

Once he was alone, Nicklesworth went into the next cabin and began collecting up the various files that he needed from his desk. He was trembling with anger – an anger aimed at himself as much as anybody else. With the same passion that he disliked Dollimore, he wished that he could be more like him. It was clear to all now that the enemy must have been planning this invasion since the *Altmark* incident back in February and Dollimore had been one of the only people who had envisaged that.

Curse him for his insight, thought Nicklesworth, except, for God's sake, we're both trying to pursue the same bloody thing – to protect Britain, her people and their Allies from this totalitarian horde punching out from Central Europe.

It was just that that infernal man did it so much better!
****

The first day was spent steaming slowly northwards in moderating weather, the ship's company keeping a steadfast watch and conducting drills, and the second was well and truly begun when Lieutenant Irwin took over the bridge once more in this never-ending cycle of watches. The men had been stood down from Dawn Action Stations and were back in the lessened grip of Defence Stations. Hopefully he would be dealing with nothing much more than the forever-shifting grey that seemed to characterise this part of the world because he did not feel particularly upbeat.

He had not slept well and was suffering from anxiety born out of the fact that his brain was more muddled than usual because of that lack of sleep. It was a vicious circle of mental torture though he kept trying to tell himself that it was all rubbish. He understood everything that was going on around him, came to the same conclusions as the other men but was then crippled by the fear that he did not. To make matters worse, every time he managed to stop being silly and was able to calm himself down, his tired worries sneaked back into his head via a circuitous route and brought him low again.

He wished that he could have been somewhere else right now and not on the way to carry out this hazardous operation. Paradoxically, he was glad that he was involved. If he could just get through this, he might be able to look at himself in the mirror and be proud – prouder than anyone else would be of him at any rate.

Looking out over the small, crawling convoy, he wished that they could move faster but unfortunately they were limited to *Corona Lawrence*'s top speed of twelve knots and even that was kicked into touch by the currents and wind. Even then, he reasoned, *he* might want to reach the destination quicker but their course and speed were set in order for them to arrive at their objective at nightfall, no sooner, no later.

He clenched his fists, yawned and tried to concentrate on the watch-keeping.

Quite suddenly, his swirling tension burst into shocked reality as he watched a fiery geyser erupt from the far side of the freighter. The *Corona Lawrence*'s hull shook unnaturally and plunged for a few seconds, her low waist briefly awash. As the roar of the explosion belatedly reached Irwin's ears, the ship corrected herself to a her proper draft and tried to appear normal except for the crashing water, flame and smoke running amok amongst the deck housings.

A petty officer shouted, 'Sir!'

Of course, as Officer-of-the-Watch, he was supposed to be raising the alarm but he was standing here just watching the calamity unfold. Jolted from his shock, he pressed the alarm button and the bells and rattlers sent the resting half of the exhausted company back to their Action Stations.

As Captain Dollimore appeared on the bridge, tugging on his duffle coat to guard against the falling temperature, that unfortunate freighter was four hundred yards off the starboard quarter and dropping further behind. She was gradually rolling onto her side and her crew were jumping into the sea or climbing down the portside in the faint hope of staving off the inevitable.

He looked at Irwin and guessed from the look on his face that the helplessness in his heart was magnified tenfold compared to that which was in his own. Focus was required. 'We carry on as we are.'

Irwin found himself calmed by Dollimore's simple words. The Old Man was in effect taking responsibility for all that was occurring. If the *Burscombe* was to do nothing to aid those men in peril back there then it was not his fault.

The destroyers had been tasked with dealing with survivors. However, the submarine threat came first. *Crayhorn* and *Catterley* were already racing off to the east, throwing out great foaming wakes. Did they have echoes from their ASDIC equipment detecting a hidden enemy? Irwin's mind was blank on the possibility.

The *Corona Lawrence* was sliding beneath the waves fast. Once lying on her starboard side, she disappeared mostly at that angle until the last few seconds when her stern finally raised up and violently blasted out her trapped air. Then she was gone and the desperate survivors either clung onto the wreckage or floated away surely to perish unless the destroyers came back soon.

It was the most sobering of sights for Irwin. Watching the *Castledown* explode had been bad enough. Why was he witnessing it again? Why were they even at war? Why did the other men consider him so mad to wish for negotiations to end all this? The men pursuing this had to be insane and that went for Dollimore too. It was definitely the one thing he could not understand about his revered captain.

'This changes nothing,' said another strong voice from behind him. He turned and saw that Rear-Admiral Nicklesworth had come up to the bridge and, yes, a chief petty officer had announced his presence. Irwin had just not acknowledged it.

Nicklesworth was letting everyone around him know that, whatever happened, they were on course for doing everything in their power to succeed in this mission, and letting Dollimore know that he would not waver in the face of adversity.

The cruisers ploughed on to the almost gentle sound of depth charges being dropped at about two miles' distance. With any luck Fulton-Stavely had positively identified his target and got the sneaky pirate that lurked somewhere in his steel tube beneath the waves. These U-boats were notoriously difficult to destroy but not impossible.

As they turned onto the next pre-arranged leg of their zig-zag course, now at liberty to increase the speed a touch, Irwin dragged his attention away from the plight of the *Corona Lawrence*'s last few men and busied himself with the reports coming in stating that no further threat was detected ahead. Then he saw Lt-Cdr Digby looking at him out of the corner of his eye.

It was a concerned look his friend cast as he asked, 'Are you okay?'

'Y… yes, I am.'

****

Lt Philip Dollimore sat in an armchair staring at the glass of whisky that had just been placed in front of him. This wardroom at HMS *Cochrane*, the shore establishment of Rosyth, was full and bustling. Officers were chatting, laughing and playing cards or darts. Some were meeting up with old friends, others were introducing themselves to new faces and sharing their war experiences, news or simply the buzz. It was coming at him from almost every direction. Norway was the hot topic.

Tired from the long journey coming north and aggravated by the fact that he had missed the *Crayhorn* by a matter of one day, he sat there feeling aloof. He had finished stuffing the tobacco into his pipe, had lit that and was now wondering about the wisdom of allowing this drink to enter his body. He had not touched a drop since arriving in London and to all intents and purposes he thought he had lost the thirst for it.

However, his muscles were now tense, the apprehension building up in every sinew of his body. It was daft because he was not afraid of the Germans. He was not afraid of the ships. So what was going on? He had noticed a downturn in his spirit when he had had to accept that he would not be in a position to help Patricia any further, or to admire her mother. But the final crunch had come when he had realised where he was going next. When he had enquired about HMS *Crayhorn*'s return, he had been informed that that flotilla had been designated to operate out of Scapa Flow of all places.

That was where the *Royal Oak* had gone down; where she still lay with over eight hundred men dead inside her broken hull. He had travelled many miles and been to many places since that terrible night and the only place that had truly comforted him had been the house in Belgravia where his late friend's widow still needed his help.

Here, in this place which was jolly for all but him, he did not know or understand anybody. They were just more faceless men en route to their own destinations and who might possibly die getting there.

He scooped up the glass and knocked back the entire shot in one gulp.

# TEN

# Fire in the Fjord

The loss of the *Corona Lawrence* was a severe blow. For the seamen it brought back the nightmare of the *Castledown,* and for the soldiers it was a deeply thought-provoking introduction to the war. Enough of them had seen the ship turn over and sink to understand that this was no game. The panicked men splashing about in the sea could well have been them had the torpedo hit the *Burscombe* and it would be pointless to deny that a soldier would prefer to die on dry land if he was to die at all.

One could become quite melancholy thinking about it so the sergeants went round the decks telling their men that the only emotion worth having was hate. Hate for the Germans was to be the key to their soldiering. They had started it so the KOYLIs were going to finish it. The sentiment worked. That was how, when Pincher asked one sorry-looking young soldier over a game of cards if he was worried, the reply was, 'Worried about Jerry? Sod that. We're gonna murder 'em.'

'What yer looking so upset for, then?'

'It's the food.'

'Not good enough for yer?'

'Oh, just fine. Where else could I get six meals a day?'

'Six?'

'Yeah, three down, three up.'

'Oh,' replied Pincher, laughing at the unfortunate man's propensity to seasickness.

\*\*\*\*

Four decks above, in his enclosed bridge, Nicklesworth was busy monitoring the various signals which had been coming to him. He felt very uneasy. Reports were suggesting that the army was still not moving on Trondheim, that they were having trouble with persistent enemy air power. Apparently they were being hampered by a frightful weapon called the

191

Stuka. It was a dive-bomber which screamed as it sought its prey, striking terror into the hearts of its victims, and was deadly accurate in its destructive potential.

He had earlier sent a signal to Admiral Forbes asking for further guarantees on air cover but had heard nothing back. As they were now due to reach the mouth of the Tjierrefjord in a little under two hours, he considered with growing aggravation that knowing what to expect might be an important matter.

One of his flag-lieutenants entered the bridge and handed him another envelope. Ah, hopefully this would be the message he was expecting. But when he read it, he turned a shade of fiery red as further frustration began welling up in his heart. Far from receiving solid news on air support, what he had got was a complete game changer:

*To Rear-Admiral Commanding 25th Cruiser Squadron,*
*Air reconnaissance by RAF Bomber Command indicates there is a*
*DEUTSCHLAND class battlecruiser, two destroyers and troop ship*
*anchored in TJIERREFJORD. Take precautions as is necessary.*
*Admiralty*

He gritted his teeth and looked at the nearest man, a sub-lieutenant who was studying the compass and writing notes. He ordered, 'Go and get me Captain Dollimore and Major Binkley-Walling.'

'Very good, sir,' answered the sub, immediately slipping his notebook under his arm and heading off to locate them.

They arrived a moment apart from each other, Binkley-Walling first finding the admiral staring angrily out of the window. Nicklesworth handed him the signal.

When Dollimore appeared, the major was rubbing his chin in deep thought and, noticing the captain enter, handed the paper on to him.

Binkley-Walling, appalled, said, 'Our plan won't work. We shall have to go to Namsos instead.'

Nicklesworth was noticeably aghast even though his initial thought had also been to abort the plan. But that was before he had asked himself what he thought Dollimore would do. 'What do you mean? We have orders to land in the Tjierreford and, without specific instructions from Admiral Forbes or from the Admiralty, the plan will go ahead.'

'But this changes everything,' argued Binkley-Walling, his cheeks glowing red.

'It changes it to a degree, yes, but it doesn't mean that we give up. Our landing is part of a wider operation and we do not have the authority to scrap it just because we've run up against some opposition.'

'*Some* opposition, sir? I think I would call three warships and a troopship *stiff* opposition. Rather more significant than a few piddly parachute troops, wouldn't you say? And as for you not having the authority to scrap the operation – well I have.'

'I beg your pardon?' asked Nicklesworth with understandable astonishment.

With no lessening of authority, Binkley-Walling stated, 'I have clear orders from my general that I have the opportunity to cancel the landing if we face any opposition.'

'That's completely absurd!' returned Nicklesworth. He could not remember another situation in the whole of his career where he had had to listen to claptrap like this. 'What do you think warfare is?'

'That's not the point. The point is that we were supposed to be there before Jerry. We were supposed to be dug in and ready to repel him when he arrived. Now the tables have been turned on us and it's not reasonable that my men and I should have to fight our way ashore. I'm very sorry, gentlemen, but this mission is over. We either go to Namsos or go home. Look, I know that what I'm saying doesn't seem right but my orders do not extend to the needless slaughter of my men. Norway is important but it's not that important.'

'Then what the hell are we doing out here?' Nicklesworth all but spat out, 'and what was the worth of the sacrifice of the *Corona Lawrence*?'

'I'm mightily upset about that – ' Binkley-Walling began.

Dollimore held up a hand to silence them both. Having reached the pinnacle of his toleration, he was finally toppling off the edge. Taking one of his invisible deep breaths in an effort to remain calm, he said, 'Right, this is exactly how it's going to happen, no ifs or buts. Now that the destroyers don't have the *Corona Lawrence* to escort to Namsos, they will guard the entrance to the fjord while the whole cruiser squadron goes in for the landing.'

When Binkley-Walling opened his mouth to object, Dollimore quickly said, 'Major, the forcing of the fjord is under navy jurisdiction and we *will* be entering it and we *will* be engaging the ships that we find there. Please feel free to join me on the bridge while this takes place. I can't think of a better spot from which to witness it. Once we have eliminated them, you can then decide whether it's suitable or not to land your troops, and not before.'

Binkley-Walling looked carefully at this navy captain. He did not really cut the most impressive figure. Not overly tall, not particularly muscular, though his movements were fluid enough for his age. The man looked haggard though not quite washed-out. Where did his strength come from? Was he simply hell-bent on getting into a fight or going out in a blaze of glory? Why did he need to take on such a powerful German force when there were alternatives? Nicklesworth must see that surely.

But the admiral too was looking hard at the major. 'I concur with the captain.'

Binkley-Walling wondered whether it could be that the navy specifically chose lunatics to be in command. Still, after giving it a second thought, there was something appealing in that. Some might say: nothing chanced, nothing gained. Thinking about his many months of inactivity about the fields of France, freezing in the worst winter for years, perhaps he could do with a bit of action; and, of course, if these men here fouled it up, he would still be free to pull the plug.

'Very well, gentlemen,' he said with resignation. 'The lives of my men and I are in your hands.'

Nicklesworth scowled, 'They have been since the moment you stepped aboard, major.' Then he turned his back as a dismissal to them both, though silently scathing of himself.

He was becoming more and more aware that he had never taken time to visualise such a situation as this through all those years of peace. The navy had consistently conducted exercise after exercise making him solidly grounded in the theories of battlefleet action. He had written a hundred reports on fleet manoeuvres and weapons handling, had studied Jutland again and again but that appeared to be a completely alien concept now. Perhaps he should have paid more attention to the lessons of other campaigns of the last war like Gallipoli, Zeebrugge, Tanga or even the Rufiji River. Norway was looking very much like an effort worthy of those difficult fights.

\*\*\*\*

Action Stations was called before the coast came into sight. No matter what the men were observing, where they were observing from or what they were doing – Dollimore and Binkley-Walling looking out from captain's bridge, Nicklesworth from the admiral's bridge; Clark, Pincher, Paddy and the Turtle scanning the sky from their pom-poms; Commander Locklin studying the coastline from the aft-superstructure; CPO Doyle waiting patiently at No. 1 Damage Control Base or WO Hacklett at his guns in B-Turret – they were all silenced by the uncertainty of dealing with a strong enemy.

The dark jagged peaks of the rocky hills were whitened significantly by bright snow and punctuated less so by the dull greenery of sparsely growing vegetation. With the wind audibly forcing a passage between the peaks and the only sign of movement being the crashing waves and fast-moving clouds, the way ahead offered itself as an eerie prospect. The immediate terrain offered no opportunities for human settlement. To men enamoured of the pleasant green fields of England and even those more used to the bleaker beauty of the Scottish Highlands, this place looked as lifeless as the mythical Underworld.

But at least the hostile welcoming party was not waiting for them right here. If they were still inside the fjord then they would find themselves at a disadvantage even if they did have a battlecruiser present.

A *Deutschland* Class Battlecruiser, thought Dollimore. Could it be? Was it the *Moltke*? The possibility was completely profound that he should keep coming up against that ship. Was there now some personal destiny developing between himself and his opposite number? As quickly as he thought that, he cast it aside. There was no time for flights of fancy. The situation was far too serious.

The low sun, having struggled to make its presence felt all day, finally gave up and sunk below the horizon. Nicklesworth decided that it was time to move and gave the order to proceed as per the revised plan. So, while the two destroyers circled in their patrol patterns within a three mile limit offshore, the three cruisers entered the fjord, steaming their way towards the next clash of arms.

The *Burscombe* cautiously went in first at twelve knots, the *Farecombe* two cable lengths astern with the *Marsfield* bringing up the rear at the same distance again. The noise of the boiler machinery and generators from within their hulls emanated like a din to the men who otherwise wished for dead quiet. It was like stomping clumsily into the open jaws of a sleeping monster, keeping them on edge as they scanned the fast-dimming rocks and peaks, trying to ascertain whether they were being watched.

After an hour and a half of cold tension, Lt-Cdr Peterson, who had been conferring with Irwin through the chart house voicepipe, said quietly, 'That was the final bend. In a couple of minutes we'll see a small bay to starboard and then the lake of Hemmeligstein ahead of us soon after that.'

'Very good, pilot. Is that bay large enough for ships to anchor in?'

'Yes, sir.'

Intuition began to gnaw at Dollimore's brain. It stood to reason that the enemy ships should be anchored in the main lake but what if they were not? 'Guns, train the main armament onto the upcoming bay, starboard side.'

Lt-Cdr Digby happily acknowledged the order and set about giving his own knowing that the captain wanted the action, if any, to happen at speed with a view to stunning the enemy with shell fire and getting torpedoes into their sides at the earliest possible opportunity.

The three ships went on, their twelve knots creating minimal wakes. Suddenly AB Smith's voice came down the pipe from the observation platform up the foremast. 'Three ships anchored green zero-nine-zero, range nine hundred yards.'

The motors of the Director Control Towers and turrets whirred as all of the ship's main armament trained to the starboard beam according to Smudge's report. Behind him, the White Ensign was hoisted.

For a good few seconds Dollimore could discern nothing of the target identified by Smith because a small promontory, a black wall of headland, was still blocking his view. That wonderful seaman above could obviously just see over the top of it and the advantage he had given them was crucial.

'Any second now,' Dollimore said to Digby. 'You may fire as soon as you see them.'

Major Binkley-Walling stood just below the DCT, excited and proud to be present. This calm, clinical execution of an attack was a far cry from anything he could expect with his infantry assaults. Whereas he had to consider hand-to-hand combat and physical survival dominated by muscle power, these men here were preparing to slay their enemy purely by means of science. All the latest mind-blowing technology for destruction was wound up in this ship – not that he had been allowed to investigate much of it – and it was fascinating in the extreme.

Then they could see the silhouettes as reported by Smith. One then two, then finally three ships sitting silently at anchor. The muffled instructions from within the DCT came through the thin armour followed by the quick hum of the final training corrections and then Digby ordered, 'Fire when ready.'

With hardly a pause, the eight guns of the two forward turrets flashed and roared their abrupt end to the stillness. Everybody jumped whether they were expecting it or not. The air all about them was displaced and quickly the disgusting smell of sulphurous smoke drifted across them.

In naval terms this range could almost be considered point blank. The shells crashed into the first and closest ship, destroying everything around her. In a sudden burst of orange fire which lit up the whole bay, steel was torn into shreds and the surrounding water was thrown skyward. That was the satisfying effect as nearly 900lbs of armour-piercing shells did their job.

Down in the smoky turrets, where absolutely nothing could be seen of the fight, sixty-plus men busied themselves with reloading the guns. In well-rehearsed rhythm, the teams rammed in shells and cordite, closed the breeches, inserted the primers then stood back as the guns were elevated for the next shot. It all took little more than ten seconds by which time the aft turrets were also cleared to fire.

Fired electrically from the DCTs, all sixteen of *Burscombe*'s guns now roared together. Although the sound within the turrets was not overbearing – for the force of the charge went out through the barrels and did not find its way inside the enclosed armour – the steel deck shook violently, shaking everybody's bones and breaking glass and fittings below. There was no time to worry about that, though. It was time to reload again.

The ship which had been targeted was already listing with her stern awash. Fire and smoke shrouded her entire upper decks and one or two flaming men could be seen throwing themselves over the side. Beyond that, nobody else emerged. Secondary explosions within the ship blew her hull open. Her magazine igniting?

'We've got two destroyers!' Dollimore shouted between the flashing of the guns and barely thinking about the ridiculously thin armour that the enemy possessed. 'But what's that third ship?'

As the guns fired again, this time joined by the forward turrets of the *Farecombe*, Peterson and Digby strained their eyes to see clearer through their binoculars. 'It's the troop ship!' reported Peterson.

'Where's the battlecruiser?' asked Dollimore. Turning to the other lookouts, he asked again, 'Does anybody see the battlecruiser?'

There was enough flame and moon to give them adequate vision for this whole stretch of fjord. Answers in the negative came from all about him.

'She must be in the lake up ahead! Keep a careful watch for her!' He was suddenly filled with a vision of that powerful German ship manoeuvring right now to be able to get in a full broadside as soon as the *Burscombe* appeared to them out of the darkness, but it could not be helped. There was no going back.

Where these destroyers were concerned, however, if Dollimore had felt any sense of sport, it evaporated from his mind at this point. The combined firepower of *Burscombe* and *Farecombe* were dropping another thirty two 6-inch shells and twelve 4-inch shells onto the two ships still afloat and their utter destruction was certain. The new instinct that took over him was that it was wrong to kill those few remaining who had no chance. Just to see that second destroyer sink first, then he would show mercy to the troop ship.

When the flaming hulk tipped over onto its side, Dollimore ordered a ceasefire.

The ringing in everybody's ears gave the impression that the night did not want to return to its old silence. Excitement was still high, the sight of the dying destroyer and flaming freighter was incredible and the idea of the ensuing calm was almost unreal. The cruisers had wreaked havoc and won in under four minutes and, even more miraculously, *Marsfield* had not even had a chance to open fire.

But now for the big fight. Dollimore ordered, 'Give me revolutions for twenty knots! Guns, when we're in the lake I'm going to turn to port. Be prepared to get off a broadside. Chief Yeoman, signal *Farecombe* and *Marsfield* to adhere to the admiral's standard divisional attack.'

There's not going to be much room for that, thought Peterson, but, oh well, here we go.

With the burning troopship left far behind, all they could see ahead was a solid wall of black hills above dark grey water. Dollimore looked up at the moon as it struggled to be noticed, much as the sun had done during the day. It was just enough. Eventually the shoreline a couple of hundred yards off the starboard bow with its lapping waves began to spread to reveal a large body of water stretching out ahead of them.

The *Burscombe*, her forward turrets trained either way off the bows to cover the A-arcs, thundered her way into the open expanse of the lake, the lookouts and officers straining their eyes to see the main enemy, but all was peaceful ahead. No silhouette presented itself and no gun opened fire.

'Come two points to port,' ordered Dollimore, and was soon convinced and relieved that they were not about to be blown out of the water like those two destroyers they had left back there. 'The *Moltke*'s not here,' he finally declared, letting slip for the first time that it had been that particular ship which was on his mind. 'Reduce speed to six knots and signal the squadron to proceed to Hemmeligstein with caution.'

As the ship gradually manoeuvred and Peterson gave the necessary orders to arrest her otherwise reckless speed, Dollimore looked over at Binkley-Walling and, with much more irritability than he meant, asked, 'Well, major? What say you about the situation now?'

At that moment, the admiral was announced as being on the bridge and Nicklesworth came to stand in the already huddled space to repeat, 'Yes, what say you now?'

'I must understand every aspect of our opposition,' insisted Binkley-Walling. 'For instance, the men from that troop ship. They could be in that village waiting for us. We'll be dreadfully exposed as we row ashore.'

Nicklesworth looked briefly at Dollimore. No, don't pause, he thought. They don't like my pauses. But what would Dollimore say right now? Yes, that's it. Going on authoritatively, he said, 'I for one am willing to fire on the village. A crying shame for the people, I know, but if there are Germans that need to be neutralised, well… you've seen what our guns can do.'

'Yes,' said the major, sickened yet emboldened, 'and very impressive they are too. Order the landing to commence.'

Triumphantly, Nicklesworth nodded to Dollimore, 'Captain, see to it.'

'Very good, sir.' There was nothing like a fresh burst of activity to take his mind off the fact that he had just slaughtered possibly as many as four hundred and fifty men without giving them a chance to fight back. It was difficult but necessary, best practice in warfare in its clearest guise: surprise, daring and ruthlessness. After all, was that not how the Germans had been operating? It was high time that hesitancy in the British forces was done away with.

Dollimore ordered a leadsman into the chains – whereby the said operative threw his line from the foc's'le – and listened to his reports on the depth. He then reduced revolutions accordingly as they neared the inshore end of the lake with its silent, blacked-out village. When the leadsman called a depth of six fathoms, he ordered the engines slow astern for dropping anchor and had the Foc's'le Part of Ship men lay one shackle of cable along the lake bed, the blackened barrels of the big guns behind them now facing to starboard, still giving off their residual eggy cordite stink after their hefty action.

They were still three hundred yards from the shore but, knowing that they were at the height of a spring tide with a maximum drop of 10.4 feet for a ship whose current draft was 21. 5 feet, it was as close as he was willing to go. Even then it was little risky.

While the other cruisers followed suit in every detail, Binkley-Walling's soldiers were ordered to the waists. The whalers and cutters were then swung out on their davits while a small stream anchor was dropped abaft Y-Turret to steady the *Burscombe*'s stern for the task to hand.

The major gently shoved his way through the mass of men, saying, 'God bless you all! Good luck! I'll see you ashore! Keep your weapons at the ready! Give 'em hell!'

He received happy looks and nods all the way from the familiar faces of the men who barely managed to make proper room for his passage, such was the crush.

Very quickly the boats were lowered into the still water, the lines detached, then the midshipmen ordered their oarsmen to get them underway.

Clark had command of that boat into which Binkley-Walling had climbed. Before the ritual discipline of silence had been established, the major had shaken Clark's hand and said a quick, 'Thank you, young man.'

The oarsmen pulled hard and Clark's boat came abreast the first whaler that had already proceeded. Commanding that other boat was the hunched figure of Midshipman Farlow. It was noticeable that he did not acknowledge Clark's proximity. There was no race to the finish line as in front of the *Castledown*, just an exhausted effort to get the job done.

Glancing about him, Clark noticed that the starboardside boats from the *Farecombe* and *Marsfield* were not far behind while the portside boats were beginning to emerge between the great ships' black hulks. One boat, packed with seamen, headed straight for three small fishing trawlers that were anchored not far away. Those trawlers were evidently to be commandeered. So, within fifteen minutes of their anchoring, some hundreds of men were already on the move.

The soldiers and marines in the bows of each boat sat facing forrard with their rifles trained on the confused shadows of the houses ahead. While the moonlight still intermittently disappeared behind thick cloud, they just managed to observe the movement of a huddle of people gathering on the snowy shore. Enemy soldiers? No. Binkley-Walling called out to his men, 'Hold your fire!'

In the middle of the cluster of people was a white sheet raised atop an oar. It was attempting to flutter in the wind, a clear sign of surrender; and so they should surrender, the major thought, with the guns of the three cruisers pointing straight at them.

None of the men noticed the cold. Their minds were completely focused on what their reaction would be if the night erupted into flame ahead of them. Then the bows of the boats were sliding noisily across the gradual slope of the shingle and every man not charged with responsibility for the craft themselves were jumping across the gunwales and running up the beach. Not far away from the water's edge, the shingle was coated with snow and the scrunching of many a boot echoed about them.

His revolver in hand, Binkley-Walling strode purposefully up to the small crowd gathered before him. There were about a dozen of them, already protesting or pleading in their own language. The major held up his hand to silence them. He wished he could see their faces clearly but he could not so he would just have to suppose from their tones that they were nervous of his presence.

'Are there any Germans nearby?' he asked, which paved the way for a fresh bout of unintelligible pleading.

Up ahead, the village was still shrouded in black silence, a few curtains being pulled aside where worried occupants were staring out. The surrendering representatives jabbered on.

'Good God!' the major snapped, 'Doesn't anybody speak any English?'

Then, looking around at his men, he enquired, 'Does anybody here speak Norwegian?' In the darkness, he assumed that they were all giving him blank looks, so he cried, 'Why the hell don't we have anyone who can speak Norwegian?'

'Sprechen sie Deutsch?' asked the man holding up the makeshift surrender flag.

'He's asking if we speak German, sir,' said Captain Avery, who had crept up beside them and was feeling very annoyed about the time being wasted on this impromptu negotiation.

Binkley-Walling fumed, 'Do I look like I speak German?'

'Parle vouz Francais?' asked Avery, but got nothing but a shrug from the civilian opposite.

'So everybody speaks something but not the thing that we want!' shouted Binkley-Walling. 'Top hole!'

Knowing that it was hopeless, he turned to his gathering officers and said, 'Captain Burghley, you and I will take Able and Baker Companies, and the marines, and start moving eastward to take the valley, check on the condition of its access and see how we might guard against parachute troops. Tomlinson, Charlie Company will move up these two lanes to our left and right and begin searching houses. If there's no opposition I want billets and adequate places for supply and ammunition dumps identified and designated by dawn.'

'Yes, sir,' came the chorus of answers.

He then left the huddle of civilians standing chilled in the snow while he heaved himself up onto the roadway and advanced up the steep lane to the left of the hill-surrounded Hemmeligstein, his boots threatening to slide unhelpfully on the patches of ice that peeked through the snow.

\*\*\*\*

Clark's oarsmen were finally flagging. The heavy work had continued throughout the short night and the sun had now been up for about an hour. On this, their last trip, they had taken in the remaining crates of ammunition from *Burscombe*'s multitude of stowages and behind them was the now familiar strip of land where the snow-covered wooden buildings, adorned with bright and uplifting coloured paintwork, sat snugly in the only rocky cove where the ground could possibly hold them. Off to the left they now clearly saw the gap between the hills where the track led through to the valley and the wild land which linked Trondheim to Narvik. The snow looked thick up there and they could distantly see the persevering KOYLIs trying to traverse it.

Back near the ship and the prospect of a rest, Clark looked out to the west across the lake to where a large pillar of black smoke poured skywards from behind the hills. This was the first time he had really paid any attention to that trouble scene from last night and began to wonder how terrible it was there. Then he noticed the faraway dot of a boat heading towards them across the lake and he rubbed his eyes to look harder. He could just see the oars breaking the water's surface either side of the small vessel. Germans?

With the fenders of his boat finally bumping against the *Burscombe*'s side, his men moved to hitch their blocks and tackles to the davits' lines but Lieutenant Selkirk – the First Lieutenant – standing on the deck above, stopped them. They looked up with enquiring and appalled looks.

Commander Locklin appeared from forrard, weaving his way between men pulling on ropes or clearing up scattered equipment. He looked over the side and saw Clark below. 'Ah, some volunteers.'

He motioned vaguely towards the expanse of the lake, 'The admiral wants you to find out if there are Germans in that approaching cutter. They're not answering our requests to identify themselves so they either comply or we machine gun them. Clear?'

'Very good, sir!' Clark called back, noting that his oarsmen were looking extremely unhappy; not that they said a word for it was not their place. How sympathetic should he be? He looked back up at the commander and said, 'Sir, these men are all done in! Can I have fresh oarsmen?'

Locklin frowned. He was not used to being questioned after giving his orders. However, he was not completely ignorant of the requirements either. These same men had been pulling on their oars for hours while other men back here had had a relatively easy time of it. What was more, fresh men would be better placed to have their wits about them if they were dealing with a possible enemy.

A few minutes later, the exhausted men had climbed up the rope ladder while the new lot, armed with rifles, descended upon the lines. Pincher and the Turtle were amongst those assembled. That was handy, thought Clark, for he knew them to be good men in a sticky situation.

As they pushed off from the *Burscombe*'s side, the men could see that Clark was desperately fighting off sleep. He did not want his senses to seem impaired in any way so he put his hand into the freezing water and scooped some up over his face. Yes, that was better.

The boats began to draw near to each other and Clark strained his eyes to see the occupants of the other. He drew his revolver and held it at the ready, the oarsmen watching his movements. 'Ahoy there!' he yelled. 'Heave to!'

Then one of the mysterious crew ahead stood up above his companions and Clark thought that he recognised that bearded face and sturdy posture. 'It's Michaelsen, isn't it?'

'Yes, I am Michaelsen,' came the heavily accented reply, 'and you are HMS *Burscombe*.'

Clark suddenly had a feeling of dread creeping over him and he just had to know the answer to what he suspected. 'Is that the *Dagrand* burning over there?'

'Yes,' answered the ancient deck hand. 'The fire is nearly out but we are much damaged by your guns.'

The boats pulled alongside each other and Clark noticed a blackened German naval officer sitting amongst the Norwegian oarsmen, his right arm hanging bloodily in a dirty sling. Michaelsen said, 'That's Kapitan-Leutnant Schulze, come to surrender. We have forty two Germans still on board our ship.'

Clark thought of the German destroyer crews who had had little chance of escape during last night's lightning attack. 'Just forty two?'

'Yes, all the rest are dead.'

That was approximately four hundred men perished in just a few minutes. Clark felt momentarily sickened but then calmed his mind with the stern thought that they had started it. They had to reap what they sowed. He then asked, 'What of Captain Bakkevig?'

'He's all right... well, nearly all right.'

Nearly all right? Clark could well imagine what that meant. He decided that Bakkevig might need an offer of assistance so told Michaelsen to take his German to surrender to Rear-Admiral Nicklesworth while he went on to the *Dagrand*.

He lifted his torch up from the thwart and begun to flash the morse as well as he was able back to the *Burscombe*, guessing that the yeoman on the receiving end was probably wincing at the shaky effort. Once a reply was received, Clark ordered his men to pull off in the other direction, towards the pillar of smoke.

****

They exited the lake and rounded the shoreline to slowly approach the damaged ship. Some of the rails up forrard had been smashed, some deck ripped up and a sizeable hole punched in the hull above the waterline. The jagged steel was twisted outwards so a shell had obviously exploded within her thin frame. The ageing paintwork along the length of the upper decks was ruined further by scorching, evidence of the hell of the previous night's conflagration.

Clark had been able to smell the smoke a long way off. He watched as a mixed crowd of bedraggled men appeared at the side rail – German seamen standing alongside the Norwegian merchant sailors. It was an eerily peaceful approach, these spectators staring forlornly. The inaction told of the Germans' continued shock at the severity of the attack. What could they really do? Their ships were lying wrecked under the surface and the Royal Navy dominated the fjord.

A figure pushed in between those standing at the rail and heaved a rope ladder over the side. Clark, Pincher and the Turtle immediately recognised the young lad, Oskar, who had been so helpful to them the last time they had met. He was waving enthusiastically, saying, 'Hey, hey, Turtle.'

Clark led his men up onto the deck, coughing as the filthy air swirled about them. While the Germans watched passive and subdued, he asked the boy, 'It's Oskar, isn't it?'

The soot-streaked boy replied, 'Yes.'

As the prisoners were gently herded together, Clark continued with Oskar, 'You have my utmost apologies for what happened. Are any of your crew hurt?'

'Two hands are killed,' Oskar said in his clumsy accent, looking like he might want to cry but stopping himself ably, 'and Bernie, the radioman, is injured with his leg.'

'We have surgeons who will take care of him. What of the Germans?'

'These are okay,' said Oskar, nodding at them, 'eleven in the cabin are hurt and we have twenty eight bodies on the stern.'

That meant that most of the four hundred dead were still inside those two wrecks under the surface not that many yards away. Bubbles were still rising, swishing the surface where air was escaping from one of them. Once again he had to reason with himself on the nature of war to stop from being overly concerned.

He walked over to the officer who looked to be in charge, a man who was wearing torn epaulettes of the rank of leutnant. This officer said wearily, 'I congratulate your captain on his attack. May I have the pleasure of knowing his name?'

'No, you may not.' Clark understood that this campaign was far from decided and he was not going to yield a single piece of information to a man who might yet be back amongst his own very soon, not even for the sake of honest chivalry; and definitely not while he was this tired. 'One of our ships will be picking you up very shortly and then you'll be taken to Britain.'

The leutnant, offended at not having his question answered, narrowed his eyes and said, 'You will not be so happy with yourself once you've lost this war.'

Clark did not want to think about the wider subject of the war right at this moment. 'I advise you not to speak so freely about us losing. After all, it's *you* who's about to be put into a prison camp.'

'We'll see. Your English arrogance far outstrips your practicality.'

'Shut up.'

As the leutnant smiled back, Clark turned to Oskar and asked, 'Where's your captain?'

'On the bridge,' said Oskar. 'He will not talk to you.'

'He has no choice.'

Clark walked on with purpose, climbed up the ladder and pushed open the burnt hatch to enter the bridge. Oskar followed, his face still showing sorrow and worry but his actions demonstrating decisiveness.

As soon as Captain Bakkevig saw that his bridge was being invaded, he turned and glared at the midshipman, the impertinent young man who thought he was some sort of authority on board this ship. Well, damn him! Bakkevig shot forward, truly a man possessed, grabbing him powerfully by the front of his coat. There was to be no more talk. These last few months of fear and caution had got them nowhere and pounding this boy was going to make up for it beautifully.

Clark attempted to break away from the captain's grasp but he was too strong. Then somebody else intervened.

It was the Turtle. He reached out and caught Bakkevig's wrist, matching the Norwegian's strength and more. 'You wanna try that with me?' he asked menacingly.

Bakkevig's maniacal eyes were bloodshot and surrounded by heavy, dark lids. His chin was unshaven and the corners of his mouth pushed down. There were more lines on his face than they remembered and the ghoulish figure erupted into a furious tirade. The flow of words thundered from him to the accompaniment of angry hand gestures.

Clark looked to Oskar.

The round-eyed lad said, 'He tells you to go.'

'We came to offer him assistance.'

'He wants nothing from you.'

Clark shook his head and tutted. 'Are the engines working?'

'Yes.'

Bakkevig then launched into a diatribe aimed at his young apprentice. Beyond the understanding of Clark and the Turtle, the nature of Bakkevig's words was this: 'You keep thinking that these people are your friends. English? German? There's no difference. Every few years they fight each other and drag everybody around them down. Wake up, Oskar, the one is as bad as the other and I forbid you have anything to do with them. What will your father say if he hears that I let your attention be diverted to some stupid loyalty to people that want you dead? I mean, look at what they did to my ship last night. They fired on me like I was German too.'

Oskar, deeply ashamed to have to hit back at the man he had once revered and still thanked for stooping to give him a job, felt that things had gone way too far. In high emotion, emphasised by his barely broken voice, he said, 'Please, sir, see who is at fault here. We were fired on by accident and they stopped their attack as soon as they realised we were no threat. The Germans are invading our country...'

'The Germans are protecting us from the British, you fool!'

'That's all horseshit! The British were never going to invade! And who would *you* want as a friend? Hitler or Chamberlain? Eh?'

The very second that Oskar had let slip his profanity, Bakkevig's body had nearly ruptured with rage. Here was somebody who really needed to be taught a lesson.

But the Turtle had been watching closely. He may not have understood the words going back and forth between them but the body language was unmistakeable. He took a step forward and halted the captain with a definitive shake of his head before he could do anything stupid.

Bakkevig looked at him with shocked surprise. He shouted in Norwegian, 'Who the hell are you to stop me doing what I need to do on the deck of my own ship?'

'That's enough!' came another gruff shout from the door.

Bakkevig paused and looked to see his old radio man, Bernie, standing there, leaning slightly to one side as he painfully held himself up with the aid of a wooden crutch.

He said, 'Captain, you will profit nothing from beating the boy. He has a point about who we should consider to be friends and enemies.'

'You too?' said Bakkevig, his shock deepening.

'You know that our government has ordered us to make ourselves available to the British...'

'Our defeated government?' cried Bakkevig. 'Quisling is our prime minister now and he has ordered no such thing.'

'I've worked for you for twenty years and I love you like a brother but you've got to get your perspective sorted out on this one. You've been under a lot of pressure in your efforts to keep us all safe. A lot of other captains have failed and died but you are still here. Now, we'll stand by you if you won't help the English Navy but at the same time we should not hinder them.'

In that moment, Bakkevig begun to feel like a fool. He knew that Bernie was right. He turned and walked slowly away, mostly as an attempt to hide the shame that filled his expression. He hated himself. Why, after everything he had been through, was he so scared? Why had everything become so complicated when all he was trying to do was deliver goods from one country to another? Furthermore, how much was he still in control of his own ship? It was his by law after all.

Changing his expression to the charade of considered anger, he turned and pointed at Oskar. 'You are fired. I want you off my ship now.'

Tears suddenly sprung from the boy's eyes and streaked down his dirty face. Of all the things he had seen, believed, done or had done to him, this was the ultimate disgrace. 'Please, captain, I beg you don't fire me!'

'Get off my ship!'

\*\*\*\*

When Michaelsen's cutter reached the *Burscombe*, orders had already reached the waist for the Master-at-Arms to take the German kapitan-leutnant down below where they could keep his prying eyes away from the continuing operation. The Norwegian himself, stressing that he had important information about the geography of the fjord, was held in the waist until Nicklesworth and Dollimore appeared with Peterson and Irwin in tow.

From there, they went aft and crossed the brass bar onto the quarterdeck.

Noting with interest the activity on the ships and shore and the multitude of anti-aircraft gunners standing by their weapons on this bright but freezing morning, Michaelsen followed the formalities of introductions with, 'You were very lucky to get your ships into the lake but not so lucky, I think, now.' He pointed out across the water to where these waters flowed into the narrows of the fjord itself. 'Under the water there, there is a terminal moraine, just over twenty four of your feet at high tide.'

'There's a what?' asked Nicklesworth.

Dollimore immediately looked over at his navigating officers. 'Perhaps one of you two would be better placed to explain.'

Peterson purposely paused because he suddenly perceived a surge of confidence appearing in the lieutenant standing beside him. Irwin happily explained, 'A terminal moraine is, in effect, a large mound of rocks and the like pushed into a wall by moving glaciers over the course of thousands of years. This lake here was formed by the force of melting glaciers and that terminal moraine marks the final point where the land was churned up before the overflow formed the fjord itself. It's dashed unfortunate we didn't know about it before.'

'And, by the sounds of it, damned lucky we didn't run aground,' commented Nicklesworth, his satisfaction with the landing now turning extremely sour.

Michaelsen nodded. 'This is what I'm trying to say.'

'Well, why didn't we know about it?' continued Nicklesworth, glaring at Irwin.

As the young officer gave a perplexed look and a shrug, Peterson explained, 'The chart's only as accurate as it is, sir.'

Dollimore, wanting to deflect from that pointless line of questioning, asked Michaelsen, 'Are you local to these parts?'

'No.'

'Then, please explain the basis of your knowledge.'

'You don't trust me?'

'It's not a question of trust, old man. If you were receiving intelligence that would affect your operation, would you not enquire after *all* of the facts?'

Michaelsen calmed a little when he considered the argument and cautiously explained, 'It's why this lake is not used as an anchorage for large vessels.'

Nicklesworth let his head lean slightly to one side as he frowned, 'But that still doesn't explain how you know about this moraine thing. Did the Germans have a pilot with them?'

'No. We were led up the fjord by a big German ship – what was it named? – *Moltke*. It hit the rocks and had to reverse back out.'

'The *Moltke*?' repeated Dollimore, as usual hiding his excitement and the resulting shame of that excitement. 'Her draft is much deeper than ours and so is the *Dagrand*'s. That's why you anchored in the side bay and didn't enter the lake. Was the *Moltke* damaged?'

'I don't know. I don't think so.'

'Not significantly, then,' stated Nicklesworth. 'I wonder where the bugger is now. Why were the Germans in this fjord in the first place? How did you come to be mixed up with them?'

'We were in the wrong place, wrong time – as always.'

Nicklesworth considered that for a second and then turned to Irwin. 'Send a boat over to the lake entrance, one of those motor fishing boats. That'll be faster. Get them to take soundings to confirm these reports.'

Michaelsen started angrily, 'I said you didn't trust me! What does it take to convince you of my helping?'

'Calm yourself, Mr Michaelsen, don't take it so personally. By the way, we need an interpreter on the shore. Would you be in the market to help us out?'

The grizzled old Norwegian grumbled, 'Ah, help yourself out,' and stalked off towards his boat, there to get himself back to the *Dagrand*.

\*\*\*\*

A couple of hours later, Clark leapt over the gunwale of his cutter onto the shingle at Hemmeligstein and then proceeded through the trampled snow to Lieutenant Eddington's miserable command shed. One of the houses further up the slope may have been a better billet but this sizeable shack was best placed to command the comings and goings on the beach for the time being. Piles of ropes, nets and hooks had been thrown out into the snow and a small coal-burning stove set up in their place. Steaming away merrily on top was a kettle with a teapot standing by.

Accompanied by the Turtle, Pincher, Oskar Fjeldstad and a few other seamen, Clark quickly updated Eddington with the latest on the terminal moraine, then asked, 'The captain wants to know if you're still having trouble finding an interpreter, sir.'

'Yes, I am,' replied Eddington, 'I've not come across a people so cut off from civilisation since I was trying to order a Pimm's in Glasgow.'

'In that case, sir, this lad here has offered his services.'

Eddington stared past his shoulder and smiled, 'Ah, good-oh. You're the boy from the *Dagrand*. Awfully sorry about what happened last night.'

Oskar could not share a reciprocal smile. Still upset by Bakkevig's dismissal of him, he just wanted to get down to work.

'All over some bloody valley,' the Turtle moaned, careful that the officers were out of earshot.

'It's the only one way to get to Narvik and to Trondheim,' explained Oskar. He had been staying close to the big ugly man because there was an unspoken accord between them which obviously stretched back to their first meeting on that long-gone wintry day. He still had with him the cap tally that the Turtle had given him. It was one of his prized possessions. 'Norway here is getting thinner and thinner. You go the other side of these hills, then another twenty miles and you are in Sweden.'

'Really?' The Turtle's frown was mistaken for being that of surprised interest but, of course, he was immediately contemplating his desertion. He glanced over at Pincher. Thankfully that busybody was more interested in filling the teapot than watching over him.

# ELEVEN

## The Stukas Attack

The tension created by the race in getting the men ashore and scouting the valley for the enemy eventually crumpled into a relieving anti-climax. Apart from the two sunken destroyers in the bay, there was no evidence to suggest that this part of the country even existed in the minds of the Germans. Their aircraft never appeared and there were no echoes from the fighting which they knew was taking place fifty miles to the south. Everything was so peaceful that it was almost as though Major Binkley-Walling had landed for nothing more than some sort of impromptu exercise.

If what the captive Kapitan-Leutnant Schulze said was true, his admiral in the *Moltke* had led his little force up the fjord then retreated having sent word that this place was unsuitable for his purposes. Why Schulze himself had been ordered to stay he could or would not tell. Nicklesworth and Dollimore concurred that the German's story was suspicious and neither rested easy until the 25th Cruiser Squadron was able to leave the fjord and get back out to sea with Fulton-Stavely's destroyers, keeping an eye out for the return of the battlecruiser.

Ashore, instead of flinging themselves head on into a duel to the death with Nazi parachute troops, the only excitement in the many long days following the landing was afforded them by the fact that the KOYLI's equipment was a great bloody shambles. Captain Tomlinson of Charlie Company stalked about Hemmeligstein for hours at a time full of an indefatigable rage which was emulated by the sergeant-major who was constantly at his heels. Their problems had evidently begun with the fact that everything had been packed by some unknown persons who neither knew nor cared about what they were doing.

It did not help that there was very little chance for anyone to get dry and warm either. The families living here in their picturesque houses had opened their doors – they had very little choice in the matter – but nobody was permitted enough down-time to truly benefit.

'Thank God for your signallers, Lieutenant,' Tomlinson told Eddington, not for the first time, his voice thundering as he and his sergeant-major half walked, half slid down the icy path to the shed on the beach.

The orders for the navy semaphore signallers to brave the elements atop the surrounding hills had gone out within the first day and they had positioned themselves accordingly but that did not prevent Tomlinson from constantly feeling the helplessness that the expedition's planners had foisted upon him. 'What do you suppose they were thinking when they sent us up here with no radios?'

Eddington, puffing away casually on a cigarette, said, 'The admiral's informed the War Office so we'll see if anything gets sent up in the next flotilla.'

Tomlinson glared at this infuriatingly blasé navy officer and had to bite his tongue. They had already had the conversation about borrowing short-wave radios from the cruisers but Rear-Admiral Nicklesworth had flatly refused, citing the workload that his telegraphists had to contend with. Wartime radio traffic at sea was constant and demanded all their available resources for they could not afford to miss a single message. It was not his fault that the army could not get its act together.

Believing that succumbing to bad temper also would help no one, Eddington had long since decided to stay calm and do only what he could to alleviate the situation. 'A cup of tea?'

That question made Tomlinson want to howl with anger. However, he had enough reasoning power left to understand that he could solve nothing more now and so temporarily laid aside his anger for the sake of a little warmth. 'Yes, thank you,' he sighed in defeat.

Eddington turned and called inside the shed, 'Martin, bring Captain Tomlinson and I a brew and make sure they've got a couple of sugars in them.'

Once Pincher had brought out the cups of steaming liquid and the two officers were seated on damp stools, Tomlinson naturally calmed somewhat as he sipped away. Shuffling uncomfortably, he said, 'My mother always said that sitting on cold surfaces would give me piles.'

'You didn't believe that hogwash, did you?' asked Eddington.

'Me and my lads have spent this last winter with our arses stuck to cold surfaces …'

'And how many of them have piles?'

'One of them does, actually,' Tomlinson laughed. 'No, seriously, though, where do they get off sending us up here half-cocked? Our heaviest weapons, the 3-inch mortars, only have five rounds apiece, we only have six anti-tank rifles and no land mines. Our air defence? Ten Lewis Guns and you know they're vintage.' It was true, those heavy-barrelled machine guns with their distinctive circular magazines had been used by the British Army since 1915. 'So, we're dependent on our personal weapons and a couple of heavy machine guns with ammunition enough for three days of fighting – provided we don't run up against anything more than the blasted parachute troops that we didn't find here – and don't get me started on the rations. If we don't get resupplied soon, we're going to starve. The bastards at the War Office want their heads knocked together.'

'Hopefully the admiral's got the point across,' said Eddington. 'Anyway, should the operations around Trondheim succeed then Jerry's invasion will be stalled and we should be able to just pack up and leave this place without a fight. I've caught the buzz that we'll easily defeat them there, so chin up.'

'I shall pray for the capture of Trondheim when I take my boots off tonight,' said a much-placated Tomlinson. Then he stood. 'Thank you for the tea.'

Nodding to his sergeant-major, who had procured a cup of tea and a cigarette at the shed door, he moved on to his next irritation.

\*\*\*\*

Major Binkley-Walling considered the three hills straddling the northern end of the snowbound valley of paramount importance. On the reverse slopes were where he placed his few 3-inch mortars, their spotters just above the highest trees on the forward sides where they commanded a view of the open ground to the south. He had placed Able and Baker Companies in the woods with the marines and had ordered them to dig in, a task made difficult as they found the ground under the snow not just frozen but rocky as well. Finally, he had set up his headquarters in a shack built of wood taken from homes in Hemmeligstein. This was covered by a heavy machine gun at the start of the uneven track which led to that village.

Marine Sergeant Burroughs and his new pal, Sergeant White, pushed their way up the tree-covered slope and stopped in front of the makeshift HQ. There, they stooped down and began to undo the short, thin lengths of rope which held their tennis racquets to their boots.

The other blokes had laughed at them the first time they had put on these 'snow shoes' but then everybody had had such a hard time working their way along the two mile track that they had since asked repeatedly where they had got them from. But only a total of seven racquets had been scoured from the officers of the 25th, including Captain Dollimore's, along with the nineteen pairs of actual snow shoes taken from the locals. More pairs had been placed on the list of required equipment to be sent out from Britain but, as the days passed, the soldiers gave up any hope of receiving them. They came to the conclusion that this, along with all the other shortages, was the consequence of not being part of the main force down south; and so there was added a strained sense of being forgotten by the authorities.

Captain Avery of the Royal Marines, having just finished making his latest report to the young major, stepped out of the shadowy, crooked doorway and regarded the sergeants with a look of disdain. He always wore that look whether he was fed up or not.

'Sir,' Burroughs said directly, 'are we likely to be here long?'

'Why's that?' asked Avery. 'You have somewhere you need to be?'

Burroughs was cold and had long ago decided that he either wanted a fight or the order to go home. One was just as good as the other, but he said, 'No, sir, it's just that me and Whitey have had an idea for the Lewis Guns if we're stopping here much longer.'

'Oh yes?'

'Well, they're all we've got to have a go at enemy planes and there's only a couple of places where we can elevate them effectively. We thought that the *Burscombe*'s artificers could easily knock up some gimbal mounts in their machine shop.'

Avery put on his usual frown, the one he used to let a man know that his input was a hindrance. 'You know that Captain Dollimore can't give us anything that rightly belongs on board.'

'With respect, sir, it's the admiral what won't help,' said Burroughs, Avery's warning frown having had no impact on him whatsoever.

'Sergeant, don't presume to know what the policies of your officers are.'

'I wouldn't, sir,' replied Burroughs, unperturbed, 'not in month of Sundays. But if we can put the guns on decent mounts then we can train and elevate them much easier and, let's face it, we ain't gonna see those Hurricanes, are we?'

'You don't know that,' said Avery with growing anger, but that was just a usual part of the dynamic between these two men. Captain Avery would get angry with his pushy sergeant but he never stopped listening to him. 'And anyway, to go behind the captain's back and simply take what we need is a serious offence. What exactly have you got in mind?'

Burroughs took on a triumphant look and nodded at Sergeant White to take over the explanation. He had told him that his officer would be okay about it.

White pulled a small notebook and pencil from his greatcoat pocket and began sketching a crude diagram, saying as he went, 'All you need, sir, is a base-plate, a pillar on some sort of bearing so it can swivel, and a large horse-shoe shaped piece at the top that we can attach the gun to. Then we can stand and use the gun in any direction at shoulder height, sir, turning whichever way we want.'

Having taken the sketch and stuffed it into his tunic pocket, Avery went back into the shadowed doorway saying, 'I can't promise anything.'

But next time he was in Hemmeligstein, he passed it onto Lieutenant Eddington, who immediately beckoned Clark to join them.

Clark looked at the sketch and asked, 'What's this, sir?'

'A gimbal mount,' explained Eddington.

Avery, disgusted at the idea of being questioned by a 'snotty', said forcefully, 'I want one of these for each of the Lewis Guns we have. Our artificers can make them easily enough.'

Looking confused, Clark said, 'Have the restrictions on taking equipment from the *Burscombe* been lifted then, sir?'

'Don't get smart with me, boy. Take that sketch to Warrant Officer Hacklett. He owes me a few favours.'

'Hacklett?' Clark asked, genuinely surprised. 'But I never knew a man more of a stickler for the rules.'

As Avery clenched his fists and raised his shoulders, Eddington butted in with, 'Clark, just do as you're told and don't blab about it. Just your sort of caper, no?'

Clark smiled and trudged off across the ice to the water's edge where one of the commandeered fishing boats sat, its black bow lodged gently upon the shingle. With the help of the stoker, he pushed it out and leapt up onto its slippery deck. Soon he had the engine running.

As the boat turned to chug away, Avery noticed a name crudely painted on its side in light blue lettering. '*Free Spirit*?' he asked.

'Yes,' sighed Eddington, 'that's how that young man sees himself; and he knows better than anybody else that it's his free spirit which has prevented him from being promoted already. That said, I still think he shows great promise.'

A scowl was the only reaction Avery could muster.

\*\*\*\*

Clark also had on board three soldiers – two with influenza and one with a broken wrist – who he had been due to deliver to the *Burscombe*'s sick bay before picking up provisions and rum for the sailors working ashore, so those jobs could easily cover his more clandestine requirements. One wondered why the army had not been given more support in the first place but that was another matter. Having made the long journey down the fjord, he found the ship hove to in choppy waters being guarded by the other circling cruisers and destroyers. He steered the boat to come along her leeside.

Leaving his men to carry out the other tasks, he wasted no time in locating WO Hacklett, who was presently conferring with an artificer about the explosives for the Walrus catapult on the flight deck. He walked up to the otherwise unapproachable man and immediately held out the piece of paper. 'From Captain Avery, sir, says he could do with ten of these for his Lewis Guns and says you'd know what to do. I'll pick them up tomorrow morning.'

Needless to say, Hacklett had never really warmed to Midshipman Clark; seemed to think he knew an awful lot more than he did. But then, Dollimore appeared to hold a grudging respect for the lad and *his* opinion was almost on a par with God's. Hacklett raised himself up to full height and twisted his already twisted face into a look of disgust. 'Ah, eav' a i'e. Na, u'a oa!'

Clark was unimpressed. Sowing the seeds of confusion and doubt just for the sake of it might rattle the men of the lower decks but it did not wash with him. 'Yes,' he replied, 'I understand that to be the sentiment of the day, sir.'

Hacklett watched him go. That bastard handles himself well, he thought. Maybe he might be due some of that grudging respect so long as he doesn't do anything too stupid. We'll see. He's never been in a real battle yet. That'll decide the issue.

As for Captain Avery, Hacklett would happily see what he could do about his gimbal mounts. Their brains operated on the same level.

Everything was about service, loyalty, winning and taking to task any man who thought otherwise; that and the fact that Avery had recently somehow supplied him with some Cuban cigars. Hacklett had smoked just one of the precious things so far and now knew it to be everything it had been reputed to be – pure bliss.

Once he had finished with the artificer on the flight deck he took himself off below to see ERA Jones, one of the more senior artificers and very crafty whist partner who did not mind a sneaky challenge.

\*\*\*\*

The following morning, Captain Dollimore was seated in his sea cabin when he was informed that *Free Spirit* was once again alongside. 'Thank you,' he said to the waiting seaman. 'Please ask Midshipman Clark to report here immediately.'

Of course, Clark was a little stunned to be summoned like this. He had been making these runs out the *Burscombe* every day since they had arrived and the captain had not seen fit to acknowledge his presence until now. Why today of all days? Had something gone wrong with their plan? Had Dollimore discovered their underhanded activities? He steeled himself for the confrontation, thinking through the various arguments which he might need and was duly relieved when the captain did nothing more than place a thick envelope in his hand. He was not sure, but was the captain looking graver than usual?

Dollimore said, 'This is for Major Binkley-Walling, Mr Clark. You are to place it in his hand and no other, you understand?'

'Yes, sir.'

Aware that Clark was likely to become inquisitive, Dollimore cursed himself for the possibility of giving away any emotion. Yes, there had been plenty for him and Nicklesworth to think about in the last hour or so but that was no excuse, so he immediately cleared up his expression, saying, 'Tell me more about the conditions ashore …'

Clark talked him through the various deprivations. He was not informing the captain of anything he did not already know and felt that he was just being fobbed off. But that was the captain's right. He had given his orders and asked a question. Nothing else was Clark's business.

Before too long had passed, a message came down the voicepipe from Peterson on the bridge. 'Sir, Fulton-Stavely's relief has arrived. Three more destroyers.'

Once again, the *Crayhorn* and the *Catterley* had reached the end of their endurance with barely enough oil fuel to reach Scapa Flow. Also, their rations had been supplemented by the 25th for some days now.

'Thank you,' Dollimore replied then turned back to Clark. 'Well, away with you, boy. Keep up the good work.'

'Very good, sir,' Clark answered, thinking that the captain would not be so nice if he knew what they were up to.

Once the midshipman was gone, Dollimore tidied up the papers on his desk. But putting everything back in its place was just a gesture to orderliness while his brain was otherwise engaged upon the news which Clark was now carrying to the major. The massive pincer movement with which the British Army had been planning to capture Trondheim had never happened. The two ports of origin, Namsos and Andalsnes, where they had been due to push out from, had been bombed heavily by the Luftwaffe and the army had been evacuated by sea. But that failure was only the beginning of the problem.

The most sinister part of the story was these orders from the War Office, those which Clark was conveying to Binkley-Walling at this very minute – orders effectively telling him to stand and fight where he was. They were nothing short of murder and Nicklesworth, finally showing keener judgment, had rightly signalled a personal objection to them.

Dollimore could not bear to think about it any longer and decided to go to the bridge to observe the approaching destroyers and bid Fulton-Stavely a good luck farewell. Once outside in the cutting wind, he looked at the ships, feeling their power but also their vulnerability in the eerie gloom. As a sudden moment of light burst through the shifting clouds, his eye caught the fishing boat, *Free Spirit*, as it made its way towards the fjord, bobbing heavily on the high waves.

He pointed down to her and asked Peterson, 'What do you suppose is lurking under those canvas sheets?'

'I'm sure I don't know, sir.'

Dollimore called for Commander Locklin and very quickly the EXO climbed out onto the wet bridge, his breath emerging as vapour. 'Sir?'

The captain motioned to the boat entering the fjord on the ingoing tide and said, 'They've embarked something a little more than their usual provisions. Please look into it.'

'Very good, sir,' answered Locklin. Thus he snooped around the ship and questioned the men, appalled but intrigued at the fact that some conspiracy was at work right under his and the captain's very noses. He asked a few questions, got no solid answers and wondered that, if he checked certain stores' paperworks, he would probably find discrepancies.

But did he give the investigation his all? The fact that stopped him pressing too hard was that the army and marines had been sent ashore to do a very difficult job with hardly any working equipment and that just was not on. Still, he wrote something in the form of a report and typed up his suspicions. 'Sir, my investigation,' he said, eventually handing the brown file over to Dollimore in his cabin.

The captain read through Locklin's findings in short order and said, 'It's a little sparse. Some equipment has been removed from my ship but you have no idea as to the identities of the perpetrators? Evidently Midshipman Clark is in on it; but on his own or for personal gain? Never. That's not his style.' Because he thinks too much like me, he reasoned. Clark was certainly growing to understand that the wider picture was more important than one's self.

Eventually, he closed the file and laid it down on the desk. 'Clearly some sort of punishment is in order for, if proved, it's no less than theft of Admiralty property. Thank you, EXO. Please leave this with me.'

\*\*\*\*

Albert 'Les' Gordy climbed fitfully up the rope ladder serving the whaler at *Burscombe*'s side then waved back down to the lads who were hitching the mail bags to a line, there to be hoisted aboard. 'Thanks for the lift!' he called.

'Any time! See yer 'round!' came the answer – a brother Irishman, albeit one from the north.

Les was looking healthy and happy with himself, which he knew was very different from how his shipmates would remember him. He had always been stick-thin and pale before, confused and wandering around with a gormless look on his face. There had been just so much he did not understand that he should have been ripe for the slaughter if Pincher Martin was not always watching his back. But today he wore a look of fresh understanding backed up by exuberant colour. That was what happened when he spent time with people who showed him a little patience. From Lieutenant Hanwell in the Walrus to the seamen of the destroyer he had just arrived in, they had treated him very differently to… well, Smudge and the Turtle. It was they who generally set the tone that the other bullies in the *Burscombe* went by.

After reporting to the office of the Regulating Branch that he was back aboard, he passed the torpedo tubes and catapult and entered into the passageway which led to his mess. He was just attempting to decide whether he was actually happy to be back when he walked past the idiotic Smudge waiting in a queue outside the provision issue room. Of course, it was nearly time for 'Up Spirits'.

The usually comedic able seaman, presently disposed to irritability since this mission had devolved into something as commonplace as those endless patrols, was suddenly very dismayed to find Les looking so well and put out a hand to stop him as he went by. The boy had colour in his cheeks! Christ, he even had a bit of tan! Where the hell had he been able to pick up a tan from? 'What you doin' back? I thought you'd been lost in action.'

Already, one or two of the other men in the queue were preparing to laugh as they witnessed the exchange.

'I don't know about that,' said Les, his voice almost singing with happiness, 'but I'll tell you what did happen...'

'No, there ain't no time for all that. You should be dead. We even auctioned off all your kit to send the money back to your mum; all apart from than weird stick you've got with the knobbly bit on the end what we don't know what it's for. Your mum can have that back.'

'I ain't got no stick,' said Les, his freshly confused face dropping.

Suddenly, Paddy Walbrook appeared, climbing through the nearby hatch clutching his fanny in preparation to collect the rum issue for his mess. His hard, brown eyes stared out menacingly from his wide face. 'Les, it's good to have you back,' he said, with more than a hint of warning to those wanting to bully him. 'Where you been?'

Relieved, Les replied, 'Well, when we flew...'

'Hold onto it, lad,' Paddy suddenly said, holding out a hand to silence him. 'Tell me later. Rum's up.' With that, he made a point of pushing in front of Smudge in order to let the attending chief and lieutenant measure out his mess's ration, then disappeared forrard.

'Oh, aye,' said Smudge, staring at Les, his nose even more out of joint. 'Paddy's new 'ammock buddy, are you? All right, so you was captured by the enemy, escaped and'll probably get a medal too. What sort of justice is that? I bet you busted the Walrus an' all.'

'No...'

'But you did bring the spur-lash back with you, didn't you?'

This time Les was completely stopped dead in his tracks. Desperately trying to picture the spur-lash which he could not even remember taking with him, he began to wonder what he must have done with it. 'Er, no...'

The colour started disappearing from his cheeks as the other men laughed at him.

\*\*\*\*

When Captain Tomlinson climbed up onto deck of *Free Spirit* and took in the weight of one of the gimbal mounts by pulling at it, he all but shouted, 'How the bloody hell are we going to get these things down to the valley; let alone up the hill to the signaller's position?'

Lieutenant Eddington, having walked along Hemmeligstein's beach with his Hollywood-like swagger, asked of him, 'Have you never heard of the siege of Ladysmith or the Royal Navy Field Gun Tournament? No? Then let me educate you...'

So it was that, under his direction and using the skills of the able seamen and equipment to hand, the gimbals were dragged across the dreadfully uneven ground – made more treacherous by the snow's gradual thaw – on small purpose-built carts or, with jackstays and pulleys, up the slopes of the hill. Tomlinson was impressed with the sailors' prowess and vowed never to doubt Eddington again.

\*\*\*\*

Clark got out of that work thanks to the urgent nature of the dispatch that he had been charged with delivering. However, he still found the two miles tough going, the sliding about on the ice placing strain on his knees and hips; and his boots were wet through again. He had heard the horror stories of men having had their feet amputated thanks to the rigours of trenchfoot during the last war. The affliction had been so called because of its prevalence in the waterlogged trenches of Flanders Fields and the Somme. This in turn made him long to get his boots off in front of Eddington's hot stove. He shivered in spite of his exertions.

He eventually descended along the steep track to the HQ, passing from the open air from where he could observe the southern valley, into the trees which concealed the heavy machine gun post. Soldiers were moving about here and there, working hard or punching at their own arms in an attempt to keep warm. Clark noticed that the holes they were living in were only covered by branches and natural foliage pulled from or about the trees. There were no tents; another oversight.

At the doorway to the ramshackle HQ, he had his presence announced by one of the aides and was then asked to enter. The damp, smelly interior was dimly lit by carefully placed candles since the weak daylight could not penetrate deep enough into the corners. The place was just big enough to hold a desk, two seats and two camp beds. On the desk was a pile of reports and a telephone, Binkley-Walling's only modern link to his front line which was nearly a mile to the south.

'Ah, young Clark,' he said jovially. 'Always at the forefront of everything, eh? It's the only way to get on, you know.'

'Yes, sir,' the midshipman replied. 'From the War Office, sir,' he continued, handing over the large envelope. As for his actual desire to get on, he decided to allude to it no further. While he could claim strong loyalty to the *Burscombe*, he could not give two hoots about the navy. It was only in his blood because his father had told him it was; and he had hated his father.

Binkley-Walling sliced open the envelope with the letter knife that lived amongst his papers, unfolded the sheets and read every word carefully, making grunting noises and twitching his face unhappily as he went. His already red nose and cheeks went redder as his moustache jerked from left to right. 'Loggins,' he eventually said to his aide, the private who had been waiting patiently alongside Clark. 'Take down this message and have copies sent to all company commanders, marine detachment commander and beach commander: "The front around Namsos has collapsed. It is reasonable to expect the German Army to drive on our position in the near future. We are to hold this valley at all costs".'

He could hardly hide his dismay as he said the words and now Clark understood why Dollimore's feathers had been more ruffled than usual. It was not his place to say but, how were four hundred freezing, poorly fed, ill-equipped men to hold off a victorious enemy that undoubtedly would come at them with tanks and artillery, not to mention the full fury of the Luftwaffe?

He could only venture a token, 'I suppose Chamberlain needs us to hold on to the north of the country, sir.'

'So it seems.'

'After all, he gave guarantees to the Norwegians ...'

'Quite,' barked Binkley-Walling, 'but there's no sign of *their* bloody army anywhere either.'

Clark gave a frown. 'They were in the south, sir. If they've not been evacuated too then we should assume they've been defeated.'

'Probably shouldn't have depended on them anyway. It's their fault that the country stood open to attack in the first place.'

In that moment, Clark felt distaste for this major. He might be in a sticky situation but what was the worth in blaming the Norwegian Army for this predicament? The blame surely lay with Westminster's and Oslo's wishy-washy politics and the Germans' superior organisation. However, all that unspoken argument aside, Clark himself was more concerned about what could potentially happen right here in the name of political expediency.

Eager to change the tone and direction of the conversation, he asked, 'Has the admiral offered you the use of the squadron's guns, sir?'

Binkley-Walling gripped the paper tighter as though he never wanted to let go of it. 'Yes, he has, God save him. There's much work to be done. I need to meet with one of your gunnery officers to formulate a bombardment plan and I also need to impress upon the War Office the precariousness of my situation. Repel a few parachute troops, they said. Bloody hell! Loggins, have you finished those orders yet? Send them on their way. I have another dispatch to dictate for Clark here to take back with him. Why the hell don't I have any radios?'

\*\*\*\*

On the next day, during which Lt-Cdr Digby sent his 2nd Gunnery Officer ashore to confer with Binkley-Walling on the need for a possible naval bombardment, the heavens brightened considerably as the cruisers and destroyers continued to circle off the Tjierrefjord and, in light of the newly credible threat from the air, Dollimore began to wish that they could have more of that stormy weather which had been the bane of their lives for so long. But it was stupid to think that he could influence the actions of God. The Lord did what He had to do and if He decided this day needed to bring forth a clear sky then so be it. Dollimore felt that it was time for a taste of the trials to come anyway, so he was not surprised when one of the lookouts called, 'Enemy aircraft bearing green zero-four-zero!'

Lt-Cdr Peterson turned, looked off to starboard and immediately recognised twin-engine bombers of the same type that he had seen coming at them in the past. He immediately pressed the alarm button and announced through the ship, 'Enemy aircraft off the starboard beam! Enemy aircraft off the starboard beam!' Then he had orders relayed for the ERAs to lay on higher revs for manoeuvring.

Of course, the Oerlikons, pom-poms, 0.5 machine guns and 4-inch guns were all loaded and ready. Most of the men had seen this apparition before and found they were not as apprehensive as they once might have been. Sick to death with the quiet monotony of sea, squadron and mountains, they just wanted to shoot some stupid sod down.

Once the bombers were getting close, all the high-angle guns of the cruiser squadron opened up, spitting their cacophony of fire into the sky. Little black puffs appeared all around the aircraft and white tracers wormed their way to find the targets but then, quite inexplicably, the formation, unscathed, turned in a landward direction and flew off to circle round again, the pitch of their engines straining to the acceleration.

Nicklesworth, who had just come up onto the bridge, saw this happen. 'What on earth are they playing at?' he asked after the guns had fallen silent. 'Why did they not complete their bombing run?'

Many of the deafened men, like Les and Paddy, were standing by their smoking guns, grinning proudly at each other. They were not wondering, having come to the conclusion that the barrage they had put up had simply been too heavy.

But Dollimore remained uneasy. Some inkling that these slippery Jerries were up to something came to him but he decided to stay silent until his suspicions were confirmed. He watched as the planes completed their circle and came in again on the bombing run. The anti-aircraft guns thundered out more of the usual shrapnel and lead amongst the planes. Their defence, as before, had begun at extreme range; and that might just be the problem, he thought.

What he was thinking was suddenly fully justified when the formation of bombers turned away again. Now he knew what their deadly game was.

He turned to Nicklesworth as the guns all along the threatened waist fell silent. With some urgency, he said, 'They're purposely depleting our ammunition, sir.'

'What are you talking about?' returned the admiral. 'They just don't like the odds, that's all.'

Again, Dollimore felt that hideous temper rising in his chest. How much more effective would this squadron be if this admiral refrained from being present? He turned to Lt-Cdr Digby and, with tones unmasking his impatience, ordered, 'Guns, get me an estimate of ammunition used so far – and order your men to hold fire until the enemy are much closer.'

Immediately understanding the nature of the order, Digby swiftly went about his work while Dollimore turned back to Nicklesworth and said, 'And, sir, I would suggest you order the rest of the squadron to do the same.'

By now, Nicklesworth understood just what Dollimore was getting at but as ever, he did not appreciate being told what to do by this infernal man. Only, he was always right, damn it! Whatever was the right thing to do, his irritated pause delayed the signal enough so that the anti-aircraft guns of the other ships fired away hundreds more rounds of ammunition at extreme range without a hope of hitting anything just for the enemy to circle away for a third time. Only the *Burscombe* had held back.

As the next silence fell, a voice came up one of the voicepipes and Digby, after acknowledging receipt of the message, turned to the captain and said, 'Estimated twenty five per cent of our ammunition has been used, sir.'

Dollimore looked sharply at Nicklesworth but did not have to say anything. The admiral could do the maths as well as anyone else. At this rate the bombers only had to circle a few more times before they had three nice targets who would not have the ability to fire back; and it was not just today that they had to think about, but every day that was left of this deteriorating operation.

Chief Yeoman Ross flashed the orders to fire at a shortened range and then they waited once more. Soon the bombers were coming back over them and it was clear that the Germans had realised their little game was up for, when the ships held their fire until they could be sure of offering something more lethal, they simply decided to complete their run.

The bombers dropped their payloads from a high level. Those little black dots, as most had seen before, seemed to be coming straight for the *Burscombe*. Teeth were gritted, muscles were tensed and trigger fingers pressed harder in the ridiculous hope of deterring the course of the falling bombs.

The fury of the guns was then augmented by the sight and sound of the sea exploding all about them, fiery blasts seen within the frothing water. But somehow all the bombs dropped wide, much wider than their trajectories would have suggested and all six ships continued on their way unharmed. It was becoming clear that, with these high-level bombers, damage like that done to the *Castledown*, was actually the rarity and she had only succumbed because she had dropped out of line and slowed down.

Over the *Marsfield* a plane caught fire. An orange glow flashed out from one of its engines and the spluttering machine immediately flipped over to one side. Leaving a trail of black smoke winding in its wake, the plane spiralled out of control down to the sea and disappeared in a violent splash. Nobody had managed to get out and deploy a parachute. That was just their bad luck.

Cheers came up from the gun platforms just below the bridge and down in the waists. Dollimore would let them have their moment. They all knew that there was a lot worse to come before this was over.

'Sir,' one of the Yeomen suddenly said, 'a signal from shore. "Enemy planes approaching from the east".'

The officers swung around and raised their binoculars to their eyes. Sure enough, there were more little black silhouettes approaching. But they were behaving differently this time. They were advancing just above the peaks as opposed to the high altitude of the last formation. Straining their eyes, they soon realised that they were looking at single-engine aircraft with a strange crooked angle to the wings and fixed undercarriage. Fighters?

'Stukas,' Dollimore informed all about him. 'This should be somewhat different.'

They watched in awe as the dozen attackers casually gained a little height then rolled into their dives. One after the other, with precision timing they came down. Again the anti-aircraft guns fired out their spirited defence but they kept coming. A hideous screaming siren sounded from each plane, heightening in its nerve-shattering pitch and the seamen, who otherwise knew the awesome sound of naval gunnery, were completely unprepared for it. The noise seemed to speak of a personal vendetta. The sirens rose to a terrible crescendo, rattling every exposed man in the squadron, until the planes swooped across the tops of the masts, releasing their bombs.

It felt as though the ships were sitting ducks but it transpired that the Stuka pilots had actually been put off their aim by the barrage offered and they had dropped their bombs wide. Only one exploded near to the *Burscombe*'s port side.

The surface of the sea was blown sky high and the sound of jagged steel clashing against steel came from all around. Down below, hot metal splinters ripped through the thin unarmoured section of the hull and tore holes in mess tables, benches and seamen's lockers. Just above that, similar pieces wreaked havoc in the aircraft hangar, wrecking some equipment and pipes but fortunately there was no precious Walrus inside.

On the bridge, a few surreal seconds passed in which a heavy spray rained down upon them. Then somebody shouted, 'Sir!'

It was one of the young lookouts, kneeling next to the crumpled figure of Lt-Cdr Peterson who was lying unconscious with a deathly agonised look on his face. There was a significant wound to the top of his head and blood was spreading thickly about the wet deck, drifting to port and starboard with the ship's gentle roll. Where was his tin hat? It was lying upon the deck a few feet away with a gaping hole in it.

With no further attack immediately threatening, Dollimore knelt alongside the man who was already inspecting the wound and asked, 'Is he alive?'

'He is, sir, but barely, I should say.'

'Have a couple of men take him down to Surgeon-Commander Lawson straight away.'

'Aye aye, sir.'

Dollimore, realising that he had not credited in the past just how much he actually liked Peterson, personally and professionally, forced himself to turn his back on the scene. He felt a tense charge of hurt driving through his whole body but he was not going to let anybody know it. It was his job to be aloof and master of his emotions in times of crisis. There would be time enough to enquire after him, send his regards and say the right thing later. The ship's company would appreciate that approach.

With a dry throat and the smell of gun smoke still lingering in his nostrils, he stood with his lookouts as he began to appreciate that the sky had emptied of planes. He turned to Lieutenant Giles. 'Bosun, please pipe for Mr Irwin to come to the bridge.'

'Very good, sir.'

Dollimore well understood that Lieutenant Irwin was not and never would be flavour of the month with these men, or anyone else in the ship, but that pettiness had to go by the wayside now. He was the man best placed to take over from Peterson and that was that.

\*\*\*\*

In an almost casual way, a second flight of Stukas sauntered along above the wintry hills and valleys until they finally spotted the houses of

Hemmeligstein sitting on the eastern shore of the lake of the Tjierrefjord in their merry colours. The airmen, highly confident because they had consistently swept aside all opposition since Poland last year, knew that British troops had entered Norway through this place and quite rightly assumed that the village was still occupied. They simply tipped or banked their planes into their dives and screamed down to bring death to whoever was within.

On the beach, Lieutenant Eddington, Clark, Pincher and the Turtle had heard the growing sound of aircraft engines and swiftly ran into the shed, pulling their tin hats on as they went.

When Clark peered back outside, he observed a couple of civilians walking along the pathway in front the nearest house: one of the fishermen, a rude old fellow who had cursed the English on more than one occasion, and his equally rude wife. Clark cupped his hands to his mouth and shouted, 'Get under cover!'

The couple picked up the pace a little but they were not as spritely as the young servicemen. Clark could not watch any longer. The Stukas were almost upon them. He turned away.

He and the men with him threw themselves down and gritted their teeth. The ground shook under the roar of the engines and the screams of the planes' sirens and then came the detonations of the bombs. The hut swayed and threatened to be torn away from the beach as they were attacked by nine successive aircraft.

The teapot fell from its perch as the old shelving collapsed, nearly spilling boiling liquid across Eddington's face and decades-old dust was dislodged from the roof beams. They shouted and hollered their fear or abuse as the air was dragged from their lungs and smoke replaced the breathable air. Then, all of a sudden, there was silence.

The German airmen, hardly registering the piddly Lewis Gun bullets that blasted out from the hilltops, had done what they came here to do and flown off at their leisure.

Clark was the first on his feet, stumbling out across the cold shingle where the snow was gradually melting away. The village was in shock, ruined by scattered beams and wreckage and shrouded in black smoke. The colours so much loved by the Norwegians looked to have been dulled in an instant and one house was completely obliterated, its broken timbers fast being consumed by flames. Smashed cups, plates, pans, chairs, tables, a clock, torn paper and linen were strewn everywhere before it – and what was that just there? Was it a leg?

Eventually, he became aware that men and women were crying and screaming in the lanes behind the houses. On top of the forty or so inhabitants – which included no Norwegian men of fighting age since they had obeyed their country's call to arms and since disappeared – there were nearly a hundred of Binkley-Walling's men billeted here taking their turn for a brief respite in relative warmth.

Eddington stalked angrily along the beach and quickly ordered the Turtle, 'Tell those idiots to get that fire pump working before we lose the rest of the village!'

A little way up the slope on the right-hand side, an old fireman kept his horse-drawn pump in a shed. Eddington had long since warned him that it might be needed but he was not sure that the unhelpful man had even paid heed to Oskar's desperate translated cajoling on the matter. He had even gone so far as to suggest that Eddington had been making 'a mountain out of a molehill', as the English were so fond of saying. Well, now he had a series of fires to deal with and ample evidence that the proverbial molehill had been overshadowed by the mountain.

Pincher and the Turtle raced over there and had to physically shake the old boy into action. The only dramas of all his years had been when fishermen had been lost at sea. He had never seen anything like this before and he deployed his fire pump in a state of shock.

Soon, a line of soldiers and civilians were passing buckets from the water's edge and dropping the contents into the barrel at the back of the pump while two men heaved on the handle. The old fireman, crying the tears of a man truly grieving, directed the hose. To the sound of collapsing timbers and the frightened whinnying of the horse, everybody's hearts were still pounding from the suddenness and ferocity of the attack and many, rightfully and fearfully, kept glancing up at the sky.

Now it felt like they were losing another battle. This eons-old pump was not designed for the work required and the flames claimed two other houses before the wind shifted the fire back the other way. Thankfully, the rocky shoreline made it so that the people of times past had not been able to build their houses in close-knit rows. This loose planning turned out to be as much of a saviour as the wind.

Eddington passed a quick thought through his mind that portable pumps like those that the ships were carrying might have been adequate for this job but then he had to remind himself that they were essential pieces of equipment for Damage Control on board. The admiral would no more consent to let them go than any of the other equipment he had refused them; and Eddington had condoned enough 'theft' already.

Wounded men and women were being carried across to the big house on the eastern edge of the village which had been designated as the first aid post. There were groans all around and screaming from the more severely hurt. The army stretcher-bearers, their little white armbands with red crosses appearing stark against the khaki and soot, were working as quickly and diligently as they could, reaction to their training quelling the shock of seeing action for the first time.

One soldier was limping along the track holding onto the outer thigh of his left leg. Blood was seeping through his fingers and he was grimacing with every movement. Clark stumbled across the uneven ground towards him, his own various discomforts all forgotten about, and said, 'Here, let me give you a hand.'

'Na, that's all right, fella,' said the soldier, his thick Yorkshire accent lined with forced humour, 'there's other blokes back there need more help. I could do with a fag, though. Got a fag?'

Clark reached into his pocket and pulled some out. 'Here, keep the pack.'

'Thanks, fella.'

It barely registered with Clark that the man should have been calling him 'sir'. However, this was certainly not the time to go into the technicalities and respect of rank; and the lack of any gold rings on his dirty sleeves probably did not help.

He wandered back down onto the beach where Pincher and the Turtle were helping direct the hose onto the burning buildings, marvelling at the fishermen and women who were creeping right up to the crackling timbers in an attempt to throw buckets of water uselessly into the inferno.

Eddington spotted him and walked over, ironically lighting up a cigarette as he came. 'Clark, go and see the doctor. As soon as he says it's okay, start getting the casualties into the boats. I'd like to get them out of here soon.'

'The civilians as well?'

'If they want to leave, yes, but God help them if they don't. Jerry'll be back soon enough.'

Clark frowned. 'Wouldn't it be nice if we had some way of fighting back? Wasn't it Vegetius who said: "If you want peace, you must prepare for war"?'

'I beg your pardon?' asked Eddington.

'Well, it struck me that, not only did we fail to prepare for this war – as you see we do not have the means to fight it – but that if we had, Hitler might have thought twice about causing all this bother.'

Eddington looked at him askance. 'Can't think of a bigger waste of money than to prepare for a war you're never going to fight.'

'But, that's what Vegetius was getting at, a way to preserve the peace.'

'Fat lot of good that does us now.'

'Exactly.'

Thoroughly confused, Eddington pointed at the first aid post. 'Go and do what I told you to do before I tell the doc that it's your brain needs checking out.'

'Yes, sir,' said Clark, wondering why the other could not see his logic. But then people only ever see what they want to see. Even as his mind pondered these things, he heard the distant whirring of the Stuka engines once again and looked up to see more of those dreaded machines appearing over the southern hills to the chatter of the Lewis Guns. The next stage of the German advance had begun in earnest and, what was more, they were pursuing it with impunity.

# TWELVE

## Matters of Deep Concern

Lieutenant Philip Dollimore stood upon the deck of the struggling auxiliary vessel and looked out across Scapa Flow. If you cleared out all the warships that were anchored here the place might look innocent enough. But it still gave him the chills. Of course, his eyes were inexorably drawn to the north east corner of the anchorage where his old ship, HMS *Royal Oak*, was lying in her watery grave. He stayed looking for some while. What did he expect to see? Part of her hull breaking the surface? A salvage team working on her resurrection? The ghost of his best friend? There was nothing there but still water and the distant speck of a buoy marking the spot.

This was the first time he had been here since that awful night when they had been torpedoed. He did not care that the Admiralty had now furnished the Flow with adequate protection from the scourge of the U-boats because the damage had already been done, not just to the pride of the fleet and the nation, but to his personal commitment. Coming back to the scene of the crime had done nothing but rekindle his distrust in the authorities.

Also, one of the other lieutenants travelling the same direction this day had upset him. While he was taking tea – secretly laced with a little whisky – in the wardroom, a certain Lieutenant Watkins had sat opposite him and asked if he was a Dollimore.

Stupidly, Philip had answered, 'Yes, and you are?'

'Percy Watkins, captain of the *Grey Tor*, and the reason I ask is because I just wanted to extend my regards to your father. He once took passage aboard my ship, you know, when he was first off to take command of the *Burscombe*, and what a name he has made for himself since.'

'I'll be sure to remember you to him,' said Philip, pursing his lips in annoyance.

Fortunately, this Watkins fellow had quickly realised that Dollimore the Younger was not going to be such prestigious company, so took himself away and sipped his tea elsewhere.

Now at Scapa, lonesome and bothered, Philip was taken by motor launch to the destroyer HMS *Crayhorn* where, after his bags were lifted aboard, he climbed up onto the port waist. After trading salutes with and identifying himself to the Regulating Petty Officer, a message was sent along with an ordinary seaman to announce his presence. His first feeling was a sharp and unwelcome reminder of the *Cossack*. He was not going to get any better treatment here. Then he noticed a couple of men painting over some black streaks in the bulkhead just forrard of the torpedo tubes. There were four nasty holes in the steel. They had been in action – real action.

'Some of the Jerry aircraft have pretty powerful guns on them,' said a cheery fellow who appeared from behind a team of men working a derrick. 'The bastards pounced on us off the Norwegian coast.' Then he held out his hand, saying, 'I'm Tony Thorogood.'

Philip shook the hand of this wavy-haired man who was dishevelled of appearance, stripped of cap and tunic and sporting a dirty white submariner's jumper. But he was obviously an officer for the posh accent said it all.

Thorogood continued, 'So, Lieutenant Dollimore, great to meet you and all. The captain's waiting for you in his day cabin. You know the way?'

Philip nodded in the affirmative. He did not feel much like launching into any pleasant chit-chat here anyway. What would be the point in getting to know anyone too well when it probably would not be long before Fulton-Stavely wanted rid of him as well.

Commander Fulton-Stavely was standing at the big table in the cabin, leaning over a chart in close scrutiny. 'Come in,' he said to Philip without looking up.

'Lieutenant Philip Dollimore reporting, sir.'

Then the commander straightened and looked the newcomer up and down. So, this was Philip Dollimore. A little haggard perhaps, but that was to be expected given his history. The bottom line, though, was that Fulton-Stavely did not really judge a man on his appearance, only by his ability to do the job. There were certain allowances for slacker regulations in smaller ships providing a man's service was up to scratch. However, what was clear at first glance was that Philip had an insolent air of cynicism about his face in the way that he would not look his new commanding officer in the eye.

Fulton-Stavely, hoping deep down that he had not made some massive blunder by speaking up for him, instantaneously decided that he would dispense with the usual respect for the Dollimore name and treat him like he was any other old replacement. He somehow felt that he was unready to link him with his father. He would never know how fortunate that feeling was.

In strong tones, he said, 'Welcome on board. Forgive any urgency I might have at this time but we're under orders to proceed again in a couple of hours. Well, I understand that what happened in the *Oak* has thrown your career a tad out of kilter. Convalescence leave, then influenza followed by a hastily cobbled appointment in the *Cossack*. I trust that you're ready to get back down to some real work?'

'Yes, sir,' Philip replied, though in truth, he was not.

'Good. As it was I was losing two of my officers due to appointments and sickness anyway but I lost my Number One to air attack two days ago as well. Bullet in the shoulder.'

For Philip that was a sobering thought, remembering the punctured steel he had seen when he came aboard. He imagined the scored and stripped paint being supplemented by a gratuitous splattering of blood.

'Lieutenant Thorogood would have been the logical choice to take over but you have seniority by a whole year,' continued Fulton-Stavely. Staring Philip in the eyes, he half stated, half asked, 'Number One?'

Totally taken aback, Philip began to mumble a response.

Fulton-Stavely, right in thinking that the other's mind was whirling, was not going to give him a chance to let the situation get the better of him. 'If there's a problem, inform me right now. I don't want to find out it's all been a ghastly mistake in the middle of the Norwegian Sea.'

'No, sir, no mistake.' Philip actually found himself appreciating this particular captain's type of directness. All other approaches had been completely exhausting.

'Good. Go and find Lieutenant Thorogood. He'll show you what's what and then you can start overseeing the final preparations for sea.'

'Very good, sir.'

Philip left the cabin and wandered back down towards the port waist. The mucky Tony Thorogood, gave him a light-hearted nod and asked, 'So, it's 'Jimmy the One' for you, is it?'

'It would appear so, yes. So, bring me up to speed.'
\*\*\*\*

Hundreds of miles away, in the strained hulk of HMS *Burscombe*, Captain Dollimore slumped down onto his bunk. He even dared to take his boots off to rest his feet awhile though it was almost a certainty that some event would cut his rest short. That had become part and parcel of this affair since those wretched Stukas had begun taking an interest in them. What with their persistence and the inevitability that the German Army must be nearby, the matter was going to come to a head soon. There was no doubt about it.

But those thoughts were encroaching upon the fleeting minutes he had given himself. He reached over and picked up a letter from the desk. It had been in his possession these two days past and he had been thwarted in his attempt to read it too many times already. It was from Jennifer so whatever news it held could only be welcome. Her words would be well balanced and free of any trivial concern which could wait until he was back in port. She understood that, when he was at sea he would have troubles enough to contend with without her adding to them. He wished every other wife or mother was the same but that was not how the world was. There certainly were the occasional few who knew how to heap misery on a man already under strain.

Anyway, he opened the envelope and began to read.

*Dear Charles,*

*I hope my letter finds you well. All is fine at home. The evacuated children are a little homesick but they get to see their mother at least once a week. Thankfully, the Germans haven't started bombing the town but we still don't think they should go home as yet. Some are beginning to think the bombing won't happen at all now. Whatever happens, I won't let the children go home until we are certain how it's all going to turn out. Their mother and I are of the same mind on that. Anyway, their experience of the countryside has been positive. They have helped out on both farms nearby.*

*However, my biggest news is that Betty is in a relationship with a very fine young man that you will remember – Mr Barclay-Thompson. They first met in February and are now quite serious about each other. He has been having the most positive effect on her and she appears to be maturing in a more satisfactory way. In fact, she may hardly be recognisable to you when you next see her.*

*I hope you will not be too judgmental of the fact that I tried to warn him off her for his own sake, not that I was able to him put off. I like him a lot. I will keep a very close eye on her so that she cannot mess it all up in a way of which only she could be most capable. I'm sure it will do your heart good to know that she is beginning to find a direction for herself.*

*As ever, call when you can. I don't know what to believe in the news but I am sure that you'll be okay,*

*Yours forever with love,*

*Jennifer*

As usual, she had written as much as she dared. She was as conscious about security as the best of any serviceman. Of course, he knew that the town stated was Portsmouth and that Mr Barclay-Thompson was a Royal Navy sub-lieutenant. Those little facts need not be divulged to any prying eyes that might have happened to see the letter.

So, that young officer had taken Betty under his wing. Dollimore was immediately comfortable with that. Barclay-Thompson was a very well grounded individual and had been a welcome influence in the *Burscombe*'s gunroom during his time aboard. Providing he did not become a casualty of this war, he looked set to have a very good career ahead of him for his conduct had been good and his official diary had contained many a shrewd observation or comment.

Dollimore wondered if there was a marriage in the making. That was the question which he would begin to discuss when he got the chance to phone home. With much guilt about his feelings, he had long hoped that Betty might be able to get by on her looks and charm because her brain did not look set to cut it.

Inadvertently, the idea then made him think of his elder daughter, Victoria, who had married a seemingly very charming young man two years ago only to use the arrangement to distance herself from her family. What with her doing that and Philip experiencing the troubles that he had been, could he really be certain that Betty was headed for matrimonial bliss? Also, what did it say for his and Jennifer's parenting skills? Please let Betty be the one to be truly happy.

Suddenly, the weight of his more immediate responsibilities caught up with him again in the guise of the flag-lieutenant asking him to attend on his master.

'Of course,' replied Dollimore, immediately putting away the letter and reaching for his boots. He had managed to steal all of six minutes for himself before being summoned to see Nicklesworth.

The admiral was seated at his desk as usual, putting his signature to various documents, and started talking even before he had finished writing. 'And how is Mr Peterson?'

'If he makes it home, he's going to have a very difficult time of it, sir,' replied Dollimore.

'I'm very sorry to hear it,' said Nicklesworth, but he had other things on his mind so proceeded, keeping it short and to the point, 'Charles, I would like your take on the coming action.'

Dollimore, noting the use of his Christian name, was not going to let him off that easy. 'It's simple, sir, we're to bombard the enemy when they come at the infantry.'

'Well, obviously,' said Nicklesworth, immediately letting his irritation get the better of him. He looked up at Dollimore and regarded that cold, hard face. The intelligence was all-consuming but there was now this immovable arrogance. Although this man had kept his temper in check, he certainly looked as though he was bursting.

Nicklesworth, despising the fact that he so often asked of himself, 'What would Dollimore do in this situation?' and doubly despising the fact that he was now asking him outright, reminded himself that this was the angry officer who had been responsible for that accident in the Clyde back in '33. But he still had a dilemma of conscience to solve. 'You don't need to remind me of the objective. What I would like to know is how you would go about it.'

Dollimore frowned briefly. What was going on? Did Nicklesworth have no plan? 'Perhaps if you were to tell me the extent to which you are prepared to risk the squadron, I could answer more honestly, sir.'

'Don't be insolent,' replied Nicklesworth, standing up so that he could look down upon him from his superior height. 'Let's just have absolute honesty. We may not particularly like each other very much but I chose you to be my flag-captain upon Admiral Forbes' recommendation for advice on the very type of situation which we face now. We're staring into the eyes of disaster here and I have a very risky plan which I'm going to put into action if I can't come up with anything better. The plan involves a certain amount of damage and loss, which means that a few of our chaps are going to be none too happy about it. Now, are you the smart fighting captain that Forbes takes you to be or are you not? Eh?'

Dollimore looked hard at Nicklesworth. Was the admiral out of his depth? No, not exactly. He would fight and have no problem taking responsibility for anything that went wrong; that was for certain and was much of what being an admiral was all about. But his mind was very limited as to the possibilities of the weapons on offer.

Dollimore sighed and suddenly looked weary. 'If I may sit?'

'Please,' said Nicklesworth, motioning to the chair that was tucked away in the corner by the bunk.

Dollimore pulled it out and sat himself down whilst the admiral also took time to reseat himself. Now they were on a level playing field. It was so much more civilised.

'Right,' Dollimore began, 'our main problem is that the top range of our guns is only fourteen and a half miles – twelve and half if we're to achieve proper accuracy – and the distance from the sea to the bombardment area is more than twenty four miles. This evidently means that we need to be in the fjord to be able to bombard the enemy. The lake in daylight is a deathtrap, certainly to anchored ships and almost as certainly to those effecting manoeuvres as slow as that which a ship of this size must make in that relatively confined space, and that's not even taking into account that terminal moraine; which brings us to the point that the idea of *three* cruisers manoeuvring in there under fire is utterly ridiculous in the extreme – and this is notwithstanding the point that we need to be in a position where the flight of our shells can safely pass over the hilltops, otherwise there's no worth in the operation at all.'

Nicklesworth nodded. 'That's exactly how I see the situation. What's your answer to it?'

Without a pause, Dollimore continued, 'Well, word on the whereabouts of the Germans would be nice but I think we can discount that. The RAF evidently has better things to do and I wouldn't send a Walrus into the viper's nest alone. No, Major Binkley-Walling will have to do his best to give us at least three hours' notice to bombard at which point we steam up the fjord stern-first.'

Nicklesworth's mouth fell open, his face a picture of surprise.

'In that time,' Dollimore went on, 'we should be able to get in range, ideally just beyond halfway up. The advantages of this are that we won't immediately be exposed in front of Hemmeligstein so the Stukas might take a bit of time to find us. Of course, there's the danger that they'll notice we've disappeared from the estuary and put two and two together, but that can't be helped. So when they do come for us, we'll be faced downriver and will be at liberty to withdraw at high speed, but we can judge that at the time. The longer we can stay in the fjord the better it will be for Binkley-Walling. Then, of course, on his signal we unleash the bombardment to the plan already agreed with.'

While listening to this, Nicklesworth had forgotten all about his loathing and his admiration for the idea simply overrode all else. 'I say, that's supreme! Much better than my plan! You see? This is why I asked you the question.' Plus, of course, there were no witnesses either to ever suggest that he had been at a loss over the matter.

But Dollimore had more to add. 'Beyond that we're going to have to look at the best way to extricate our forces from the shore ...'

'Except, that's not what our orders are. As you know, I've made the recommendation for a withdrawal and I've received no answer, so there's an end to it. Thank you for your input, captain. I shall set everything in train.'

Then, as Dollimore was just making to leave the cabin, Nicklesworth suddenly added, 'You didn't just come up with all of that off the top of your head, did you?'

'No, I thought of it days ago, sir.'

'You rogue.'

After the captain had gone, Nicklesworth smiled to himself. His own plan had certainly not been as good and it was just as well he had not needed to air it for it revolved around the *Marsfield* supporting the infantry from within the lake during a tidal period which could have been fatal to her. He had chosen her because he did not want to risk losing one of the two newer cruisers. While ever the *Marsfield* was in there, the Germans would never have a better opportunity to sink her or run her aground and some thousands of men would know that he had purposely sacrificed her for a marginal gain.

Thankfully, Dollimore's plan offered not just greater fire support but an equal chance of survival for all three ships involved. It was perfectly Nelsonian.

\*\*\*\*

On their voyage north to the Tjierrefjord, *Crayhorn* and *Catterley* paused only once to drop depth charges on an echo that had been picked up by the

ASDIC teams. Blasting to the surface hundreds more unfortunate fish and not much else, they attempted to reaffirm the presence of what they thought might be a U-boat and, failing in that aim, carried on to their destination. They had to make do with hoping that they had scared some Germans half to death in their claustrophobic machine.

Philip Dollimore knew that he should not care to be in a submarine with those charges going off yet he had no sympathy with the fools who were.

But his mind was soon back on his own awful conflict. He was still highly frustrated to say the least and the only thing that seemed to bring clarity and calm was a good shot of whisky a couple of times a day – or was it more?

They arrived off the Tjierrefjord as the sun was setting and almost immediately received a signal from the *Burscombe*. It turned out to be his father allowing himself a slight break in his strict discipline to enquire if Philip was on board and if he was well.

Philip said to his Yeoman of the Signals, 'Tell him, "I am well".' He would say nothing more, nothing less. At least he did not have to go across and meet him.

Then came, "Have you brought supplies?"

"Affirmative; bound for Hemmeligstein."

"Acknowledged. Proceed at your discretion."

\*\*\*\*

As soon as the sun was settled enough to ensure full darkness within the hour, the two destroyers made their way into the fjord at speed. The night was set to last no more than two and a half hours so they knew that they would be badly exposed at dawn. At least they did not face the depth restrictions placed upon the larger vessels on account of that terminal moraine. With drafts of only twelve feet, the destroyers could safely be deployed in the lake at any time.

The night was calm and there was just enough moonlight to steer by. The two companies stayed at Defence Stations all the way. Thankfully, reports from this theatre of war so far indicated that most, if not all, air action had taken place during daylight hours, the Germans not yet having satisfactorily perfected precise night targeting.

When they finally entered the lake, Philip, Thorogood and Fulton-Stavely were greeted by the sight of intense fires burning ashore about two miles distant.

The captain glanced at the compass and said, 'That's where we're going.'

Philip was not frightened. He felt himself being drawn to those bright orange flames in the blackness as though he were a moth. Would he be burnt there? Would this place be the death of him? He would not care if it was, but decided that, no matter what the outcome, the Jerries were going to come off worse just as they had in the Jossingfjord.

As the *Crayhorn* and her sister ship glided across the smooth surface of the lake, the sound of her machinery emanating softly from within her hull, Thorogood took a closer look at the fires and the men moving amongst them through his binoculars and said to Philip, 'Does it not remind you of the sinister artwork of the renaissance?'

'What, you mean their depictions of Hell?'

'Exactly; and I think there's something inherently evil in the human mind that makes it appealing. It's shameful ...'

'Macabre,' added Philip, 'but evil begets evils, hate begets hate and violence begets violence. Revenge and the harnessing of Hell to one's own will are most important. That is what I've learnt since the beginning of this war. That – and that the only good German is a dead German.'

He fell silent as Fulton-Stavely glanced across at him. The captain never said a word and his enigmatic look did not hint at approval or otherwise.

At about eight bells tolling midnight, the anchor and cable was laid across the lake bed and Philip and Thorogood were down flitting between the waists, organising the many crates of food and ammunition needing to go ashore. *Crayhorn* only had two small boats so Fulton-Stavely signalled the shore party to send assistance and any wounded that they might have.

Before too long, the commandeered fishing boats had come out from the beach, silhouetted against the fiery backdrop and the men in the bows were throwing lines to the waiting sailors.

'Here, catch this!' called a young man on one of the boats. Thorogood was the nearest and he put out his hands, catching the rope easily as it flew over his shoulder. He and a chief then pulled on the line and the boat was dragged alongside. The young man once again piped up with, 'I've got forty wounded, seven of them stretcher cases.'

As if to emphasise the point, a cry of pain shot up from somebody, but to Thorogood's surprise, the cry was that of a female. The young officer explained, 'Some are civilians. We convinced them that they would stand a much better chance if they allowed us to help them aboard our cruisers, what with our operating theatres and all.'

'Very good,' replied Thorogood.

Then Philip appeared at his side and screwed up his eyes in a determined effort to try and see better in the dark. 'David Clark, is that you?'

'Yes, sir,' came the reply. 'Philip Dollimore?'

'The very same. I should've guessed you'd be somewhere in the middle of all this.'

'Not by choice,' laughed Clark. Remembering the tense man who had sat sullenly in the *Burscombe*'s gunroom back in February, suffering the intrusive questions of the midshipmen, he added, 'How do things go for you?'

But Philip had no intention of talking about himself. The very idea of that was abhorrent. Instead, he leapt straight to, 'I have messages for you from home. Please step aboard for a few minutes. The chief will see to your wounded and then load you back up with stores.'

Clark paused for a second. Messages from home? No doubt a plea from his mother and perhaps an insult from his sister. What could either of them say to change what had happened? Then he reasoned that he should not shoot the messenger so extended his arm. The pair of them grabbed each other's wrists and Philip hauled him up over the railing onto the *Crayhorn*'s deck.

Even by this light Philip could see that Clark's uniform was of rather an untidy form, it being discoloured and boasting a large rip on the left sleeve. 'You've had a rough time of it,' he said.

'Yes, I'm heartily ashamed of these rags,' replied Clark, fingering the unsightly flap of material. 'As soon as I get a moment I'll sort them out. But constantly being dive-bombed and – '

'Excuses, excuses,' said Philip.

'I know, we must always have a reason, never an excuse.'

'And damned right too, otherwise where would we be?'

Philip was then about to say, 'It's good to see you,' but he did not. Was it good to see him? Was he a good friend? No, a good acquaintance, yes, but not a good friend. He had only met him for the first time last year and it had been obvious straight away that the courses they ran were different: their ages were different; their outlook was different; their sense of respect was different. Even with the tumultuous changes wrought on them by their similar experiences, they were still different.

He said, 'I got in touch with your family like I said I would; found them in London in fact. In Belgravia.'

'London?' The town house had been meticulously maintained these last couple of decades but Mother had not been there for years. She did not particularly like it.

'It's safe enough,' said Philip, 'Jerry's too interested in this place here to be bothering with London.'

'But why are they there?'

Philip sighed. 'Well, it's Patty, you know. She wasn't doing so well since John died.'

'I'd gathered that much…'

'No, you don't understand.' Philip was already getting quite short-tempered on this matter which meant so much to him. 'She wasn't doing well at all. Her grief was so deep that she was neglecting herself terribly; and the baby within her too. They went to find better help in town. I spent some time with her too and I think she's improved somewhat, but I'm still not happy about it.'

Clark stood staring in silence. To say the least, he was uncomfortable with the subject being spoken of. It was true, some part of him did want to go back there and see if there was anything he could do to help – but it had been they who had tried to destroy his life. Not the other way around.

Philip continued, 'David, your mother begs you to get in contact with her. Whatever went on between you, she's fully desirous of making amends. These are horrible times we're living in and she needs you back. She's a great and humble lady …'

'*Humble?*' Clark said, the incredulity dripping from both syllables. 'I can quite guarantee you, whatever she may be, humble she is not.'

Philip felt his temper snapping. He could not equate such contempt being expended upon so gracious a lady as Dorothy Clark. 'I think you should be just a little more respectful when you speak about her. She has a genuine desire to be reconciled and you're behaving like a spoilt child.'

Thinking about the girl he had wanted to marry and the way in which his mother had chased her off, Clark had long ago decided that any reconciliation with his family would have to have serious terms and conditions attached to it and he did not believe his mother would even try to live up to them. She was great in many ways but she was still a snob – a born and bred snob.

But anyway, talk of respect was rich coming from Philip Dollimore. Clark was not appreciative of his hypocritical righteousness. 'Right, so how are things in your own family?'

'What are you talking about?' Philip asked, stunned and angered. They were not here to talk about him.

'The buzz is that you want to be like your father but it's not exactly working out.'

Philip, conscious that a lot of men were working not that many feet away, dropped his voice to a paranoid growl and asked, 'Who's been talking about me?'

'This is the navy,' said Clark, not half so discreet in his tone. 'Everybody knows something about everybody else. Your father's considered to be a great captain but for some reason, you don't come up to the mark.'

'You don't know anything, but I can see that the rumours of your insolence are very well-founded.'

Suddenly a voice came down from the deck above. It was that of Fulton-Stavely saying, 'Number One, there's work to be done! And you, young sir…' for he could not see Clark well enough to recognise him, '…if you would please desist and remove yourself from my ship before I cause you a real problem.'

'Very good, sir,' said Clark, glad for the order, but then paused. 'Oh, sir, are there any radios or 3-inch mortar rounds amongst this lot?'

'That would be a question for the men who packed it,' answered Fulton-Stavely dismissively. In other words, he hadn't a clue.

Clark moved instantly to take himself away from here. As he climbed over the railing and leapt back down onto the deck of the fishing boat, accidentally brushing against the men loading boxes, he reflected that Philip had probably entered into their conversation in the right spirit but could not possibly know how much of a tangle he had actually been caught up in, an unwitting tool of the Clark family. However, he should have kept his personal opinions to himself.

With all said and done, when the boats had run back and forth a few more times and the handover of wounded and stores was complete, David saw him one last time and said, 'Philip, good luck out there.'

Philip picked out the shadow of David Clark amongst the men crowded on the deck of the small craft. He had a hot flash of anger surging through his body. He felt like he was being goaded. How could somebody insult him and then wish him luck just a couple of hours later? The inconsistency was too confusing so instead of returning the compliment, he answered with, 'It's you who'll need the luck; and besides, once your mother's had a proper think about it, she'll realise she doesn't need you. If you can't be bothered, then there are others who can. Her needs are being taken care of.'

'What's that supposed to mean?'

'She has good friends, you know, not least myself and Commander Crawshaw.'

Clark paused. He was not sure that he had heard correctly. After all, life had become very intense what with this odd campaign and the growing persistence of the Stukas. Had Philip Dollimore really just dropped a name which he thought had long since disappeared into the ether? 'Do you mean Derek Crawshaw?' he asked.

'Well, of course. You're old commander; a family friend.'

Clark was about to say that Crawshaw was nothing of the sort but reverted to silence. Philip had again imparted information of which effect he was completely ignorant. Well, Clark was not about to enlighten him. That really was none of his business.

He ordered his stoker to get the motor going and, while the fishing boat chugged its way back to the beach, he sat on the boxes in the stern, aware of a chilly breeze cutting through his scarf and coat. It was exacerbated by the sight of the sky lightening already. These short nights would take a lot of getting used to. By his watch the time was only just past 0200. He turned and watched as the destroyers weighed anchor and proceeded, picking up speed and making their way towards the fjord and the highway to the sea; and he did wish them luck because they might only be but halfway along when it would be light enough for the Stukas to come back.

His mind then went back to Derek Crawshaw. Just when he thought things could not get worse, that name had been thrown into the mix as well. So, he has managed to style himself as a family friend, he thought. It's perfectly feasible that he and Mother could have some sort of accord for she was once a close acquaintance to Crawshaw's brother until Father suspected them of having an affair. But that was twenty years ago, a sordid history which had ended in tears for everybody concerned.

There was one thing that was for certain here and now. Derek Crawshaw was a cad and a womaniser and if he was posing as a friend then he had an ulterior motive. He had always been held back in his career by the late Rear-Admiral Harper Clark and David himself had been partly responsible for his dismissal from the *Burscombe* last December. Crawshaw was obviously after what he considered to be his dues. Respect, revenge, perhaps even money.

Clark wondered if the smooth-talking commander had actually wormed his way into his mother's bed and felt sick thinking about it. Reason dictated that she was too proud to ever allow that to happen. But, damn it, had she not been full of surprises already?

By the time the bows of the boat scraped up against the shingle, he knew that next time he had leave, he would be heading south to sort out this situation once and for all. To an extent, his brother had been right in that letter he had written. Clark should have been behaving like the head of the family whatever his grievances were. He was the closest in proximity to their home and should have been keeping an eye on matters. Instead, he had left a void into which the confidence trickster, Derek Crawshaw, had skilfully advanced.

But when was his next leave going to be? He quickly thought through this Norwegian situation and decided that, unless the Germans suddenly and miraculously sued for peace, he might just be dead before the week was out.

****

'You're a good lad,' the Turtle said to Oskar as they sat outside Eddington's shed in the growing light. They were both tired and dirty and there was to nowhere that they could escape from the constant stench of smoke, fumes and charred bodies in this crumbling place where there was no longer a single building left unscathed by the bombs.

Oskar had just wandered along the beach to be greeted by the Turtle holding out a steaming cup of tea for him. He slumped down onto one of the stools and sipped at it appreciatively, deciding that he had never tasted anything so sweet. He gazed back and forth at the destruction and wondered why he was here, especially in light of the fact that he seemed to be distrusted by most of the British and the Norwegians. It was because they were all suspicious of spies, he knew, but that did not help him when he had to translate messages or try to offer advice. At least the Turtle was above all that. He was a moody, solitary man yet somehow compassionate at the same time. Oskar would not doubt him in any matter.

'Where's your mum and dad?' asked the Turtle.

'In Bergen,' answered Oskar, giving a little despairing look because everybody knew that that had been one of the first towns to fall to the enemy.

'What are you gonna do when this show goes tits up?'

'When what?' enquired Oskar, not understanding the reference.

'When it all goes wrong,' said the Turtle gently. He was not his usual, miserable self today. He was actually smiling, if the contortion could be called a smile.

'This is not going wrong,' said the Norwegian lad pompously. 'With the English Navy and Army we'll win. We'll shoot every Nazi dead.'

'Don't you believe it, my son. This is what my dad would call a classic stuff up 'cept that he was an 'ypocrite otherwise – had a lot to say about stuff ups in the last war without actually being there; idiot. Anyway, I'm sayin' this because you're a decent lad and I care about what 'appens to you. No matter what 'appens here, don't ever give up. There's a way out of everything and there's solutions to everything. Stay one step ahead of the bastards that wanna do you wrong and that's all I can tell you.'

Oskar suddenly looked even more despairing. His sleepy, blackened face and his shaggy mop of hair made him look younger and more fragile. He was only fifteen after all. 'Are you saying that Jerry will rule this country?'

'Unless twenty aircraft carriers turn up with two hundred planes to help – and I'm talking about soon – we're stuffed, so just you be ready to look after yourself.'

'I come back to England with you, Turtle.'

The Turtle looked down, almost ashamed. 'Na, that won't be possible. You'll have choices to make shortly. Use your instincts and you'll know what to do. You've already saved lives and done more work than most men twice your age. I reckon there's more for you to do before the world settles back down again.'

'Why can't I come with you, Turtle?'

'You just can't.'

They continued chatting while the day came about in its unhurried way and at about 0430 they heard the first droning of aircraft in the distance.

Men everywhere looked up and, after a slight pause, began to dart for cover. Shouts came from those who were trying to shift the last of the stores to safety. One or two dazed men seemed not to register that they were about to be bombed and got an earful of abuse from the sergeant-major.

'Here they come,' said the Turtle matter-of-factly, standing up with a sigh and straightening his coat.

Oskar was on his feet as well, looking at him in a confused way. 'Are you all right?'

'Absolutely tickety boo, my son. You go and get undercover.' With that, the Turtle picked up a satchel that had been lying on the ground beside his stool. It was a particular satchel which he had secretly taken from an injured man during the night. It bore the medics' red cross so anybody observing him would think that he was off to help the wounded during the coming raid. Only he knew that he had discarded all but the barest of first aid essentials and had concealed some spare socks and four days of rations in the resulting space underneath.

The Stukas appeared over the peaks from the south and, as before, they hardly took any time to think about the objective before they fell into their dives and swooped down, their sirens screaming as they came.

Oskar ran into the shack as the Turtle looked about. He knew that Lt Eddington and Pincher were up at one of the company stores a few houses back and a quick glance down to the water's edge showed Midshipman Clark and his men hiding in or underneath the angled hulls of the beached fishing boats.

It was now or never. He started running towards the track leading out of the village, fighting the urge for his bladder to empty itself for the Stukas screams. He did not think he had run this fast at any other time in his life. But he had to keep going and not take cover. Taking cover would cost him time that he did not have.

The deafening roars of the Stukas shook the ground and then the bombs exploded. They seemed to fall indiscriminately everywhere and chunks of debris flew all about him. He felt the heat of the blasts, the air being displaced all around and the shockwaves which threatened to flatten him. He felt stones hitting his back and stinging his legs as they nipped at him. One or two clattered off his tin hat – but he kept running and he never stopped. He was going to desert and had thrown his all into this moment. He was going to get to Sweden. Short of being killed in action, nothing else was an option.

\*\*\*\*

'Has anybody seen Haggerty?' Clark asked after the furore surrounding the last spate of bombings had abated. With his ears ringing and the exhaustion of helping with the wounded just settling in, he had suddenly noticed that the Turtle was not with them. He cursed himself for the unforgiveable oversight.

When they had been lifting people out of the ruins of their homes or trying to keep that antiquated fire pump going, he had not once seen

Haggerty anywhere. There were already two casualties amongst the naval shore party and he really did not want there to be a third, although another niggling doubt began creeping into the back of his mind.

Eddington turned this way and that, letting his tired eyes scan the scene. 'When was the last time anyone saw him?'

Pincher said, 'He was sitting here with Oskar right before the air raid, sir.'

'Go find Oskar and ask him if he's seen him since. If not, check the aid post up there.'

Pincher found the boy busy trying to reason with a distraught elderly woman who plainly wanted the soldiers and their equipment out of her house. She and all her possessions were covered in dust and she was clutching the unrecognisable remnant of some posh ceramic object. Whatever it used to be, it had been important to her.

'Oskar,' said Pincher, 'is the Turtle with you?'

'No,' Oskar replied, briefly turning his attention away from the woman, 'I thought he was helping the wounded.'

'Well, he wasn't.'

'He had with him the first aid bag.'

'Really?' Then, regarding the woman who was slumping exhausted into a chair, her expression one of unsurpassed despair, Pincher asked, 'Is she all right?'

'Not really. Her son is missing with the army for three weeks and she wants the English to go home.'

'Believe me, I could do with going home right now.' He walked across to the aid post, looked about at the pitiful casualties – thankfully low in number because there were not many people left in Hemmeligstein – and then peered under the blankets which covered the dead. Until now, he had resisted looking at the faces of the deceased but he had to know. The Turtle was not here. That left two possibilities, neither of which sat well with him. Either he had received a direct hit and was scattered to the four winds or he had made a run for it.

Pincher walked slower than he should have back down to the beach thinking back to that night in Rosyth when he had had his altercation with him. If this was a desertion then he was pretty much involved having never broached the subject with anyone in authority. He considered himself to be as honest as the day was long; it was one of the foundations on which his family earned its respect, but he was also not a grass.

He approached Eddington and Clark on the beach and shook his head at the senior officer. 'I can't find him anywhere, sir.'

Then Clark held up a brown satchel, saying, 'This was Haggerty's, the one he brought ashore with him. I found it in the shed. It's stuffed full of medical supplies.'

'Oskar said that he was helping with the wounded, sir.'

Clark looked hard at Pincher through his thinning, black-rimmed eyes. 'You know as well as I do that he kept a change of clothes and rations in this bag; and more than one man saw him with a Red Cross bag right before the air raid, so he switched the contents. What do you say about that?'

Pincher could not hide his troubled expression but continued to keep his mouth shut.

Eddington's face was red with fury. 'Are we talking about desertion here?'

'It would be wise to consider it a possibility, sir,' replied Clark, just as furious.

'Over that police affair?'

'That's certainly worth a punt.'

'Right,' Eddington said, turning to the half dozen or so who were gathered a few yards away. 'Spread out and look for Haggerty again and, Clark, go along to the valley. If you don't find hide nor hair of him, talk to the major's military policemen, but be sure to state that he might be wandering around concussed. There's still some scope left for the benefit of the doubt.'

Not by much, thought Clark.

But Eddington revealed his true feelings by shouting, 'God damn it! We don't have time for this!' as he walked away from them.

'Martin, wait here a second,' ordered Clark, glaring at the AB. Once everybody else was out of earshot, he continued, 'You understand my position? I reported to the captain that there was no sustainable case against Haggerty and I don't appreciate being dragged into this business just to be hoodwinked. Don't tell me again that you know nothing. You're a terrible liar.'

Pincher tried to maintain a blank expression but it was just as Clark had said. His indecision still showed through. The trouble was his own disgust at the possibility that the Turtle had deserted. Eventually, he said, 'Sir, for what it's worth, I believe that whatever happened to him when he was on leave in January, the situation wasn't of his making.'

'That doesn't matter now. He's most likely on the run, and it makes him the prime suspect.' Then he stopped short and rubbed his tired eyes with dirty fingers. 'Except that the police knew the time of the murder and he had an alibi. But somehow he *did* do it. Otherwise, why would he run? I mean, his jack knife matches the wound on the body – as any jack knife would, I suppose – and … I don't know.'

'Jack knife, sir?'

Clark suddenly remembered that Martin was not privy to any of those details which he had picked up during the interview with Detective Sergeant Crosbie; and he really should not be either.

'The knife he's got now isn't his own, sir,' continued Pincher cautiously.

'What's that?'

'Sir, I've not been totally up front with everything I know.'

'You surprise me,' snapped Clark sarcastically.

'It's just that desertion's going beyond a limit, sir, but there's more to it all. Listen, in the newspapers there was all the fuss about the murders. Peter Averell one week and Cliff Parker the next. 'Orrible bastards …'Scuse my French, sir, but they weren't nice people, know what I mean? Now, the police were looking at Parker's murder like it was some sort of revenge killing, and the Turtle – was he somehow roped into it? If not the actual killing then some sort of complicity?'

Clark sighed. 'Martin, these are all questions for the police so stop rambling.'

'But there's another angle, sir,' Pincher persisted and with that looked even more troubled. 'I don't say that I know the Turtle's family all that well but my mum does. Same community an' all.'

'Just get to the point.'

'He's got this cousin – lovely little girl she was – called Mary Sewell. Now, she was Cliff Parker's girlfriend; wanted to marry him an' everything, but for some reason they never got 'itched. Rumour has it, though, that about three years ago she got pregnant and he forced her into having an abortion. That's the word what went around anyway. But I do know that she stayed with him and somehow her name hasn't come up in any of the newspaper articles anywhere. You can bet your life that she's got something to do with it.'

'All conjecture,' said Clark, busily digesting what he had just been told.

'And you said he had an alibi sir,' said Pincher with greater directness.

'So, you think that this Mary Sewell murdered Parker and that is what Haggerty's complicit in?'

'I told you there was another angle, sir. It's a possibility.'

'Christ!' muttered Clark. 'This is a complicated world.'

'Too many people in it, sir, and we just ain't all alike.'

'You said that the jack knife that Haggerty possesses is not his own. Whose is it?'

'He took it from Les ... er, Ordinary Seaman Gordy, sir. He's been bullyin' him these last months. But Les is tougher than he looks, sir, so that's not an official complaint.'

'Right,' Clark acknowledged. 'Thank you for the information but you would have been wise to have told me sooner. These are police matters which you've held back on.'

'Yes, sir,' said Pincher, looking away. 'But perhaps I ain't got the same faith in the law what you've got, sir. Those gangs are part of our lives in East London and if the police were any good, they wouldn't be, would they?'

Clark nodded his understanding. This case had certainly built up a picture for him of how vulnerable London's poor could be. It was something he had never really credited before, but how could he with his background?

'Isn't it also ironic, sir,' Pincher then asked, 'that we're standing here agonising over the details of the murder of some malicious thug while scores of innocent people are being killed or made homeless in this war? I mean, who's actually mourning the loss of Cliff Parker?'

'It's still part of what we're fighting for. Justice, liberty and holding people to account when they step out of line. Sometimes the scale just differs. Prosecuting a murderer or fighting the Nazis – they're both part of the same struggle.'

Pincher nodded his understanding and thought on it. Those of the midshipman's superiors who kept saying there was no hope for him would have been proud to hear that come out of his mouth, to know that he was definitely maturing to a naval officer's standard.

'Where do you think he's gone then, sir?' Pincher asked.

Only taking three seconds to turn full circle and scan the extent of his surroundings, Clark finished by facing the track to the east. 'If it were me, I'd try for Sweden, and Sweden is *that* way.'

# THIRTEEN

## Resisting the Inevitable

Once he was descending the eastern end of the track into the wood and a biting wind, Clark again observed the pitiful entrenchments that the soldiers had clawed out of this unforgiving ground. Although the temperature was ever so slightly warmer than it had been this time last week, the waiting about and the cut rations cancelled out any positive effect that might have brought; and there was still plenty of snow on the ground. The soldiers and marines were living miserably in this damned wood but the one saving grace it had was that the Germans had not yet managed to identify it as a target. That was not to say, though, that none of the blokes were praying for Jerry to get a move on and attack. It was high time they got this business over and done with.

Set up on a rocky outcrop about fifty yards to the left was a machine gun emplacement, its thin stick of a barrel poking out from a pile of large stones. Its field of fire was all across the track where it snaked to the gap between the hills that Clark had just emerged from. This was an obvious place for him to start asking questions for the soldiers here would undoubtedly have seen Haggerty had he tried to pass.

He clambered across the uneven ground, sometimes through knee deep snow, and was greeted by a couple of shivering privates and a corporal. 'What does the navy want?' the NCO asked in a thick Yorkshire accent.

'We have a missing man, possibly concussed,' explained Clark.

But before he could continue, the corporal said, 'Treacherous country this.'

'All right, no need to be flippant, and address me as 'sir'.'

The corporal looked Clark's dirty uniform up and down, not seeing any insignia or rank that he recognised. 'Yes, *sir*,' he answered sarcastically.

Clark shook his head and, eager to get to the matter in hand, continued with, 'Has one of our men come by here with a first aid satchel in the last three hours?'

'On some sort of goodwill humanitarian mission is he, sir?'

'Just answer the question or I'll report you to the military police for obstruction.'

The corporal raised his eyebrows and, too fed up to be rattled by the threat, simply said, 'No, sir, one of your blokes has not passed this position this morning with or without a first aid satchel. I'll stop him if I see him but, in the meantime, there's some other rubbish going on, sir.'

Deeply dissatisfied as Clark was with the man's response, he decided that he would leave this place and let him get on with his job. Soon enough this corporal would be fighting for his life for nothing much more than Westminster's political reputation.

As he walked away, he heard the corporal asking his men, 'Do you reckon it costs less for a whore to stay the night here than it does in England? I mean, the crack of dawn comes a lot earlier for a start.' Then the laughter drifted between the rocks.

Clark walked back up towards the track and observed the ground again. There was no way that Haggerty would have been able to sneak past that machine gun post without being seen so it stood to reason that he must have been hiding somewhere back along the two miles between here and the village. The worst thing was, with all the craggy rocks, outcrops and defiles, there were a million places where he could have been concealed. Plus, the snow itself would offer no clues. Where it had not been flattened entirely by the comings and goings of hundreds of men, it was still churned up by the deviation of a further few so trying to look for Haggerty's footprints was pointless.

After wandering back down to Binkley-Walling's rickety HQ and lodging a report with the two MPs he found there – who admittedly expressed their surprise that it was the navy that should be the first to suffer a possible desertion – Clark started on his way back to Hemmeligstein.

He reached the track's summit panting from the uphill exertion and looked back out over the tops of the trees to the south. That was when he heard the familiar sound of aircraft engines. Already wincing at the thought of being bombed, he stood stock still, knowing that he was in a completely exposed position, and let his eyes travel across the horizon. Ah, that was why he had not seen them straight away. They were coming in at just over tree-top level and had been almost perfectly camouflaged against the mountains opposite. There were two twin-engine bombers of the Junkers variety flying in a straight line across the woods where the KOYLIs were hidden. The machines sped past, large and with every detail perfectly clear in a momentary rush of power. They passed unmolested.

Clark wondered for a second why the soldiers with their Lewis Guns mounted on those painstakingly supplied gimbal mounts did not open fire, but then it did not take him much longer again to realise that those airmen were searching for the next line of resistance and it would profit nobody to give the position away precipitately. That was true discipline, for the soldiers to be offered such a target but exercise restraint especially in the light of the fact that they had many an axe to grind.

He waited there for a few more minutes until he was sure that the skies were well and truly clear then continued on his way, walking across another small rise in the track. As the next stretch unfolded before him he was astonished to see Harry Haggerty coming towards him. He was right there within thirty yards of him!

They had seen each other at the same moment and stopped, staring for a brief, tense second. There was suddenly murder in the big man's eyes and Clark reacted by drawing his revolver from its holster. Looking all about him, he realised that they were alone, just the two of them. So be it. Pointing the weapon squarely at him, he asked rhetorically, 'And where do you think you're going?'

Taking a few steps closer with his hands out away from his sides, the Turtle was angered that this stupid lad should dare to stand in his path. It was true that he had nothing more against Clark than that he was an officer and was just adhering to the rules of the service, but he was resolved to hurt him if that was what it took to get away from here. He quickly decided that he would not beat about the bush and try to spout some feeble story of what may or may not be going on. He had no time for any of that. Instead, he leapt straight for, 'Sir, they're gonna hang me if they catch me.'

'And you think desertion's going to help your case?'

'Actually, yes.'

'I've told them that I believe you're concussed so I'm going to take you back and we can sort this out.'

'You ain't taking me back, sir,' said the Turtle, taking further steps toward him, the anger and desperation showing more and more clearly upon his face. 'They're gonna hang me and there ain't no two ways about it.'

'So, are you admitting to me that you're guilty of murder?' asked Clark with his own menace. 'Did you murder Cliff Parker?'

The Turtle gritted his teeth, his whirling mind threatening to make him see red and charge. With almost all reason gone from the features which had spawned the names Turtle and Lizard Face, he no longer resembled the leading seaman who had served HMS *Burscombe* so well in the past.

'Or are you covering for somebody else? Are you covering for Mary Sewell?'

The Turtle stopped, momentarily dumbstruck.

Clark pushed further with, 'Mary Sewell did it and you're deserting to ensure the blame lies with you!'

'Who you been talking to?' growled the Turtle. 'No, don't bother answering that. I've got a pretty shrewd idea.' It must have been that brown-nosed arse-licker, Pincher. That man's loyalty had always been questionable.

Clark, his revolver still aimed carefully, said, 'Right now, all that matters is that you're coming back with me. Turn around and start walking back to the village.'

The Turtle cautiously took another step towards him instead. He was determined that this had to go his way because he just could not be foiled for a second time. But he knew enough about Midshipman Clark to know to be wary. 'Sir, you're barkin' up the wrong tree about Mary. Leave her out of it.'

'I said turn around, Haggerty.'

The Turtle sighed and made as if to turn but suddenly lunged at Clark in the quickest, most unexpected way he could, just as he would have done back in his pub fighting days. While his whole body pushed forward, he concentrated his left hand on dashing the revolver to one side and that was when he knew he was right to be wary of Clark because the weapon fired with a deafening crack.

Clark had pulled the trigger the very second he realised that the stronger man was going to try and best him. Haggerty fell heavily against him, knocking him to the ground and causing the back of his head to hit the sharp stones that were poking through the ice. His vision momentarily flashed white as sparkling pins shot across his eyes but he was soon aware that he was being held to the ground by Haggerty's superior body weight.

There was that and a great muscular hand threatening to constrict his throat.

'You shot me!' gasped the Turtle, his face a mask of shocked anger. Blood was oozing from his forearm and washing down onto Clark's throat. 'You was gonna do it! You was actually gonna kill me!'

His hand tightened its grip and Clark, finding that one of his arms was unrestrained, punched his assailant in the ribs. But the blows did not even register. They just made the Turtle shift his position until Clark's movement was limited further.

Somehow the damage to the Turtle's arm had no lessening effect whatsoever to the pressure he was placing on the lad's throat, and with no breath finding its way into his shuddering body, Clark's eyes began to close.

It was at that point that the Turtle fought to calm himself and he let his fingers loosen. He leaned in close and stared straight into Clark's vacant eyes. 'You see, I could kill you just like that. That's what you're expecting, isn't it? Sorry to disappoint you. It's not who I am.'

Clark felt the relief flooding through his body. For a few seconds he had been certain that he was finished. However, with fatigue and exhaustion from the struggle finally catching up with him, he did not see the fist coming which knocked his head sideways, sending his consciousness falling into a void of black.

\*\*\*\*

'Right, that's enough of the binoculars,' said Sergeant Burroughs, lowering them and letting them hang about his neck. Whilst looking at the distant enemy, he had done what he could to shield the lenses from the glare of the sun and now decided he had seen enough not to take any more chances. He turned to Sergeant White who sat in the snow next to him, keenly awaiting the report of his closer observations. 'You said you wanted a fight. This is gonna be a good'un.'

They had crept southwards down the valley to the extent of some three miles into the open and had waited for the enemy that they knew must come soon. Here, what passed for a road lying just beneath the receding snow turned off sharply towards the west and some other twisting fjord which neither of them could be bothered to remember the name of. Between the never-ending scattering of rocky slopes and peaks the Germans were finally advancing.

They moved cautiously, because of the terrain as much as the threat of opposition, and led with small, light trucks, cars and a few tanks. Burroughs had scrutinised those tanks carefully and was glad to note that they were not the beasts that he feared might be coming. These things moved on fairly small caterpillar tracks and only boasted double heavy machine guns mounted in turrets that were barely more than shoulder height of a man on foot. There were no large canons amongst them.

'Mark One Panzers,' stated White when Burroughs described them to him. 'How many?'

'I saw at least five but they're still too far away. I couldn't make out the whole column. There'll be hundreds of troops as well.'

'Today's the day, then,' said White, turning and leading the way a short distance down a concealed slope where they could not possibly be observed by the enemy. He unfurled the three foot red flag on a stick which he had brought with him and began waving it heftily above his head.

Burroughs raised his binoculars to his eyes again and looked northwards to the far hill upon which a couple of Eddington's signaller's were perched. 'They saw you, Whitey. They'll be signalling to get the squadron into its bombardment position now. Let's get back.'

'Watch out,' White suddenly cautioned. He had noticed a flight of Stukas passing high across the valley. Were they heading towards Hemmeligstein again? The collective hum of their engines was soon bouncing off the surrounding hills in a persistent echo. 'The bastards know we're here somewhere.'

As soon as the immediate threat was gone they gave each other a quick grin and started pushing their way back through the snow as fast as they were able. Thank God it had thawed enough for them to have been able to discard those comical tennis racquets.

\*\*\*\*

The untimely incapacitation of Lt-Cdr Peterson had thrown Mr Irwin into a whirl of personal turmoil. But while the loss of the senior navigating officer was upsetting on an emotional level, in the sphere of professionalism, the absence of his mentor had created an equally giant void; and the most annoying thing was that that void was completely irrational.

Throughout his nine months on board Irwin had not managed to make any blunders which could be considered dereliction of duty. In fact, he had hardly made any blunders at all but he just did not have the confidence to accept that he could continue with such an unblemished track record for long. He had also not been able to relax in the wardroom since his elevation to 1st Officer-of-the-Watch. He had partaken in conversation with those few officers that he considered to be friends but had done so absent-mindedly. He could not smile at a quip or a joke and he certainly made no jokes of his own. He was now living day to day with the fear that he was going to mess everything up at any moment.

At times he visibly shook under the weight of the responsibility on his shoulders and it was threatening to crush him. There had to be a solution and, thinking on it, there was one thing that he could do. He requested to have Able Seaman Barrett, the foul-mouthed mathematician of the lower decks, posted to the chart house on a permanent basis.

The captain summoned Irwin to his cabin and strongly reminded him that the seaman had other duties to attend to, but Irwin was so eager about this request that he had to pipe up with, 'Sir, I would be greatly reassured if I had him checking my facts and figures as we went along.'

Dollimore screwed up his face in annoyance and said, 'It's about time you stopped selling yourself short. What is it that you think you can't do?'

Irwin wanted to shout about how he had been beaten as a boy, his father telling him he was useless from the word go, how his mother had taken the view that the head of the house was always right; how his teachers at school had punished him hard for innocent mistakes while others had seemed to get away with outright insolence; how his views were routinely dismissed even when they matched whomever's he was talking to; and how insulting it was that the captain himself had only ordered him to show his daughter Betty around the ship because he was the only one without sufficient charm to turn her head.

Even as all that went through his mind it sounded mad but they were the things that made him so, thus leaving him without the confidence to suppose that his performance as an officer could actually be good. Inevitably, he put a stopper on that flood of emotion before it erupted and minimised it to, 'Sir, Barrett has a faster brain than mine. I will do the work but I would like him to be given leave to check what I do.'

Dollimore thought that Irwin was probably right in what he was asking but decided that it would be sending the wrong message to the ship's company. They wanted to know that their officers knew what they were doing, especially now that they might be on the verge of a major action. A show of weakness anywhere near the top could be highly detrimental to the fighting efficiency of the ship. He said, 'Our numbers are depleted enough with having men ashore. Barrett can't be spared from his other duties. Mr Irwin, I have faith that you can deal with whatever's coming. If I didn't, I would just have to appoint the next qualified officer to take your place and I'm not going to do that. The knowledge of that fjord is ingrained in your mind; you know it is. You are going to fight this campaign to a successful conclusion and then, if you so require, we can have this conversation again when you've got us safely back to Scotland.'

Irwin was highly uncomfortable, his skin flushed and his throat dry when he answered, 'Very good, sir.'

He went away thinking how little good it would do anybody if, at the crucial moment, the facts and figures on the chart and note paper became a meaningless jumble of scrawls before his eyes, because that was what could happen if he became too stressed.

It was just as well he did not know that many a mess below decks had men grumbling about that 'idiot' that had inherited the navigating officer's post because that would have tipped him right over the edge.

However, for the moment he had to summon all of his mental powers to survive the new situation which was arising. Within an hour of his conversation with the captain, the expected word came through that the German Army was advancing.

He did what he could to steel himself for the fight, put on his tin hat and took up his position on the bridge. Was this going to be the day that he made his blunder? Come on, he told himself as he warred with his doubts – I know the plan; just get it done.

\*\*\*\*

With no more prevarication than that foisted upon them by the limitations of the engines, each of the three cruisers moved to get into their designated positions directly the signal was received.

Earlier, when the Commander of the Engineering Department, Bill Bretonworth, had listened to the captain's plan, that greasy Scotsman had immediately become worried, describing the idea as 'a bit ticklish'. The astern turbine was designed for short bursts of power, he explained, and prolonged running may well overheat and damage the engines, therefore they would have to proceed in stages; and he could only guarantee thirteen knots – fifteen if they were lucky.

*Burscombe* went in first as was her right being the flagship, followed by the *Farecombe* and the *Marsfield*. They had everybody required at Air

Defence Stations while the hundreds of men responsible for the 6-inch and the 4-inch guns prepared themselves for the coming work. Busily loading up with shells – albeit of the armour-piercing type because the squadron was geared up for fighting other warships, not bombardment work – they were looking forward to laying their barrage. Forty of the larger guns and thirty two of the smaller were going to knock merry hell out of the Germans.

Captain Dollimore had also suggested that the admiral refrain from sending a signal to the Admiralty about their plan until the last minute so that Their Lordships could not have a chance to interfere. The Trondheim campaign had been muddled by too many cooks spoiling the broth and it was going to take months, maybe years, to untangle what had happened there. But would Nicklesworth then be disciplined or praised for his audacity? The only thing they knew right here and now was that something daring was required; this was it, and nobody should be allowed to make matters worse from a distance.

On the chart, beyond the series of thin bends where the fjord narrowed to as much as two hundred yards, there was a stretch which continued almost straight to the north east for over half a mile. Irwin suggested it as a bombardment position and Dollimore had not hesitated in declaring it so. At that point they would be able to position the three ships end to end and, angled slightly with their starboard quarters and port bows towards the banks, present full broadsides against the enemy. Helpfully, the summits of the nearest hills were spread out enough for their low-trajectory shells to fly between them. After all, naval guns were not howitzers.

As they proceeded stern-first, Dollimore asked of Irwin, 'How are we doing?'

Barrett was gone and Irwin was alone with his calculations. His legs as stiff as tree trunks and despising the emotional infirmity which threatened to make him a laughing stock, he replied, 'The tide is currently on the flood, sir, so we can take advantage of that for a while. Though it will turn just before we get into position and the ebb will be six knots coming back the other way. Not ideal. Our thirteen knots of way will be reduced accordingly. I predict our passage shall take no more than one hour and fifty minutes.'

There, the words had come out seamlessly and professionally and even Lt-Cdr Digby, who knew something of his stress, looked over and gave him a discreet wink. He could do it. He would do it.

After dealing with the strangeness of proceeding for so long in this fashion and pleased that the wind was carrying the boilers' disgusting exhaust gasses off in a different direction, they reached their chosen position and hove to, carefully dropping their anchors and shackles of cable. Stream anchors then went over their sterns to steady them against the tidal flow.

Dollimore wondered what the keel looked like up forrard since he had felt the bow scraping along the rocks more than once during those tricky manoeuvres. There were no reports of damage internally so hopefully there was not yet another spell in dry dock beckoning. Something like that really would beg scrutiny from Their Lordships.

Finally, there was no sign of detection from the Luftwaffe. That was the biggest blessing of all.

When his men reported they were ready, he ordered, 'Have the engine room reduce to fifteen minutes' notice.' That would allow Bretonworth to take some of the pressure off the machinery while they did not know how long they were going to be here. 'And have the Fo'c'sle Part of Ship men ready to weigh as soon as I give the order.'

Then they waited.

Smudge relieved the previous lookout up the foremast. He took a yeoman up with him and, from this post nearly ninety feet above the waterline, studied the hill four miles distant which held the intermediate semaphore signallers in the communication chain that led all the way back to the valley. Even through the binoculars they were incredibly small but he had no problem with that. His sight was known to be amongst the best in the ship with people marvelling at how he could detect a rusty pin on the deck at ten yards or even a ship from the mast at ten miles. To bolster this quality, he possessed a natural state of self-assurance which meant that he would never be prone to indecisiveness or hesitation; or rather, he usually did.

He would not admit to anyone that he was feeling the strain of this campaign and he was tired and irritable, but what really did not help was that he was growing bored. Les had returned from his little adventure somehow emboldened in his thinking and was not half as susceptible to the taunts as he used to be. It was no fun when the Irish boy let the abuse go over his head and wash off his back. He would shrug it off, the other men would then not laugh and Smudge would have to think harder about how to hold their attention. In other words, Les was attempting to make him look stupid.

\*\*\*\*

The marines and Baker Company of the KOYLIs were dug in beneath the tree-lines straddling the road about a mile below the track to Hemmeligstein. They held their fire when they saw the familiar figures of two men jogging across the frozen ground in front of them.

Both Burroughs and White were amused and relieved all at once when they dived into the first shallow defensive scrape that they came across. Hearing the engines of the tanks and the rumbling of the caterpillar tracks not that far away, just out of sight in some dead ground behind them, they shared a little laugh to the confusion of the two marines they had just landed on top of.

White held out his hand and the other shook it. The former said, 'Gotta get back to my lads. Hope to see you again soon.'

'You too, chum,' returned Burroughs, and then White was gone.

He then looked down and saw that one of his men, Yates, had in his possession a hefty 0.55-inch Boys anti-tank rifle. Its bipod was resting on the rocks, its impressively large barrel pointing out front. 'Where'd you get that?'

'The infantry just passed it along about an hour ago, sergeant,' was the reply.

'Nice. Ever fired the bloody thing?'

'No, sergeant.'

'Give it here. Let me have a go.'

Soon, the lead tank was in plain view. The grey machine with its occasional streaks of rust might have been small but it was perfectly capable of sweeping them with devastating machine gun fire and then driving over the top of them. With its commander standing with almost the whole upper half of his body out of the small turret, it advanced menacingly towards their hole. This was going to be the first place to be hit. Burroughs knew that the nerves of all those around him were going to be squirming and shaking and, if he was to be honest, he was questioning himself right now about what the hell he was doing. But two things he knew overrode everything else: he was not going to let Jerry pass without a fight; and he was not going to be seen to withdraw until absolutely necessary.

The tank paused about two hundred yards away and, from the column behind, grey-uniformed infantrymen started running out to the left and right.

'They must know we're here,' said Burroughs. He looked up to the sky but could not see their aircraft anywhere. That was something to be thankful for at any rate. It looked like they were going to probe this wood first before calling in the heavy stuff. The caution made sense.

The tank then came on, its looming shape appearing larger in their imaginations than it actually was, its guns pointing with menacing accuracy. Two more appeared, driving a little way out to the flanks.

'Sergeant,' said Yates in an almost pleading fashion. How could he just sit there watching that thing hunt them?

'Just let them come a little closer.'

So, with the enemy at about fifty yards away, Burroughs pulled the trigger and the powerful recoil slammed into his shoulder. With the opening shot sounding like thunder, an armour-piercing bullet flew out and clanged sharply against the steel. It visibly ricocheted upwards in a white flash.

'Shit!'

With rifles and machine guns suddenly clattering all around him, he pulled back the bolt and ejected the cartridge as quickly as he could. Then he fired again, the bullet this time tearing through its victim low down between the caterpillar tracks. The tank stopped, its brave commander slumped dead, as smoke poured out everywhere. Burroughs felt his original burst of desperation just as suddenly turn to elation. We can do this, he kept thinking. Hardly registering what he was doing, he pulled back the bolt again then let off another round into the already stricken panzer.

Suddenly there was an explosion within. The ground all about it shook violently and some of the rocks in front of the marines' holes fell or were pushed aside by the blast. The heat that washed over them was incredible.

Burroughs looked out all across the front. German infantrymen were dropping to find cover wherever they could but they were so exposed that they had few choices. Torn and bloodied soldiers were lying motionless or writhing all around the place as the snow turned red – and the firing went on and on.

Then one of the marines tugged on Burroughs' arm and pointed upwards. The Stukas had arrived and with their morale-busting sirens wailing, dropped towards their feeble entrenchments.

\*\*\*\*

Clark was sitting in an uncomfortable and shadowed corner of the HQ when the sounds of action erupted in the distance but the noise did not surprise him or any of the other officers present. They had been all fired up for it since Sergeant Burroughs' first sighting of the enemy some four hours past and another report had come in on the single field telephone from the front line not ten minutes ago. In many respects it made his own little matter with Haggerty seem completely insignificant and that was what had gone through his mind when he fumbled with the words of the report he had pencilled on the scrap of paper he had procured.

But, no, Haggerty was not of secondary importance for, if you give up on one man, you may as well give up on them all and then where would you be?

Besides, he now wanted to see him about the way he had assaulted him. If somebody could be knocked for six then Clark certainly had been, and he was not sure whether he would have frozen to death if one of Binkley-Walling's men had not walked up the track to find out who had fired off their weapon, discovered him and led him unsteadily down to the HQ. Needless to say, Haggerty had once again absconded.

The major entered and said to Clark, 'It seems as though your mission is over for the moment, young man. Now, if you would be so good as to rejoin Lieutenant Eddington.'

Clark stood up, mastered the wobbliness in his legs and stuffed the paper and pencil into his pocket. 'Very good, sir.'

But just before he got out the door, Binkley-Walling grabbed his arm and stopped him. 'Listen, if we get cut off from you, I've told the men to head north or try for Sweden. Please tell the admiral that we did everything we could.'

Above the roaring of bombs, machine guns and rifles, they could now hear the unmistakeable screams of those damned Stukas diving on the front line. Clark suddenly pleaded, 'Withdraw towards Hemmeligstein, sir, and let us get you out of here now!'

Binkley-Walling frowned and said, 'I'll put your insolence down to the hiding you've received. Now, be on your way.'

Clark made his way back up the slope and, once above the trees, saw the pillars of smoke rising in the distance upon bases of expanding flame. High above, the Stukas were rolling or dropping into their dives unchallenged. There was a military disaster unfolding just over there and the words 'criminal negligence' filtered through his thoughts. Would Chamberlain be able to sleep tonight if he were here to witness what he had done?

Once those planes had gone, it only seemed like minutes before the next lot appeared. What was clear was that all the heavy fire was concentrated one way – against the British line. What had been the outcome of Captain Dollimore's attempt to get his cruisers into the game?

Clark had been so wound up in his own business that he did not even know the answer to that question. The only thing he did know for certain was that if Dollimore did not turn up it meant the *Burscombe* had been sunk.

\*\*\*\*

The gunners of the 25th Cruiser Squadron only had to wait another half an hour after the sounds of battle, rumbling like a distant thunderstorm, had started to reach them along the twists of the fjord. Fire Control had given them their training and elevating instructions and they had been standing patiently at the ready, once in a while making corrections if the ships dragged slightly against their cables or the wind changed direction. Their target area was the open ground in front of the woods where they knew the enemy was presently trying to break through. The advent of that breakthrough would be the moment the big guns were needed. If they could create enough carnage, it might hold them up for a few hours, maybe even a day.

Once in a while, from his blustery position up the foremast, Smudge could see the enemy aircraft circling miles away and was not looking forward to the moment when their attentions were turned his way. He would never forgive the RAF or the Fleet Air Arm for this travesty. Just wait until he met one of those bastards in the pub on his next run ashore.

Suddenly, the Yeoman next to him started saying, 'Our man's signalling. He says, "Comm-ence bom-bard-ment A".'

Without a pause, Smudge lifted his hands to either side of his mouth and shouting down to Dollimore on the bridge, 'Commence Bombardment A, sir!'

Dollimore acknowledged him with a thumbs up and turned to his gunnery officer, 'You may open fire, Mr Digby.'

'Very good, sir,' Digby replied with relish. Into his voicepipe, he called, 'Open fire all main guns and portside 4-inch!' He wanted to add, 'Let the bastards have it,' but he checked himself on pain of being admonished by the captain over what he would otherwise consider a trifle.

There were about two more seconds of quiet before the day was ripped apart by the roar of the guns blasting fire, smoke and shell from their muzzles. As soon as *Burscombe*'s shells were on their way, the gunnery officers from the other two ships gave their orders and thunder rippled from the length of the squadron.

In the turrets, well-drilled orders for sequences and procedures were shouted as the next shells were rammed into the breeches and soon they were ready to go again. There was no pause. As soon as the men in Fire Control knew the guns were ready they fired them again – and again.

****

The telephone cable had been cut by an explosion in the opening skirmish of the battle so when the KOYLI's Captain Tomlinson judged that the moment for the bombardmcnt had come, he had had to send a runner back through the trees with the order. By that point, two of the Panzers had made their way into the gap between the trees where the road innocently wound but Burroughs, still half dazed from the Stukas plentiful near misses, had managed to blast one of the tracks off the lead vehicle with the heavy Boys Rifle.

It was the German infantry which concerned him more though. They were expertly pushing their way towards the tree-line and attempting to eliminate the defensive holes with their grenades. The only good thing about the situation was that they were paying dearly for it. The white ground was already extensively scarred with smears of black, brown and red and the litter of steel and flesh lay everywhere.

The Panzers' machine guns kept chattering, their bullets whipping up dirt and stones and taking chunks out of men's bodies.

Burrough's himself was already cursing a hideous gash of five inches across his left bicep. Although the fight was diverting his attention away from the pain, he was aware that he could not use his arm properly. It refused to move where he wanted it to and he had a suspicion that the blood soaking down his sleeve was blood he could ill afford to lose.

Dragging a field dressing from his pack, he kicked Yates up the backside in order to get his attention and ordered, 'Tie this on my arm! And tight, like a tourniquet!'

At that very second, they heard the screaming of more Stukas overhead and Yates looked up in terror.

'Worry about my arm first!' shouted Burroughs. God, how these men needed to be kept in line.

But as the 500lb bombs dropped from the cradles beneath the Stukas onto the cowering troops, something far worse came out of the heavens onto the advancing German soldiers. Somewhere in excess of two tons of naval shells suddenly dropped all across their advance, grinding and mincing rocks, steel, road, snow and flesh alike.

The noise was horrendous, making soldiers of both sides duck and grimace, certain that the ground was going to open up and swallow them. Never had they felt it so violently quiver before. This must be what an earthquake of devastating magnitude must be like; and when the shelling seemed to subside, it started again.

Burroughs knew of the ten or so seconds it took to reload the cruisers' 6-inch guns so understood the pause but the bombardment gradually intensified, the minor differences in the ships' rates of fire making the fall of shot more constant. As he looked up through the branches and smoke above, he observed the Stukas and fancied he saw one swoop and swerve as though caught in the powerful downdraught of a passing shell. Whatever the case, the pilot dropped his bomb wide and it exploded harmlessly on a nearby unoccupied hillside.

In front, three more German tanks were on fire and the only other one he could see was reversing back along the pitted road as fast as its tracks would take it. Still gallantly firing as it went, it somehow dodged between the explosions and disappeared into the thick black wall of churning earth and smoke.

He watched it go, experiencing a strange mix of disappointment that it had got away whilst wishing the crew the best of luck. But what was that to the right? Enemy soldiers were sprinting into the tree line past the forward entrenchments. They did not fire, just ran.

Burroughs shifted his body round and, yelping with the pain that jarred through his arm, snatched up a .303 rifle and fired at their backs. But they disappeared into the smoke between the trees unharmed to one man's cry of, 'They've got behind us!'

'They won't get far!' answered Burroughs above the continuous roar of the fighting. 'Able Company's back there!'

After what seemed like a lifetime, the shelling suddenly ceased, leaving not much more than residual noise hissing in many painful ears occasionally disturbed by machine gun and rifle fire coming from behind them. That had been a full two minutes of incredible intensity during which as many as six hundred shells could potentially have been fired, though the exact tally was probably much less.

Captain Avery, unhurried and bold in his purpose, strode fearlessly across the exposed ground and eventually lowered himself into the crowded hole. Filthy and annoyed but unhurt, he pushed his way past the men to get to Burroughs and said, 'That bombardment worked like a charm. Though I do think, sergeant, that you should get yourself back to the first aid post.'

'Can't do that, sir,' replied Burroughs, trying to ignore the sharp pain which was now rising in the wake of his combat exhilaration. 'What if that lot come again?'

'We'll stick it to 'em, won't we lads?' Avery said, his voice raised in fully accepted bravado.

'Aye aye, sir,' came the replies from around them.

To Burroughs, Avery finished with, 'Get that wound sorted out then I'll see you back here.'

The sergeant smiled, nodded and took himself off towards the rear, more than proud that this marine detachment had been able to teach the Germans and the Yorkshires a thing or two.

****

His ears still ringing from the explosive sound of the *Burscombe*'s main armament, Les Gordy looked about at the men standing ready with him at the pom-pom guns and decided that he was not missing those that he would usually find here with him. Pincher was a good mate, sure, but the Turtle and the others were not; and that Smudge! Well, thank God his action station was up the foremast. He was something else and Les could not imagine what everybody thought was so funny about him.

Thinking on that, however, people's attitudes had cooled a bit towards him after Les had accused him of 'self-imposed retardation', a term he had just happened to pick up from that wonderful pilot fellow, Lieutenant Hanwell. Smudge had reacted with unprecedented fury at the slight but Les had still been too inspired by his little Walrus adventure to care much about the backlash. A lot of the other men were beginning to whisper that Smudge should be able to take the abuse if he was willing to dish it out.

Things were changing.

Having spent some time away from the ship and its bullies Les was definitely making personal headway. He had been involved in something which had appeared more important than cleaning, polishing, painting, heaving and pulling and it had shown him a possible future. A better one. For the first time since volunteering for service in the navy back in the autumn of 1938, he was sensing the return of the original driving enthusiasm he had felt over the confusion which had plagued him ever since.

Everything had seemed so possible when he had first joined up. In Ireland he had been brought up peaceably enough in a proud but quiet family. He understood that there were divisions of a sort between his people and those of the UK but he did not have a fully rounded opinion on the matter because his father had thought him too stupid to absorb it; and he had had no other friends to spell it out for him either. There had only been a girlfriend but she had understood less than him about life outside Belmullet and had forcefully told him to get lost because apparently he refused to satisfy her. He still had no idea what that had to do with anything.

But Les liked ships and, knowing that war was likely, had signed onto the Royal Navy. His father had accepted it, even if reluctantly, and had sent him on his way, saying, 'I'm probably wastin' my feckin' breath but take this copy of *Les Misérables*. It's a classic. Never forget the spirit of the barricade. Come back to us one day when you've become a man and I'll see if you've learnt anything.'

What had he learnt? Nothing from that book because he had not understood a word of it – the fifteen or so pages that he had struggled through anyway.

Back to the present, Leading Seaman Paddy Walbrook was perhaps the man that he most wanted to look up to. That big brother-Irishman was standing just a couple of feet away, patiently waiting by his station at these pom-poms looking formidable in his anti-flash hood and tin hat. Better him than the Turtle, that was for sure.

Paddy noticed Les looking at him and suddenly asked, 'So, what happened when you went up in the Walrus?'

Les looked at him almost in shock. He had a genuinely interested look on his face. Pleased to be able to tell the story to somebody reasonable, Les began, 'Well, we had to …'

His voice was suddenly drowned out by an announcement from an officer which was cutting out through the nearby loudspeaker, 'Enemy aircraft off the port quarter! Enemy aircraft off the port quarter!'

'You'll have to save it for later!' said Paddy to the scathing command from a nearby petty officer of, 'Pipe down! No talking!'

The enemy were coming from the opposite direction to that which Les and his mates were facing so they looked up over their shoulders to watch the Stukas getting into position to dive. He jumped when the portside anti-aircraft guns started spitting their shells and bullets skyward but soon calmed his nerves again. He was slowly getting used to all this even if they were anchored here, a stationary target, instead of manoeuvring outside the fjord's estuary.

That said, the planes' screams still made his body shake. It was the one thing which really grated on him but he knew that he was not the only one. Before he hardly understood what was happening, the first Stuka was swooping low over the masts and a small black bomb was dropping in an unnaturally slow manner down towards them. It crashed into the gently rippling surface of the water and blew it upwards in a deafening blast. The frothy grey-white rose up and then crashed over the starboard pom-poms and flight deck.

Some of the men cowered under the nearby deckheads and one or two more were knocked over by the downpour but Les and Paddy stood by their guns, their pride the only casualty.

Half drowned, Les gasped, 'Like I wasn't cold enough already!' and the other man gave him a grin. Things were just getting better and better.
\*\*\*\*

Bombs fell all around the three cruisers. Shrapnel and water flew everywhere, which should have been more devastating but for the very heavy barrage they were able to put up.

Nicklesworth and Dollimore stood alongside each other on the *Burscombe*'s bridge watching the planes making their attacks. They both felt the tension. Each bomb was very close. The upper and fo'c'sle decks were wet and chunks were being nicked out of the thinly armoured sections of the ship all over the place, probably out of some of the men as well. It was just a matter of keeping their nerve. This otherwise foolish venture was given its perspective by the fact that they had vowed to stay in the fjord for as long as they were able.

But now their barrage was weighing heavily on Dollimore's mind. It was depleting their ammunition at a much faster rate than he would have liked and there was the possibility that they might run out of shells and bullets before this little episode was over. Earlier calls to the Admiralty for these particular fresh supplies had simply come to nothing.

When the Stukas had finished their work and were flying off to the south, Nicklesworth turned to Dollimore, his face an angry shade of red, and said, 'When the ammunition is down to ten per cent we are weighing and proceeding at full power.'

'Sir ...'

'And even that is cutting it too close to the bone!'

There had been no need for the hard tone because Dollimore fully agreed with him. Leaning over the voicepipe, he ordered, 'Engine rooms come to Immediate Notice to Obey Telegraphs.'

\*\*\*\*

A little later, while things were still relatively quiet, Dollimore passed the word that this was the moment to get their Action Messing sorted out. They had to make the most of the time they had in order to get the men fed.

As oggies, soup, tea, kai and a chance to buy nutty or cigarettes appeared, the ship's company were appreciative. There was nothing like such a diversion to lower the tension and serve to fill the stomach at the same time. But it was while they were enjoying this that fresh sounds of distant battle began to drift down to them from the valley once more.

\*\*\*\*

The front line had been silent for a while. Now, nearly two hours later, the dampened sounds of a fresh assault were emanating from the shadowy spaces between the trees. Machine guns, rifles and pistols of varying types were rattling their unique reports from everywhere and bullets were even hitting trunks near to where Major Binkley-Walling was standing, adding flying wood splinters to his list of worries.

He began to feel helpless. He could not leave this command position and yet was itching to know what was happening at the front.

He had hoped that the Germans would have withdrawn to lick their wounds until tomorrow but, as that was not to be the case, he had sent orders that Baker Company and the marines should fall back through Able's positions to allow him to initiate Bombardment B, a shelling as devastating as the first but adjusted to wipe out the southernmost quarter mile of the woods – that was providing the cruisers still remained in the fjord. There had been no signal to the contrary.

With every minute that passed he expected a runner to arrive telling him that they were ready for the bombardment but there was nothing. After a while, wounded men, shocked and bloody, began appearing, walking up the slope towards him. They were saying, 'They're everywhere, sir,' or 'They flanked us somehow,' and 'They were in amongst our holes, sir.'

'You're A Company, aren't you?' asked the major, duly concerned.

'Yes, sir,' replied a corporal who was holding a shaking hand up to a shattered eye socket.

Binkley-Walling gave it a few moments of thought. If the Germans had got that far then Baker Company's runner must be dead and the men up front must be wondering what had happened to their next bombardment. He cupped his hands to his mouth and faced up the slope to where his navy semaphore signallers were waiting in the clearing. 'Commence Bombardment B!'

'Aye aye, sir!' came the reply and the Yeoman smartly pointed his flags in a series of precise movements for the benefit of the recipients on the hill and beyond.

\*\*\*\*

It did not matter to Smudge that the Yeoman next to him commented, 'At least they ain't bloody Stukas this time.' He had long ago wearied of this fight.

A formation of twelve high-level bombers coming up from the south turned towards them and unleashed their payloads at exactly the same moment that the 6-inch guns roared out again to the orders for Bombardment B. Smudge, covering his ears as he continued to sit up the shaking foremast, watched unimpressed as the bombs fell.

The *Burscombe*'s array of anti-aircraft guns had also belatedly sent up their barrage, purposely limited to a very short window of opportunity because there was just not much ammunition left.

Bombs fell in the water all around them. Some even fell on the shore a couple of hundred yards away and Smudge found himself waiting for the one that was going to knock him from his perch. He suddenly and quite inexplicably had an attack of vertigo. His mind kept telling him that he was shortly to go crashing down onto the myriad of steel fittings below and it caused him to tense up in a way he had not experienced since that first day five years ago when he had climbed the mast at the shore base of HMS *Ganges*.

Not sure about what he had been capable of as a raw recruit, he had cautiously crept up the ropes, certain that he was going to fall and eventually just as cautiously descended. When the chief at the bottom had shouted, 'Are you taking the piss? Too slow! Do it again!' he had thrown his vertigo to the wind and heaved himself to the upper yardarm and down again in what must have been a record time. The fact that the chief then shouted, 'Too fast! Do it again!' only opened up his mind to the wondrous possibilities of paradox and hypocrisy – but that was another matter.

Right now, the crashing of the bombs and guns were jangling his nerves and causing his imagination to stoop to the concept of a vertigo that had long ago been banished. He forced himself to think of how he was going to punish Les later on and that went some way to making him feel better.

Down on the bridge, Lt-Cdr Digby watched his guns perform and savoured the gratifying noise and stench of cordite smoke. He had rarely seen so many weapons in use all in one go and never ceased to be amazed at what these ships were capable of. However, the time came all too soon when he had to order a ceasefire. The bombers had run away after only scoring more superficial hits and the two minutes allotted for the main bombardment in the valley was up. His ears still pounding, he sent out the order, 'Get me an anti-aircraft ammunition report!'

Very soon reports came up from the gun crews and magazines all over the ship and, after jotting down some figures in his notebook, he was able to turn to Captain Dollimore and say, 'Sir, we've dropped below fifteen per cent remaining.'

'In the magazines? What about the ready use lockers?'

'Fifteen per cent overall, sir.'

'Very good.' Dollimore then turned to look at Nicklesworth.

The admiral did not react for a good few seconds. Could he push this further? Dollimore clearly wanted to go. God damn it! The blasted man was right. They had been more than lucky to have managed two bombardments under this pressure. That luck could not hold out.

As if to accentuate his doubts on the matter, AB Smith's voice came to them again from the voicepipe reporting on another formation of bombers circling in towards them a few miles away. Nicklesworth nodded at Dollimore. 'You know what to do.'

Dollimore issued his orders, 'Weigh both anchors! Obey Telegraphs! Signal *Farecombe* and *Marsfield* to weigh and proceed immediately!' Finally, to the Yeoman up the mast, he ordered, 'Send a signal for Major Binkley-Walling: "25th withdrawing".'

While the yeoman next to Smudge waved his semaphore flags in their precise configurations, the hatches down on the fo'c'sle and quarterdeck flew open and the men who had been standing by to assist with the anchors ran out to achieve their tasks next to the smoking barrels of the main guns. Their sense of urgency had never been greater. Down below, the capstan motors whirred heavily as they pulled up the cables.

\*\*\*\*

A strange silence had fallen all across the battlefield. Sergeant White, light-headed, confused, his legs aching and blood dripping from his right ear, hauled himself uncertainly to his feet and tried to comprehend what had just happened. He barely remembered leaving his hole after shooting down a grey-clad infantryman, trying to follow the order to retire. The Stukas had done for at least five of his men and he had been attempting to get back to the line that he knew was occupied by Able Company when the whole wood had exploded about him.

He had thrown himself to the ground as it shook and heaved and had felt the debris of torn earth and branches raining down on his body. Amidst the cacophony of destruction he had also heard whole trees crashing down. He thought he was a dead man and, when the explosions suddenly ceased, had finally hauled himself up with utter disbelief when he realised that he was somehow not. He stumbled ahead, seeing the pockmarked and cratered snow littered with branches, bodies and discarded weapons. He felt sicker and sicker with each step of understanding.

Bombardment B had fallen on him and his men. Yes, it had fallen on the Germans too since they were everywhere amongst them but the shelling was supposed to have begun only after Baker Company had fallen back. What the hell had happened?

A dirty figure appeared a few yards away, calling, 'Sergeant, come this way!' though the man's voice was barely audible through his battered eardrums.

He turned around and around, looking every which way. There were no Germans chasing him.

'You wait 'til I get my hands on those bastards,' he muttered murderously. It was clear he meant the navy.

# FOURTEEN

## The Moment of Crisis

In the wider and straighter sections of the fjord it was possible to bring the cruisers up to full power and, keeping at least two cables length of distance between them, they charged for the open sea at thirty two knots. This meant that they were heading into relative safety within half an hour of weighing and proceeding. Not a man in the squadron was sorry to see the back of those miles of dead, rocky hills and mountains. They certainly never thought they would be so happy to see the sea.

But the Luftwaffe continued to hunt them all the way. The airmen would by now be filled with such vindictiveness – if they were not already before – at the destruction the ships had wrought amongst their comrades on the ground.

Dollimore and Nicklesworth watched as the Stukas, still confident in their victorious invulnerability, changed tack and concentrated on the lead ship, the *Marsfield*.

Captain Iggenham had his anti-aircraft gunners putting up all the defence that they were able but the Germans had finally figured out that that smaller cruiser possessed but half the guns of the others. To make matters worse, Dollimore could tell that there were no pom-poms in action and that the Oerlikons and 4-inch guns were firing very conservatively. Their ammunition was almost entirely spent.

Now that there was room to manoeuvre in the estuary, Nicklesworth ordered, 'Signal the squadron to form line abreast! We must be able to support each other better!'

But even as the Chief Yeoman was flashing the message with the morse lamp the *Marsfield* turned hard-a-starboard in an evasive move against the Stukas which were practically upon them.

At the same time there was a sudden flash about one of the diving planes and a bright flame shot out from its nose. With bits of metal flailing out to

277

left and right and trailing black smoke, it went into a steeper dive than it already had been and violently exploded against *Marsfield*'s port waist. Chunks of the plane flew off in every direction as a fireball shot across the aft superstructure and enveloped the bases of the funnel and mainmast.

The roar of the explosion reached the *Burscombe*'s bridge soon after and when the maelstrom of the original impact cleared, they could see the tail of the aircraft sinking in the white froth it had churned up in the water. The afflicted cruiser sped on with fire and smoke pouring from her side. It was inconceivable that there could have been no casualties and Dollimore continued to watch with the mixed anguish of victory and despair as the last Stukas pressed home their attacks.

Thundering fire blasted out from her once more as a bomb struck her up forrard. How much easier it was for the Stukas when the ships could not give anything back. But the *Marsfield* continued out into the open sea with *Burscombe* and *Farecombe* eventually conforming either side to cover her with their guns.

****

'Altogether a successful action,' said Nicklesworth an hour later when he had summoned Dollimore to his bridge.

'Yes sir,' the captain agreed because the admiral was not wrong for all that the *Marsfield* had been pretty badly mauled. Damaged she was with twenty-eight casualties but she was not sunk and the squadron had managed to get off two effective bombardments on the valley. The latest semaphore signal to be received from Binkley-Walling had simply read: "Thank you. Enemy retired".

Dollimore looked at Nicklesworth closely. He saw tiredness and strain there but perceived that the other was seeing the same thing in him. No matter. There was still plenty of work to be done and he suspected that he was just about to find out what that work entailed.

The rear-admiral said, 'A couple of things from home, Charles. Firstly, the radio is broadcasting that the government's in crisis. Apparently, Chamberlain made some sort of a public speech about the advantages gained from the evacuations of Namsos and Andalsnes.'

'What advantages?' asked Dollimore, immediately unable to comprehend such wicked delusion and too far tried to prevent his past, suppressed character from rising to the surface. 'He handed the whole southern half of Norway to the Germans on a plate. He must know better than anybody the implications of his folly amongst the other neutrals and the French. They were looking to us to repel the invader; and now here we sit, Binkley-Walling's men the last thing standing before the enemy and the north. He may well have stalled them today but tomorrow he'll be annihilated!'

'Charles, Charles,' Nicklesworth said, holding up a hand to stop him. Throughout this campaign he had knowingly been testing Dollimore's patience but now that patience was on the verge of snapping, he took no pleasure in seeing it. He had grudgingly come to respect this captain too much. 'I'm with you on this. It would appear that both sides of the House of Commons are calling him out. They're probably sick of his procrastination and compromise.'

Reining himself in somewhat, Dollimore still fumed, 'Fobbing the Opposition off is all he's been doing. You shouldn't be allowed to play party politics in the middle of an international crisis.'

Nicklesworth shrugged. 'Well, I don't know too much about that but the situation seems to have had some bearing on our predicament. We have new orders. We were fighting here so that Chamberlain might save face, but wiser counsel has prevailed.' He handed a slip of paper to him.

Dollimore squinted tiredly in the dim light and read:

*To Rear-Admiral Commanding 25th Cruiser Squadron*
*TJIERREFJORD is to be evacuated of all Allied troops without delay.*
*W.S. Churchill, FIRST LORD OF THE ADMIRALTY*

'Good,' said Dollimore with noticeable relief, 'although this should have happened the moment Trondheim was given up on. I will see this done tonight.'

Then, for the first time in the three months since Nicklesworth had set foot on this ship, he smiled. 'Inform Binkley-Walling of the order and work out the details. I'll endorse whatever you decide.'

'Very good, sir.' Dollimore rose, invigorated but confused. Being given a free hand to bring this matter to a close? Was the admiral playing some new game with him? No, the man seemed less arrogant and more genuine in his outlook today. Anyway, even if he was wrong, those men still ashore came before all personal considerations.

\*\*\*\*

Fulton-Stavely's two destroyers were going to bear the brunt of the evacuation and so tasked, the small ships headed into the fjord at full power as this tortured day slowly drew to its end. The tide was on the flood so, if everything went smoothly, they would be in the lake by the time it got dark.

The Stukas attacked them when they were about three quarters of the way up. A flight of six aircraft screamed down and bombed them, narrowly missing them and adding an element of desperation to the mission in hand. All the men knew that the situation was coming to a head and they were becoming less and less certain about their chances of making it out alive.

Soon the light had faded significantly enough to stave off further attacks. The Luftwaffe still did not come at night. Fulton-Stavely knew he had perhaps three hours before the final onslaught began.

To add to this, the Germans' spotting of the destroyers had also taken their attention away from the cruisers, a blessing since Dollimore had been manoeuvring to take the *Burscombe* back into the fjord again in order to be on hand when the sun rose.

Leaving the *Farecombe* and the damaged *Marsfield* behind patrolling the estuary, Dollimore and Nicklesworth stood upon the bridge, guiding her for the last time towards the conclusion of this degrading affair. In the chilled darkness, the officers and lookouts had a forlorn air about them.

Lieutenant Irwin was numb. He was not quite sure what he felt other than that he could not reconcile himself with the various forces that had brought them to this point. Such a vicious clash of arms between civilised societies should have no place in the modern world. Why did educated men behave in such a fashion?

When they had been planning this final incursion, Captain Dollimore, another educated man, had, as ever, shelved any question of morality in order to get straight down to business. 'What will be the state of the tide in the lake during the night?'

Irwin, trying to dampen his own fears and doubts, had replied, 'It's a risky business, sir. It will be on the flood the whole time and high tide will be forty three minutes after sunrise.'

'No doubt Fulton-Stavely will still be evacuating the troops at that time, so we'll need to get in close.'

'We won't have long to turn and get out again, sir,' said Irwin in such a tone as to suggest the foolhardiness of going in there at all.

'How long are you giving me?'

'Erm, thirty … thirty minutes, no more.'

\*\*\*\*

Lieutenant Philip Dollimore narrowed his eyes as he tried to recognise the features of the shore ahead from the *Crayhorn*'s previous venture into the lake. His memory was a little fuzzy on the subject. Perhaps he should not have had those shots of whisky earlier on. But then, if they dulled his memory for detail, they had also served to give him whatever clarity he needed to fight the enemy. He thought about the little hip flask he had in his pocket. Something in the back of his mind was saying to him that he really should have thrown it overboard. But then the devil on his shoulder kept equating that with stupidity.

For the moment he could hardly make anything out on the shore. The fires had finally been extinguished and a dark tension pervaded everything. The nothingness was even more sinister than those visions of Hell; or that other night of long ago when they had cornered that tanker in that other fjord. What was the name of it now? Not the fjord, the tanker...

They had a man down on the fo'c'sle calling out the depths and as both destroyers busily got to laying their anchors, Philip could just see the fishing boats approaching them as before. Of course, there would be many more wounded before the fit troops started coming aboard. He had already told his men down below to prepare to receive soldiers and berth them in every conceivable space. Hammocks were slung everywhere to accommodate stretcher cases. It was going to be bloody awful for them but there was no choice if they were to cram everybody in.

'Look lively, chaps,' Philip said irritably as the fishing boats came alongside and lines thrown. 'Start passing those wounded up here. Come on, come on.'

After a little more cajoling which became evermore impatient, Lieutenant Thorogood appeared at his side and motioned for him to take a few steps away from the work parties. The young man with his innocent ways, fresh face and high voice seemed like such a boy to Philip, but he was deadly earnest when he said, 'I know you've been drinking and I think you'd best calm it down before the captain notices too.'

'What the hell do you know about it?' Philip said with a scowl.

'I need you to calm down.'

'Or what?'

Thorogood showed his palms in despair, 'I must say, I've not known a person be as confrontational as you since I was in the playground.'

'And when was that? Last year?'

'Just calm down or I'll tell the captain what you're about.'

'You devious little shit,' said Philip, squaring up to him.

'No. Think about it. We're in the middle of an operation here. I don't give a damn if *you* come a cropper but you're risking all of our lives too.' With that, Thorogood was gone, back to his own job.

Philip looked at the groaning soldiers being helped over the railing. Just like the last lot. There were so many of them; and he suddenly felt ashamed. They were coming aboard as quickly and as quietly as they could knowing that the odds were stacked against them. Not only were they about to be stuffed into a space below decks that they would not be emerging from if they got sunk but you could almost guarantee that they had all lost comrades in today's fighting – and he had not heard one complaint from any of them.

Why did he think he was so different from other men who had fought and lost?

His mind whirled and he cursed himself for his selfishness, for that was what it was. He did not remember being that selfish before the *Royal Oak*. Why was it that the sight of these men made him feel this shame? He had felt a similar humility when he had been faced with Patricia's plight in London; and suddenly it came to him that his perspective of his own problems changed whenever he saw people who were worse off.

Was this a moment of understanding? He would not be throwing the hip flask overboard just yet.

\*\*\*\*

On the dark beach, Lieutenant Eddington tramped along the wet shingle, now nearly devoid of its thawed ice, and came to stand alongside Captain Tomlinson, who had recently arrived with the first of the healthy soldiers from the scarred valley. He reported, 'All of your wounded are embarked now, sir. This lot will go in the next boat.'

'Thank you.'

Then, as Eddington went back along to check on other progresses here and there, he came across a group of marines with a familiar, if scruffy, man at their centre. 'Sergeant Burroughs? Good to see you back here. Are you hurt?'

Burroughs gave a short laugh and looked down at the bandaged arm which he kept pressed to his front without the aid of a sling. 'It's all rather painful really, sir, but I shouldn't complain. Pain lets you know you're alive.'

'You're easily one of the most incorrigible rascals I've ever met,' Eddington said fondly. 'Get in the next boat and get going. It's supposed to be wounded first.'

'Thanks for the sentiment, sir, but I ain't seen the officers from our detachment yet so I'll wait here with the rest of the lads. We were the first here so we're gonna be the last to leave.'

'As I said, an incorrigible rascal and a fool too.'

'Born and bred,' agreed the sergeant. 'I was built for this, me.'

As Eddington turned to head off elsewhere, he was suddenly stopped by the voice of another man striding aggressively across the shingle. 'Oh, here they are!' came the angered voice from the shadowy figure, his indiscretion ensuring an audience. 'Bloody navy! Shell our blokes, will you?'

'Belay that!' Eddington answered back.

'Don't come the old senior service jargon with me!' cried Sergeant White. 'You dropped your fuckin' bombardment on our heads this morning!'

Eddington was quite certain that he had never been spoken to like this in his entire life – if you discounted some of the things that the senior cadets might have said once upon a time at college.

'First off,' he fired back without a pause, 'I never dropped anything on anyone and second, I would consider walking away before you get yourself into something that's going to cost you dearly. Believe me, one more word and I shall call the MPs over.'

'You …' White began, wanting desperately to carry on.

But it was settled by another figure coming in between them. It was Burroughs, incensed and appalled by the behaviour of the man he had considered a kindred spirit. He grabbed the front of White's tunic with his good hand. 'Welcome to the war, pal. Sometimes shit goes wrong but there ain't no point in stomping up and down about it like a child. I thought that you of all people would understand that. Our squadron took a massive risk to get you a bombardment at all; and who do you think's taking another risk to lift you off this bloody rock?'

'Yeah, well, you're all mad,' was all White could say. He was getting no support from any of the other blokes mustered nearby. Somehow they too were accepting this war for what it was.

'Yeah, well, walk on,' Burroughs retorted, effectively ending whatever association they had fostered in this unforgiving country. Finally, he added, 'We're done here.'

As White walked away, Eddington said, 'Thank you, Sergeant Burroughs, but I was quite in control of the situation.'

'Sorry, sir, I'm not sure what came over me.' But he and Eddington knew perfectly well that it was offence at the criticism of the 25th that had come over him. No one was going to get away with that.

\*\*\*\*

Binkley-Walling had secured the help of a few volunteers to stay put in the forward positions in order to react to any movement of the enemy while the rest of the men moved off at speed along the track to Hemmeligstein. He then had the mortars and machine guns displaced from the mountain on the left flank and had them bolster the defence on the right, closer to their route of escape. Thank God he only had hundreds of men to move instead of thousands. Otherwise, he would have been much less sure about their chances.

This last day had been one which he would not forget in a hurry. The fighting, while proving the mettle of the troops involved, had shown up the deficiencies of the wider British effort – as though he had not understood them before – but worst of all, it had shown up his own deficiencies. He would never forgive himself for misjudging that bombardment. However, he must try to concentrate on the evacuation and the only honourable thing he could do now was command the rearguard action.

The night went very quickly but all his troops were at least heading in the right direction by the time the sun rose. Even the volunteers out in front were beginning to filter back through the trees undetected by any scouting force. If only it would all go this smoothly.

Wishful thinking that was as, once the daylight was lifting the valley out of its macabre gloom, he could hear tanks starting to rumble cautiously along the road a mile distant.

He looked up behind him and saw the backs of the escaping men disappearing along the track between the hills. He would need to give them at least an hour before he started falling back. He suddenly felt very calm. This was going to be the encore of his performance before he handed everything over to the navy. Casting one last look down the slope to his HQ, that odd hut in the middle of nowhere, he decided that he would not be sorry to see the end of that poky, draughty hole and hoped that next time he was on campaign he would have something more substantial to operate out of.

It took about thirty minutes for the leading elements of the German infantry to reach the foot of the slope atop which sat Binkley-Walling's last line of defence. He watched as a couple of cautious men in field grey had a quick discussion, obviously coming to the conclusion that this was the way they wanted to go if they were to find where their foe had slipped off to.

He looked to the left and right and saw his men waiting in their semi-concealed positions amongst the rocks. Some were visibly nervous, others cloaked in the perfect façade of calmness. The latter helped the former to function and his own bravado gave them all purpose. The responsibility of command was a great and precious thing to him and that more than anything else gave him the control that he wanted.

He let the enemy come so far and then he shouted, 'Open fire!'
****

The decks of the *Crayhorn* had never been so packed with men. It was a good thing that so many stores had been depleted because they were even cramming themselves into the closest of storage spaces and, to make matters worse, such was the worn-out condition of the soldiers that had come aboard, they had no idea how badly they stunk. After so long living out in the open and then fighting hard, they were oblivious of the plight they had got themselves into in matters of hygiene.

Also, in the interests of safety, Philip Dollimore had to tell them more than once to steer clear of the fo'c'sle and the stern. 'If we have to open fire, we won't be buggering about asking you to move before we do. You'll be going over the side if you stay there.' What was it they did not understand about that?

Stalking about the decks seeing that everything was just so and growing uneasy about the daylight, he looked across to the *Catterley* and saw more men hauling themselves out of a fishing boat onto her deck. It should not be too long now.

At some point he realised that he had got by without taking another swig of his drink. In fact, having reasoned that some of the exhausted soldiers looked like they could use the whisky more, he had allowed them to have it.

As he squeezed along the waist, the sound of machine guns, rifles and mortars came to him on the morning breeze. He gazed over to where a last trickle of soldiers were running down the track towards the devastated village and the beach. The enemy was practically upon them.

'Just about time to leave?' asked a soldier who was crouched nearby smoking a cigarette.

'Soon,' replied Philip. 'We can get a few more on board yet.'

'Jesus Christ. Where?'

'This is nothing. We had a hundred more men than this stuffed into the *Cossack*.'

The dirty soldier looked impressed. 'You were on the *Cossack*? I read about that. "The navy is here!"'

\*\*\*\*

The beach was almost clear of men. What still remained were pieces of scattered and broken equipment, wreckage and empty crates of all sizes, the sad detritus of mankind's worst folly. Anything that was not worth salvaging was staying in this heap of discarded rubbish. Perhaps the few civilians still cowering in their scorched houses nearby would come and tidy everything up once the soldiers were gone. It would probably take years for them to restore their lives, if ever they could.

At the end of another return trip to the destroyers in *Free Spirit*, Clark jumped into the shallow water from the prow and waded ashore. He had just spied the boy, Oskar Fjelstad, coming down from the houses looking confident and proud. He had forgotten all about him in the confusion of the last few hours. 'Oskar, get in the boat,' he ordered.

As if to emphasise his urgency, there came the sound of a particularly large explosion from the east and both of them looked over to see smoke rising from somewhere along that hotly contested track between the hills.

'I'm staying,' said Oskar with considerable finality.

'You're mad!' Clark all but cried. 'This is your only chance to get out of here.'

'He's right, Oskar,' said Eddington, whom neither had noticed approaching. 'We've given space to other civilians so you should come too.'

'No,' said Oskar, 'the right thing is for me to help my country.'

Clark shook his head. He thought too much of this boy to see him trap himself here when the rest of them were getting away. 'Oskar, your country is lost. The best thing for you to do is leave with us and come back to fight another day.'

'I fight now,' replied Oskar just as vehemently.

286

'No,' said Eddington, 'I'm telling you no. You're still a boy and as such belong in a place safer than this. Get on the boat.'

'I'm fifteen!' said Oskar strongly. 'And there's nowhere else to go. This is my country and I want to stay and fight. Not here on this beach but to …' He tried to think of the word and eventually said, 'I have to resist!'

'Oskar!' Clark made one last plea.

'What would you do if this was England?'

Both Clark and Eddington's argument was stopped dead. They both knew that if German soldiers set foot on British soil then they would be fighting to the death before they saw the bastards settle in. At the same time they were both saddened by the fact that this was the last they would ever see of this brave boy.

Clark undid the belt holding his revolver and ammunition pouch and gave it to Oskar. He could barely utter the words, 'Don't do anything stupid.'

Then Eddington, who was not happy about it but had decided not to admonish Clark for giving up a serviceable weapon, said to the boy, 'Go. Fight on but don't get caught. Get away from here.'

Without another word, Oskar turned and ran back up the shingle towards the bombed wrecks that had once been the simple fishermen's houses before the British had arrived to save them.

Neither man could watch him any further so they turned away.

As they did so they saw the soldiers of the rearguard running along the beach, their wretched figures muddied and bloodied. Two of them advanced as fast as they could bearing one of their pals on a stretcher and finally Eddington and Clark were urging them to get on board the boats as quickly as they were able.

Another big explosion made them look up towards the track.

'Where's the major?' asked Eddington.

'He'll be the last man down here as long as he's alive,' answered an out-of-breath corporal. 'Chances are he won't be, though, sir. Jerry's getting a bit lively.'

'*Getting* a bit lively?' answered Eddington in disbelief. He could see the muzzle flashes of light weapons through the drifting smoke. The fight was very close now and soon the German infantry were going to be able to fire on the beach. Things were getting very interesting indeed.

But even as he thought that, a heavy, thunderous roar made him jump and he had not yet recovered when part of the track exploded in a tumult of fire, rock and dirt. Initially he wondered whether Binkley-Walling's men had managed to set off some great mine that he did not know about, but then suddenly reasoned that the first roar had sounded like a salvo being fired from large naval guns. He glanced out to the west and made out the dark grey shape of HMS *Burscombe* standing sentinel just beyond the terminal moraine. His heart immediately lifted. Whatever anyone said about that terrible business of yesterday's bombardment, nobody could accuse the navy of hanging the army out to dry.

The tired men clambered aboard the boats as quickly as they could while more shells exploded across the German advance. Judging that his boat was full, Midshipman Trent had four of the seamen help him push it off the shingle and finally climbed aboard with them. 'Away you go, cox'n!' he ordered. The old engine came to life in a swirl of petrol fumes and the coxswain turned the boat in order to make good their escape.

Eventually, the last few men came running along the beach. Major Binkley-Walling approached, his revolver drawn and his uniform as torn and dirty as all those around him. He was glancing behind him every now and then as if expecting to see the Germans hot on his heels but he knew that the cruiser's guns had ultimately kept them at bay.

Looking at how the men were throwing themselves into the boats, Clark called to Eddington, 'Sir, get going! I've got room in *Free Spirit* for the last few!'

Eddington, immediately employing his men to push off his boat in the same manner that Trent had, frowned at Clark and called back, 'I've warned you about that 'free spirit' business! It shan't get you anywhere, you know!'

'Off this beach will be a good start!' Clark laughed.

Eddington shook his head and had his coxswain drive them away.

With the remaining soldiers climbing aboard *Free Spirit*, Binkley-Walling came to an exhausted stop after his rough retreat across such difficult terrain and regarded the waiting midshipman. 'Mr Clark, I can only thank you for your diligence in this affair. I'd like you to know that this debacle has taught me one valuable lesson amongst many: the navy doesn't know the meaning of the word 'impossible'. Bravo, young man.'

'Yes, sir,' replied Clark as cordially and patiently as he could. Why had the major stopped to make a speech in the middle of a desperate evacuation which was being conducted on a knife-edge?

Binkley-Walling climbed aboard with a sigh and sat on the bench. The planks were wet and he guessed that they had been scrubbed down for a good reason – there were still traces of blood hereabouts. He looked up, saw Sergeant Burroughs sitting there with his smashed arm and said, 'It's unforgiveable. I left too many behind.'

Burroughs nodded his understanding. Captain Avery had not reappeared from the valley either.

As *Free Spirit* rattled out towards the *Crayhorn* with the occasional 6-inch shell soaring overhead to their explosive destinations, Clark looked back at the village, this poor Norwegian backwater that should never have been involved in such a fight. When he had arrived, the place had been peacefully alive for a hundred years, its inhabitants living in houses painted in extravagant colours to a jolly style one would be hard pressed to find in the staid land of Britain. Now, the whole place was a black and grey ruin with household items, broken military equipment and rubble littering every spare space that may have been a road, a courtyard or a dwelling.

Destruction and subjugation is our legacy to the Norwegians, thought Clark sadly.

\*\*\*\*

Philip reached down and pulled the last man over the *Crayhorn*'s railing to a gasped, 'Thanks.' It was David Clark – an older looking David Clark with dirty, weather-beaten features and more than one hefty bruise on his face.

Philip nearly said, 'Good to see you,' but nothing came from his mouth. He needed to avert his eyes away from the man who had so recently made him uncomfortable so turned and waved to Fulton-Stavely on the bridge, the signal that it was finally time to leave this place.

He suddenly heard the sound of aircraft. This was what everybody had been waiting for. There were profanities and exaggerated murmurs all around the decks with the necessity to express: 'Why don't we just get out of here?'

The Stukas appeared from the south and circled once while the pilots, so well practised in their murderous art, observed the ships below and wasted no further time in rolling into their steep dives.

Philip watched them come straight down at him and looked upon them with scorn, willing them to do their worst.

Clark threw himself into a crouch against the bulkhead, covering his head with his hands.

Philip laughed at him and the soldiers. Such panic all around.

The few guns of the *Crayhorn* and *Catterley* that could be elevated far enough chattered out their lethal fire but it did not seem like anywhere near enough. Suddenly he heard heavier guns firing and saw white tracers cutting across the course of the Stukas. Small explosions rocked the aircraft and they swerved to the left and right, the pilots duly perturbed by the new threat.

Philip pushed through the cowering clump of soldiers and climbed the nearest ladder so that he could stand atop the next deck to see where the barrage was coming from – as if he did not already know.

Staring out across the port beam, he saw the great hulk of HMS *Burscombe*, that powerhouse of dark grey steel turning slowly not two hundred yards away. He heard the soldiers' cheers until they were drowned out by the crescendo of Stukas screaming and bombs hitting the water.

The cracks and clattering of shrapnel tearing holes in the *Crayhorn*'s steel and ripping flesh in their destructive passage through the mass of stained khaki silenced the euphoria and gave way to pain and terror, but Philip stood up on the deck by the mainmast thinking about nothing more than that he wished his father would go away.

Clark stared up at him, wondering that he must be either the bravest man he had ever met, barking mad or drunk. What was the possibility that it was all three combined?

\*\*\*\*

Captain Dollimore scanned the whole scene through his binoculars from the bridge of the *Burscombe*, watched the great geysers of water go up around the destroyers, the Stukas banking away and climbing with bullets and shells chasing them. But what was that he was seeing on the aft superstructure of the *Crayhorn*? An officer staring out at him, careless of the fact that everything was exploding around him. The frame of the body was familiar. It was Philip. For the love of God, did he have a deathwish?

'Get down from there, you madman!' he shouted, knowing that his son could not hear him.

But luckily for his own anguish, he was distracted by the sight of Lt Irwin glancing nervously at his watch, not once, not twice but three times. He knew at that moment, beyond the shadow of a doubt, that Irwin would never command his own ship. Such a waste; a thoroughly decent brain trampled by a weak character. But he knew what the basis of Irwin's present worry was. They were fast running out of time before they would be trapped in the lake and he would be shouldering the weight of the responsibility in the most negative way possible. It had already taken them nearly fifteen minutes to steam in, turn and engage the Stukas.

Dollimore quickly glanced back at the destroyers and saw that their anchors were being weighed. Good, they were preparing to leave. 'Steer three points to port! Revolutions for twenty knots!' he ordered into the voicepipe.

The *Burscombe* left behind a frothing wake cutting down the middle of the glassy lake, her aft turrets trained slightly off the port quarter with their barrels elevated, ready to fire if German soldiers appeared on the beach.

Dollimore looked back and was relieved to see that both destroyers were getting under way. Up above, the Stukas were heading off to replenish with new bombs so that they could come back and continue the onslaught.

In a very few minutes the *Burscombe* was nearing the western end of the lake and the narrower stretch that led into the main course of the fjord. Now was the time to slow down because, while Dollimore did not want to be caught by the tide, neither did he want to leave the destroyers behind. He leaned over the voicepipe and gave his orders.

But suddenly, the deck plates began shuddering beneath their feet, the vibrations travelling up through everybody's bones as the ship's momentum was curtailed in a more violent fashion than the normal cutting back on the throttle should have dealt. What was going on? What was making that awful grinding noise?

As if one needed telling? Irwin's mind froze as he took in the blank looks from some of the other men but he was under no illusions about what was occurring. He had made his fatal mistake. He had got it wrong and had finally, after all these months of doubt and apprehension, proved himself right.

The captain clung onto the bridge casing as he fought to maintain his footing then, whilst the grinding continued and the ship came to a gradual stop, he ordered, 'Stop all engines!'

The *Burscombe* was suddenly helpless with black smoke drifting forlornly from her after funnel. She was ever so slightly bow down, motionless with her stern stuck hard against the terminal moraine, that ancient mound of stones and fused rock which had so long ago been swept down here by the melting glaciers.

'How could it be?' muttered Irwin. He had taken such careful consideration of the tides in order to avoid this obstacle. How could it be that the water level had dropped more than he thought it would by this time? The answer must lay somewhere between the paperwork and his thought processes but he could not put his finger on it. In the meantime he knew that the men around him were cursing him behind his back. Here it was that, despite his best efforts, he had led them to disaster.

'Snap out of it, Mr Irwin,' said Dollimore, his voice full of warning. 'There's much work to be done.'

But surely the captain must blame him as well?

'At what rate will we lose the depth?' continued Dollimore.

'Er, approximately, er, one foot ten inches an hour, sir,' replied Irwin, his voice shaky. But how much could he really trust that?

'Mm, we'd better get cracking.' Leaning over the voicepipe, Dollimore ordered, 'Full ahead all engines.'

Nicklesworth and all the other officers and men on the bridge silently prayed that this would work, that the *Burscombe* could heave herself off the rocks under her own steam – but what of the propellers and the rudder? Would they be clear? It was too bad if not. To do nothing was not an option because if they were stuck here for the next eleven hours then the game would be over for all of them. There was no two ways about that.

The artificers down below turned their throttle wheels and allowed super-heated steam to push through the largest turbines at the maximum pressure they could attain. The light whine which was peculiar to the turbines spinning in a vacuum against nothing more than labyrinth glands grew in intensity as they willed the ship to move. Under their feet the deck plates shivered enough to tell them that all was not right.

Commander Bretonworth, the stolid head of the engineering department, prided himself on the fact that he knew every little whim of the old girl's style of performance from her sounds and movement and quickly convinced himself of one thing. Picking up the phone, he was put through to the bridge in order to report, 'Sir, I'm suspecting that there's damage to at least one of the propeller shafts. I need the opportunity to be certain.'

Up above, Dollimore glanced at the torrent of foam being thrust out from the stern and answered, 'If you're suggesting that we put a diver over the side then I can quite guarantee you that this is neither the time nor the place.'

'I understand, sir, but we must take action if we're to prevent greater damage to the shafts,' Bretonworth continued in the receiver.

Dollimore looked out as the ship inched her way ahead and said, 'It's either the shafts or the whole ship, Mr Bretonworth. Just give me a little longer at this power.'

The engineering commander hung up and was glad that the captain could not see him shaking his head when he muttered, 'Ah, what a fine pickle we're in.'

As he walked to the back of the portside engine and looked down at the thrust block, he noticed the steel shuddering here more than anywhere else and he fancied that he could hear the reduction gearing straining in the unit behind him. That was not good.

Suddenly, there came the distant sound of screeching metal through the many bulkheads aft of him, a heavy clang of something hitting the keel of the ship and then the shaft spun with a greater whine.

Within seconds, he was on the telephone again informing the captain that their propellers were crashing against the rocks and that they were more than likely losing their blades.

Dollimore digested that and looked down to the stern. The water was still frothing up but they were no longer moving. The engines had done all they could so he immediately ordered them stopped. He stared for a brief second up and down the length of the ship.

Nicklesworth, noting the perplexed look on Dollimore's face, wondered if he too was grinding to a halt and felt bound to say something. 'I think perhaps ...'

But many a man had judged Dollimore wrongly at one time or another. He was far from out of ideas. Shoving as respectfully as he could past the admiral, he picked up the microphone for addressing the ship's company and ordered, 'Fo'c'sle Part of Ship men prepare for towing forward.'

Then, 'Chief Yeoman, signal the *Crayhorn*, "We are aground. Take us in tow".'

'Aye aye, sir!' Without further ado, Chief Yeoman Ross started flashing out the message with the small signal lamp. It was only a few seconds before he received the reply: "Understood."

Lieutenant Irwin wished that the deck would open up and swallow him. You never knew, perhaps it would.

\*\*\*\*

Commander Fulton-Stavely turned and said, 'Number One, get down to the stern and prepare the cables for towing aft.'

'Very good, sir,' replied Philip, expertly hiding the sense of amusement which was threatening to overwhelm him. With yet another problem somebody else had got themselves into, he was feeling quite happy with himself. He took himself off down to the *Crayhorn*'s stern, barely able to push his way through the crowds of soldiers now helping their comrades who had been hit by shrapnel in the last attack. Blood was running quite freely down through the scuppers but somehow he did not notice it.

'You men help me prepare the lines for towing aft,' he ordered the ABs helping wounded near the starboardside depth charge throwers. They quickly broke away and assisted him.

The *Crayhorn* passed easily over the terminal moraine and slowly down past the *Burscombe*. How pitiful it was to see that great ship helpless with that sad diminishing plume of smoke drifting up from the funnel to no purpose. Men of the cruiser's company looked over at their comrades in the battered destroyer and cried, 'Good old *Crayhorn*! Think you might be able to handle our weight?'

Philip shouted back, 'You certainly know how to get yourself into a bind, don't you!'

As they passed *Burscombe*'s forward superstructure, he looked up and saw his father looking back down at him. The Old Man just stood up there as motionless as his ship, staring and waiting to see what he would do next. Well, here's the way it is, Philip thought: this time I'm coming to save you. Then he realised that there had never been another moment like this in the whole of his life. Both of his parents had been in such control of everything that there had been no room for him to add anything to the mix. A great sense of satisfaction ran through his body as he considered that. For the first time, perfect old Charles Dollimore needed his son and not the other way round.

Then he saw the men on the cruiser's fo'c'sle preparing their equipment and lines. This should not take too long. To attach a tow line was a simple affair.

\*\*\*\*

With steel wires now attached to the cables or deck clamps aboard both ships, Philip shouted to the nearest chief, 'Let the captain know that we're ready to tow!'

The chief passed the word through the voicepipe at the depth charge station and soon they could feel the boilers and engines gathering power through the deck plates. The water was gradually churned up at the stern and the wires pulled taut as the little destroyer tried to extricate its big sister from her present predicament.

Watching carefully as the ship began to sway and shudder, he eventually became satisfied that the *Burscombe* was indeed slowly moving from the rocks. The soldiers packed along the upper decks watched with wonder at the operation, marvelling at the power of this small ship. With a crescendo of high pressure steam power from below, the *Crayhorn* kept dragging until the other's bow rose and stern fell back to their normal trim along the plimsoll line. Cheers went up from both ships. With the *Catterley* already much further ahead and not stopping for anything, the *Crayhorn* was soon towing the cruiser down the fjord.

But nobody was surprised or in any doubt about what was going to happen when they heard that familiar drone of Stuka engines echoing once again over the hilltops. The buzz had already gone round all decks that the *Burscombe* had all but run out of ammunition and too few guns on the *Crayhorn* could be elevated for a spirited defence. They were nigh on defenceless against the coming onslaught.

Fulton-Stavely said to Philip as the latter reached the bridge, 'We're just going to have to hope that our speed will be enough. *Burscombe*'s rudder and screws are out of action so we'll not be ditching them any time soon.'

'A pretty state of affairs,' replied Philip, looking up at the Stukas that were preparing to come into the attack. There was nothing about them that frightened him. They were just a fact of war and nothing else.

Fulton-Stavely, noticing the de-sensitisation in him, said, 'By the way, well done for the speedy work on the tow wire. It may make all the difference.'

There was no reaction.

The anti-aircraft guns of both ships opened fire and the last of the ammunition blasted its way into the sky, passing between the growing silhouettes of the planes. Those damned pilots were getting good. They were not as deterred by the barrage as they had once been. They had learnt that their chances were still fair even when being shot at. Their losses in this type of action had been light so they had figured that, if they could just hold their course and aim, they should get their direct hits and hopefully still get away unscathed.

'Here it comes,' said Fulton-Stavely, gritting his teeth. But for *Crayhorn*'s very small number of pom-poms and Oerlikons, the guns were silent now, smoking and useless and there was a hard tension along every open deck as the planes swooped down. They were dead on course and there was nothing anyone could do about it.

But, just as it seemed like the bombs must be released onto their heads, the Stukas broke off their attack and roared off to gather height. They had not pressed home their attack! As if from nowhere, heavy machine guns bullets ripped up the water and peppered the rocks on the shore, startling soldiers and sailors alike.

'Skuas!' laughed Philip. 'Would you look at that?'

Silvery-white planes sporting the British roundels on their long, thin fuselages and wings banked and swooped as they fired their guns at the Stukas. With roaring engines they mercilessly chased those hitherto feared machines into the heavens and began teaching them a lesson that they would never forget. Even though they were a doubtful cross between fighter and dive-bomber, the Skuas immediately gave a good account of themselves. In only a few seconds, fire belched from one of the Germans' exhaust pipes which then crept menacingly along its side. The Stuka was soon burning all over. The dying enemy lost speed, the airframe bent and what was left spiralled down onto the hillside to explode into a million pieces.

The spirits of every man in the ships were automatically lifted, not just those on deck but also those closed away in compartments deep below the waterline to whom the word had quickly filtered down that the Fleet Air Arm was on hand at last. Just the very idea that those Stukas could be chased off and hurt was of paramount importance.

Swirling streams of smoke filled the clear sky as Skua bullets damaged their enemy's engines, leaving the pilots with dying machines. The sun glinted off the bright paintwork as the planes darted this way and that in their desperate bid for supremacy of the air. It was clear that the Skua was a better fighter than the Stuka. The Germans tried desperately to gain the upper hand but failed and in short order, they fled.

'Well,' said a visibly relieved Nicklesworth, 'I never thought I'd live to see the day. We've only been asking for the buggers for two weeks. I almost feel tempted to say that they've redeemed themselves. What about it, Charles?'

Dollimore, barely able to break away from his assessing of the ship's damage and far from safe situation, ventured to say, 'We're all in need of redemption at times, sir.'

The men about him, even Lt Irwin, who was shaking for his less than exemplary conduct in this affair, took some heart at the captain's forgiving words. They all knew him for a man who did not say anything lightly, whatever or whoever he was talking about. If it was not for him they most likely would have been sunk long ago. Under his command, HMS *Burscombe* was still the Home Fleet's luckiest ship.

# FIFTEEN

## Beyond the Fjord

The companies and passengers of these three worn and battered ships, more than happy to see the back of Norway, were encouraged even further when they finally pushed their way into heavier waves and saw what was ready to receive them beyond the estuary. Steaming about a mile offshore and protected by a small group of destroyers was an aircraft carrier, her Skuas circling high above and preparing to land on her flight deck.

'HMS *Glorious*,' said Dollimore. 'God bless her timely intervention.'

Lt-Cdr Digby, more prone to think that she had been rather late on the scene, raised his binoculars to his eyes and looked at her more closely. 'Bit of an ugly beast, isn't she, sir?'

'I hardly find that relevant.' Dollimore and some of the older members of the service may well have remembered *Glorious* from twenty years past when she had lived life as a 15-inch battlecruiser. As part of Britain's tentative dalliance with naval aviation – that concept which too many people in the past had thought distasteful – she had had her big guns and superstructure removed to make way for a 550 foot flight deck and small island.

Digby was too young to remember her old configuration. 'Not like the new purpose-built carriers, sir.'

Dollimore looked at him sternly. 'Did she not prove her worth already? Purpose-built or not, that's the future right there and we should count ourselves lucky that Hitler doesn't have any of them.'

Digby did understand what the captain was getting at but he had spent a whole decade studying naval gunnery and was still not convinced that a few squadrons of planes could be superior to the power of the battle fleet. This question was still being asked at the highest levels: why, if aircraft were so important, was every nation on the planet still investing in the big gun?

To Dollimore, however, the question was something very different; and one with which he would never admit publicly that he was in complete accordance with young Midshipman Clark, of all people. The Royal Navy still placed an overbearing emphasis on the battleship, the big gun and the battle line – in other words the tactics of Jutland – as opposed to the developing areas of aviation, submarines and inter-service cooperation. Did not true mastery of the sea require proper attention to be paid to the control of its depths and the air above, not just its surface?

It seemed that more harsh lessons were required.

****

Under clear blue skies, where the Skuas continued to fly their constant patrols, casualties were transferred from the destroyers into the care of the surgeons of the *Burscombe* and *Marsfield*, Eddington and his men returned to their ship and Rear-Admiral Nicklesworth transferred his flag to the *Farecombe*.

When the admiral stepped out onto the *Burscombe*'s quarterdeck for the last time, he paused to look at the patient sailors standing to attention at the top of the steps leading down to his waiting boat. They looked fresh and smart, clean and alert and not like they had just spent the last few days being dive-bombed by Stukas.

He turned to Captain Dollimore, who had been walking a few paces behind him. There was a calm, professional appreciation in the way the two men now regarded each other. There was none of the animosity of old, only a new understanding.

Nicklesworth said, 'I very much hope to serve with you again one day, Charles. You can take it from me that I consider you did everything you could have done and more.' He held out his hand.

Dollimore took it and they shook as brother officers do when standing on common ground. 'Thank you, sir.'

'It just remains for you to get these damaged ships home. I'm taking *Farecombe* and *Glorious* to Narvik. You'd never believe it but there is a massive effort being made there to get rid of the Germans in the town; tens of thousands of troops, British and French, proper air cover, tanks, actual anti-aircraft guns – the works.'

'Sounds almost too good to be true, sir.'

'Well, perhaps old Chamberlain's woken up.'

They saluted smartly then Nicklesworth stepped onto the stairway to the piercing whistle of the chief piping the side. Then the rear-admiral's pennant was struck from the mainmast. HMS *Burscombe* ceased to be the flagship.

\*\*\*\*

But had old Chamberlain woken up? If he had not then he was never going to be given the chance.

As the *Burscombe* was towed slowly southwards down the Norwegian Sea to a zig-zag pattern and screened as best as possible by *Marsfield* and *Catterley*, Dollimore looked at the details of a news report that had been picked up in the Sound Reproduction Equipment Room and called the department heads to his cabin. For the first time in a long time, his most senior officers were gathered before him. Their old eagerness of days gone by was missing and they all appeared more serious and advanced in age but they were still companionable and at ease with each other; except for Irwin. He was the only one who did not seem to fit as they sat or stood hereabouts, waiting for his words. The rest were good men and solid leaders – Commanders Locklin and Bretonworth, Surgeon-Commander Lawson and Lieutenant-Commanders Digby and Gailey.

Dollimore wasted no time in saying, 'The prime minister's finally stepped down, gentlemen. Chamberlain has succumbed to attacks from both sides of the House. They voted, it was decided that his party did not hold the support that it must to govern and he's been unable to form a National Government that are prepared to trust him. So he has made way for another to take his place – Winston Churchill.'

All expressions in the cabin changed whether they were in the form of surprise, resentment or satisfaction. In fact, the varying looks reminded Dollimore of just how different these men were for all that the navy tried to mould them into the same thing.

He continued, 'I'm going to allow the BBC News to be broadcast through the ship this evening but I didn't want you to be taken unawares …'

Irwin's face was as white as a sheet as he started shaking his head.

Dollimore looked at him. 'What is it, Mr Irwin?'

'Does nobody see that we've just lost all chance of a peaceful solution to this war?'

'That's enough!' snapped Locklin in what was probably the first time he had ever divulged an inner feeling. 'That's just the sort of defeatist rubbish – '

Dollimore held up a hand to silence the commander and said to Irwin, 'I'm sorry you still feel that way but I think the rest of us are in general agreement that that chance was lost when Hitler attacked Poland last year. Only God can forgive us the fact that we've also allowed the same thing to happen to Norway; and yet there's more. The Germans have attacked the Low Countries and France as well. Does that surprise you?

'Now, I want all of you gentlemen to disseminate this news amongst the ship's company before they hear it from the radio. You shall tell it matter-of-factly and in the least sensational tone you can manage because our first priority is to get this ship home. Mr Irwin, you need not prepare or give the men a lecture on these developments.'

'I understand, sir,' said Irwin, his chin shaking from the insult. His liberal reasoning had ultimately got him nowhere. 'Need there be any more lectures at all, sir?'

'I think not.'

\*\*\*\*

Coming down to the mess after four hours of watching the sea for torpedo tracks in this interminably slow passage home, Smudge was near to exhaustion. '*Crayhorn*'ll bust a boiler dragging us halfway across the ocean,' he muttered to no one in particular. 'Irwin should be hung from the yardarm for sabotage, he should.'

He was especially despondent because of the news that had been circulated and broadcast about the government. He had never been a great fan of Chamberlain but he just could not come to terms with the idea that the men who were supposed to be running the country did not know how to cover up the fact that they had no clue what they were doing. Of course, he knew that politicians were not infallible but it was part of their job to smooth over any ineptitude by shrewd talk or actions – in effect, talk shit and lead the way forward. Chamberlain had sorely disappointed him on all counts this time round.

He had not got halfway to his locker when he saw Les sitting at the mess table, concentrating carefully on the needle that he was threading in preparation to darn the row of socks that he had laid out in front of him. What was he so happy about?

'Judging from the smell, you didn't wash 'em first,' said Smudge with hostility.

Les looked at him in confusion, held a sock up to his nose and shrugged. 'Can't smell a thing.'

'No, I heard tell that your brain needs to decipher messages from round your body so's it can function properly.'

Les continued with his confusion but then quickly decided that he was not going to give this man any more attention than he deserved. He brushed Smudge off with, 'Once I've done these I'll have earned an ounce of tobacco.'

'Ooh, more than you've earned in the whole rest of your life.' Smudge sat on the bench opposite, leaned across the table and stared hard at him. These days the staring was far more menacing. 'One wonders why you bother. You'll never be one of the heroical types like in your book which, incidentally mirrors your use to the navy – always hovering around the first few pages 'cause you don't get it.'

'Well, you wouldn't have any more luck with it!' Les fired back, perplexed. Then he remembered something Pincher had once told him. 'Anyway, you've never read anything heavier than a *Beano* or a *Daily Sketch*!'

'Infinitely more informative than that Irish claptrap you've been trying to read!'

Then, for perhaps the first time, Les had a completely original thought in confrontation. '*Les Misérables* just happens to be French.'

'No wonder you can't read it, then!' shouted Smudge.

'But it's in English,' continued Les, determined not to falter.

'Well, make up your bloody mind! English, French or Irish? Though all three'd be more like Greek to you!'

Suddenly, Smudge was shunted along the bench by someone sitting down heavily next to him. 'Here, watch out!' he exclaimed as he noticed that it was Pincher who had descended upon him, clumping a bucket of soapy water down on the deck.

Pincher then picked his tattered shirt up out of the water and began to ring it out right next to him, allowing some of it to spatter on his uniform.

'Careful!' cried Smudge.

'No, you be careful,' said Pincher. 'Just because you're having an 'ard time, don't come in here and take it out on Les.'

'I haven't even started on him yet,' declared Smudge, only to find another man suddenly sitting down very close on his other side. He turned and was not so happy to see Leading Seaman Walbrook grinning at him. 'Evening, Paddy,' said Smudge more cautiously.

'You been hackin' on my mate,' stated this large killick of proven strength and wit. Nobody ever purposely tried to get on his bad side.

'Course not, me old china.'

Pincher frowned. 'And stop with the ol' cockney slang. You're from Epsom.'

'Free country,' Smudge muttered feebly.

'Les, got anything you wanna say to the Smudger?'

'Not really,' said Les, though strangely discovering that he was taking some pleasure in the moral force being exerted against his nemesis. 'Except, bugger off, you idiot.'

'Well, that's nice, I must say!' protested Smudge to the laughs and 'ooh's' that emanated from the other men working hereabouts. He was careful not to be too passionate in his protest, though.

Suddenly emboldened, Les decided that he wanted to say more. He went on to use another insult he had picked up recently. 'You're as worthless as one of those chocolate gerbils.'

But that silenced everyone and had them looking at him in wonder. Smudge wanted to be the first to quiz him on what he meant but Paddy beat him to it. 'What the feck are you talkin' about?'

'Oh, well ...' stammered Les, finally realising that nobody else understood the context. Lieutenant Hanwell had used the term when they had encountered some troublesome lascars back in Scapa Flow. But now Les was red-faced. Why did he always manage to get himself into these predicaments? It was almost as if Smudge was right about him.

Pincher shook his head in disbelief and immediately decided to hark back to the original message. 'Right, so just lay off him, all right, Smudge?'

Still tightly sandwiched between his two antagonists, Smudge looked at each of their warning faces and raised his hands in submission, 'Whatever you say, though I have to tell you that I'm no fan of coercion. I'm a reasonable man and Les is an old friend.'

'Pleased to 'ear it,' said Paddy, finally taking his leave for he had other things to be getting on with.

Still uncomfortable with the proximity of Pincher and his bucket of water, Smudge also removed himself from the bench and went to open his locker. 'So,' he said conversationally, 'the Turtle's a murderer after all and he's managed to escape to Sweden. Who'd have thought it? Totally hoodwinked the police, though that's not 'ard. The buzz is that they wanted to release an artist's impression of him but the editor of *The Times* lodged a complaint on account of the fact that the drawing looked like a squirrel what had been hit by a car.'

Pincher sighed, thinking on the intimate knowledge that he had of the Turtle's case. It was not proven that Haggerty was a murderer but he had no desire to get into it here and now.

All that aside, Smudge still had a smooth way with words and Pincher felt the hint of laughter welling inside him. Other laughs were already being chorused around the mess. The tension which had been building during those arduous days in Norway seemed to be dissipating slowly and a little bit of normality was returning to the mess.

'The Turtle should get together with Neville Chamberlain,' continued Smudge, 'and collaborate on a script for RKO Pictures, something along the lines of *Beauty and the Beast*. Throw in a couple of rampant Nazis, preferably with Hitler moustaches – those like national treasures Chaplin or Olly Hardy – add a chocolate gerbil into the mix and you've got an instant all-time favourite. What do you think, Les?'

'What about?'

'God give me strength!'

\*\*\*\*

Clark was briefly dazzled by the daylight after he emerged from B Turret. Having just spent the last two hours crawling around in the machinery compartment underneath the gun mountings with Midshipman Trent and an Ordnance Artificer, he was pleased for the fresh air. He stepped over to the side rail and saw that the gun barrels were slightly depressed so that the seamen standing on top of A Turret could sponge out the last of the black cordite residue from the muzzles.

He wondered whether the job was being done a little too soon for they were still nowhere near home and the guns could be wanted at any moment. What then would be the worth of the effort? But, of course, the captain liked everything shipshape as much as possible, flagship or no flagship, steam or no steam.

As he cast a glance out to Fulton-Stavely's hardy little destroyer which was still towing them, and then at her sister ship burning up fuel in her constant circling vigil, there suddenly came an announcement from the loudspeakers: 'Do you hear there? Midshipman Clark to the captain's cabin.'

Clark quickly stripped off his greasy overalls and threw them towards CPO Doyle, who was standing nearby. 'Look after these for me, chief, and pass me a cloth.'

Doyle did as he was bid and watched the 'snotty' enter the hatch into the superstructure, wiping his hands as he went. The CPO muttered under his breath, 'Yes sir, no sir, three bags full, sir.'

The cabin was only two decks above, tucked behind the chart house and the admiral's plot so it did not take Clark long to reach it.

'Come in,' said Dollimore. The various files of paperwork piled up on his desk told the invariable story of the thousand and one issues which he was gradually addressing. In the middle of it all was a familiar document, Clark's own blue-bound diary which, as a midshipman, he had been required to keep. Keeping a diary was forbidden in war unless you happened to be a midshipman; it was considered to be too vital an assessment of a young man's progress to be put on hold.

Had he been called to discuss that? As far as he was aware, he had not put anything controversial in it, not for a long time. He had been keeping his head down.

'Very orderly statements with good insights,' said Dollimore, immediately handing the book to him, 'but you have plenty of catching up to do. There are two weeks or so missing.'

Well, of course there are. During those two weeks Clark had been a little preoccupied but the inference was clear. Now was the time for *everybody* to catch up on the work which had been delayed due to circumstances.

Looking up at Clark, for he did not invite him to sit, Dollimore said, 'It has come time to discuss your future, young man. Especially in the light of the good report which Lieutenant Eddington has put in about your conduct in this Norwegian affair, I'm pleased to be able to tell you that the exam for your promotion has been set for tomorrow afternoon, as soon as we reach Rosyth. As you well know, if you pass, that means you will be leaving the *Burscombe* forthwith.'

'Very good, sir.' There were lesser authorities on board who would normally have been imparting this information and, undoubtedly, there would be other boys set to take the exam as well. Why had the captain singled him out like this?

'As I'm sure you understand, greater events than those we have experienced so far have yet to unfold. The Low Countries and France are under attack and, if the Germans proceed with the same precision that they showed in Norway... No, I should say, if *we* proceed with the same indecision that we showed in Norway, then the most difficult tasks are going to befall every one of us thereafter. God-willing I'm way off the mark.'

'You're rarely wrong, sir.'

'Don't interrupt. You have shown a consistent flair and aptitude towards the kind of work that we are involved in. Your courage is undoubted, your reactions and solutions to the problems are good and those under your command trust you. Now, it just remains for me to add that your otherwise good performance is still at times marred by a certain disrespect for authority and hierarchy. I do appreciate the improvement that you've made since the New Year but it's as though you still sometimes place little value on the accepted traditions of the service – a need to display something of a 'free spirit'.' He raised his eyebrows in gentle derision. 'What do you have to say about that?'

Clark thought about saying nothing but figured that Dollimore was deserving of the facts. 'I know that there were times when you did not want to tolerate me being on board your ship, sir, and quite honestly, I am sorry for the times I have caused offence. It's just that I find it hard to automatically judge men on nothing but their rank. What I mean is, I judge them by their characters and their morals and I also see myself as exactly the same as any man in the lower decks with whom we are facing these challenges. I am no better and no worse. We are all in it together.'

'Yes, we are. But those thoughts don't go hand in hand with good discipline. What's more, the men down below can ill-afford to think that way. A 'free spirit' can get them into an awful lot of trouble, more so than you, I should think. They have been given little choice in any matter regarding their future and they will never see you as the same as them. They expect you to be superior.'

'But *I* feel like I was given little choice, sir. It's just my misfortune to have been born into the family that I was. They forced me into the navy against my will in order to make me into something that I'm not. That said, sir, I have come to accept the position that I've been put in. I might be rough around the edges and not everything that the snobs would want me to be, but to fail the ship that I serve in times of need would be the biggest disgrace of all and that's the reason why I've persevered to be better than the boy I was when I first stepped aboard.'

'Good, then I'm satisfied that you've at least been developing in a positive manner.' This was not the time or place to get into the question of the snobbery that Clark so detested in society. Dollimore had always been comfortable with the British class system and was fully able to function within its bounds without being covetous or contemptuous of those above or below. To him it was one of the bedrocks of society. Even his own personal and professional troubles over the years had not shaken his belief in that.

'Now, concerning the case of Leading Seaman Haggerty,' he continued, picking up another sheet of paper from his desk. 'I'll not lie; but because of your views it had crossed my mind that you may have been slightly less than diligent in your pursuit of him than you were and perhaps let him get away – until I read this. Are you certain this is what you want to submit? Are you certain this is what you think? This puts it squarely back into the hands of the police.'

'Yes, I'll want to talk to them about that.'

'*They'll* want to talk to *you* about it. I'll send it along when we reach port.'

When he was dismissed, Clark finished his work about the turrets and finally returned to the gunroom to find some food and relaxation. He had not been seated for too long with cigarette in hand and the smoke swirling about him when Midshipman Farlow, pale and thinning, entered and sat opposite him.

It had been questionable whether Farlow had fully recovered from the knock on the head he had received when the *Castledown* blew up. His sense of animosity and mischief towards Clark had all but disappeared of late for he never felt well enough to goad him. A regular propensity to muscle aches and sickness had taken over most of his attention these last few weeks while he was just trying to scrape by in his job.

This change in the heated dynamics between them – dynamics that had been standard since they had first entered Dartmouth at the age of thirteen – had secretly bothered Clark and so he had actually taken it upon himself to confront Surgeon-Commander Lawson about why he was doing nothing for him. Lawson, that impossibly unhelpful Cornish ex-general practitioner, had erupted with fury at his impudence before Clark stooped to playing the class card and reminded him that Farlow was high-born and had a powerful father that would be deeply interested in his neglect.

Consequently, the surgeon-commander promised to look further into his case when they reached home.

'The buzz is you're leaving us,' Farlow said, looking at Clark through thinned eyes.

'I must say that got around quick enough; so yes, you're getting what you've always wanted – me out of your hair.'

'Good,' nodded Farlow, though lacking in any conviction. 'Well, what I mean to say is, it's inevitable that our paths will cross again and, believe you me, I shall endeavour to give you as much trouble as you would care to take.'

Clark had to stop himself from laughing. The threats had been ridiculous even when he had been on par, but now? 'Farlow, what the devil are you trying to say?'

'In short,' said Farlow, wrinkling his brow, 'I never thanked you properly for pulling me out of the sea and saving my life and, whenever we meet again, I shall be honoured to continue our battle of wits.'

'One could hardly call it a battle – more like a rout.'

Farlow stood and pointed at him in a semi-intimidating manner, saying, 'One day, Nobby Clark, one day, I'll get you.'

Then he left the room, leaving Clark to the laughter he could no longer contain.

\*\*\*\*

Three more destroyers were sent out to meet those dragging *Burscombe* back through the dangerous seas. There could be no thought of the navy losing another major warship if it could possibly be helped. Furthermore, it would be a great boost to morale to hear that the cruiser had made it back from the warzone against all the odds, especially since the German radio and press had already reported that she had been sunk.

The ships were brought to Action Stations each dawn and two other times concerning shadowing aircraft. It would have been an easy thing for the Luftwaffe to guide its aircraft or a submarine onto them but somehow an attack never materialised. The enemy obviously had its hands full elsewhere.

After nearly three days of this steel-straining work, a pair of powerful steam tugs rendezvoused with them thirty miles down the estuary of the Forth from the railway bridge. Minesweepers led the way upriver in the final effort to ensure the damaged old girl got home to Rosyth.

'You're not an old girl just yet,' muttered Dollimore.

'I beg your pardon, sir?' asked Lt-Cdr Digby, who had just finished taking photographs of the men around him on the bridge. He had many a strip of negatives hidden away for the future when this tormented present could be viewed in glorious peace, free from the restrictions of security. Of that eventual outcome he was sure, no matter the terrible news coming out from Europe. 'Is everything all right, sir?'

'Of course,' answered Dollimore, snapping out of the tiredness that had threatened to ensnare him. There was no way that he was going to let slip his feelings in front of these men while he was still in command of them. He and the *Burscombe* had managed to achieve great things in their short time together but he was well aware of the relief that was flooding him now that this mission was finally over.

But on to the remaining items of business to hand: de-ammunitioning before going into dry dock was going to be a quick business because most of the magazines were empty; some compartments were full of sick and hurt soldiers that needed to be sent on to hospital; Lt Irwin had slipped into a deep funk over the silencing of his voice amongst other things; and finally, it was not certain that Lt-Cdr Peterson would ever regain consciousness again. Dollimore secretly saw that last item as far too high a price to pay for a politician's credibility.

The rest of the ship's company were in no mood to think about anything like that just now anyway and most were just waiting for the moment that they were free to find some booze, women and the chance to post their letters home.

Unfortunately, the subject of their liberty was needed to make an example of another matter first. When all other tasks had been completed and the *Burscombe* was sitting anchored in the Forth awaiting her turn in the dry dock, Dollimore ordered the lower decks cleared.

Everybody who was not currently engaged on a job somewhere within the ship was crammed onto the quarterdeck beneath the guns of Y-Turret. The White Ensign fluttered in a breeze which, for once, carried with it a late spring warmth, and Dollimore stepped the few inches up onto a closed deck hatch. He was thus surrounded by them, these brave lads who had followed his orders into the turbulence of war and held their nerve and discipline in order to fight to the finish and make it back. They stood at ease, their heads inclined towards him, calmly wondering what this was all about. Silence and undivided attention ruled over every other compulsion.

Dollimore loved them all. He saw many faces he knew well: the officers Locklin, Hacklett, Irwin, Selkirk, Giles, Gailey and Bretonworth; the senior and lower rates Ross, Vincent, Doyle, Walbrook, Smith, Martin and Gordy; amongst hundreds that his forced aloofness dictated that he could not know so well.

'Men, thank you for all you have done. You did everything in your power to assist the army in what, up to that time, was its greatest challenge of the war. I cannot commend highly enough your conduct through the course of the Norwegian campaign. For the moment, your work is done. You should be temporarily resting on your laurels and enjoying a run ashore to do whatever you feel it is necessary to do. That is why it pains me to be forced to remind you of the nature of the very precise institution that is the Royal Navy.

'When we were in the Tjierrefjord, certain items and materials were removed from this ship in an act which I can only describe as theft. It is no matter what the materials were needed for. The fact is that they were stolen and I am going to be asked by my superiors to account for them.'

He looked on as some faces dropped in shame and others flared red in anger, especially those of the Regulating Branch who were hearing about it for the first time.

After a pause, he went on, 'Because of this unfortunate situation we find ourselves in, I decree that all liberty from HMS *Burscombe* is stopped...'

Gasps and muttering sprung up all around him, men flagrantly interrupting and not caring that they were seen to be talking over him. However, he could see they were more hurt than angry. That was what he had hoped for.

He held up his hand to silence them and, just as he knew they would, they gave him their full attention once more. He was all powerful here; just he, one man amongst hundreds. 'It only remains for me to admit that I knew about the theft even as it was happening so I am complicit in your crime, fully understanding why it was you perpetrated it. Therefore, this stoppage of liberty applies to me also. Now, consider yourselves fortunate that the punishment is no worse. For the next two days, those rostered to go ashore at the start of the First Dog Watch will not be able to do so. We shall all be doing penance together for a period of two hours after which, at the ringing of eight bells, the remainder of your liberty will be restored to you.'

In the next second, the men erupted into a mashed chorus of cheering and laughing. Dollimore wanted to laugh and cheer with them but he remained standing stock still, his expression stern and unchanged. He would never let his guard slip.

\*\*\*\*

On the following afternoon, Lieutenant Philip Dollimore watched the whaler pull alongside the jetty and threw his spent cigarette butt down on the ground. As the men shipped their oars, David Clark stood up from the thwart and leapt onto the steps before the bow line was even secured. He climbed them stealthily and the two men came face to face.

'Whatever was said between us out there,' Clark began straight away, for he could sense that Philip was still going to be sparing of conscience and might need prompting, 'I'm glad you made it.'

Philip looked down at the bags that a couple of seamen were putting by their feet.

Clark continued, 'I passed my exam yesterday so I'm off to Pompey.'

'Pompey, you say?' said Philip with a frown.

'By way of London, yes. I'm taking your advice and I'm going to sort everything out with my mother.' Though not in the way you think I should, he thought.

'I'm pleased to hear it,' nodded Philip, moving past Clark and making his way down the steps towards the whaler. There he ordered, 'Take me out to the *Burscombe*.'

Clark supposed that he must be heading over there to sort everything out with his father. Whatever he was doing, he still looked to be the same troubled man who had not come to terms with all that had happened to him. Deciding to cast him from his thoughts, Clark waved down to the midshipman in command of the boat. 'Trent, it was good serving with you. I'll see you again sometime.'

'Undoubtedly,' replied the grinning, baby-faced lad, 'thanks for everything,' for Clark had been one of those who had made it easier for the younger boys to fit into the gunroom life.

But then Trent had to busy himself with the task of transferring this more morose-looking officer here over to the ship. He still remembered the captain's son from that day back in February when he refused to divulge any details of his adventures in the Jossingfjord. Trent swore that, whatever happened to him, he would never be so dismissive of any younger chaps who were in need of some inspiration.

\*\*\*\*

'Just talk to me,' Dollimore demanded of his son. 'Say what you're thinking.'

'What good would it do?'

'It would help me to understand. No, not your pain, but what I have done wrong – what *I* have done wrong.' The man standing before him now may have been proud, sober and clean-cut but he still no more resembled the happy family man in the framed photo on the cabin bulkhead than the pasty drunk he had been nearly four months ago.

'Very well,' said Philip. 'Firstly, I didn't appreciate you and Fulton-Stavely pulling strings to take me away from my appointment in London. I was making such progress there that you could not imagine. I was helping someone who was helping me – '

'That I understand was not your wife.'

'Father!' shouted Philip. 'Isn't this just the crux of the matter? How can I explain anything to you if you're always trying to take the upper hand?'

For the first time ever in Philip's memory, his father, the great naval officer Charles Dollimore, buttoned his lip. It was not anger, shame or defeat that showed upon the Old Man's face but a determination to exhibit patience. Mother was right. It was possible for a person to continue growing no matter their age.

Philip now felt able to continue. 'I've managed to moderate the drinking presently, though I know that you're not going to like what I have to say next. I've had to replace the desire to do so with something else. If I should not be allowed to be in a position to help those less fortunate than me, then I shall devote myself to the destruction of the enemy. The quicker we get this business over with the better, for then I can get on with my life; but until that time comes, there's no room in it for you, for mother, nor even Sarah or little Charlie.'

Dollimore was aghast but careful not to show it by way of expression. He cautiously asked, 'Do you understand what you're saying?'

'Yes. I'm saying that I do not have the mental capacity to effectively fight this war while people try to pull me to and fro in distraction. I don't wish to be told that I'm neglecting my family; I don't wish to be measured up by people according to *your* reputation; I don't wish to be told that my priority is anything other than winning the war; I don't wish to be told anything.'

Looking upon this monster that somehow he and circumstance had created together, Dollimore put his hand on his son's arm. 'It doesn't have to be this way.'

'Yes, it does. I'll reconcile myself with you all when the fighting is done.'

'And what about reconciling yourself with the *Royal Oak*?'

'I'm past all that,' Philip lied, his expression unchanged.

Finally understanding that Philip could not be reasoned with through arguments of loyalty to the family, Dollimore vowed that he would attempt to discover the thing which would bring him round. Until then, he had to be content with saying, 'That's not good enough.'

'Too bad.'

When Philip left the *Burscombe*, he was sure that he had left his father in turmoil though, as ever, the Old Man did not show it. Perhaps that suppression of emotion had forever been part of the problem.

He made his way back to the *Crayhorn*, not even feeling any shame about the other significant thing of which he had not been entirely truthful. He had not cut everybody out of his life. The one person that he was still able to write to with any sense of comfort was Patricia Bushey.

\*\*\*\*

The destroyers were not known as the 'maids of all service' for nothing. No sooner had the dockyard workers patched up the damage to the put-upon *Crayhorn* and *Catterley* and the men had painted over the scars with yet more dark grey, than they were ploughing their way through gentle seas towards a new destination. They had been told that they would be anchoring the following night in the Humber. Beyond that, no one knew anything.

But it did not take a brain surgeon to figure out that they were being earmarked for operations concerning the great battle which was fast eclipsing the effort in Narvik: the battle for Holland, Belgium and France.

Up on the *Crayhorn*'s creaking bridge, Thorogood breathed deeply of the salty air and said happily, 'It's likely we'll need to transport more troops to France.'

'What troops?' asked Philip as patiently as he could. 'Don't you remember we already cleaned Britain out looking for men for Norway. And you saw the state of Binkley-Walling's mob when we disembarked them. They're not going anywhere for a while.'

'Then, what do *you* think we're doing?'

'What *I'm* doing is trying not to think about it.'

Fulton-Stavely appeared from aft having decided to join his two lieutenants on this pleasant evening. He was tired and aching inside but was heartened to find that they looked as bad as he felt. 'Sorry that there was no opportunity to get ashore this time,' he said. 'What with things going from bad to worse ...'

Philip shrugged and gave him a hard look. 'It rather suits me fine, sir.'

'Speak for yourself,' grinned Thorogood. 'Thanks to the navy, I've not actually spoken to my wife for the best part of six weeks.'

Fulton-Stavely was surprised. 'We've been on the go for that long? You're right. Well, I never. I do empathise with you, Mr Thorogood.'

'Only empathise, sir?'

Giving an uncharacteristically mischievous look, Fulton-Stavely explained, 'What is an inconvenience to you is a blessing to me. I've not spoken to my wife in just as long and I don't mind telling you that I'd rather fight off ten flights of Stukas than subject myself to the level of nagging, self-serving, attention-seeking and complaining that she's capable of.'

All three men laughed together.

Philip had successfully suppressed his guilt at the way in which he had treated his own wife and was quite dead to it, and what he appreciated here in this ship was the fact that nobody was prying after knowledge of her, even after these two men's candidness about their own relationships. His private business was his own unless he was prepared to bring it up.

However, there was one thing which was not so private. Fulton-Stavely asked, 'Mr Dollimore, is the hip-flask still full?'

Philip's face instantly became more serious, if that was possible. 'Yes, sir.'

'Okay. While the booze is in the flask it's not in your belly. I've been watching you, Number One, and I've noticed something of a change in you ever since we pulled the *Burscombe* out of the Tjierrefjord. Now, you can tell me if I'm wrong because I'm not running this ship in the way the exalted captain of a battleship would, or in the way our old friend Vian would, but you effected much greater control of yourself after the fact became apparent that it was we who saved your father's neck.'

Philip said nothing.

'I'm not going to say that you were daft for disliking living in your father's shadow because, who knows how the human mind works? It's certainly one of God's crazier designs. But, hopefully, you can see that you're every inch as good an officer given the right circumstances to prove it. *Royal Oak* doesn't count. It doesn't count, I say. You poor sods never had a chance. But I'm just hoping that, having had the upper hand, having been in the forefront of the battle and realising that your father is as dependent upon you as you on he, you can moderate your feelings a little. *Everything* in moderation, Number One – except the killing of the enemy.'

With that, Fulton-Stavely gave him a gentle pat on the shoulder and took himself away from the bridge. Significantly, he said no more about the hip-flask, did not even try to take it from him.

Philip looked out at the sea and reflected that this had been the first time the captain had mentioned his father and then it was for something other than praising him or suggesting that Philip be praised just for being his son. He had also been right about killing the enemy. Philip knew that if he had a revolver pointed at the face of a man like Captain Dau of the *Altmark* again, he would most certainly pull the trigger.

He looked at the sky with its scattering of white and grey clouds turning red. It was a good day to be alive.

\*\*\*\*

Work on HMS *Burscombe* proceeded without too many complications. The collision with the terminal moraine had had less negative effect than the violence of the accident had originally suggested. There were hideous dents and scrapes along the otherwise flat red keel but, as Dollimore had already appreciated at the time from the Damage Control reports, no oil or water tanks had been breached. The worst of the damage was a total of five propeller blades lost from two of the shafts, the rudder bent slightly out of alignment and various bits of damage to the machinery in the tiller flat. They had been lucky.

Of course, to rectify these things would take a little time but ships of this worth were a priority at the moment. With dockyard workers scrambling all over her battle-scarred hull, her turnaround time back to duty was going to be good.

In the dry dock, the ship's company finally had plenty of opportunity to give her a deep clean, maintenance, further treatment for rust and lots of fresh paintwork. Her boilers were completely shut down for a thorough clean and her other machinery checked and overhauled where necessary. As in peacetime, the work was done with professional satisfaction coupled with personal irritation, though it was now given greater impetus by a desire to get the ship back into action.

Then a necessary Board of Enquiry was convened aboard ship even as she sat on the blocks, a small number of solemn-faced officers arriving as if from nowhere to question all concerned about the incident of the ship running aground.

Dollimore sought to take full responsibility himself. It was the only right thing to do. After all, Lieutenant Irwin had risen to the challenge of the action even if his calculations were slightly out. It was Dollimore who had insisted upon the course they had taken – with Rear-Admiral Nicklesworth's agreement, of course – and to add to that, there was no doubting the fact that their timely arrival in the lake had very likely saved two destroyers and the lives of hundreds of soldiers and sailors.

But Irwin's evident discomfort told a much deeper story. How he appeared before them, worried and indecisive, did not help at all.

The humourless officers of the Board pondered the matter thoughtfully then delivered their verdict. The chairman, a man named Pearce who bore the single broad stripe of the commodore, first passed judgment upon the unfortunate lieutenant, saying, 'You have accepted the fact that the hazarding of the ship laid within your power to avoid and that you did, through navigational error and subsequent advice given to your captain, place the *Burscombe* in such a position that she should run aground within the zone of battle. This shall be entered onto your record and Their Lordships will be left to decide for you a more appropriate appointment.'

Irwin was neither upset nor relieved. It did not matter whether he remained in the *Burscombe* or was sent elsewhere. He was inwardly crying out for a complete reconditioning of his character. Dismissed, he finally went off to his cabin to calm down as privately as possible.

To Captain Dollimore, the commodore said, 'The Board finds that there is no questioning your commitment and skill as regards the commanding of HMS *Burscombe*. She was placed in her precarious position by the mistakes and authority of others. Therefore, no comment of any negative kind will be placed on your record of service.'

In fact, when Dollimore walked up to the gangway with the investigating officers, a general pleasantness having replaced the earlier po-faced formality, Pearce stopped, turned to him and said, 'Rear-Admiral Nicklesworth already submitted a report in which he took full responsibility for what happened so our findings would have been the same anyway whichever way you look at it. We have to keep everything in perspective, you see. Worse things are happening to other ships every day. Don't you worry, when *Burscombe* is seaworthy again, the Admiralty has one or two ideas for you, mark my words. I have it on good authority that even Churchill asked after your safety; quite something given the amount of things piled onto his plate at the moment.'

'Thank you, sir,' replied Dollimore, happy but unsure how he felt about having been scrutinised quite so closely.

'Like I said, thank Nicklesworth; and Admiral Forbes. He, above all, values your efforts.'

Dollimore was aware that he did. The Commander-in-Chief had said as much in the past and now Pearce had just passed on the pleasing acknowledgement that he was still standing by his word. If only the rest of his life was so rewarding – or had he truly not put the same effort into his own family as he had that of the navy?

Not wanting to be drawn off at any tangent over his personal concerns, Dollimore decided to return to other, more practical matters. He just happened to know that one or two of the larger ships had been fitted out with a new electronic detector which could see formations of enemy bombers a long time before the human eye and other optical devices, even through cloud, giving ships more time to prepare for or evade an attack. Therefore, he dared to ask, 'Sir, when might we receive that new Radio Direction Finder?'

Pearce looked at him as though he was mad. 'Radio Direction Finder? What a fanciful idea!'

What, receiving it or the existence of it in the first place?
****

Lieutenant Irwin packed up his belongings into the two large suitcases that had accompanied him everywhere since he had first found his way into the navy. He had come into the service through the Special Entry Scheme at eighteen and what a journey it had been since then. Being accepted had been a great boost to his fragile state of mind and he really had believed that he could flourish once he was free of the stifling grasp of his parents and schoolmasters. His understanding of maths and navigation had been far above average and this had given him the hope that he might be able to add something to the navy.

He knew now that there was much more to this business than being able to do a few sums. Wardroom life, politics and war had taught him that.

Strength of character was everything. There were officers all around him both socially adept and inept who seemed to slide smoothly between the myriad of egos and prejudices that were constantly probing them. He could not do it.

He had just managed to get by in peacetime but the war had made everything far too serious. As the responsibility on his shoulders grew, so did the intolerance shown him by other members of the ship's company. But then again, were they actually being extra intolerant of him or was that just the way he perceived it? As in everything, there was doubt.

The only thing he knew for certain was that he did not belong in HMS *Burscombe* so being sent ashore for a little while was probably the best development.

Just as he was finishing up, Lt-Cdr Digby appeared in the doorway to his cabin. He too was very serious but it was presently more to do with emotion than business. 'I wanted to say good-bye, old boy. Christ, it sounds so final, but it's not. You'll go on to bigger and better things, I'm sure.'

'It's men like you who go onto bigger and better things. Even if I'd not run the ship aground I'd still never have been able to fill the shoes of Geoff Peterson – I pray to God he makes it.'

'Listen, I'm going to tell you what you ought to do for your own sanity. The captain would agree even if he'd put it in different words. We all know that your navigation is fine. You just need to be less high-strung. When you get a spot of leave, ask a girl out. Any girl will do. Take her dancing, get her phone number and arrange to take her out again. Talk with her and laugh with her.'

Irwin smiled nervously and gave an unsure laugh. 'You know that's not me.'

'Well, it bloody well ought to be,' Digby fired back, wondering in the back of his mind whether the rumours of his sexual preferences were true. Come to think of it, he had never known Irwin to compliment actresses, singers or models when the other chaps discussed them in the wardroom. But then, neither had he been ungracious about them. No, don't think about it. There was no evidence either way; and besides, he probably just simply meant that he did not have the confidence to ask a girl out.

Digby continued, 'For whatever reason, you're carrying far too heavy a conscience around with you. It's weighing you down. Try and switch off and, like I said, get some decent company and laugh for a while.'

But suspecting that the damage done to his confidence as a child was probably irreparable, Irwin was eager to change the subject. 'Hey, after all this is over I'd like to have copies of all those photographs you've been taking.' He knew better than to add 'if we win,' in front of his friend, the arch-optimist.

'Of course,' agreed Digby. He walked Irwin down to the gangway and hoped that he would heed his advice. There was a sturdy character in there, honest and dependable, if only he would allow it to come to the fore.

Irwin left the ship, relieved but very self-conscious when he was finally walking away across the quayside. He had not been able to shake the feeling that, while crossing the gangway, everybody from the ordinary seamen scrubbing the deck to the officers overseeing them were staring at his back and mouthing: 'Thank God that Jonah's finally gone.'

# SIXTEEN

## No Place like Home

The world was changing and Clark journeyed south filled with a determination to influence what he could of it. London was waiting for him in the form of unfinished family business and once there, that business would take precedence over everything else; and he had to be swift and brutal because he only had three days before he was expected in Portsmouth. For the moment, however, here in this jolting railway carriage, he had to exercise a little patience so he perused the other changes over which he had no control. Looking at the war news in the paper, he tried to read between the lines for clues based on his own experience with Britain's foe.

Holland, attacked by German parachutists, had fought hard but capitulated after Rotterdam had been flattened by the Luftwaffe. Clark tried to imagine the extensive forces that the enemy must have needed to achieve that. Thousands if not tens of thousands of men would have had to drop from the sky in order to fight the Dutch Army and many hundreds of bombers would have been needed to flatten that town in so short a time. Why had British and French forces not met the Germans and repulsed them in equal strength and inventiveness? Again it was that twenty-year peacetime neglect of the realities of warfare.

Even so, it was reported here that the British Army was moving in strength through Belgium and great success was expected, as with the French around the Maginot Line, their extensive network of fortifications along the frontier with Germany. Clark thought, have they encountered the Stukas yet? A shiver went down his spine even as he thought about them.

Then there were the many German mobile units of tanks in play and he thought on Binkley-Walling's men being sent in to fight with no vehicles, heavy weapons or air support whatsoever. He dared to suppose that that had been the case in Norway because all the choice equipment had been in France.

What was clear was that the Germans were taking their full frontal attack against Western Europe's greatest powers much more seriously than they had Norway because the stakes were so much higher. But would the western governments take it just as seriously? The appointment of Winston Churchill as prime minister was a step in the right direction, if for no other reason than that he understood that peace and Adolf Hitler were not compatible. The big questions were, had Churchill had time enough to chew through the aftermath of Chamberlain's policies to get better prepared, and would his decisions be any better?

Clark did not like it at all and, visualising further defeat, found himself echoing Captain Dollimore's sentiment of hoping that he was dead wrong.

Within the realms of this first class carriage, with the beautiful rolling green of the British countryside basking in the early summer sun just outside, he listened to two elderly gentlemen debating the situation. One man was entirely upbeat and contemptuous of the Hun, but was he being so for the benefit of his wife, who sat beside him listening intently? Or did he just have blind faith?

The other gentleman had three fingers missing from his left hand and continuously warned he who sat opposite not to underestimate the Germans. They deserved respect as a first class enemy and may just astonish the world with their new ideas. Then, after declaring that he was going to enlist with the latest organisation that was hastily being formed, that of the Local Defence Volunteers, he smiled and apologised to the lady if he seemed unduly pessimistic.

She replied graciously, 'Not at all, sir. I have never been of a mind to shy away from the truth. There's not much point to a stiff upper lip if it's attached to a head that is buried in the sand.'

Her husband 'harrumphed' heavily.

'And what do you think, young sir?' asked the single man, who had the evident look of a veteran of some long past encounter.

Clark, realising that he was being asked a question, looked up from his paper, 'Evidently, I commend you to your caution, sir. I too have such respect for the enemy as you've described and believe your intentions to join the LDV as completely correct.'

The other gentleman sitting opposite tutted and said, 'More defeatism!'

His wife tutted just as heavily. 'It's called prudence, dear!'

Then the veteran leaned closer in to Clark with excitement in his eyes and, looking at his bruised face, asked, 'Have you fought them already?'

'In Norway, sir.'

Then came the disappointment. 'Oh, that sideshow.'

Clark sighed and quickly found the opportunity to become deeper immersed in the newspaper once again, trying to forget the insult and yet observing that, from every viewpoint, Norway had been relegated to the realms of ignorance. Their entire effort had somehow become irrelevant. But at least this veteran was going to stand up and put his money where his mouth was. That was something at least.

****

He knew that his mother would be waiting impatiently for him at the house in Belgravia. He had not sent a letter stating his intentions for he wished to say everything that was on his mind in person, but the sending of his luggage ahead from the station was announcement enough of his imminent arrival.

By the time he climbed out of the taxi in front of the neat Georgian terrace with its white front walls and iron railings adorned here and there by neatly cut bushes, the shadows of the late evening were already stretching out along the pavement. He banished all thoughts of the war and kept his mind to the task in hand.

The maid, a longstanding member of the household called Jean, opened the front door and ushered him inside with a familiar smile. The hallway was spacious and well lit with the eyes of the most respected Clark ancestors looking down upon him from their imposing portraits. Nobody had thought to put a likeness of his father here just yet. Perhaps one of his brothers would be the one to bother.

The house was just as he remembered it from the rare visits they had made before his college days. The last time he had been here was easily nine years ago. It crossed his mind that it was amazing how much scattered property the Clarks had sitting empty while large families like Pincher Martin's were stuffed unapologetically into some tiny hovel that was owned by someone else and only kept respectable by the tenants' sheer hard work and personal pride.

But that thought was detracting from his purpose.

Jean motioned for him to enter the sitting room and he did so to be immediately confronted by his mother, standing there with a mixed look of hope and perplexity on her face. Her hair was a little greyer than it had been before but her features were just as elegantly smooth and complimentary to the good living she had enjoyed, notwithstanding the troubles brought upon her by her late husband, the war and he himself.

Dorothy looked at him and thought his face to be more rugged than it had used to be. It was certainly more filled out and more manly. Significantly, the look in his eye was more calculatingly shrewd and the self-belief was less boyish. This she recognised straight away. A lot had happened to him in the last eight months. She felt like she wanted to cry for the loss of her baby but she did not. She never cried in front of anybody. She never had.

Looking at her intensely, David felt the inevitable tearing of his soul between relief at being reunited with the woman who had shown him such love in the hostile world of his upbringing and hatred for the woman who had dictated the ruin of his future happiness.

But then she held out her arms, begging him to come forward and hug her, saying, 'I'm so, so sorry. Please forgive me. Forgive me, David, you must forgive me.'

Damn this woman! He found himself drawn to her and before he knew it, he was locked in an embrace of reconciliation. Eventually, he broke away and began slowly pacing the room. No, he would not forget his purpose quite so easily. 'You've done much which I don't find acceptable, mother.'

'But you must understand how things are...'

'I didn't say I didn't understand. I said I don't find it acceptable.'

Remembering the daft young girl that David had fallen in love with, a pretty little thing to a fashion but still a publican's daughter, Dorothy was careful not to let her condescension show when she said, 'You were so young and seemed so determined to have everything your own way. You needed guidance so that you did not harm the family.'

He immediately felt the indignation that had been the cause of him staying away for so long. 'Well, therein lies the problem. It seems to me that it's perfectly acceptable for the likes of you and father to do what you please while I must live by a completely different set of rules.'

'You are at the beginning of your life, David, and the choices you make now will affect everything that comes after. I believe that you should allow a greater amount of time still for a proper reflection on all the implications of the marriage that you were proposing.'

David looked hard at her. 'If I remember correctly, you did not ask me to reflect on the implications last September. You let me think you were on my side and then saw to it that she was chased away once I was not in a position to do anything about it.'

'It was for the best,' she persisted, though her tone was not so definite as it might have been.

'I'll never agree with you on that. I'm here to tell you that you no longer have any control over me. I am a man in my own right and you will be saying and doing nothing to influence my situation ever again.'

She in turn felt the displeasure welling up inside her at that, saying, 'How dare you? You are still my youngest son and you were brought up to respect your elders.'

'Well, something must have gone wrong with my sense of compliancy, mother, because this whole infernal world is full of inconsistencies which I can barely get my head around and one of those is the fact that I am to respect you while you show scant respect for me. It doesn't add up. I've watched you and father for years at each other's throats, at loggerheads with each other, scheming against each other, disrespecting each other while at the same time both trying to drum into me the attributes of being a decent human being. Well, who the hell were you to try to teach me that?'

'There's no need to swear!' she rebuked him.

He thought that it was a good job that she had been nowhere near the Tjierrefjord. The language used daily by the men up there would have given her a heart attack.

'You're going to have to excuse my language.' That was not an apology.

Dorothy regarded him closer still. His features and his intelligence had certainly matured but he was still possessed of the wayward spirit which had landed him in hot water so many times in the past. To her mind this might make him more dangerous than before, unless he felt that things were going his own way a bit. She could not bear to think of any of her sons off fighting a war filled with an utter hatred for what home stood for.

She said, 'My actions last September when you had placed such faith in my words I see were deplorable in your eyes. I know that now and I'm deeply sorry. But you have had all these months to think about what might have been had you married Miss Gufford. Are you clear where your mind is on the subject?'

'I would like very much to know where she is except that I know you engineered it so that her family should hide her away from all of us; and God knows they were happy to oblige. So, unless her father has a miraculous change of heart or I spend my life searching for her myself, the one person who made life bearable has been lost to me forever.'

Furrowing her brow through some inner pain, Dorothy said, 'That's how life is, David. I once saw your father as the person who made my life bearable until drink and paranoia got the better of him. I can still barely comprehend how it all went wrong.'

'So, if you understand misery, why do you visit it upon others?'

'I still believe I was protecting you,' she said, the strength that he knew so well returning to her demeanour.

He could see that there was going to be no arguing on that point. She was just as stubborn as him. Or was it the other way round? He continued with, 'All that aside, the main reason I came back is because a certain Derek Crawshaw has been worming his way into your company and, if the reputation of the family is all that you keep saying it is, then I am ordering you to drop him.'

She smiled. Here was the situation that she had been canny enough to foresee when Crawshaw had first recognised her at the Savoy. Knowing a little of her son's animosity for the man, she had allowed the commander to think he was getting close to her. What better reason for David to come running home than to introduce a malign influence that even he could not ignore? 'In rather a clumsy way,' she said, 'I think you're saying that you wish to protect me.'

He could not bear the thought of the commander taking advantage of his mother, even after everything she had done. He shrugged. 'If you like. He might have an old connection to our family but I can quite guarantee you that his intentions are not correct. He's not to come here again and you will disassociate yourself with him entirely.'

'What do you mean 'he's not to come here again'? He has never been here.'

David studied her face carefully and decided that he believed her. However, that did not change the fact that she had been seeing Crawshaw, a man who was exactly the type of person to work an injurious angle on her.

Dorothy continued, 'He has offered words of support for Patricia and we talked about his poor late brother who, I gather you understand, Harper and I once knew. I certainly have got no closer to him than that. The very thought is nauseous. Has anybody said anything to the contrary?'

He thought about that night Philip Dollimore delivered his message and opinion to him in front of the burning village of Hemmeligstein. 'Not exactly,' he said, everything suddenly falling into place, 'but there was some suggestion, heartfelt on the part of the man who spoke to me. You have Philip Dollimore wrapped right around your little finger, don't you?'

She frowned and said, 'I cannot be held accountable for the actions of others.'

David glared at her. 'Well, here I am, as gullible as the rest, mother. I would be tempted say that you were a stone cold, heartless old woman were it not for the fact that you seem to be driven by the need to have me back into your life.'

'My children mean everything to me.'

'No doubt, but if I am to live up to your wishes then we're going to need to discuss finding the girl who will make me happy – Maggie Gufford, who is your equal in every way save for your selfish deviousness.'

Dorothy stared hard at him in distaste and was about to hit back when she was stopped by a ghostlike figure appearing in the doorway.

David saw her eyes being distracted across his shoulder and turned quickly to see his sister standing there, all but propping herself up against the doorframe.

Patricia was dressed only in her white cotton nightdress which served to accentuate the whiteness of her skin and the soft greyness of her facial features. Her pained expression was similar to those of some of the wounded soldiers they had brought back from Norway and she was given an even more maniacal look by her shocking hair flowing in unkempt blonde tangles across her shoulders. Her free hand was clutching at her heavy belly.

She was just beginning to say, 'Philip, you've returned ...' when she stopped, realising that something quite different had invaded their home. This new apparition before her was nothing less than a ghoul. Her breath taken away, she stared in horror at David's dead face, his eyes lifeless yet somehow goading. He had obviously drowned and, what was worse, he was not going to rest in peace. He was filled with hatred and a desire to haunt her. She stared in shock and gasped through a burning throat, 'He's dead!'

'Who's dead?' asked Dorothy, perplexed. 'What are you talking about?'

Patricia pointed at the animated corpse wavering in her panicked vision. 'He's going to destroy us all!'

'Jean!' shouted Dorothy even as the worried maid appeared at Patricia's side. 'Take her out of here.'

Close to tears, the unfortunate maid dragged Patricia away to the stairs, the young mistress trying to convince her of the presence of the Angel of Death with every step.

David looked back at his mother in deep shock. 'It's worse than I thought.'

For the first time in a long time, Dorothy felt too weak to stand. Letting herself fall into the nearest seat, she put a hand up to her forehead and said, 'She's getting worse and worse and I don't know what to do. The doctor is talking about committing her. Over my dead body, I say.' She looked up at David. 'The only person who has had any positive effect on her at all is Philip Dollimore...'

She did not add that she was ruing the day that she had engineered Philip's return to active service. It now looked as though that single action had been selfish in the extreme.

\*\*\*\*

It was getting quite stuffy in this office and it was putting Commander Crawshaw right off the idea of getting any work done. He had delegated as much as he dared and diligently continued with the rest knowing that, whatever his failings, he would never accept an accusation of being lazy. He pushed the window open even wider, as if that could make any difference, and briefly looked on the thriving dockyard that sprawled down to the Thames. Many ships were heading to and from the wharves, there to unload their wares ready for distribution throughout the country, and he wondered if the Germans might actually possess the strength to take control of them all – the ships and the wharves. No, it was unthinkable.

Subjugation and military occupation was a classically continental problem and Britain had been the one true haven of common sense ever since... well, for a long time anyway. He had never paid much attention to history. He could not see how it helped the present.

The telephone connected to that of the secretary rang and he stepped back over to the desk to answer it. 'Yes, Brigitte?'

Really, he should have been addressing her by her surname of Merryweather or maybe even her rank of petty officer, but he wanted this particular Wren to feel more at home while working for him. The appearance of women in uniform over the last few months had been damned interesting. A branch of the Royal Navy in skirts? A pleasant development so long as they were not expected to man any ships.

'Sir,' she said, clearly annoyed, 'I have Sub-Lieutenant Clark here to see you. I've told him that he must make an appointment but he is most insistent.'

Crawshaw felt a surge of mischievous pleasure go through him. 'It's all right, Brigitte. Let him come in; and you remember the matter we discussed?'

'Yes, sir.'

The door opened and his gorgeous little red-head ushered the newcomer into the office.

Once the door was closed, Crawshaw, still standing, regarded Clark's stern face and smiled. 'Congratulations on your promotion,' he said. Long gone were the days when the very sight of this boy had sent him into taut agitation. 'A whole month ahead of your twentieth birthday. I seem to remember I became a sub just after my nineteenth. Halcyon days. Harsher days; not so much molly-coddling.'

'I'll make this short and sweet,' said Clark, for being in the presence of this man was not particularly nice.

'*Sir*. You call me *sir*.'

'That would be suggestive of the fact that you deserve respect.'

Crawshaw was actually a little stunned. He knew the boy had some gall, but this much? 'You realise that you're signing your own death warrant even as you speak?'

'What does that matter to me?' said Clark, and somehow the greater part of his conscience meant it. 'But it's you who removes us from professional understanding and into the personal. I know what you are trying to do – trying to get at my mother for recompense over what my father did to you and your family. I'm here to tell you that you will never see her again. Your pretence, your feigned friendship in her hour of need, is over. You will take nothing from her and I will see to it that she offers you nothing.'

'Too late,' said Crawshaw firmly. 'These last months, she needed companionship and male guidance. There has been a void in her life and, strangely, all three of her sons have been unable or unwilling to become the man of the family since the revered admiral died. She needed somebody to help her so then there was me. I gave her a shoulder to cry on; I advised her on her business matters; I helped cushion the blows during your sister's worst madcap episodes. In fact, I have provided *all* her needs.'

Clark expertly held back his urge to laugh at the revelations. Crawshaw's implication was that his mother had been completely unable to cope since Father's death but the idea was completely preposterous, as was the idea that anybody might actually believe it. 'I'm going to make this easy for you,' he said, taking a few steps closer to Crawshaw, staring menacingly into his eyes. 'Just don't go anywhere near my mother again or I shall make it seem like my father was a saint. I believe I once told you that I was sorry for the way he'd treated your family but what he did does not condone what you're doing now.'

'I've explained myself to you, sub-lieutenant. You're completely out of order and now I think its best that you leave before you say something you'll really regret. For the sake of your mother, I shall not take official action against you for your insubordination, but if you insist – '

'I do insist!' Clark snarled. Thinking on the way that Harry Haggerty and the people from the East End of London seemed to settle their disputes, he clenched his fists and continued, 'Stay away from my mother or be prepared to spend the rest of your life looking over your shoulder. Believe me, I have a few ideas about what to do about persistent blackguards like you.'

'And you have just threatened me, your superior, in my own office!' gasped Crawshaw.

'Stay away, Crawshaw,' said Clark and turned, leaving the office.

Crawshaw paused for a second, thinking on the immense power of the Clark family and decided that he could still make a splash in this little conflict. He made certain that he was quick to follow, though not immediately to catch him up. He stopped at Brigitte's desk, where she sat with a worried look on her face and the phone still at her ear. 'Did you hear every word?' he asked.

'Yes, sir,' she said shakily, for the awful conversation had come clearly through the receiver and Clark had never noticed that the one in the office was still off the hook thus leaving the line open.

'Good girl.'

Then he picked up the pace and trotted down the hallway after Clark. Passing the stunned chief at the security desk and the blank-faced sentries at the sand-bag covered entrance, he caught up with Clark a little way down the lane. Being so close to the docks, this ancient thoroughfare with its high brick buildings either side was teeming with labourers and sailors moving to and fro.

'Clark!' he called above the din, making the young man stop and look around. 'I do have one thing to add. It's amazing how people conduct their affairs according to what they *think* they know as opposed to what is the truth. When we were in the *Burscombe* last year, you made a mistake about me and it cost me my position.'

Even remembering that, Clark's irritation still drowned his sense of guilt. 'What are you trying to say?'

'They're still keeping secrets from you.'

'My family?'

Crawshaw shook his head, saying, 'The Admiralty. Let's just say that the official reports of your father's death are slightly departed from fact.' He could not help his face from falling into an expression of malice as he said those words, such was his hatred of the Clark family.

Clark considered punching this sad, ageing commander right here. It was something that Haggerty would probably have done and something that would probably have solved the problem, or at least made him feel better. What a different world was that of the officers where the sparring must be done by words. Besides, if he hit him here, then a whole raft of witnesses would be produced to attest to his aggression. Instead, he leaned closer and finished with, 'Ever the liar.'

'I don't think so.'

Walking away, his muscles tense with consternation, Clark thought about the reports of his father's death. Last December, Rear-Admiral Harper Clark's flagship, HMS *Godham*, had been in action against the superior German battlecruiser *Moltke* and her destroyer escort. It had been a hard-fought engagement but the *Godham* had inevitably succumbed to the relentless shelling and torpedo attacks with the loss of the whole ship's company bar twelve. The rear-admiral was finally sleeping peacefully within Davy Jones' locker to accolades of courageous resistance to the foe in the physical world. How could that be a lie?

As Crawshaw headed back into his office, the impossibly naive Petty Officer Merryweather jumped to her feet and all but cried, 'Are you all right, sir?'

'Well, of course,' he answered with a grin. Then, taking on a mock look of concern, he continued, 'Oh, my poor Brigitte. It's so wrong of me to get you mixed up in my business. Anyway, no more harm can come of it. I didn't catch him up. He's walking too fast and I'm not so energetic as I once was.'

'But you'll bring a charge against him, sir?' she asked.

He pretended to think it over for a few seconds. 'No, not this time. One last benefit of the doubt perhaps. Little as you'd suspect from his barbarous attitude, he's actually a very good officer and I think he'll be needed at sea again. What would it profit me to deprive the country of his service just now with all that's going on?'

Brigitte smiled. She had never known a man to be so forgiving.

He smiled back. 'Now, how about a cup of tea?'

\*\*\*\*

Clark finally returned to the Belgravia town house, weighing up the pros and cons of asking Mother whether she knew of anything concerning the Admiralty's alleged lying. By the time he was back in her presence he was leaning towards not taking anything Crawshaw said with more than a pinch of salt, and it was all put from his mind anyway as soon as he realised that there was another visitor waiting for him.

He looked over at the settee closer to the window and, standing respectfully to acknowledge his arrival was Detective Sergeant Crosbie. The red-headed man still looked worn out and rough by way of his clothes and hair but that said nothing about his eagerness to do his duty to justice. With a broad grin, Crosbie said, 'Mr David Clark, good to see you again.'

Clark shook his hand, remembering the last time they had met. 'Indeed? I must have missed something considering your last words to me were something to the effect of minding my own business and letting you get on with the police work – and I've tried not to get above my station but, as you can see, it's quite difficult.'

Crosbie gave a quick glance at the fine furniture, silver service on the coffee table, the ornaments on the mantelpiece and the paintings hanging from the walls. This was about the twentieth glance he had given them since he had been sitting here taking tea with this very fine lady, Dorothy Clark; and she herself had been so beguiling that he had very nearly discussed the case with her, something which would have been quite unprofessional. 'You'll have to excuse the way I was, young sir. I've spent a lifetime chasing down criminals and I have a natural aversion to anybody telling me my business. I get protestations of innocence or accusations of persecution on a weekly basis so my mind leaps forward to that eventuality... er, a little hastily perhaps. But, I've come to let you know that we followed up on the question you asked concerning Mary Sewell in your report on Haggerty's desertion – and that is a nasty bruise he gave you there.'

Dorothy sighed. 'Do get on with it, Mr Crosbie. My son has many other matters to take care of besides whatever it is some fool has foisted upon him.'

'Agreed, ma'am,' smiled Crosbie. 'I had noticed that the war has finally broken out since the young sir and I last spoke in March.' To Clark, he continued with, 'I and my colleagues at Scotland Yard have talked at length on your ideas but we have a problem with alibis.'

Clark immediately knew what he meant and, with no hesitation, removed his watch from his wrist. 'It's presently quarter past four,' he said then quickly twisted the tiny brass knob with his fingertips. Thereupon, he showed the watch face to Crosbie. The hands now showed 9.58 and, without any further ado, he stepped forward and smashed the watch with a determined crack against the corner of the coffee table to his mother's cry of, 'David!'

He then held the watch up to his ear and listened for the ticking. 'Yes, it's definitely stopped.'

The two men talked deeply on the matter for the next half an hour, after which time Crosbie made to leave. At the sitting room door, he shook hands with Clark once again before absent-mindedly wiping the sweat from his brow with the sleeve of his jacket. 'Thank you for your input. It's been most welcome,' he said, then turned back to Dorothy. 'Ma'am, it's a shame that this lad's insisted on joining the navy. He would make a very, very fine detective.'

'How dare you!' she replied, staring down her nose at him. 'He's doing something important with his life.'

Crosbie gave her a charming smile and retreated, wondering where it was he had heard that a policeman's lot is not a happy one – not while everybody thought that he was the scum at least.
****

Twice Harry Haggerty had tried to cross the valley which ran through these rugged stretches of Norway but there were German patrols everywhere so he had decided to head further south instead. He now considered that a mistake because it seemed like they were more concentrated here than anywhere else. His reasoning had been to head in the opposite direction from the fight which he knew would be escalating around Narvik and then to sneak across the border into Sweden. He had climbed all the way over a mountain to achieve that and in so doing, had used up all of his provisions. He had since killed the odd chicken and stolen eggs and vegetables here and there as he went.

Otherwise he had been careful to steer clear of the scattered dwellings. He was not desperate yet and he did not want to get turned in by the frightened locals.

There had been a moment, early on, when he had seen Oskar climbing down the mountainside not a hundred yards away from where he had been hiding and nearly called out with a mind to join forces and use the boy's knowledge of the country. But he had quickly thought better of it, having resolved to disappear completely into the landscape and not reappear until he had found the ways and means of changing his identity.

For now it was just enough that he had been able to run, thus drawing police attention away from his cousin Mary, who might just have been fitted up. She had been so stupid it was incredible; right from the beginning when she had fallen in with Cliff Parker's crowd and thought that she was tough enough to influence 'The Fox' in his little empire just by means of her sexuality.

The unfortunate truth was that Parker had valued no one who strayed from his very strict idea of what loyalty was. She should have stayed away instead of thinking she could change him to suit her ideas and live that slow descent into the mental hell she had created for herself.

Haggerty had plenty of time to think about all of this now he was alone, wandering this strange land, hiding from the world. His own past was destroyed just as the future he would have liked was, but he was strong enough to take care of himself; Mary not so. Since this whole business began, he had resisted being the infuriating type of person who always asked, 'What if?' to everything but the questions were there nevertheless. What if he had got his leave at a different time? What if he had decided to go drinking in the West End that night instead of in the local? What if he had not forgotten to take his jack-knife out with him when he had said, 'See you later,' to his mum?

It had been his last night at home in the town of his tortured youth, Bethnal Green, and he had decided to go to The Camel for a couple of pints to oil the war nerves a bit. It had become easier to wear his uniform in public with the introduction of conscription since more and more of the lads who had made fun of him in the past were beginning to appear in military attire themselves. But there were still some who thought they were untouchable by the war and carried on as though it was not happening. A couple of Parker's lads had recognised him straight away from the old days – how could they not with a face like his? – and immediately began with their immature jibes. However, once they found they were unable to ruin his evening, they changed tack and started trying to cajole him into joining them on a job.

Of course, he was not having that either and so had to put up with all of those ridiculous arguments about his betrayal of their way of life, turning his back on their cause and thinking he was better than them. Inevitably, still unable to get their way, they came to the conclusion that it was simply more sporting to beat him up instead. Finally having been thrown into one of his old style furies, he gave a damned good account of himself, though he would have been better still had he not forgotten to take his knife with him. That was an unforgiveable oversight for somebody of his experience. For some reason he had emptied his pockets at home leaving only the shillings for his drinks.

So it was that he had found himself walking home with a gashed temple and a headache to find his mother in a torment of worry. 'Oh, thank God you came 'ome,' she said wildly. She was a tough woman but could still rise quite terribly to a drama. 'I was about to send round to the pub to fetch you. What've you done to yerself?'

'Usual gash. What's happening?'

'Mary was 'ere. Says she found out that Cliff ordered the murder of Peter Averell.'

What that had to do with Mary had made no sense to Haggerty at first but he was soon enlightened to the fact she had recently started playing up to the rival gang leader in rather a friendly way, presumably because she had finally realised that life with Parker was not going to be what she had wanted. Haggerty could imagine Averell gloating in triumph at having stolen such a powerful man's woman and so had probably walked into his own murder.

Haggerty sighed. 'She's made her bed, mum. What do you want me to do about it?'

'She's taken your knife!'

'Shit!'

His mum's hand instinctively came up and slapped him on the mouth. 'Say that again an' I'll shove soap in there!'

'Sorry, mum,' he said, soaking up the rebuke in instantaneous forgiveness and guilt. 'Where does Parker operate out of at the moment?'

'He generally 'ides out in the back of Garry's Butchers but nobody's s'pposed to know that.'

That was a little way down Green Street. Good, it was not too far away. 'I'll go get her back before she does anything stupid.'

But before he went, he looked down at the sleeping form of his dad slumped, prematurely old and feeble, in the armchair by the front window. Giving him a kick on an inanimate ankle, he asked his mum, 'I take it he was no use you?'

'He's finished 'is bottle of gin and that's as much as 'e knows, the pig,' she replied, her words dripping with disgust. 'Don't you worry. That gut rot'll do for 'im sooner rather than later.'

It was only a matter of ten minutes later that Haggerty was creeping along the alleyway behind the small row of shops, the smell of discarded food fortunately not as bad as it used to be, firstly, because it was so cold out here and secondly, because the rationing had made waste not only rarer, but a cardinal sin. The ice underfoot was cracking noisily making him fear discovery but he kept going forward anyway.

He reached the door and was a little stunned to find it lying ajar although a blackout curtain was solidly in place within. Even criminals abided by that rule. He could hear Mary's voice emanating from somewhere inside, full of emotion and scathing chastisement. She was accusing Parker of murder. Then came his voice, angrily warning her off before she too fell foul of him – as if she had not done so already.

But then what was that? The sounds of a scuffle. Up until now Haggerty had been desperately trying to think of a way out of this that would be peaceful to all but now the fight had started. This no longer being the time to consider the rights and wrongs of Mary's choices, he rushed in, surprised to find no presence of the two or three bodyguards that one would expect a man like Parker him to have around him. He must have demanded privacy from them when confronted with his melodramatic woman. Well, more fool him.

Haggerty arrived in the room just in time to witness him, his sweaty face fronted by the streaks of his long black fringe flopping in front of blue eyes, taut with fury and mindless hate, easily taking the jack knife from Mary's failing grasp and turning it back on her. She was very nearly done for when Haggerty grabbed hold of his wrist and crushed it with all his considerable might.

'Lizard Face!' was all Parker could gasp before his murderous expression turned to a grimace and his painful hand let the weapon go. It clattered to the floor and there should have been the end of it but for the fact that Haggerty knew how this man's mind worked. He would feel wronged, insulted and itching for revenge. It was his way and the only thing that Haggerty could do was knock him unconscious and get himself and Mary out of town and somewhere completely discreet within the next two hours.

He lifted up his fist to do the deed but suddenly became aware of another hand appearing from the right with a blade flashing in the lamp light. Forced to divert his fist from its original task, Haggerty deflected the thrust of the blade, seeing that it was his very same jack knife, quickly snatched up from the floor by Mary and aimed for Parker's neck. Looking at her maniacal expression, Haggerty swiftly took it from her and shouted, 'What the bloody hell are you doing?'

Parker immediately realised his reprieve and wasted no time in saying, 'She's gone barkin'!' while at the same time side-stepping in order to reach for a large kitchen knife that lay nearby. He had obviously reasoned that he was in a fight for his life and somebody was not going to be walking out of here alive.

'Watch out!' cried Mary through Haggerty's distraction.

He spun round again, his right arm ruining Parker's aim and his left thrusting forward to punch for the abdomen. But the jack knife was still in his grasp and the blade slid effortlessly and deeply into the other's intestines. It had all happened so fast, he barely had time to comprehend what was happening until it was over.

Parker immediately looked weak. His legs buckled and he fell heavily onto the floor. He was visibly trying to ignore the pain, forget the damage and fight on but his body was failing him fast. How? Why? Other people went on for much longer with worse injuries than this. Haggerty had seen it many times.

He was immediately distraught and offering a string of shocked profanities even as Parker tried to give him his cue. The dying man said to him weakly, 'You'd better run, boy. Run and keep on running.'

But he did not. Bundling Mary out of the slaughterhouse and telling her to wait at his mum's place, he sat and waited the few short minutes until

Parker's life had expired. During those minutes, he came to wonder how circumstances swallowed people up without them even realising what was happening. This old life which he had turned his back on had caught up with him anyway.

Leave from the navy was supposed to be a rest from aggravation. All he had wanted to do was see his mum and enjoy his few days in London. What a complete cock-up.

For a few moments he was unable to comprehend what to do next and even the good sense to run as hard as he could eluded him. But after a few more minutes had passed, something in his mind suddenly clicked and the necessity of not giving in to the inevitable gave him strength.

He grabbed a cloth that was hanging on a nearby hook and gave his knife a quick clean before slipping it into his pocket. Thinking on how to shift attention away from his own blade he carefully manoeuvred the knife that was still in Parker's hand about the wound, pressing down to extricate more of the thick blood, all the while keeping his own hand covered by the cloth to eliminate the chance of fingerprints.

Then, thinking on how he might possibly draw unwanted attention away from his presence in the first place, he drew to mind a cheap detective novel he had read a couple of years ago where a murderer had calculatingly smashed a clock at the scene after setting it on a particular time, demonstrating what the police would take to be the time of the murder, thus giving the felon an alibi. To be honest, in the story, the murderer did not get away with it, but that was a novel, not real life; and detectives in novels were often smarter than the real thing. That was what he hoped anyway.

He slipped Parker's watch off his wrist, rewound the hands back to show the time that he had been brawling with those other scum in The Camel and smashed the face of the time-piece on the corner of the table. After checking that the thing had indeed stopped he gave it a wipe and put it back on Parker's wrist.

Now it was time to run. Before stepping out, he took one last look at the corpse. It was already significantly grey with perhaps a tinge of blue about the mouth and eyelids; or was that just a trick of the light? Again, he cursed Mary and his bad luck and swiftly headed off into the night.

Looking back and forth along the blackened alley, he paused long enough to be satisfied that he was not being observed then bound his jack knife in the folds of the cloth he had been using. He stooped over the gratings of a nearby drain and dropped the small bundle through one of the slits. He could just about hear it splash in the water somewhere below, so hopefully it would be washed out into the Thames at some point in the next couple of days to disappear forever.

Then, walking home at a slow speed which was completely at odds with the pounding of his heart, he was confronted by a policeman, who questioned him about the dried blood which marked one side of his face. It had been there the whole time since he had left the pub but matters had persisted so fast and so foul that it had been of secondary importance until now. He spoke to the policeman with a calmness which surprised even himself and was then allowed to go on his way.

Trying to talk to Mary about what had happened that night was useless. She had become so tense that she was unable to sleep and the greatest sense that he could get out of her was, 'It wasn't meant to be you what did it, but I'm glad you did. He didn't deserve to live. Not after what he done. I would've done it myself. I definitely would've done it myself. Should've done it.'

'Just keep your head down,' said Haggerty. 'You never know, they might not even link you to the thing and I can fob 'em off an' all. Parker had so many enemies that it might take some time to get round to us. Christ, there's a war on and people have got better things to worry about! Hopefully they'll overlook the bastard entirely.'

Nobody had come knocking that night or the next morning. Haggerty checked his uniform for any signs of his scuffle, gathered his things together and rejoined HMS *Burscombe*, unfortunately in a much darker mood than the one he had left with.

Back with his shipmates, he had been living the whole time under the shadow of that night, hoping against hope that the whole incident would just go away. Things had been bad enough when that Crosbie man eventually came sniffing about but finally, when he had received that letter from Mary, warning him that the police were looking into her past relationship with the deceased, he had known it would not be long before he was back in the spotlight; hence his attempt to desert in Rosyth, where that boy scout Pincher had confronted him.

Now, alone and wandering in this Norwegian valley, he gradually worked his way through the problematic German-dominated landscape, and got to wonder if he should have strangled Midshipman Clark to death as well. He looked down at his painful arm along which the bullet had skimmed when that meddling boy had fired his revolver but still managed to reason that he was glad he did not have another murder on his conscience. Clark might still try to cause trouble for Mary but Haggerty's mum would swear that the young woman was with her all night; and his dad would shrug and agree too.

He looked up as a formation of bombers flew overhead towards the port of Narvik. 'Keep it up, boys,' he muttered because, dangerous as they were, they were beautifully creating the confusion into which he was going to envelop himself and disappear.

\*\*\*\*

Detective Sergeant Crosbie walked away from Belgravia tiredly scraping his heels along the pavement. He was deeply pleased to be able to nominally close this case because it had not been the easiest thing in the world to make his enquiries amongst a community that habitually hated him.

Nearly two months ago, he had begun looking into the rumours of a link between Mary Sewell and both murdered gang leaders and he felt like he was beginning to close in on the right solution when he had received a copy of David Clark's report into the desertion of Harry Haggerty. The young officer had remembered Crosbie saying that Parker's fatal wound had been in the right side of his abdomen and later, during his struggle with Haggerty, Clark had registered that the ugly brute had lunged with his left hand first and continued to choke him with the same even though the bullet had damaged that arm.

Mary was right-handed.

But whatever the evidence of left or right hands, Crosbie was satisfied that Haggerty's desertion was enough to condemn him. But as for bringing him to justice? He had lodged paperwork with the Admiralty and the War Office declaring Leading Seaman Harry Haggerty wanted for murder and Scotland Yard had informed the Swedish Government of their desire to apprehend him should he turn up in their territory. Until then there was not much more he could do.

Anyway, it was time to head over to Shoreditch where there was some suspicion that an elderly gentleman had been poisoned by one of his sons. Apparently it was a matter of inheritance. This one should be a bit easier to figure out.

# EPILOGUE

Rear-Admiral Nicklesworth was exhausted, deflated and empty. There were hundreds of things that were presently in danger of clouding over his mind so he cleared his thoughts and settled on the immediate situation, that of getting his cruisers and destroyers back to Scotland. They had just extricated another battalion of battered and bruised soldiers from the fight, this time from the region of Narvik. As far as Norway was concerned, this was the end of the campaign. They were finally admitting defeat.

The idea of holding onto that last corner of the country so that the British could have a front against the Germans and ensure the supply of Swedish iron ore for the Allies had been given up on. It was true that the Narvik effort had been better than Trondheim and that the enemy had finally been held at bay on the ground but it was not enough. Churchill wanted all available forces back home in what was set to be a gargantuan struggle for mastery of the British Isles themselves.

Nicklesworth had the *Farecombe* and her attendant destroyers proceed at twenty three knots across these relatively calm seas so that they might reach safety sooner rather than later. The ships and men were worn and battered and in much need of attention.

The fleet was dispersed. Other ships had gone on ahead as soon as they were ready, just as there were still others lagging behind, breaking out westwards away from the occupied coast before turning south. Somewhere beyond the horizon, making good speed, was HMS *Glorious* with her escorts. She had stuck around long enough to embark the two squadrons of Hurricanes that Nicklesworth had not seen until it was nearly all over and then she had left. One of the last, still behind them somewhere, was HMS *Devonshire*, which he understood was carrying the Norwegian royal family to safety.

Essentially, British and Norwegians alike were running like dogs with their tails between their legs but at least this final passage was peaceful. The Luftwaffe was not harassing them any longer and that was a most welcome change. It was almost as if the Germans were finally happy with their gain and too exhausted to make any more fuss.

Having given the orders for the zig-zag pattern that he wanted his ships to steer, Nicklesworth relaxed and climbed out onto the open bridge to the acknowledgement of Captain Craine. He suddenly found himself in a position to enjoy the heat of the sun and its radiance as it shone across the flat sea. There had been so much work to do these last two months that he had hardly noticed the changing of the seasons beyond the way that they affected military operations. How lovely it was now.

'So, what next for us, sir?' Craine suddenly asked, in turn hoping to suppress his sense of failure by enjoying the good weather. 'Britain, I mean. I thought we'd had it bad up here but, by all accounts, France sounds twenty times worse.'

'Indeed,' said Nicklesworth, thinking on the latest disconcerting news that the British Army had been routed in Europe and had needed to be rescued from the port of Dunkirk by the navy. He then put on a meaningful expression and stated, 'But let's not talk of France as though they're finished. They're still resisting Jerry in the heart of the country and might yet establish a solid Western Front.'

Craine looked doubtful. 'Like the last war? God forbid. Sir, is that your gut feeling on the subject?'

'The French will fight to the death before they capitulate,' stated Nicklesworth, 'and we'll lick our wounds and get back into it. We must. British involvement on the continent has always been about maintaining a balance of power, that no one country should dominate the others because that would spell doom for us. If Hitler defeats France then he will be in possession of three thousand miles of coastline bordering the British Isles.'

'The odds sound awesome, sir.'

Nicklesworth smiled. 'We may have had a shaky start but the Royal Navy is stronger than the Kriegsmarine and every battleship, cruiser, destroyer, submarine and everything else we have will be waiting for the bastards in the English Channel. Not one German soldier will ever set foot on British soil.'

Craine nodded and returned the smile. 'In that case, sir, how can we fail?'

The admiral looked out over the water and wondered what Dollimore's take on the situation would be. No doubt that strange and precise man will have already worked out how he was going to foil all German designs on the British Isles. It was funny to think how much he had despised that captain only to end up learning more from him than anyone else in this entire fleet. His thoughts were suddenly interrupted by the sound of one of the lookouts informing the captain, 'There are men and wreckage in the water dead ahead, sir.'

Nicklesworth watched closely as the ship eventually slowed amongst a scattering of blackened wood and rubber debris with rafts holding very weak men. The summer may have begun but it was still cold enough for the sea to have nearly killed them and, through the stinking layer of oil that covered them, one could see the vestiges of Royal Navy uniforms.

While the other ships continued circling, Craine brought the *Farecombe* to a stop and ordered his men in the waist to report to the bridge as soon as they had the numbers of survivors and knowledge of what ship they were from.

When it came, Nicklesworth was appalled. 'The *Glorious* is sunk?'

'Yes sir,' replied the unimpressed chief who had climbed the five decks filled with grim resignation. To him the loss of that much-needed aircraft carrier represented nothing more than blindly stepping in the turd that was the Norwegian campaign. 'They were attacked by a pair of German battlecruisers, sir. They had no chance.'

Nicklesworth said, 'Do we know which direction the enemy went off in?'

'No, sir.'

With the survivors safely aboard, they continued on their way, knowing that they could not be any more vigilant than they were. Double lookouts were always posted and the companies of all four ships were at Defence Stations anyway. But, even still, they could not prevent the incident which sent up the cry of, 'Torpedo track, green zero-eight-five!'

Craine, who had just been about to retire below, looked out and quickly judged the speed and direction of the torpedo, whose white bubbly trail could clearly be seen in the calm water. It was coming in at a slight angle just forrard of the beam and he figured out his evasive manoeuvre as fast as he could. 'Helmsman, steer three points to starboard, quick as you can!'

The order was repeated from below and the *Farecombe* immediately leaned out of her ensuing turn. Hopefully, the torpedo would shave past the stern but it was soon apparent that the turn was too slow and that the warning had come too late.

Craine, Nicklesworth and everybody else who could see the approach of this terrible weapon tensed their muscles and helplessly waited for this fresh disaster to befall them. The Germans did not need the Luftwaffe to chase the Royal Navy home. The Kriegsmarine was perfectly able to make its own mark after all.

The torpedo sped in at forty knots and, with a great metallic bang, thudded against the side of the ship before it sunk out of sight, somehow undetonated.

In his confusion, Nicklesworth saw the last four months flash through his mind and remembered the day that the whole emphasis of the war had shifted onto Norway. The 25th Cruiser Squadron had stopped the *D/S Dagrand*. That had then led onto the storming of the *Altmark*, the German invasion of Norway, British intervention and finally retreat. Significantly, the whole episode had started and finished with dud torpedoes. So much depended on sheer luck.

Hardly knowing whether he was relieved or not but sure that he was more deflated than he had ever been, he mumbled, 'If anybody needs me, I'll be in my cabin,' and with that he walked stiffly off the bridge.

# Glossary

**binnacle** – the fitting on the bridge which holds the compass

**cable length** – the length of one anchor chain, one tenth of a nautical mile (approximately 100 fathoms – equal to 200 yards or 183 metres)

**chains** – originally small platforms on either side of a hull where the shrouds (part of the rigging)were attached and where a leadsman could stand to take depth soundings. More relevant to the days of sail but a term which survived in later years

**fanny** – the pot used to collect the rum issue

**gash** – rubbish

**kai** – hot chocolate

**labyrinth gland** – reference to the particular packing in the turbine shafts, the only part of the turbine which makes contact with the casing

**lascar** – Indian or South East Asian sailor

**leeside** – side away from the worst of the weather

**nutty** – chocolate and other sweets

**oggie** – cornish pasty

**snotty** – midshipman

# About the author

M. C. Smith is a tour guide aboard HMS *Belfast* in London, an associate member of the *Belfast* Association and a volunteer at TS *Constant* (Sea Cadet Corps).

Printed in Great Britain
by Amazon